ROYAL DECEPTION

SOPHIA THORNFIELD

Contents

1. Chapter 1 — 1
2. Chapter 2 — 11
3. Chapter 3 — 23
4. Chapter 4 — 39
5. Chapter 5 — 55
6. Chapter 6 — 69
7. Chapter 7 — 85
8. Chapter 8 — 102
9. Chapter 9 — 123
10. Chapter 10 — 130
11. Chapter 11 — 153
12. Chapter 12 — 163
13. Chapter 13 — 178
14. Chapter 14 — 190
15. Chapter 15 — 210
16. Chapter 16 — 230
17. Chapter 17 — 251
18. Chapter 18 — 274

19. Chapter 19   287

20. Chapter 20   322

21. Chapter 21   335

22. Chapter 22   349

23. Epilogue   367

1

— • —

CHAPTER 1

F allon

(4 years ago)

"My queen, please don't be sad. In my departure I want to bring your smiling face with me." He wiped the tears of his wife's face."T hen why don't you remove mother's head and bring it with you?"

"My god, Fallon. Why do have to be so sarcastic, dear?" He said weakly.My mother glared at me for interrupting their moment. I just chuckled weakly with tears in my eyes. I had my husband beside me and our little son, Louie. My husband, King Marion, was an apprentice of my dad and loved him dearly.King Jethro, my father.He was well-known in many ways. He was known for his kindness, sagacity, and how he is always happy. He comes up with festivals, and balls so that everyone in Sorah, our beloved kingdom, and even foreigners from other lands, will enjoy.Being one of the greatest kings in the kingdom, his portrait hangs in Sorah's Hall of Greats along with the kingdom's greatest rulers.During his reign, never was there an attack nor did Sorah engage in war with other kingdoms. He was the first Sorahian king who didn't need to win a war to prove his greatness.Even in his death, he spoke as if he had a lot of breath left in him. He still made us laugh.

He had a weak body and we knew, even with the best physician, he wouldn't last long. We lost hope but we didn't show it in front of him. He didn't get rid of his smile, that I adored ever since I was a child, even on his death bed. Being the eldest, I had the longest time with dad, and for that I am thankful.My sisters, Genevieve and Blair, came to me and we comforted each other as mom was speaking to our dying king. When she was done, dad kissed her and she wept. Her tears never left her, no matter how hard she tried to stop them, as she sat on the edge of his death bed.Finally, the time for his most important words has come. He called my brother, the youngest among us.Aspen, our only boy, went forward with tears and knelt down in front of him and kissed his hand, "Father."

He whispered.Aspen loved our father for dad spent the most time with him. He personally trained him. He has always adored our father and was aiming to be like him in all ways.He placed a hand on my brother's hand, and focused his eyes sternly on him."My boy, a son born from Sorah's own flesh and blood. The time has come for you to take my place as king of this nation." He said in his once mighty voice. "I am proud that I am able to leave this kingdom a king who has power in knowledge, strength, wisdom, discipline, justice, faith, but most of all... a heart."

"You forgot looks, father." Aspen jokingly said, trying to smile at a great man's death. We all managed a light chuckle except for dad, who laughed heartily. It's true that he got his looks from our king, who was a very handsome and dashing man. Blonde hair, chiseled teeth. Everything. The two of them resembled each other any more ways than one."I see in you a prosperous Sorah, my son. I raised you to be a wise and strong king and I know that you will love, lead, and serve this kingdom well. Yet, I don't want you to live in the shadow of greats, Aspen.

"He was catching his breath, feeling weak. "I want you to be your own great for you can never have someone else's. Sadly, I don't have enough days left to watch you surpass me." A tear fell from their eyes as father said that."Just remember every word of mine. I know they'll guide you. Oh, And you must also remember..." Then father whispered something that we weren't able to hear. Whatever it was, it made the both of them laugh and smile before he shook his brows.He'll be the first man in history to be able to joke this much in his death. I mentally face-palmed but I quickly shrugged it off and smirked lightly.He looked at Aspen intently, " Aspen, never forget...-"

"A great man isn't always a king but a great king is always a great man." They both said and smiled before father added, "And that's what I really want for you, my son. For you to be a great man."It was dad's life motto. It served him well. I've known it ever since and I've always said it to Louie. He's gonna be king too someday. I want him to live by that. Whatever my father was, the world needs a lot of it, that's why I want my son to be more like him. Marion also wanted that.After they said that, father placed a hand on Aspen's head and said a silent benediction. It was a tradition every time the crown was passed on to it's rightful heir. The king gives his blessing to his son."Now, take this." He took his crown that was beside his bed and placed it on my brother's head. Aspen bowed his head as the crown was placed."Your highness." Father whispered. "My son, I am so proud of you.""I haven't even done anything yet, father."

"You were born, you became my son. You don't know how happy I am because of that."Aspen cried. His tears were streaming down his face. The sight of them warmed and broke our hearts. My husband embraced me as I watched the scene.Aspen took my father's hand as his voice started breaking,"Father, I promise. I'll be a great man and a great king. I'll lead Sorah in your honor. I promise you."My father nodded. Then he gestured to all of us. My sisters, my mother and I went to him. We embraced him and he held our hands and he cupped mother's face. He looked at us with tears. I placed my head on his chest, hearing his heartbeat weaken.

"Because of you, I am able to greet death with a smile. I wanted more days with all of you. I wanted to see Louie grow up-" He touched my son's face- "I wanted to see my future grandchildren, I wanted to see my son, and my sons-in-law rule their kingdom and prosper. Still, what we've had is more than enough for me.

"Our husbands fell on their knees and knelt down as a sign of honor, which was indeed suitable for my father. We tightened our hold on his hand."As I depart, please smile. And keep on smiling. Through that, I can always be with you."Even if it's hard, we'll try. We'll try to live on as if he was still alive, because he is and he'll always be.A tear fell from his eyes as he said his final words," I love you.

"Then...he breathed his very last.I felt it as his heart stopped.I felt it as his breathing seized.He closed his eyes and stopped moving. It took us mere seconds to wake up from the heartbreaking stupor and finally accept that our loving father is now gone.Like every loss of a loved one, it was unbearable. It was like a canon firing. Now, our father is no longer, and it destroyed us.Although a king, his last words weren't for his kingdom. It was for his family.Not a moment too soon, we started crying, grieving, whatever you do to show the pain and bitterness you feel. We howled as if were being skinned alive. We tried to cry quietly but the more we suppressed it, the more it wanted to come out.We were ready for this day. But, turns out it's more painful than we expected. My sisters, my mother, my brother, my husband, my sisters' husbands cried as if they never cried before, and so did I. It was just too painful. We wailed, hoping to ease the wound. Tears weren't enough to heal though.

"Goodbye, dad." I said silently.I stood up and went to the window. I saw General Eric, Blair's husband, on the flat roof of the castle where he let down the flag of Sorah and raised a plain black one. The people knew what that meant. That's what we do every time our kings die.When the people saw, they stopped what they were doing, knelt down, and grieved. The Sorahians loved my father. You won't see one standing up right now. All were down on their knees in respect to King Jethro's death. Carriages stopped moving, the soldiers stopped their training for a while. All you can hear on that day was wailing, mostly my father's name."Your Majesty!""King Jethro!"Then, it started to pour. Even the skies are crying. But, no one moved. They were still on their knees. They cried over the kingdom's loss, over the loss of a great ruler.It was a very sad day for Sorah.

Two days later, we had the public funeral. We had one yesterday, where the royal family and all the king's staff were required to attend. Today is where the Sorahians can pay their final respects to their king. And by final, we meant final.Here in Sorah, when someone dies, we celebrate their death once only by their funeral. It is treason to celebrate one's death anniversary or any other occasions that are connected to the deceased, including their birthday. However, that law only applies inside the kingdom. If one wants to celebrate a dead loved-one, they journey to the Valley of The Fallen

Sorahians, which serves as a cemetery and is far away from the kingdom.

Why?King Regulus, one of Sorah's late kings, believed that anything associated with the dead brings pure bad luck to the kingdom's future. He wanted to cease the celebration of the dead but it would oppose the idea and tradition of honoring our deceased citizens and especially those who died for the kingdom, which was an idea supported by the former kings. So, to keep the tradition as well as keep the said bad luck away from Sorah, he came up with the Valley of the Fallen Sorahians.Me and my family were at a balcony inside the church as we watched the ceremony. My heart warmed at the sight of the many people who loved my father. Suddenly, a messenger came with letters in hand."Sorry to disturb, your highnesses.

"He bowed."What is it?" I asked.He then handed me the letters, " I believe this is for you, princess Fallon."I sighed, "Thank you."Then he excused himself and left.I looked at the letters. From the looks of it and given the occasion, I believe that it was just letters of condolences from other kingdoms. But, I'm not wholly sure of that so I still have to read em.I excused myself and before going to my room to read. I took one last long look at my father in his coffin. I smiled genuinely then I left. As soon as I got to my room, I started reading. As I expected, mostly were condolence letters. That's very thoughtful, I'll give them that. But, the other letters were about the crown, Aspen to be exact.

They wanted to know when is the coronation, and some were even questioning about the future of Sorah in my brother's hands.What the?Those kingdom-oriented spawns of a-"Fallon."I turned around and saw my sister, Genevieve."I'm pretty sure knocking was created circa this century, Gen.""Yeah, so is answering a knock." She chu ckled."Sorry." I turned away.She walked closer to me and held my shoulder, looking at the letters I was holding, then sighed,"Fallon, you don't have to worry or be sad alone. We all feel what you feel. Don't carry everything like it's yours. Dad said that we should always share, right?"

"Unfortunately, he also taught us that there are some things we must keep to ourselves for the greater good. There are some things we can't share with one another, Genevieve, because we love each other too much." I uttered."Even though it could kill you on the inside?" She questioned, worried."Even if it's torture." I answered with my back still facing her. I then turned to look at her and snickered, "Hmm. The things that father taught us are kinda contradicting and confusing, don't cha think?"

"Aww, I'm sure he means well."With that, we both laughed. I'm really grateful that she came here to comfort me.Genevieve was the most lady-like among the three of us sisters. She was sweet, caring, thoughtful, optimistic, and attracted princes from foreign lands with her charm. But, father said that marriage was sacred and not for business, so she did marry for love. We all did.Dad doubted us a little because I married a king, Gen married Prince Zhou of the Han Yu kingdom, who was coincidentally one of the richest and most powerful princes, and Blair married General Eric.

I suspected that he was expecting us to fall in love with commoners like in those fairytales. He even questioned our love, but he was happy nonetheless.Guess he just didn't want to be that kind of dad in those tales who got in the way of his daughter's love affairs with commoners. It made us love him more.I suddenly felt a tear roll down my cheeks. I touched it and realized that I was crying. Then more rolled down. Soon, I was silently weeping.Genevieve walked to me and hugged me tightly. She too, was crying."I miss him." She whispered.

"I know. We all do, obviously."Suddenly, we heard a knock on the door. It opened without warning and saw Blair, our sister."The funeral's that way, you know." She silently smirked."Blair." I rolled my eyes and wiped my tears."Sorry." She shrugged."What's wrong?" Genevieve asked."It's time.""What? It's not even sundown." I excl aimed."They wanted to go early to the valley so that more important events can be held." Blair said. And by that, I'm guessing she meant the coronation."They didn't consider honoring the king important?"She shrugged as I sighed in frustration."Fine. Let's go."We nodded and walked out the door. When we reached the ballroom, the generals and the ministers were already down there. About 100 foot soldiers and 100 on horses accompanied us. The coffin was carried by 8 soldiers, our husbands and Aspen was with them. We went outside and climbed onto our awaiting carriages. We sat together with mother, who refused to speak. We just let her be. In the meantime, we rode in silence as we head off for the valley.

Once father's coffin was in it's place and now covered, we, his family, were given a few moments with him. I just bowed my head down, prayed, and bid farewell, since there's nothing more I can do. I know that it wasn't a total goodbye. In body, he is no longer, yes. But as long as we're here, his family and his people, he lives.Aspen knelt down in front of the tomb," I promise, father. I'll be a great king for our kingdom. I'll live up to Sorah's greatness. I'll be everything you wanted me to be. I promise you."

He whispered. After that, he got up."I'll miss you, my love." Mother said as she caressed the tombstone of our father. " See you soon."I held mom by her shoulders, "But please not too soon, mom." She chuckled softly at my remark.Blair came to us, " Dad, will always be right here." She said pointing at her chest, referring to her h eart.Genevieve and Aspen came close to us too and hugged us. "And here too." Aspen reached for mom's lips and curved it into a smile."There. Now, it's like he's still here." He said as we laughed at his gesture."He is here." Mom suddenly said. We looked at her and she gently touched our faces one by one,

"All of you are a part of him. He left me the four of you and for that I couldn't be happier. He lives in you, in us."Our hearts warmed at her words. We feel honored to be born into this family. Loving parents, and great people surround us.It made me wanna cry again. But, I already used up all my tears at the funeral, besides if I start now, I bet it won't stop.We looked at Dad one last time before we exited the tomb. The soldiers straigtened themselves up and went to their places as we climbed onto our carriages.

Aspen rode his stallion as he went on ahead, leading the people.I looked at him from behind, through the window of our carriage. I remembered his face, the way it looked like our father's. The way he smiles and his attitude resembled my dad in his youth. The way our father rode horses and the way he thinks, everything, all of it still lives through my brother.King Jethro lives in Aspen.The aura of a king, you can feel it from both my brother and my dad.With that, I can tell how great a king Aspen will be.He should be. He learned from the best. And I bet that he'll take Sorah higher than before, higher than where father took it.I smiled. Looking back at the tomb as it disappeared from my sight,"Dad, you left Sorah in good hands. I'm sure they'll be pleased." I whispered."Fallon, who are you talking to?" Blair asked.I chuckled, "Dad."

"Sweet Turkey, he's a ghost!" Then she started screaming and sliding to the side in horror. She rolled her eyes, searching for a ghost."Calm down, stupid. I didn't mean it like that.""Aww, look. I can see him smiling at you." Mom stated creepily."Ma! Not you too." Blair exclaimed."I bet he can't wait to kiss you goodnight later." Genevieve added."Stop it!" Blair demanded.Then we all started laughing at our family's youngest girl. Did I forget to mention that she was a little bit childish and scared of ghosts? Yes. Yes she is. Every time we had tea, she would always tell hilarious tall tales that would either make us doubt or laugh."Stop laughing!

"She commanded like a baby, if babies can command."I can't help but wish your dad was here. Only he could make this better." Mom said."But hey, as mom told us, he lives in us. Therefore, he's still here." Genevieve pointed out, making us grin."Yeah, b-but just to make clear, not as a ghost, right?" Blair added."It depends." I teased."Fallon!"With that, we laughed once more.This family really is Sorahian, being able to smile in times like this.

Though being sad would be much more appropriate for the occasion, it would get us nowhere but....well....sadness. So, we would smile instead, like dad told us too. I'm pretty sure, he's doing the same right now as he guards us, as he guards Sorah.And as soon as we get back, we're gonna have a new king, a new era.

2

CHAPTER 2

FALLON

The coronation took place a day after Father's burial."Sorah, I now give you your new king!" The high priest exclaimed as he placed a crown on Aspen's head.He stood up and the people roared in his name and they cheered for their new 16 year old king. My brother was dressed in this beautiful ceremonial robe, which was only worn during coronations. It suited him perfectly. He looked much like dad."Make way for King Aspen!"

The people shouted as they saw him. We were at the carriage on the way back to the palace where Aspen will deal with his first royal matters. And by that I mean choosing the new council, staff, and stuff if he wants to. He rode his white stallion as he lead the parade to the palace gates. There was a festival everywhere in honor of my brother.It touched our hearts that our people did their best to celebrate. Everyone knows how hard it is to be happy today when you just came out of devastation yesterday. It's not the best feeling in the world, trust me. It hurts just trying but hey, these are the perks of being a great ruler. You earn great people who will stop at nothing to show their love.Finally, we reached the palace. My sisters and my mom went to their respective ways and affairs.

"So, King Aspen?" I teased him as we were walking.He chuckled," I'm still not used to it, Fallon."I sighed in happiness, "As if it was only yesterday we were still calling you Prince Aspen.""It was yesterday and the 16 years before that.""Well, things are different now. Our little frog prince is now a king." I laughed.He grunted in irritation, "Please don't remind me of that incident in Diora. I swear I'll sent a battalion to wipe them away."I laughed again as I remembered that event in Diora. He was seven and tagged along with dad to that place.

It was a strange kingdom. They served fried frogs and Aspen ate it not knowing what it really was. He liked the taste and ate some more, even joined an eating contest. He won and was declared the "Frog Prince." When he asked why it was the title given, let's just say some frog legs were found clogging one of their toilets. It was really funny but he didn't like it one bit. He was so angry at the people for laughing at him.

"Aww, I'm sure they forgot it by now." I assured."Yeah, right." He smiled. But then it was turned to a worried expression."Aspen," -I held his arms- "You're gonna be a great king." I said calmly.He looked at me in confusion," Of course I know that." He smirked.I blinked, "Then why do you look so worried?""Well, I'm not sure if the council will agree to my plan."

"What plan?" I asked.He didn't answer and kept looking at the ground as we walked."If it makes you feel better, there's nothing they can do. Perks of being a king. They have to agree." I said, trying to ease his worries."Hmm. I guess you're right." He smiled, making me feel relieved. We continued to walk towards our destination.I, being the eldest and also the secretary, accompanied my brother to the king's court. One of the joys of being the firstborn. That, and because though wise, he can't really handle all of the matters alone. He has a whole lot of homework.

You see, Sorah's fairly a large kingdom. Sometimes we are even seen as a small country. We did well in wars, as our history proved, but not necessarily great. If anything, we are best known for diplomacy and negotiations.Where we live is the capital, which was also called Sorah. So, our location is well....

Sorah, Sorah.In addition to that, our kingdom has 5 main cities, named after our founders. There's Sorah, Kenan, Zohar, Aldon, Reevas .We can't really place our entire territory in one big metropolis so we divided it instead throughout the whole kingdom. Each of our cities are special due to it's location. Others are for barter trades with other kingdoms, others are for resources, one is a city for training, or for tourists, and other special stuff.It's ruled by our chosen leaders, which would mostly be our relatives.

They're automatically a member of the royal council, which is composed of 20 members.So, if you don't think that's enough pain to manage for Aspen, there are still things he needs to worry about like alliances, the court, defense, economy and things that'll probably give him headache.See why he needs me now?But, based on how wise, fair, and did I mention he's a prodigy? Yeah, finishing almost all the books in the royal library and having the mind of let's say 15 scholars put together, I bet he'll just look at these matters as if it were horse stool. Still, he's just one person, no matter how good he is."Your highness."

The ministers of the council bowed as they welcomed my brother to the King's court. I never really liked some of the council members. Some act as if they rule the king, sharing and interfering in his decisions. In short, they're pretty crappy people. I even heard that some opposed the idea of Aspen being king.Aspen sat at his chair in the table and so did the others. He sighed heavily as he started to take in everything around him. The council was staring at him intently, waiting for his next actions. He then smiled,"Take it easy on me. I'm barely a king yet."

He said, probably getting creeped out by the stares. The council managed a faint chuckle though."Of course, your majesty.""We wouldn't want to pressure you but-"

"You have to." He finished. He then straightened himself up."So, King Aspen, the first thing you-" The minister was cut off when Aspen raised his hand."Whoops. That's kinda my line and I know what I have to do." He grinned. The minister coughed in embarrassment but he didn't give it a second look. Aspen stood up from his table and walked around the room as he spoke."I was trained for this, though I didn't know it would be this soon."

He bowed his head and so did we as we remembered my father."I promised to rule in his honor and I may be a lot like my father but we're not entirely the same. Now that I am king, things will be different around here, better, and if possible, best."He walked back to the table and sat as he clasped his hands together."

I saw some faults and some things that used to tick my father off when he was around..... and I want to eradicate that first. I don't want it happening again." He looked back at the council mischievously.I rolled my eyes and smirked as I anticipated what he's about to do. I watched as the ministers seemingly swallow a stone in nervousn ess.He continued, "So, as I presumed, first things first is... I have to select the people I can trust.

The council, for example." He grinned sadistically.The ministers' eyes widened in horror and some of them was close to leaving the chairs to beg for the king's mercy on their position."Your majesty, I have served for 20 years straight, you can't just-""Yes, I can. Don't you dare question my authority."

He rolled his eyes."King Aspen, there are other more important things to discuss." The other persuaded."Aww, come on. You're more important. Don't you think? I mean you treat yourselves as if you were." He glared, scaring the man a bit."My king, I have never interfered in the kings' decisions, not once."

One complained."Well, you are now. Congratulations." Aspen gri nned."Your majesty, please reconsider!" One wailed."Not today, my lord." He said."Your majesty!" And they stood up, started bowing back and forth, begging. One was even on his knees.Aspen looked sternly at them, but couldn't resist it any longer. He finally let out his long-held laughter."Ohhh! I know that this was gonna be funny, but not this good! Hahaha!" His laughter roared.The ministers blinked in confusion. "King Aspen?"Why was he acting this way?

I guess I forgot to mention that Aspen is a little bit waggish. If you don't know what that means, here are some other translations: devilish, prankish, mischievous, and you can look up the others if you have a dictionary.Yeah, so if you put his traits altogether, you have a half king, half jester. I thought it was cool at first, but he tends to take it too far sometimes, and that's where the problems start. Because of it, some thought that he was too immature to be king.

My sisters thought he would be a fun and confident king thoug h.For this part? I go with my sisters. He maybe be playful at times but when it gets serious, he knows how to act in accordance to the situation."I'm sorry. I just had to do that, part of my own initiation as king you know."

He explained, his laughter dying down."Initiation, your majesty?" They asked."Yeah. The coronation was the kingdom's way of celebrating it. This was mine." He grinned and laughed lightly."You think the king's position is a joke?!"Aspen didn't respond and was still laughing and only looked at him after he spoke, "Were you saying something?"The minister stood in silence, as he was taken aback at the embarrassment. Aspen sighed and stood up."What I did was a joke but the idea of getting rid of the present council was not. So you better let me do the talking if you wanna stay, minister of- Who are you again?" He asked.The minister coughed, "Richard Vernon, my king, minister of external affairs."

"Hmm. Well, Lord Richard Vernon, if you don't want to be as external as your affairs, I suggest you let me do this thing my own." He glared.The minister lightly nodded in agreement and compliance, finally sitting down. Aspen stood up once more and walked around the table."I won't remove you from your position."As soon as he said that, they heaved as a sigh of relief. My brother noticed this and went to the ear of one minister but whispered loud enough for everyone to hear."I won't but that doesn't mean I can't. I'll still do it if I see any regrets in my decision of keeping you guys." He warned."When you were with my father, though some of you seem annoying," -He looked at each one of them in an irritated way- "the kingdom still prospered and was in a steady state. Nothing bad happened therefore, I've decided to keep the present council members.""BUT.." He suddenly shouted making the council flinch and making me chuckle.

"Remember my warning." He smiled."Anything more, your majesty?" I asked."Why, yes. "-He started walking around the table again- "Unlike my father, I'd like to have a right hand man, an assistant in other words.""Well, you have 20 council members, you can choo-" I was cut off by Aspen.

"I could really use someone not from this group." He said, referring to the irritated council, who was now glaring at him."Oh. Well then, I suppose you can choose others, as long as they are capable and experienced of course." I said, agreeing.Aspen grinned,

"Mmm, he's very experienced and skilled at a lot of matters. In fact, he's a royal and knows the kingdom as much as I do. He'll serve me well.""As he should. So, when are we going to have the honor of knowing this man?" I asked."Now." He smiled. He then looked at the doors, waiting for someone to enter. We looked at the door also but nothing happened.Our king coughed sheepishly, "I said NOW."Still, nothing."Ugh."

He then went to the door and opened it. We didn't see the man he was talking to but we can hear their loud whispering."Man, what are you doing? You were supposed to enter when I said the signal so it would look cool!" Aspen said."Wait, that was the signal?!" The other said."You're such an idiot. You're embarrassing me."

Aspen scolded."Oh. Sorry, sorry. I didn't quite hear.""Okay. Do it right this time or else you won't even get the job.""Yeah, yeah."Then Aspen closed the door and went back to us.We looked at them dumbfounded but I just played along, repeating my question."So, when are we going to have the honor of knowing this man?" I asked again, but this time emotionless."Now." He smiled.And like before, nothing.Irritated, Aspen shouted,

"Dang it, just come inside!"Finally, for the first time in forever, the man came inside, rushing towards us. When I got a closer look at him, I can't believe who I'm seeing."Sweet mother of- are you kidding me!?"

I looked at Aspen incredulously, who was smirking."Hey, Fallon." The man waved at me, smiling as I glared at him."Your majesty, the royal cabinet is not a jest. The council will not approve of this." They complained also in disbelief.Aspen sighed jokingly, "I knew it. I should've eradicated you when I had a chance.""I, also, will not approve this, Aspen." I said."What?! Why Fallon? Why?"

He protested."Come on, Fal. You used to be cool." The guy that Aspen brought said."Ha! No one would be cool about this. Aspen, you can't be serious?"I know you're wondering who the heck did Aspen choose that even I, the normally supportive sister, won't support.The guy he decided to be his right hand was Prince Daniel, our cousin.Sure, he's a royal and has experience in these matters, given he's a prince. But let me tell you, if Aspen is only like 40 percent a prankster, that guy is 99.9 percent!

He's Aspen's partner in crime. They share almost everything. Good looks, attitude, swords, opinions, views in life. They've been together since I don't know... since they were still not made?Yeah, these two are inseparable and have pulled off some of the pranks that are too dangerous to write in history books.

Some of their famous works was when they messed up a painting of my good friend, Leonardo, who was the one responsible for our beautiful chapels. He painted the portrait of this woman as a gift. Before it was displayed, they erased the eyebrows! The woman was cool with it but the husband was not. Well, there goes our friendship with Leonardo.In short, Daniel is bad news. He takes practical jokes too far."Fallon, trust me. He's smart, resourceful, skilled, and capable." Aspen encouraged along with Daniel who was agreeing to every word.

"Aspen, he once blew up one of our ports with his schemes!""It was not a scheme. It was just a prank....that turned into an accident." Daniel explained."Yeah, and the port was rebuilt, now stronger. He made the opportunity for that. And how bout that time he built this canon for the army? See he's even skilled at weaponry!" Aspen added."The stupid canon fired on its own and destroyed half of our training grounds!" I exclaimed, the council shaking their heads in dismay with every word."But, no one died." They defended."That's not the point!" I shouted."Look, Fallon. Trust me on this."

Aspen sighed."I trust you, but him?"- I pointed at Daniel- " I don't." Then Daniel glared at me."We have to agree with the princess on this, Your Majesty." One minister added.Aspen rolled his eyes in frustration and irritation upon our disagreement.

"Look, Aspen. You want to be a great king, right? Then, please start by making wise choices. I mean, even father wouldn't want this." I said as the council agreed with me.He chuckled lightly, "That's where you're wrong, Fallon. This is what father wanted."T aken aback, I blinked in confusion, "What? What do you mean?"He walked towards the window as he explained, "Father, before his death, personally suggested Daniel to be my right hand."That, I can't believe."Your majesty, that can't be possible. The king knows how your cousin is."

One minister said.Aspen glared at him, "Yes. He knows how he is and that's exactly why he chose him.""But, my king-" he tried to complain but Aspen cut him off by raising his brows at him."Well, that explains it. Father was dying at that time. His brain cells were dying too. Maybe it was just a lapse or you heard it wrong, or maybe he didn't think this straight." I tried to reason.

"No. As a matter of fact, I think his decision was very essential and wise according to his wishes, according to what he wants for me. He requested Daniel to be my right hand so that I will successfully grant his wish." Aspen explained.Now, the council and I were very confused, "What are you saying? What was dad's wish?"

I asked.He turned his back on us, facing the window, facing the kingdom, as he spoke."He wants me to be a great king for Sorah. But, he wanted me to be my own great and not live in the shadows of the kings before me. In other words, he wants me to be me. Because, I'm the greatest I can be when I'm myself."He then faced us."He didn't want the position and title of king to change who I am. And so do I. If I wanna be a great king, I have to be myself. I won't follow any of my predecessors' customs or standards. I don't want to be another Jethro or any other king, I can't have or share in their greatness. I want to make and live in my own. I'm gonna be greater, different yet better."

"Aspen...." I never knew that this how Aspen would turn out, a man of principle. I know that he'll be a great king just like dad. As it's turning out, he won't be a king like him."Daniel knows me best, better than myself even. If I'm gonna be myself, I need him. If I want to make Sorah known of my greatness, he's the one I need to rule this kingdom."He's gonna be different, greater.He faced the window once more, smiling,

"I want to rule this kingdom in the honor of both my father and I." He turned around and gave us a very determined look."I'm gonna rule Sorah....my way."I smiled, overwhelmed by happiness over my brother's virtue and valor.

Now, I understand. I remember now, what he promised father. He promised not only to be a great king, but a great man as well. And to fulfill that, Aspen decided to rule as himself, to do everything his style.For him, to be great, is to be different.And I couldn't agree more."Well, I can't wait to see what kind of great you'll be, brother." I smiled."I'll help with that, Fallon." Daniel said."W-well. If that's what the king wants, we couldn't be more happier." A minister smiled."A greed. I think it's about time we make things different around here. Better." Another said."My king, if you wanna do it your way, so be it." Another encouraged."Sorah is now thy clay, King Aspen. Mold it in thy most magnificent form, if you wish." Another agreed. It was minister Devon, the oldest and wisest."Okay, my lord. Thy words were too deep. I think he gets it." I joked, making them laugh.Aspen smiled widely at them.

"So, WHO'S WITH ME?" He shouted.The whole court cheered and clapped in agreement, sounding like they won a war.I couldn't be more happier and I'm sure that father is too.His son is turning into the man he always wanted him to be.At first, when I look at him, I only saw my father and our other great kings in him. Turns out, I was very wrong. Yes, he may have the blood of a king.

He may have the attributes too. But, he's very different. He's turning out to be.I'm sure that he'll be a fair and just ruler. He will lead Sorah in his own glory. He wants to be the best he can be for the kingdom. With just that, I can tell that the best king in Sorah is yet to come through him. In no time, he'll have the biggest portrait hanging in the hall of greats.With the death of a great king, comes a greater one.He loves this country and will do everything for it.That's what I thought.I didn't anticipate that he'll go this far in being different, to the point where he won't even follow the unbreakable condition essential for the kingdom's survival.Yes. He turned out to be the greatest king at his young age. He's willing to do everything for the kingdom. Everything, anything but one thing...And why is it so terrible?That one thing is the most crucial, indispensable, most important tradition that is the very reason why the royal bloodline of Sorah lives up to this day.And those struggles will bring us to the present.

3

CHAPTER 3

Isabelle

"Mom, I'll be going now." I said. Of course, as a respectful daughter, I have to inform my mother that I'm leaving. It would be rude not to.

"Okay, dear. Take care." She bid.

"Oh, mom...", I turned around once more before I step out the door, "Where's father?"

"Oh, you know that old man, always doting on his farm as if it was his own son." She rolled her eyes.

I chuckled lightly at her statement,"Okay, mom. I'll be going now, for real."

"Okay, dear. Take care...for real." She smiled.

I nodded and went on my way. Before I go out the streets, I passed by our farm to bid my dad goodbye too.

"Dad, I'll be leaving."

He looked at me and smiled with much concern, "Still going, I see."

I chuckled and went closer to him, "Dad, you know how badly I want this. I promise I'm not getting involved with any serious matters of theirs. I'm just going there to do my own thing, okay?" I said as I hugged him.

He sighed, "Fine. Take care, Isabelle."

"You know I will." Then I left.

Some people might wonder where the heck girls go nowadays. We should be at home, milking cows, sewing, feeding the animals, gardening, ending up married to knights, right? Well, usually, that's what we do and no one can beat us at it.

Now, ever since King Jethro sat on the throne, women were given more educational priveleges. Although, most women and their daughters would rather be traditional and stay at home doing their stuff, others, who would like to learn, were free to do so.

Oh, how I miss that king. Everyone was left devastated when he died four years ago. Good thing is his son, King Aspen, made up for his loss. He continued his father's ways and improved it. Sorah became well known in trades and resources. We gained popularity among other kingdoms as well. We formed alliances too.

For a king his age, I'm pretty impressed. Sorah has never been more prosperous. But, that's all I know about him.

Now, commoner women can't only be nurses, cooks, maids, vendors, farmers, or festival dancers, or anything else you can think about a woman is limited to be in this society. We can also be part of the government now and have other professions that were primarily given only to men.

The most popular were the Lady Investigators. They were like female soldiers and were very smart, the only difference was the men were for war and the women were for crime-solving. We can also be part of other guilds.

Guilds are a group of people with the same profession who work in a workshop. They are usually for businesses and all about the kingdom's economy. For example, if y'all are people who make shoes for a living, then you have a guild of shoemakers, people!

The noble women, who were daughters of landlords, merchants, and kingdom officials were given higher education by the royal clan and are the only ones who can be part of a court as judges, lawyers, landladies through inheritance, guild managers, and other higher class professions.

The lucky ones, who were mostly daughters of generals and ministers, and also the princesses, were the only ones who can be messengers, diplomats, and strategists.

I totally love this era. Lots of things to do for women.

As of now, I'm on my way to the academy. The noble's academy, at that. My father enrolled me at the ladies' academy back at our town then when I was younger. It was fine and all. I learned about medicine, investigation, history, math, and other things, given that we were all training to be Lady Investigators, or nurses, or any job in our social state's reach.

But I wanted more. I got so fascinated with information, that I went on to learn in advance and by that, I mean reading every book in the public library. And by that, I mean to every last page of every book, even the credits and references. I was so full I could explode! I even read the books from the royal library. Courtesy of.... well, I don't really like to talk about it. So, you know a bookworm if you'll ever need one.

Eventually, I began to fall asleep in classes because I already know what the lesson was. The teacher didn't like it one bit. There goes my scholarship. Well, I didn't even need those classes anyway.

"Hey, Isabelle."

"Mr. Tudor!" I greeted back, as I walked closer to him.

"Ahh, look at you. Such a fine, beautiful young lady." He commented.

"Why, thank you, sir." I said, tucking an imaginary loose strand of hair behind my ear.

"Oh, come on. Don't be flattered. I was merely stating a fact." He smiled.

I've known Mr. Tudor since I was a kid. His son, Alistair, tried to court me when I was 16, 3 years ago. I'm not really into those kind of stuff, love and white veil occasions. I'm already in love with books and learning and I'd like to be loyal. In short, he got rejected, along with everyone else.

Talk about a heartbreaker, right?

It's not really my fault. I mean, they should know me first and for those who knew me, they should consider the fact that I don't like to be courted, at least not yet. Sure, I'll get married someday, but as my father believes, it must be for love. Those jerks just wanted to get me, whom they said was the perfect girl, for bragging rights. What am I, a trophy?! Tsk. Boys.

"I heard you're going to the noble's academy." He said.

"For girls." I nodded my head,

"Wow. That takes a lot of money for us commoners." He stated in awe.

"Well, in my story, it only took a lot of guts and a little bit of brain." I grinned.

"My, as much as I'd like to hear that story, Isa, I have to go. You know me, work, work, work." He shrugged.

"I understand, Mr. Tudor. But, you seem to be doing extra work, work, work today. " I commented, referring to the doubled stack of boxes he's going to carry.

"Oh, you don't know? It's kinda a big event." He tilted his head.

"Know what?"

"Today's the prince's bri-"

"Tudor! Stop slacking around!" One of his co-workers exclaimed.

"Yeah, yeah!" He rolled his eyes, then turned to me, "Sorry, Isabella. Gotta go."

I nodded, "Of course. You work hard, Mr. Tudor."

"Obviously. Hahaha." He chuckled. I waved one last goodbye and went on my way.

Wait a second. I didn't know what he was going to say. Oh well. Guess I'll know sooner or later. He said it was kinda a big event, which means the whole town must be preparing for it.

"Where's my new shoes?!"

"Oh dear, my hair is still untidy."

"Good gracious, what happened to my dress?!"

I heard some of the noble girls yelling complaints as I pass nearby houses.

What are they getting ready for?

Deciding that I don't and I shouldn't care, I went on my way. I don't wanna be late. I've been there for weeks yet I'm still as excited as I was on the first day. This is the noble women's academy we're talking about! Maybe someday, I'll get access to the royal libraries and be able to learn new things.

"Hey, Isa!"

"Edith!" I exclaimed as I ran to embrace my long-time friend.

Edith was my bestfriend. She's now married, being a year older than me. I'm 19 as of now.

"Hey. I heard you now go to the noble's academy! Oh my goodness. You're so lucky. How much did you pay?"

"Really? Is that the talk of the town?! Well, in my case, I didn't pay even a single cent." I smiled.

"You expect me to believe that?" She said doubtedly.

"Actually, yes. Given it's the truth, stupid." I grinned.

"Seriously? How did you do it then? Knowing you, it must've taken a lot of this." She said, pointing to her head.

Well, she believes fast.

"Yes, but not a lot, only a little." I chuckled.

She then inched her face towards me and whispered in excitement, "You tell me yours, I'll tell you mine."

I rolled my eyes as I circled my arm around her elbow and told her that epic story of how I got in.

(FLASHBACK)

The girls were all sitting sloppily as if bored. I shook my head in dismay at their behavior. Some were yawning and the other was just polishing her nails. Tsk. They're missing the lesson!

"Ladies, you must remember that being part of the government takes serious responsibility. It's not a mere job that can be taken so easily. You have to learn history, investigation, philosophy, law, and other important ideals before you can be a true-"

"Madam, with all due respect, I don't think there would be any crime soon, not with King Aspen around." One retorted in a bored tone.

They all sighed as if dreaming, " King Aspen."

"He's dreamy. I wonder what's it like to be his wife.." One said.

"His wife..." They sighed dreamily.

"Yeah. I would totally forget that I'm queen as long as I'm his wife."

"Yeah."

"Girls. I know the king is great and all, especially at preventing crimes. But still, you will have to learn this as noble women. You should be thankful. Your social state gave you this opportunity. Others would die to be in your place." The teacher said.

I would.

"I couldn't agree more with you madam. You girls must consider yourself lucky. Not everyone is born a noble." The girl with the red hair said.

"Calm your horses, Scarlett. We're just kidding."

I am currently at the noble's academy, listening to their lessons. I am here as a maid, the only way I can get in and get close to the classrooms. I peek through the windows and watch the teachers. I know this is dangerous and people might see me and suspect that I'm spying, but this is what I want. I want to learn.

Besides, I'm not breaking any rules.

Am I?

At first I was guilty for not telling my parents. They do not want our family to be involved in government and politics because it was too "bloody", as my father would like to describe. They hate it. They considered it the most dangerous. But, I'm not getting involved. I just want to learn.

"Hey!" One scolded.

I thought she was talking to her seatmate but turns out they were now all looking at the window, worst and to be specific, at me!

"What are you doing here?!" She said.

My heart skipped a beat in fear. I quickly ran away as fast as I could but now, it was the teachers turn to call me. My maid's outfit shook as my body did.

"Dear, I want to speak to your supervisor." The teacher demanded in a calm voice.

Oh no.

I don't wanna get the supervisor in trouble. Well, mostly, I don't wanna get myself in trouble, although it looks like I already did.

I am here as a maid, but to be more specific, dressed as a maid.

Yes, I like to play pretend and dress-up.

So, to sum it all up, I just sneaked in everyday and get away with it thanks to this dress and my cleaning expertise.

"Please, don't." I pleaded as I went closer to her, as the crowd watched me.

"Then, why don't you tell me why were you spying on the door. You're very much distracting the class. Don't think that I haven't noticed you for the last few days." She sternly added.

"Madam, please take it easy on her. I'm sure she was just jealous of us." One commented, making the others snort and laugh in agreement.

"Stop it." The one named Scarlett said.

"Aww, come on. What any other reason would she have besides that? A poor, unfortunate girl sneaking on the rich." The girl snorted.

"It's a good thing that madam caught her. Who knows? Maybe she could've stolen something." Another added and the other's gasp.

"Check her!"

"Yeah!"

Typical. Snobby rich girls with high positions really know how to get themselves low. I've always known that but in real life, they're the worst, worse than what the books and stories describe em. Just because we don't have that kind of money, doesn't mean we don't have the dignity.

Me? Steal?!... BULL!

"That is enough, girls." The teacher sternly said, shutting their traps. She then turned to me.

"Now, why are you here? Tell me the truth, dear."

I sighed because I know that I have no other choice. I gulped and looked at her in the eyes, "It's because I want to learn, madam."

She blinked, "Learn?"

"Yes. I would like to learn here and study among this class." I confessed.

Suddenly, I heard chuckles and laughter, all due to mockery.

"See? It makes sense. She's jealous."

"She doesn't have the money to be here."

"She doesn't know what she's talking about." One dramatically sighed.

"Foolish, proposterous."

Okay.

If that won't touch all of the nerves in my body, I don't know what will. As much as I like not to snap, there are times that we just have to. Like this one.

I turned to them with fury in my face, "And you call yoursleves nobles."I smirked.

"Excuse me?" One exclaimed, taken aback.

"One should not belittle others while considering themselves highly. Isn't that what you're taught? From the book of Master Ada-iah? And that was just you're lesson a while ago."

All looked at me with sudden shock and confusion.

"Wha-"

But I cut her off, "He who mocks others as an illiterate is no better than he who is mocked." I quoted. "Saying I'm a fool makes you no different than me. You consider yourselves so honorable but what makes true honor is character. I suggest you get some."

The others gasp,

"Why you-"

"Because as far as you have shown, I don't think you're worthy of what's being given to you. It's you who don't know what you're saying. Now, tell me. Who among us is really a fool?" -I retorted with my eyebrows raised. I smirked- "There's more where that came from, more than what's in your pocket."

And I kept throwing a few other verses and lessons, some from the Book Of Masters. Those books are very essential if you're studying to be a lawyer, a court member, a warrior, or anything that requires virtue, sound judgement, and morality if you're up for it.

I can't believe these important lessons aren't being applied. Honestly, these would be better off with us commoners. We're not forbidden to read this book. It's just that it was really meant for the higher class that's why it's very rare, almost impossible, that a commoner would know these books.

It's very rare, I say, but not impossible. Proof is right here. Me

After that, they did the opposite of what they did before. They stood in silence, probably speechless. Note the mouths hanging and eyes widening.

"You-you...." one tried to speak despite the shock.

"No one talks to us like that!" A girl in the front complained.

"It's an honor to be the first one." I smiled and bowed.

The teacher suddenly raised her hands and motioned for the girls to stop what they're about to say. I looked at her as she looked at me with disbelief, shock, amazement, confusion.

"H-how is it possible?" She said as I tilted my head.

"What do you mean, madam?"

"Some of what you said, they're from the Book of Masters and the Scholar's Creed. B-but those are really advanced lessons, even the elders and teachers, especially nobles have a hard time with it. But you.... you explained it flawlessly. You really understand it?" She said incredulously.

"With all my heart." I replied with all honesty. I almost forgot that there were others in the room. Everything was dead silent.

"I don't believe her. It's just what she got from eavesdropping. Hmph." One insisted.

"That's not true." The girl named Scarlett defended.

"What?" The others asked her.

"Being one, and as far as I can see, the only one who takes this class seriously, I should know if she got that from eavesdropping. The verses she said a while ago weren't for our level, especially yours"- the girls she referred to glared at her- "In addition to that, the things she said weren't even discussed. It was from her pure understanding, right?" She turned to me, her beautiful red hair flowing with her turn.

"Y-yes." I stuttered because I was going under the impression that all of them were the same. But, as the saying goes, 'Never judge book by its cover or title.'

Everyone could use a Scarlett once in a while. She should be a role model of noble here. Wait.

I know her. She's the female captain of Sorah! The first one. Wow. I get to meet her in person. I rarely see her in some classes though. Maybe she just takes some of them. After all, she doesn't really need to study in an academy being a captain and all.

"See." Scarlett smiled.

"I still don't believe it." The others kept saying.

Not a moment too soon, the bell rang. It was the same bell used from our churches but a little bit smaller.

"Class dismissed. Except for you, miss." She said, pointing to me. As the others packed up their stuff, I sat beside the teacher in silence. The others glared at me as they passed by to go out the door. As soon as everyone was gone, I quickly knelt down in fear.

"Madam, I'm so sorry. I truly am. I didn't mean to sneak in. I just really wanted to learn. Please... I deserve to be punished." I begged.

My nervousness increased to its max level when she didn't say anything. Instead, she made stand up and sit on a chair. She got a book from her desk and opened its pages. She looked for a certain passage and started reading.

"Book of Masters, Zarah VII, Verse 9, A man who touches fire cannot remain unscathed nor will his feet won't be scorched if he walks on burning coals." She read then turned to me.

"Do you understand what it means?" She asked with anticipation.

I took enough time to think before saying my understandings,"Anyone who walks down the wrong path, does what's unrighteous, will always face consequences. They were born with it and are inseparable."

After I said it, she put down the book while she stared at me, astonished. "Oh dear god..."

"Will I be punished now?" I said in nervouseness.

She let out a laugh, "No, silly. Of course, you won't. Why do always say that?" She then stood up and went to a closet and got a box. She sat down and gave me a smile, handing me the box.

"Never in my years of teaching have I encountered an extraordinary student like you. Because of that, I give you this."

I took it and opened it. My eyes widened, my heart fluttered and started beating faster than a horse.

Inside that box brought me so much joy, more than I could've ever held in.

Inside that box was a Noble's academy's vest, exactly what those snobby rich girls wore. It was a beautiful dark red vest and it has the Sorahian crest on it's chest part. I looked at her with tears clouding my eyes.

She smiled, "I know it was meant for the nobles only but I've never met someone who truly deserves this, until you arrived. This vest was made for people like you and not those"- she leaned into my ear to whisper- "ill-mannered rich, lucky girls."

I chuckled and quickly took the vest to try it on at a nearby mirror. When I saw a glimpse of myself in it, I teared up a bit. The sight took my breath away (not because of my face). The feeling of wearing it was overwhelming. It's like officially trying on a soldier's uniform, knowing that the dream with it came true.

"It suits you, my dear." The teacher, whom I forgot to name, said behind me. Her name was Madam Amelia Yang.

But my expression quickly turned into sadness as I remembered something. "As much as I would love too, I have no money for this and my family would not approve."

She rushed to me and held my shoulders, "No, dear. With brains and will like yours, money is the least of your worries. You don't have to pay a single penny."

I turned to her in shock, "But Madam-"

"Tsk, tsk. Listen and leave it all to me. We have room for a scholar, especially someone like you. As a matter of fact, we've been waiting for girls like you. It drives us to teach. When the other teachers learn about this, they'll be thrilled. But I'll make sure it won't leak out too much."

"But-"

"Leave. It. To. Me." She looked at me intently.

I sighed in defeat.

Wouldn't that seem unfair? I will benefit here without paying anything while the others paid? I should at least pay for something to lessen the guilt of not paying at all. Hmm...

"Fine. If you want, you can pay for your books." She said.

My face lit up, "I will, Madam. That's the least I can do after for all of this."

But then again, I remembered my current situation, which changed my face.

"My parents...." I uttered sadly.

She placed a hand on my cheek, "Dear, at the end of the day, you're gonna ask yourself, "Am I happy?". If you want to answer that with a yes, I suggest you go with your heart. If you're parents really want what's best for you, they'll understand."

Instantly, her words brought me hope and I smiled, "Thank you."

"Well, you should be off now. I'll be waiting for you." She smiled.

I took the vest and bowed and gratitude, "You won't regret this Madam. I'll certainly be here tomorrow."

"I know I won't. Goodbye, miss...?"

"Isabelle. It's Isabelle, Madam." I grinned.

"Alright, Isabelle."

I went on my way, running. I was running faster than a horse. I startled some of the villagers but I just went straight ahead.

When I got home, I knew I couldn't hide it long from them so why not tell it now?

And I did.

"Dad..."

"No."

"Mom?"

"Talk to your father, Isa."

"Dad?"

"No!"

"Come on, dad. This is the last thing I'll ever ask of you."

"No."

"Don't you have anything better to say, dad?"

"Yes."

" Yes!?"

"No."

"Ughhhh..."

As expected, they rejected at first and hoped that I won't go on with it but as my teacher said, I should follow my heart. I explained that it would make me happy and that it was my dream, and that I won't get into trouble.

They soon gave up because I was too persuasive and annoying. Well, to be fair to them, it actually took me three days to convince them. They were really worried and I didn't want to give them such pressure and worry but I promised that it would be the last thing

I would ask of them. Finally, they agreed but not without giving conditions.

4

CHAPTER 4

Isabelle

"So how was your first day?" Edith asked.

"Well, of course most of them treated me as if I was different, lower, non-deserving, but there are others, like Scarlett, who became really close to me. She actually became my bestfriend in the academy." I smiled.

Edith suddenly pulled away from my grip and glared at me, "Oh, I see. You have a new bestfriend, huh? Well, fine by me."

I chuckled at her childish attitude and grabbed her arm,"You know it's not like that, Edith. You'll always be my bestfriend until the day my bones rust."

"But bones don't rust."

"Exactly."

She smiled and rolled her eyes playfully,"Fine, I'm convinced." And we hugged each other.

"So, what are you going to tell me?" I asked, remembering our deal, "I'll tell you mine and you tell me yours, right?"

"Ohhh! Right. Well, you see..." she paused a while to blush and look down to the ground, grinning like crazy.

"Edith, I'm not going to ask God to tell me. What is it?" Call me impatient but I still have some things to do.

"You know that Lione and I have been married for a couple of months now."

"Yeah?"

"Well, we've decided to take it to the next phase." She smiled.

"What?"

She looked at me incredelously before scarring my ears.

"Idiot! I'm pregnant!" She exclaimed.

It took me a minute to process what she just said and also bring my normal hearing back.

She's pregnant?!

She's gonna have a baby?!

I'm gonna be an aunt....well, a godmother!

She's gonna be a mother....

My bestfriend's gonna be a mother!

Without taking a moment, I hugged her as we jumped for joy. I was squealing in excitement as if I was the one expecting.

"Oh my goodness! You're gonna be a mother!"

"Hahaha! I know you'd be thrilled as I am." Then she let go and held my shoulders, "And you will be the second mother, okay?"

"Ha, who else will it be, silly? Of course, I will." I laughed.

We hugged once more until our excitement died down but the happiness didn't. I was so happy for her. She's moving on to a greater stage in life. Motherhood. A stage that will bring you so much pain yet so much more joy that nothing can even compare to it. I'm glad.

"Wait! Did you tell Lione?" I asked.

"No, I'll be dropping the news after he comes home." She shrugged.

"Gosh. I'm sure he's gonna sent the whole army to celebrate with him." We laughed and I sighed after, "Well, I hope the best for you, Edith. You know that."

"Of course I do." She grinned.

Suddenly I heard the bell chime and I saw other girls going to the academy. Darn, I don't wanna be late!

"Edith, as much as I would like to stay with you and plan the baby's life, I'm sorry but I have to go." I explained.

She smiled with much understanding, "I know. Go get em." She bid.

"Get who?" I teased.

"Just get out of here!" She said, faking her irritation.

I chortled, "Bye, Edith! I'll see you.!" And I went on my way.

I wore my vest over my dress and went inside. Some greeted me while others still pretended I'm either invisible or non-existent.

I noticed some of them were excited to come to school, which was very unusual. And they were dressed rather elegantly, as if their attires were brand new and some, their face looked like it was beaten up using cosmetics and makeup. They also sculpted their hair?! What's going on?

"Isabelle!" A voice shouted, hugging me from behind.

"Scarlett!" I said as I hugged her too. The girls behind her, who were also my friends, greeted me.

"Cleo! Rosella!" Once again, I noticed that they were wearing what the others were wearing, the elegant dresses, the hair, the face painted with powder, everything!

"Can someone please tell me what's going on?" I demanded.

"Wait! You don't know?" Cleo asked.

"Goodness! It's the most awaited event of every noble girl here and you don't know?!" Rosella exclaimed.

"Do you think I'll be asking this if I do?" I rolled my eyes. "Just tell me."

Only then did I notice that Scarlett was wearing her normal academy attire. It was nothing elegant at all, just simple and plain pretty. Just like another ordinary day.

"How bout you, Scar? Why didn't you-"

"Dress up like a pastry, smash ornaments on my face, and turn my hair into a tower?" She finished.

The girls looked at each other to confirm if they did look like a pastry with candles on top, which they really do by the way but I won't tell.

"Yeah that." I replied.

"Well, Isabelle. If you must know, if this is a glorious day for the noble women, it isn't for me. And besides, I don't care..." she stated plainly.

Cleo and Rosella gasped in horror, "How dare you not care?! This is a day of blessing and fruitfulness for one lucky noble girl and every one of us just might be that one. This the day where our dreams come true. Live in a palace villa, be served, be bound to the most bacheloricious guy." Cleo said dramatically.

Scarlett turned to them, irritated, "Say bacheloricious one more time and I'm gonna rip your corset out."

Her warning made the two cover their stomach in fear. I shrugged and asked once more,

"Be bound to the most bachelorici-"

Scarlett suddenly growled at me, shutting my mouth. Finally, she sighed and decided to spill the beans.

"It's the prince's bride selection."

I raised my eyebrows in shock and confusion, "The prince's bride selection?"

She nodded.

I looked down as I tried to think of a prince until one came to my head, "Prince Daniel? The king's right-hand, Prince Daniel?"

"Yes!" The two squealed.

"All the noble girls in the academy are candidates?" I asked.

"Well, no. Only a few eligible maidens were selected. Others would be princesses from other kingdoms. They were chosen according to their parent's stature, their own records, and their knowledge." Scarlett explained.

"Knowledge?"

"Yeah, at least. If a woman is educated in her duties and her responsibilities, the government and that stuff, that's a plus."

"And those two have that?" I doubtedly pointed out the two dummies behind her fixing their dress. Those two aren't really that....you know..

"Nah. Their parents are officials of the government, the highest rank a noble can have. So, they're automatically candidates."

"And you?" I asked.

Scarlett scowled, "As much as I don't want to be, I am a candidate. Darn it."

"Wow, such hardship." I chuckled.

"I don't wanna show up but if I didn't, my father wouldn't like it. Ugh." Scarlett complained.

"What are you gonna do?" I asked.

"Well, I have no worries. I'm sure that prince wouldn't even dare pick me."

I tilted my head, "Wouldn't even dare? What do you mean?"

But before she could speak, the bell sounded and we lined up instantly in front of the academy gates, facing its entrance. Scarlett was behind me. Not a moment too soon, our dean arrived, Dean Ismene. She stood on the balcony and pulled out a scroll which, from the looks of it, contains the names of the candidates.

"Greetings, ladies. As you all know, a royal event has once again arrived." She said, as the girls squealed with excitement.

The dean chuckled, "Settle down, settle down. Now, a few of you young and lucky girls have been selected. As I can see, you've really prepared, hoping to be one of those girls who will have the chance to be a princess."

On cue, a few carriages came outside the academy, making us turn.

"Very well. Seeing you have no more further patience, therefore I give you the candidates."

Once again, the girls squealed with excitement whereas I was just getting bored, waiting for this to end since it has nothing to do with me and my life. One-by-one, they started naming the candidates, who will then go to the awaiting carriages to be escorted to the Palace grounds, where the selection will take place.

"Willow Stafford." Then, she went to the carriage.

"Cleo Neville."

"Rosella Maurice."

My two friends excitedly hopped onto the awaiting elegant rig. After that, several were called.

"Stella La Pierre."

"Lucianna Safir."

"Jacquelyn Archer."

Afterwards, a certain name was called, a name, to my horror, made me wanna crawl into a shell and die. A name that made my heart skip a thousand beats in fear.

What the...

"Isabelle Almere."

I never thought that my own name could be so terrifying to my ears.

My eyes widened as Scarlett and I looked at each other in shock. How on earth did my name get there? A lot of thoughts circled in my head.

Is this some sort of a jest?

Did someone write my name by mistake?

Did the dean just wanted to tick me off?

Does the whole world hate me so much that it chose to crumble beneath me?!

The crowd started looking for an Isabelle Almere, for no one by that name is inside the carriage yet.

"Knowledge." Scar suddenly uttered. I looked at her in confusion.

"Isabelle Almere?" The dean repeated.

Scarlett started explaining, "Isa, you're the smartest girl in this academy. You know almost everything and you have clean records. That makes you an eligible bachelorette."

I was taken aback, "But Scar, I'm not a noble."

"You study in a noble's academy. Technically, you are."

Oh dear god.

I. Was. Horrified.

How could this be possible?

This can't be.

By being a bridal candidate, there's a possibility I'll be involved in the government...

That means...

No.

My parents!

This would give them a heart attack!

I can't participate in this or any event related to politics. I'll practically lose my life!

"I gotta get out of here." I muttered.

"She's here." A student pointed out before I could do anything. When this is done, I'm gonna find her and shave her head.

"Scarlett, I can't go with them." I said nervously as the guards were marching towards our direction to fetch me.

"Don't worry, I'll-"

"Scarlett de Beville." The dean announced, making Scarlett unavailable to help me. My friend looked at me with much concern as she is left with no other choice but to go, and she did. She slowly made her way to the carriage, leaving me helpless.

The guards were getting close and I didn't know what to do. Luckily, my instincts took over so I was able to maneuver my way out. In simple words...

I ran.

"Hey!" A guard yelled.

But my ears were covered by the sound of my footsteps mixing with the sound of my heart beating. Soon, I found a couple of guards chasing me, prompting me to run faster.

I kept running and kept muttering the word sorry as I crashed onto some of the people, wagons, livestock, and more. I had no choice. I was escaping. The guards kept chasing me halfway to the port, and I was getting tired so I really have to get them lost.

When I was far from them, I saw a large pile of hay. Seeing my chance, I hid behind it. The guards came and didn't see me. They split up to make the search easier. Once they were all gone I sighed in relief and I took a step backwards to go the other way.

But then, I bumped into something. I turned around only to see it was a someone. I felt caught but for a moment, my heart seemed to beat faster as I gazed into the eyes of this (I gotta admit) very handsome stranger. Good, now it's never gonna calm down.

Aspen

"The king is missing!" One soldier shouted as he rang that stupid bell that alarmed my sisters everytime I went out.

"What!? Again!? Ugh! Find him!"

"Yes, princess Fallon."

I was wearing an officer's clothes and I slipped out before they could see me. I was currently running for my life. I've been running for a couple of minutes but I'm still inside the castle! I never knew that it was this big. Darn.

I've done it now. Fallon must be pulling her hair out by now. I didn't have anymore time to rescue Daniel. (Sorry, brother.) I had a panic attack. Horses and guards started coming one after the other. This is the only time I won't be able to use my power as king.

I was still running and my feet won't stop. I ran in fear. I will never be forgiven now. But, if I went on with it, I'll never be able to forgive myself. Maybe that's why I ran.

Running away is the only option I have in which it may be wrong but at the end, I can forgive myself.

But, to sum it all up, I just wanted to get out of there!

Yeah, yeah. Fallon must be back at the castle, planning to kill me right now. Typical her, typical me. But what else can I do?

What I did was a crime....

I think.

(A FEW MINUTES AGO)

I was desperately trying to hide it.

I don't wanna leave any proof of this crime.

Gathering it in my hands, I tried to hide it in a corner at the shortest time possible.

That's when I heard the sound of a thunderous knock.

"Open the door!"

I have to get out of here or else I'll be dead in a matter of seconds. What if I'm found out?

"Wait!" I yelled.

"What do you mean wait?! I've been knocking for hours!"

Yeesh. Talk about exaggeration. I'll be checking her fists to confirm.

"If you don't open this door, Aspen, I'll have your head on a silver platter." She warned.

"Just wait!"

Even though I know she wouldn't do it since I'm the king, it still gives me chills.

"3." She started counting.

"Wait are you counting downwards?!"

"2."

She is.

I gotta hide this.

I placed the remaining evidence and covered it with a blanket.

"1!" And she swung the door open.

"Good morning, my dear sister." I greeted her.

"It's already noon, you idiot." She scolded as she marched towards me. I stepped on the blanket to protect what I've been hiding.

"What on earth are you doing here? We've prepared everything for the both of you. The guests for the engagement banquet have arrived. Are you willing to disappoint your people?"

I bowed my head, "No. It's just that.."

Fallon then held my shoulders, "Aspen, you've been saying that for almost two years now. This. Should. Be. Done. The men of the royal family are responsible for continuing the bloodline. And you're the king! I wish I could do it for you, but darn it... I just don't have the balls."

"I know. I know. I just don't wanna do it. I don't need it, Fallon."

"Of course you don't." She chuckled.

My face lightened up, "Really?"

She slapped me on the head angrily, "Of course you do, you stupid king! Now, let's get you married this instant!" She pulled my ear and dragged me outside. "Please tell my you've chosen someone already so that we can now announce the royal engagement."

Oh. That.

I stood silence and didn't say anything. She looked at me with suspicion, "Silence means yes, right?"

"Uhh, maybe?"

She stopped pulling me, placed her hands on her hips and demanded, "Have you chosen yet?" She asked in a low, anger-held, tone.

"About that.." I tried to explain but then I was cut off when we saw a black thing floating between us. Fallon caught it in her hands and inspected it. I gulped as her eyes widened, realizing what it is. She looked around the room and saw another one floating from a corner then she quickly went there. I tried to stop her.

"Fallon. Wait! I can-"

But before I could finish she went there, found and removed the blanket and discovered the ashes.

"-explaaaiinn...."

She looked at me with fury in her eyes," Y-you...YOU BURNED THE SCROLL OF CANDIDATES."

I sheepishly smirked, "It was by accident."

"Let me guess, a dragon flew by and used it as a target practice?"

"Exactly. Ugh, damn that dragon." I grinned.

She finally snapped, "What is wrong with you?!"

"Well, the dragon-"

"I give you the scroll of candidates, you trash it. I give it to you again, you throw it. I left some for you, you rip it. I gave it to you again, you burn it. Seriously, we're running out of scrolls! What is it with you and the candidates?"

I sighed, "Fallon. I don't wanna do this. You wouldn't understand." I said as I sat on a box.

Her expression softened and she too, sat, "Then tell me what's wrong? Don't you think they're eligible?"

"No. I think they all are."

"Are you in love with someone not on the list?"

I rolled my eyes at her and I almost pushed her away, "No! Where did that come from?"

Truth to be told, the idea of me falling for another is far from my mind. I put my kingdom first and my people. I know it's bound to happen but as of now, I think it's almost impossible with the rate I'm going.

"Well, are you still waiting for the right girl?"

My eyes widened and an invisible smile crept up to my lips.

The perfect excuse.

So, I look at her with much hope... hope that she'll buy it, "Actually, I am."

Fallon looked at me with a surprised face then smiled, "Really? Well then.."- she took a scroll out of her pocket-," Maybe you'll find her there."

I looked at her with a dumbfounded face, "Oh how fascinating." I said weakly.

She pinched me on the cheek, "You really thought I'll buy it, didn't you?" Then, she stood up.

"Here's a hint. Pick a name that makes your heart flutter." She said.

"Aspen makes my heart flutter." I smirked.

"Good. I'm sure there's a she-Aspen there." She teased.

I stood up, "Aw, come on, Fal. I told you I don't want to put up with this."

She looked at me with irritation, "Aspen, no king in Sorah can break that tradition, especially you. It's an indispensable rule. You have no choice."

"Ugh, just listen to me-"

She stomped her foot, "No! You listen to me. Now, you're not a prince anymore but I can and I will still lock you in this room. I'll be back for you in a couple of minutes and you better have chosen one bride or at least 5 top candidates if you're not sure."

I recoiled,"You can't do that!"

"I'm done with your charades! No more excuses, brother. Why can't you just be like Daniel? At least he went with it."

I was startled, "Daniel's having a bride selection?"

"Yes, because he knows it's his duty and he has no choice. I suggest you put that in your head so that you'll be ready when I come for you." Then she went out and quickly locked the door. I swiftly ran towards the door but I was too late. It was already locked. I banged it in frustration.

They got Daniel too. He must be looking like a criminal on a death sentence by now and now that he's tied up, I have no backup.

Why Earth?! Why?!

I won't choose because I can't get married. If I did, I would have no excuse, no escape. They'll find out about it. And that's what I can't take.

"I need to get out of here." I muttered under my breath.

I kept looking for a quick escape until I saw the window, my only hope. I ran to it and I think I can fit. I went to one of my drawers and looked for a rope that's long enough. I tied it up to a hook near the windowsill. I proceeded to escape but that's when I realized something.

I can't go down dressing up like a king. What if I get seen? The famous king Aspen of Sorah, running on the streets like a stallion... Yeesh! I don't want that out. So, I quickly looked for an outfit that will seem normal. I just took out and quickly change into my inspection clothes. It's what I wear when doing kingdom inspections and when going out.

Not wasting another minute, I swiftly climbed down from my room, thanking God that no one saw me. As I was close to the ground, I saw Fallon talking to a soldier and overheard their conversation.

"Please fetch and escort the king. Tell him that the guests are expecting him."

"Yes, right away, Princess Fallon."

Crap.

I gotta move faster.

I jumped down and ran as soon as I reached the ground. I whistled for my stallion but I remembered that it was his bath time and he doesn't let me ride him if he's disturbed. Next time, I'm gonna raise a better horse.

Left with no choice, I proceeded to run where I allowed my feet to take me, as long as it's far from all that castle chaos. Not a moment too soon, as expected, I heard the bell, signaling that I'm missing. Fallon automatically sent soldiers, ON HORSES, to find me.

"Find the king!"

I passed by the palace grounds and saw Daniel on the palace's main entrance. See, I told you he looks like he's gonna be executed. The carriage of the bridal candidates arrived and it made him look worse. I waved my hand to signal him but as soon as I heard the sound of horses, I left.

I'm really sorry, Daniel.

(PRESENT)

So here I am, escaping like a fugitive. Fallon would like to think that since I didn't show up at the banquet. For her, it's a crime.

I didn't stop running even though I was still outside the palace gates. The soldiers were getting really close and they were disturbing the civillians. As I was nearing the port, I saw a big stack of hay and seeing my chance, I hid. I overheard the conversation of the guards as they passed by. Does this make me an eavesdropper now?

"Where's the king?"

"I thought you were watching him. I didn't notice him. We were just following you."

"Don't look at me. I was just following that running man. I lost sight of the king the moment we left the palace."

"Then why were chasing that man if you weren't sure he's King Aspen?!"

"Princess Fallon gave orders. What do you expect me to do, nothing? At least we could say we tried."

"Huh. Good thinking."

"Well, we tried."

"Yeah."

Okay. What is the army training...idiots?! I'll get to the bottom of this when I get back.

Wait. They didn't notice me after all. I forgot I was wearing an officer's clothes! I could've stopped running and easily blend in!

I guess that proves I can't use proper intelligence under pressure. I just shrugged it off and once I was sure they were gone, I proceeded to go the other way. As I turned around, I bumped into something.

Looking closely, I met the eyes of the most beautiful girl I've ever seen, looking as startled as I am.

5

⸻ ◆ ⸻

CHAPTER 5

Isabelle

For what felt like an eternity but was really only mere seconds, I was staring at this noble man. I can tell from his clothes. He must be an officer or something. A trench coat, a sword, shoes, everything. We were just standing there, not being able to utter a word.

All we can hear is that crunching noise as we accidentally step on the hays and our heavy breathing due to that chase. We were like statues that can't move until we heard the sound of the guards.

"Let's go search back there for the girl."

"Yes, sir."

Oh dear. What if they see me?

My thoughts of being caught were interrupted when I heard another set of soldiers.

"We're going to find him unlike those wags the princess sent. Maybe he's there near the port. Search there!"

"Right away, sir."

The nobleman with me looked sideways and before I could run, he took my hand and dragged me with him as he ran. I didn't know what just happened. I allowed myself to run with this stranger. I could easily lose his grip, throw him like a fairy, and go the other way, but I didn't. Instead, I went with him and I didn't know why.

Crazy, right?

Heat crept into my cheeks because of his grip. Finally, we hid in an abandoned shed. We peeked throught a hole and saw no sign of the guards. But, the soldiers of Sorah are very excellent and keen. We won't be safe for too long.

Wait. Did I just say we?

I breathed heavily, trying to brush off the fact that I'm with a stanger. But I can't, given he's here beside me. I looked at him and he seemed just as worn out as I was as we both leaned against the wall.

"Were you being chased too?" I asked out of curiosity.

He chuckled, "Yeah. You?"

I laughed lightly, "Obviously." Then I peeked at the hole and sat down. So did he.

"Thank you." I suddenly uttered.

"For what?" He tilted his head.

"I don't know. I don't usually thank people for grabbing and dragging me. You're actually the first one." I grinned.

"What an honor." He smirked, and I've never seen a smirk that can look that good.

"You a fugitive?" He suddenly asked as his eyes gazed into mine.

"Me? No. I'm too good to be a fugitive. Can't you see the halo on my head?" I chuckled. "You?"

"Well, sometimes I have a halo but most of the-"

"No. I mean are you a fugitive?" I giggled. Ugh, I hope it wasn't too girly.

He laughed sheepishly, "Oh. Haha. That. Well, no. I don't think I am."

"Were you being chased too?"

"Well, yes."

"Why?"

"Because I was running away, I guess?" He shrugged. "How bout you?"

"Same." I answered.

"Why?"

"I was being forced to join something my guts can't take." I rolled my eyes.

He looked at me, surprised, "So am I! Weird..."

"Yeah. Definitely." I mumbled as I thought about it.

So we're both here because we were being forced into stuff? What are the odds, right?

"I'm pretty impressed. For you to outrun Sorahian guards? Whew. You must be an athlete." He mentioned.

I laughed, "Look who's talking! Well, I'm also Sorahian so I guess there was a pretty big chance that I could outrun them even though I'm not an athlete."

"Sorahians really are the best."

"You can say that again." I grinned.

I sighed in relief and comfort. Why did it feel so refreshing, normal, and fun talking to him? Is it because he's good-looking? Nah. It can't be. I've talked to handsome guys before and it didn't look at all like this. It would mostly resemble a war using words, me ending up as the victor, and them? Rejected flat.

Is it because I've known him before?

No, not that. His face doesn't ring a bell, not even the cowbells on the farm. He's a complete stranger. Which reminds me...

"Isabelle. " I said the same time he said, "What's your name?"

"What?"

"My name." I smiled as I held out my hand.

"O-oh. Isabelle, huh? It suits you. " He replied.

Is he blushing?

Well, who am I to judge him? I'm also blushing.

He then took my hand, "M-my name's As-"

"Ass? Like the butt?" I said, shocked, "What kind of sad parents would name their son after a gruesome body part?!"

He suddenly held my shoulders, making my weird heart stop for a second, "W-wait!" He then laughed, "I'm not finished yet." -he coughed- "My name's Aspen."

My eyes widened, "You have the same name as the king?"

He smirked, "Yeah. I get that a lot but I'm nowhere close to him."

I leaned back, "Why say that?"

"Because he's a king. He's too awesome, too handsome, too good. He must be like the greatest guy ever lived." He explained with his eyebrows raising up.

"Wow. You must really know him." I commented. Then he suddenly jerked up and sat up straight, ruffling his hair.

"W-well. Uh...ummm, I've been close to him before. I'm an...uh... an officer, you see!" He grinned nervously.

"I kinda figured that out. The outfit gives it away." I muttered.

He looked down, "Oh! R-right."

Before we could continue, we heard horses racing towards our direction, "Search there, in the trees!"

We looked at each other and I can tell that we were thinking the same thing.

"Run."

Then again, he took my hand and I just ran with him. We burst out the walls of the poorly constructed and old shed.

Should I get used to this?

"Thanks." I said between breaths as we ran.

"No problem. Now, let's go." He said, running faster and still holding my hand.

As we came closer to our supposed escape, a wall stopped us. A big wall. We heard the sound of horses getting closer and we knew we had no choice.

"Get on the ground." I demanded.

"What?!" He exclaimed in disbelief.

"Do you want them to catch us?"

"Are you serious?"

"Drop dead serious." I confirmed.

"This is treason." Is what I think he muttered under his breath as he got into postion on all fours.

"What was that?" I asked.

"Nothing."

I shrugged as I went to climb onto his back to reach the wall.

"Oh dear god!" He said as he felt my weight. "This isn't what I had in mind at all."

I looked down on him with a glare, "Do you have a better idea?"

"No. But next time, please come up with a plan that doesn't include stepping on my back." He groaned.

"Next time?" I asked.

"JUST PLEASE GET OFF." He groaned once more.

"Fine." I sighed as I finally reached the top of the wall. "And by the way, it's the dress, not me. I'm very light."

He stood up and stretched his back, earning a crack from it, "Yeah, my back doesn't think so." He grunted.

I rolled my eyes and held out my hand, "Here let me hel-"

"Got it." He said as he took a few steps back for a jumpstart and ran. My eyes widened as he jumped through the wall with ease, using the stones on the wall as footholds.

"Damn." I suddenly said.

"Damn amazing?" He raised his brows.

"No. Damn because you could've told me you could do that."

He laughed it off and took my hand again as we continued running.

"Are you made of springs or somethin?" I asked as we ran.

"No, just this." Then he flexed his arm to show his muscles. Again, daaaamn.

It was weird letting him hold my hand for the entire marathon, but I didn't seem to mind. I usually don't trust strangers but there's something about this guy. In addition to that, this was the longest time I've run, yet not even a pinch of energy was drained from me. I still feel like I could run forever.

Weird indeed. What's happening to me?

"WAIT!"

My train of thoughts were seized by his sudden halt. Only then have I realized that we've been running too long that we've reached a cliff that has a lake on the bottom.

Still, we heard the guards and horses. And my heart started pounding like it's going out of my body. No, it's not because of

Aspen. I think I can call him that now because it's rude not to use it since he's given his name to me.

It's because I'm afraid of heights. Terrified.

"We'll do this together, okay?" He said, holding out his hand.

"What?"

"On 3."

"Woah, slow down!"

"1."

"Wait!"

"2."

"A-"

"3!"

"ASPEN!"

And we were still on the cliff. He finally listened to me by the last minute. I was shaking and I was staring at the cliff's edge like it was a well.... a cliff's edge. What's more scarier and stomach dropping than that?

"Hey...hey...everything's gonna be alright." He said as he tried to comfort me, holding my shoulders.

"I can't." I whispered.

"Do you trust me, Isabelle?" He uttered spontaneously.

"W-what?"

"Do you trust me?" He repeated, holding out his hand.

Do I?

I can't say that I don't because I've already trusted him enough to drag me all the way here. I don't really know, honestly. It's just when I look at him, I get the feeling that I can trust him, that everything's gonna be fine.

So, without using the sane thinking I used to use, I took his hand. I was just focused on him and I didn't know what I was doing.

"Let's do this together." He smiled.

I nodded, my sane thinking still not coming back.

"1......2....3!"

"Wait. What?"

But it was too late when I woke up from my stupor. He took my hand and dragged me as we jumped together. We fell on the water with a loud splash. I was shaking not only because the water was cold, but also because I think I lost a kidney from the jump.

That was so damn terrifying!

When we saw the guards at the cliff, we hid underwater until they would go away. When they did, we were able to swim to a cave. It was on the shore. He first got up and helped me. We sat down inside and tried to catch our breaths.

"See? That wasn't so bad." He smiled.

"I think I lost four years of my life! How could you make me jump just like that?!" -I looked down and felt more irritated at the sight of my wet vest- "No."

"You said you trusted me! And you took my hand!" He reminded.

"Yeah, I took your hand, but I didn't say anything.

"Well, silence means yes." He grinned.

"No, silence means I'm planning how to kill you right now."

There was a moment of silence until he spoke up,

"Afraid of heights?" He asked, looking at me.

"Kinda." I muttered.

"Well, congratulations."

"For risking my life?" I raised my brows.

"No. You're able to do a thing you're afraid of. If you'll be able to do that again, without looking back, then that doesn't mean you're afraid anymore." He smiled.

"I guess. But, I don't think I'll be jumping off a cliff again anytime soon." I chuckled as I listened to him.

He laughed, "Well, if ever you're going to, just call me and I'll hold your hand."

My eyes widened at his words as my heart started pounding as loud as I could hear. He too got surprised after realizing his words.

"N-no. I meant it as....uhh, I mean I'll- I'm gonna, you know, be there, I guess, for you." He shyly stated, clearing it up.

I giggled, "Yeah, got it. Don't worry. You'll be the first one to know if that happens."

There was a moment of silence until he spoke once more,

"You're a pretty brave girl, Isabelle." He complimented.

"You mean pretty and brave, right?" I corrected him.

He laughed.

"I mean, yeah, that's given. Anyone with eyes could easily see that." He said, his head going down, avoiding my gaze as soon as he realized his compliment.

Me? I was getting more nervous by the second. I was trying so hard to be composed and be myself. I tried to change the subject by complimenting him.

"And you're pretty smart."

"Pretty and smart?" He said, giving my words back to me.

I laughed heartily. There's this thing I'm really curious about. No matter how awkward it gets, this stranger manages to turn it all around. Then, I feel comfortable again. And note, I just met him.

I was able to treat him as if we've known each other for years. I even stepped on his back! If that doesn't mean I'm comfortable around him, I don't know what does.

"Why?" He suddenly asked.

"What?"

"Why did you say I'm smart?"

Oh. That.

"What you said to me before. If I'm able to face my fears the next time, that won't mean I'm afraid anymore. That's what you said, right?"

"Yeah. What about it?"

"That's from the Book of Masters, The LionHearted, Verse 12, Fear is hard to conquer but fear is no longer it's name the second time around, but a choice to cower or not."

His eyes widened, "How do you know that?"

"Well, I kinda studied it." I replied.

Only then did he look down at my wet dress, "Are you a noble?" He asked.

So, he finally noticed my vest, huh?

"No, maybe, kinda, I don't know."

"What do you mean?"

"I'm not a noble by blood or anything, I just study where the nobles are." I explained.

"So, you're like a scholar? If you're able to study there through money, then you're a noble. But you said you're not a noble so...."

"Well, yeah I guess."

He looked at me with marvel in his eyes, "Wow. You must be really smart. I've never met someone other than a royal who knows those books. That's a pain even for the elders to understand. Those are really advanced."

"Yeah, heard that before. Guess we're just smart." I shrugged.

"I know, right. But even so.... for a commoner to know those?"

I glared at him, "Hey, a lot of commoners are very smart and good people. They work really hard and-"

"Woah, woah. I know that, okay. I didn't mean for you to be offended. I'm really sorry." He apologized, his hands in front of him.

I sighed, "Forgiven." Then I smiled.

"It's just that those books weren't really provided for commoners. So, I was really surprised you knew them. I thought that was amazing of you." He admitted.

I smiled. After that, we talked about several things, about ourselves. Suddenly, the wind blew, making me shiver.

But, the coldness was turned into a cuddling warmth when Aspen removed his coat and put it around me. He rubbed his hands against my coat-covered shoulders to make it warmer.

"Sorry. I didn't bring enough coat. I didn't know I would be jumping off a cliff." He said.

I chuckled between shivers, "Thanks, Aspen. I can call you that now, right?"

"Of course. And....and you're welcome, Isabelle."

I looked at him with sparkles in my eyes as he said my name. He looked back at me. And for a moment, time seemed to stop, waves seemed to seize, and the moon started showing, lighting our whole surroundings.

Wait.

The moon was showing?!

"Sweet mother of- IT'S NIGHT!" I exclaimed.

"What?" He stood up and looked around, realizing how dark it was getting. "Oh. It is night."

My parents might be worried sick! Dad might not allow me to go to school again. I'm so dead!

"We have to go back." I looked up, "I think they're gone."

"Uh, yeah. It's like night." He pointed out.

I rolled my eyes, "Thank you for that officer obvious."

"So any plans on how we can get back?" He asked.

"Well, I can-"

"Please tell me it doesn't include stepping on me."

"Oh. Then I don't have any plans." I said, looking on the ground.

We both sighed as we tried to think of a plan. We're like 15ft below the cliff and we have nothing, no ropes, no hooks, no daggers.

Wait. I have one dagger in my dress!

I took it out from the strap of my boots and I looked at it as if it was a lifeline, which it was according to my plan.

"Woah! You're not gonna kill me and make a ladder out of my bones, r-right?" He uttered in with fear.

"What?! I w-"

"Please tell me you won't kill me, use me as bait to attract birds that will fly you to the top!"

I paused, "Actually, that's not a very bad idea."

"WHAT!?" He cringed.

I laughed, " Of course I won't do that, silly. Where do your imaginations come from?"

"Sorry. Can't think right under pressure." He confessed.

"I see."

He coughed, "So what's your plan?"

"Do you have a dagger too?" I asked.

He went to get his dagger from his boots. "Yeah." He said, showing it to me.

"Good. But..." I scrunched up my face, "We need two more." I admitted. I eyed him and then looked at his sword. He glanced at where my eyes were, which were drawn to his sword.

He looked back at me, then his sword, then the daggers, then the sword, then at me, then at the rocks to the cliff, then at me. He widened his eyes as he finally pieced it all, figuring out my plan.

"Aspen, we really need-"

"Oh no, no, no, no, no. First my back, now my sword! What more do we have to break!?" He complained.

"Whatever it takes to get back up." I snapped. "It's just a sword and I'm sure you've got more of that wherever you came from."

"Aww, come on! Why does it have to always be mine? Why can't you break some of your stuff?" He complained.

"Because I'm a girl?"

"Only biologically."

I raised my brows at him in a questioning manner. Really, can't he just give in?

"Do you wanna be stuck down here with me forever?" I asked.

Then something surprised me. He didn't speak. Instead, I think he blushed, trying to utter some words. "Well I-"

But before he could speak, I took out his sword and broke it in half at a nearby rock. I wouldn't want to hear what he was going to say, or else my heart would explode. Will he really say....

(IN HER HEAD)

"Yes. I would. I would rather stay with you forever than go back, Isabelle." He said, without hesitation in his eyes.

"Aspen, I-"

"I don't want this to end. I don't wanna go back up there and pretend that these magical moments didn't happen."

(BACK TO REALITY!)

Ugh, come on, Isa. Don't let your imaginations get ahead of you. Besides, he may look like a son of Adonis, but you barely even know him!

Why the heck did I even think that!?

But, if that was what he was going to say, what would I answer?

UGH! OKAY. THAT WAS TOO MUCH TO THINK ABOUT. THIS IS TOO CLICHE!

"M-my sword...." he said, his voice breaking.

"Oh, get over it." I said as I ripped a piece of cloth from my dress to wrap around the piece of the sword without the hilt. I gave the one with the hilt to Aspen and I prepared myself to climb by sticking the dagger and sword at the rocks.

"You ready?" I glanced at him.

"M-my sword...." He muttered as he was sitting beside a rock, burying his head in his knees.

I sighed and went to him. "Come on, you crybaby. I'll buy you a new one."

He suddenly looked up with a smirk on his face, "Promise?"

I rolled my eyes, "Ugh, fine."

We both went to the rocks and proceeded to climb by sticking our daggers and swords to the rocks again and again. Once again, we went together.

Funny, it's just the first time we've met each other but we couldn't seem to leave each other behind.

6

CHAPTER 6

Aspen

We finally reached the top. As I was helping her up, I saw lights and I heard people celebrating. She heard it too and we went together to where the people were. And the moment we arrived, a night festival greeted us.

"What the?" I tilted my head, "Is there a celebration or something?"

If there was, excuse me for forgetting. I was chased by my own guards, my sister was being so annoying, and I broke my back and my sword. So, don't blame me for not remembering.

But at least.... I met Isabelle. Our meeting was nothing short of fate, I guess.

I was so fascinated by this girl. I've never met anyone like her. She was able to outrun the guards, she knows the Book Of Masters, and she.... she's.....fine I'll admit it.

She's beautiful.

You don't find a girl like her every era.

"Oh, I remember. I think it's a celebration for the prince's bride selection." She said.

The prince's bride selection?

Oh, Daniel!

I wonder how was he. Was he able to escape? Did he choose already? Did Fallon-

"Aspen? Aspen!" She exclaimed, waving a hand.

"What?" Only then did I notice that I was in deep thoughts. What's happening to me?

"Let's go?" She insisted, holding out her hand.

"Let's." I said as I took her hand.

I didn't even know why should we hold hands. We were now able to go our separate ways and go home. But, when she held out her hand, I get this feeling that...

I don't wanna go home yet.

"Oh, here's your sword. Well, a piece of it." She said, giving me the one without a hilt. "Thank you for that again."

I frowned "Gee, I don't know what to feel."

She laughed. The most beautiful laugh I've ever heard or saw.

Ugh! What's wrong with me? She's just a stranger. I barely know her yet I'm thinking these things about her.

"Hey, I promised I'll replace- Wait. Does that have a sentimental value?" She asked.

I shrugged, "No. Why?"

"Well, if it does, I won't be able to replace it, if you know what I mean." She smiled.

The most perfect smi-

OKAY! ENOUGH, ASPEN!

"Yeah, I know. But I was only kidding. You really don't have to replace it." I insisted.

"Uh-uh. I already promised. So, joke or not, I'll replace it."

"But I said-" I tried to protest.

"Tsk. Tsk. Ordering me what to do. Are you the king?" She raised her brows.

"WHAT?! NO, OF COURSE I'M NOT! WHO TOLD YOU THAT?!" I shouted, earning us a few stares.

"Easy on the volume. I was only teasing." She whispered.

I face palmed myself. Easy, Aspen. She was only kidding. She would never know.

Oh, about that. Why didn't I tell her I was king?

One: She might not believe me.

Two: I might scare her if she did believe.

Three: She wouldn't be acting the way she is if she knew, and I didn't want that.

And the main reason: I don't want her to avoid me.

I mean, who would want to be friends with someone powerful as the king? That would mean trouble for her, and also for me if she got in trouble. So, it's best if she doesn't't know.

I couldn't bear the thought of her avoiding me. Yeah, we just met and all, but for some reason, I was drawn to her. I don't know why exactly. I'm not very fond of girls except for my family.

I don't know why, but I like it when I'm close to Isabelle. She has something that makes her stand out. You can't help but notice and immediately wonder what it is. She's beautiful, that's given. She's smart, headstrong, athletic, and so much more that I can't tell which one of her attributes makes me wanna stay with her. And because of that curiosity, I can't help but be by her side just to figure it all out.

Which reminds me of a few moments ago when she asked me something back at the cave.

What would I say back then?

(IN HIS HEAD)

"Do you wanna be stuck down here with me forever?" She asked.

I took a breath before saying how I truly feel,"I-I would. I want too."

She gasped, "You really do? Oh, Aspen. I feel the same way."

My eyes lighted up, "Y-you do? Oh, Isabelle. I wanna stay with you forever."

"There's no place, or cave, I'd rather be."

(BACK TO REALITY!)

Ugh, what's wrong with you, you stupid king?! You can't think those things about her! You just met her today and you're being like this. This is not like me.

"Woah!"

Suddenly, I felt a strong interrupting tug on my sleeve, dragging me to a booth.

"What's wrong?" I asked.

"Hey look! It's perfect!" Then she pointed out a booth that has daggers and a target.

"You just need to hit five targets with these daggers to win this sword." The keeper of the booth said. But, the daggers were not equal in size. I see soldiers trying but no one was able to hit five targets.

Wait!

Soldiers?

Those slackers?! I'm gonna tear their-

"Aspen, look at that sword!"

Okay. I'm gonna put those soldiers aside for now.

The sword, however, was quite a work of a fine blacksmith. It was sliver with a black hilt decorated with red and white stones.

"I wanna try!" Isabelle suddenly said, pulling out money to play.

"Ah! A brave young lady. Well, may luck be with you." The keeper said mischievously as he took the money.

I tapped her shoulder to warn her, "Isabelle. It's not worth it. I think he's a cheater."

"I know." She grinned.

I took a step back and blinked, "What?"

"Please. You think they'll be giving that sword away easily? Of course, there's gotta be a cheat. How would they earn?" She explained as got the daggers.

"But how will you-"

"You just have to outsmart these losers. Watch." Then she positioned herself far from the targets. She threw one and it hit exactly at the middle. In a matter of seconds, a small crowd formed around her.

Me? Widen your eyes, let your mouth hang, look like a stupid person in awe. Yeah, that's how I look like.

She positioned herself nearer, and threw a smaller one and once again, it was a perfect shot.

Wait. I get it. She's distancing herself according to the daggers' measure. That way, she can calculate the spin needed so that when it hits the target, the sharp part is exactly on the front, hitting the bullseye.

Now, that's strategy.

Finally, she threw the last one, it flew right past the keeper's mustache, giving it a trim, before it hit the target.

Has she been doing this for ages?

When she was finished, the crowd cheered for her and so did I. The cheating keeper took the sword and gave it to her, shaking with fear.

Serves you right for cheating!

I put an arm around her shoulders and so did she, sending me chills up my spine.

"You were amazing back there." I complimented.

"Haha! Thanks and-" she knelt down in a curtsey, "Here's your sword."

I rolled my eyes, "I told you. I was just kid-"

"Take it." She demanded.

"Okay. Okay." I said, taking the sword.

We both laughed at our actions. I held out my hand and she took it. We walked together until we reached the last village near the palace, where she lived. We had a few chats on the way. For the first time, in a long time, I was enjoying myself. I was happy. And I thank her for that. I thought this day would turn out horrible but it turned out to be one of the best days of my life.

We finally arrived at our destinations.

"So, I guess, this is goodbye." She said.

I blinked," For this day only, right?"

"Of course. If time permits." She grinned.

"I'll beat up time if it doesn't allow me to see you again." I warned.

She laughed, "Well, call me. We can beat him up together."

"Yeah, sure." I smirked. "Will you be going to sleep?"

"Nah. I have some things to do. I think I'll be up til midnight."

"Okay." I smiled.

She was about to walk away and so was I but...

"Aspen." She said the same time I said, "Isabelle."

We laughed, "You first." I insisted.

"If you ever happen to be in this part of town again, don't be a stranger, okay. Find me. I'll just be around" She smiled

"I will. So, does this mean..."

She cut me off by holding out her hand, "Friends?"

My heart was pounding and I couldn't breath. But, I managed to take her hand, "Friends."

We smiled at each other before we let go. We turned our back once more to leave. But, I felt like a needed to say something. So, I turned around and called her before she could go completely far.

"Isabelle?"

"Yes?" She turned immediately.

"Thank you for this day."

She nodded, "Thank you too."

I smiled, satisfied, then left.

I was running towards the castle, no I was skipping like an idiot. I was too happy to just walk. It was night so the palace doors must be locked. Good thing my window was open and the rope I used was still there. So, I climbed up to my bedroom.

When I got up, I almost fell and died. Why? Because an idiot decided it would be nice to hang out in my room in the middle of night, looking paler than a corpse.

"What the heck, Daniel!? What are you doing in here? Do you know what time it is?" I whisper shouted.

"Where were you, Aspen?! Because of you, I'm now engaged. I'm tied up. My youth, my youth is gone!" He complained.

I held his mouth, "Shut up! You don't know what I've been through!"

"No, you don't know what I'll be going through!" He whined.

"Quit it. It's not my fault. You're smarter than me at getting away but I was able to escape." I added. I pulled his sleeve and walked him out the door, "Come visit when you're sane."

"No, please. You have to help me, Aspen. I'm doomed. I'm doomed." He said. I tried to close the door on him but he was blocking it.

"What do you mean dommed?! Who did you choose anyway?" I asked in irritation.

He gulped, "Scarlett." He whispered in fear.

I opened the doors in shock, "Scarlett de Beville?"

"Yes." He admitted, his voice getting smaller.

"Our childhood friend Scarlett?"

"Uh-huh."

I started feeling sorry for him, "The one who wants to kill you all the time Scarlett?"

"Oh dear God, yes."

"Why?!" I asked.

"She was the only one I knew there." He confessed.

I facepalmed, "You've gotta be kidding me."

"No. I'm not."

"Don't tell me you still got a crush on her." I teased.

"Shhh! People might hear, besides, that's not the case anymore."

Well, I think I have a funeral to plan. Another idiot for the Valley of Fallen Sorahians.

"You're doomed." I said as I proceeded to close the door.

"No. No. Wai-"

But it was closed.

I do feel sorry for him though. He'll be marrying Scarlett? Yeesh. Goodluck to him. There's no more I can do bout that.

Well, I'll worry bout him tomorrow.

With that, I ploped onto the bed and released a sigh. I placed my new sword on the side of my bed. I looked at it with endearment.

What a day.

But still, I don't feel tired at all. My body, my brain, as lame as it may sound, but also my heart, is still alive and awake! The events earlier, I can't get it out of my system. I can't sleep. Most of all,

I can't get her out of my head.

I can't stop thinking about her.

How amazing she is.

I can't get enough of it.

I have so many questions about her.

I wonder what she's doing right now.

She said she'll be up till midnight.

Well, it's still not midnight, and I want to see her so bad.

So, I did what a guy in my situation would do. I slipped on a warmer coat and I used the same entrance and exit I used before.

I got a horse from the stable and rode it. I used the other exit at the back of the castle and went to find her. It was night and I should be sleeping but,

There's no way I'll be able to sleep anyway.

At Daniel's Bride Selection

Daniel

This. sucks.

Why?

First, I don't wanna get married.

Second, I don't wanna get married.

Third, I don't wanna get married!

So, being the good and loyal royal I have been for years, my reward? Is to be sent to hell.

"Daniel, they're here."

"Yes, Fallon."

Yes, I was the luckiest man on earth indeed. I've been avoiding this day for 2 years by being more efficient and hardworking, not being me, only to end up where I don't wanna be. Even tradition can be a prison. This is the worst. Now I get why Aspen didn't want this. It's like watching your own funeral.

Speaking of my horrible king cousin, where is he?

He was suppose to suffer here with me by announcing his chosen bride while I'm stuck with choosing my bride in person. As I said, I was the luckiest man on earth.

Finally, after Fallon got the candidates ready, she sat beside me along with the other advisers of the court. We were at the Choosing hall, where obviously, based from the name, candidates are introduced until the bride was chosen.

Darn it.

"Daniel, I want you to choose wisely. When it's done, it's her forever. We have the whole day. Take your time. And, remember, it's for Sorah." Fallon reminded.

"I know." I agreed before muttering, "That's why it sucks."

"What was that?"

"I live for this day." I forced a smile.

"Good."

Why, Lord? Have I not been good enough? Did I do something wrong? Please, send an angel to take me to heaven now. I promise I won't play pranks on St. Peter and St. John once I'm up there. You can do everything you want with me. Just please take me away.

As I heard the thundering noise of my demise come near me, which were actually the footsteps of the candidates, I tried to figure out a way to escape. But, Fallon and the other ministers and advisers are here. These people are hard to escape.

"I'm glad you know your duties, Daniel. I know it's not easy, but at least you're here to serve your kingdom." Fallon suddenly said.

"I had no choice." I muttered.

"Because you love Sorah." She finished.

"No, because you threatened to burn my pranking tools! How could you do that?! And how did you get em?" I complained.

"As the royal secretary and the first daughter of the main royal family, it's my duty to make sure that every tradition is carried out by every royal and that the kingdom prospers." She expalined.

"That still doesn't explain why-"

"And don't leave your things lying around. " she added.

Then I remembered that time I used my tools to change the portrait of one of the ministers and place donkey ears and a pig nose on it. I heard someone coming and I left immediately, leaving my tools.

"So that's how you got it." I mumbled in depression.

"Mhm. Now pay attention and act like a prince. They're here." She commanded.

"My tools..."

"Get over it. Straighten up." She demanded.

But I slumped from my seat, disheartened, weak, numb, and I don't know what's my purpose anymore. I don't feel like living.

"Lady Stella La Pierre." The duke announced.

Then one girl came in the stage of the Choosing Hall. I just gave her a glance while she did a curtsey. The ministers talked about her records, background, and they debated.

"Thank you, Lady La Pierre." Then she left.

After her, several were called. I didn't have the energy and will to even look at them. I just sat there lifeless, as Fallon forced a smile to welcome the candidates. She was clearly irritated at me for acting this way. What's her deal anyway? She wasn't the one getting married unwanted.

Then, more came. 20 candidates, and soon 50 candidates were over. The ministers were looking at me. I haven't chosen yet. Well, like I'd want to. Fallon was losing it but was trying to keep her calm.

"Daniel, what are you doing?! You're supposed to choose a bride, not sit looking pretty." She whisper-shouted.

"You're the one who told me to choose wisely." I reminded her.

"Yes. Now, why don't you choose!? We're running out of candidates, stupid."

"I didn't like em." I stated blankly.

"You weren't even looking at them!"

"Didn't need to. Even if I did, I'm sure I still wouldn't like em."

"Look. If I find out that you're just playing this one, I-"

"You'll what? Take my princeship away? Go on. I don't care."

"You're crazy. Daniel, whether we like it or not, we are the rulers of Sorah and we are bound to this tradition. Marrying is not an option or a choice. It is a must. There's nothing I can do about it. Not even a thousand Sorahian kings can void this law for the royals."

"You just made having the royal blood sound awful, which it is." I said.

"If you don't do this, it's not me who's gonna be in trouble."

"But-"

"If you do this, you get your tools back."

I paused for a second, trying to think.

So, I if I get my tools back, that means I'm sacrificing my freedom but if I choose to have my freedom, I won't get my tools back.

These are the tough choices we have to make. You can choose only one and yet, suffer a great loss. You cannot make a way out.

You know that feeling that you're gonna be imprisoned? That's one of the negative sides of royal duties.

You can never escape.

I know that.

And if you do, you'll feel like a criminal against the kingdom.

So, we really do have no choice.

"Fine. Let's get on with this." I muttered, leaning back at my seat.

Yeah, yeah. You can call me stupid. Whatever I choose won't make a difference anyway. I'm still stuck here.

Fallon cleared her throat, "Um, Duke Wilinston, is there anyone else?"

"Well..." the duke look sideways in fear and nervousness. He went down the stage and whispered something in Fallon's ear.

"Why?" Fallon asked.

"We don't know your highness. But no one dares to come near her. They're all allergic to death." The duke said.

Who's not allergic to death anyway and what are they talking about?

"Tell her that I'm personally asking for her and don't worry," Fal chuckled, "She won't bite."

"But we don't know that, your highness." The duke doubted.

Fallon glared at him making him nod, knowing he can't do any-thing more.

"Fal, what's that all about?" I asked.

"Well..."

But before she could speak, the duke returned and announced the next candidate. I leaned back on my chair. This is just gonna be like the others. I'm not going to find any bride. I feel like I'm buying a suit at the tailors' for a ball I don't even want to attend.

"Your highnesses, I present to you, Lady...uh..Captain Scarlett de Beville."

Then, suddenly, the most beautiful girl in this messed up world came stomping, literally stomping on the stage, looking as forced as I am. Actually, she looked worse but you won't even notice it. She never looks bad. Her red hair grew to be as beautiful as she is. The sight of her made me shiver in a good and bad way.

"Captain." Fallon smiled.

She calmed herself and gave a curtsey while gritting her teeth, "Your hignesses."

I can't take my eyes off of her. When her eyes met with me, all I got was a glare for complimenting her in my mind. I instantly looked away, averting my gaze.

So she still remembers, huh? That was four years ago.

Damn. Now I'm scared.

But,

My eyes and my heart can't just seem to stop. They keep on turning towards her. I know she hates me. She's the number one threat to my life. But, when I look at her, I seem to forget that.

I don't know what's wrong with me.

My mind went blank and I just can't seem to think of anything but red. Everything red. Yes, including bloodshed, my bloodshed.

"Daniel, what do you think?" Fallon asked.

But I didn't respond.

"Daniel?"

I was able to wake up from my stupor. I shook my head and cleared my throat, "Thank you, Lady de Beville."

She raised her brows, smirked, and stomped away with heavy steps.

We looked at the duke and he shrugged, "She's the last one, your hignesses."

The ministers and Fallon then turned to me, "So, Daniel, have you chosen?"

I bowed my head, trying to think of anything but her. Unfortunately, I didn't succeed.

"Daniel, have you chosen?" Fallon repeated but I still didn't respond.

She sighed, "Well, looks like we've made the guests wait long enough. Let's cancel the-"

"There's no need for that." I said as I stood up from the chair.

"What was that?"

"Tell them, 'the prince has chosen." I stated. I was still not myself and I don't understand the damn words going out of my mouth. I can't think of one sane thought! The only thing I can hear from my brilliant mind is 'choose her.'

Fallon and the ministers smiled, "Then what are we waiting for? Let's celebrate!"

They all cheered as they went out the room to greet the guests. Before Fallon went out, she came to me.

"I'm proud of you, Daniel. May your chosen bride serve you and our kingdom well."

I nodded, unable to utter a word.

When they were all gone and I was left alone, that's when my stupid consciousness decided to come back.

What the heck did I just do?!

I was about to go out and take it all back but what I said was done, literally.

"The prince has chosen!" It echoed through the halls.

They cheered, clapped, celebrated, whereas me, the one celebrated, was trying not to think of hanging myself right now.

It was too late.

My fate was sealed.

I'm engaged.

I have chosen.

And because of that...

I'm dead.

7

CHAPTER 7

A spen

I went back to the town where I dropped her off.

Upon arriving, I tied my horse to a nearby tree. I can barely see what's around me. After I tied it, I went looking for her, trying to be as quiet as I can with everyone asleep. I can't see anything but houses, and closed stores and guild houses. I was getting desperate to find her.

Where could she be?

Suddenly, a beautiful melody broke my thoughts. It sounded sweet, yet sad and it sounded like the music came from a flute. I let my ears lead me to the source of the that sound. I wandered around, following the music. I passed all the houses and ended up in a dark place with a lot of trees.

My clothes were getting caught on the branches but I didn't care. Okay, I did, a little. It was very annoying but I just have to know where the sound is coming from.

Finally, I arrived at this small pavilion. It took me a while. It was very far from where the houses were.

There, I found a girl. She was sitting at the middle of the whole pavilion. Her golden hair was framing her sad face. Curious, I went closer. Only then did I notice...

It's her.

Isabelle!

I walked towards her but I stopped when I saw what's going on.

She was crying.

I couldn't explain this feeling I had when I saw her in that state. I felt like murdering the one who caused that. I felt shattered and weak. I don't know what to do.

Was she hurt?

Is she sad?

Why is she crying?

So many questions went on, but I wasn't able to come closer. I just stood there, listening to her, to every note she played. I was in awe. She was able to make me feel what she feels through that music. Suddenly, I felt a tear roll down from my eyes. Before I knew it, I was crying. Once she was finished, she wiped her tears and so did I.

She sighed and sat down. And I know that was my cue. I walked closer to her, my heart pounding.

Isabelle

I played the last note of the song and wiped my last tears. I felt so heavy. Although this day was one of my best days that I can never forget, I feel so blue. I miss him. I miss both of them. Look at me. All I can do is play the flute to remind me of them and nothing more.

"Isabelle.."

Someone said my name as I felt a tap on my shoulder. Needless to say, I was startled, turning around. Though it was night, I could see his face clearly. It was him.

Aspen!

What is he doing here?

"Aspen..." I let out a gasp.

"So, this is what you're up to. Hmm." He smiled as he sat down next to me.

It warmed me up a bit to know that he came to meet me, just to know what I was going to do. I wouldn't tell him this, but this was supposed to be a private time for me. But though he's here, I didn't mind. In fact, I think his arrival made this more special. For the first time I have someone to share this with.

I sighed, "How did you find me?"

"Anyone awake could've easily heard and follow the music, Isabelle. And, you're playing in the middle of the night. Who wouldn't get curious?"

"Oh. So that's how you found me?"

"Pretty much." He smirked.

We laughed lightly then we paused for a bit. He then spoke,

"That was beautiful."

"What?"

"The song."

I widened my eyes," Oh. That. It wasn't, really." I said humbly.

"Oh, it is. But, why cry when the song was so beautiful? Was it that sad?"

"Pretty much, I guess. I do it to celebrate." I answered.

He was startled by my answer. He tilted his head, "So you celebrate a sad occasion? As far as I know, celebrations are fun."

I laughed, "Occasionally, they are."

"Well, what are you celebrating?"

"Promise, you won't tell?" I asked.

"Why? Is it forbidden or something?"

I didn't answer. Instead, I bit my lip in nervousness.

Should I tell him that it kinda is?

"Well-" I tried to say something but he beat me to it.

"My lips are sealed. Don't worry, I won't have you arrested." He promised.

"That's good to hear." I sighed in relief.

"So?"

I coughed and took a deep breath, "Firstly... it's because today well, technically, yesterday since it's already midnight, is.."

"Is?"

I smiled as I mentioned his name, "King Jethro's birthday."

What I saw from his face, after I said it, got me a little bit curious. His face was a mix of shock, pain, realization of some sort, and kinda sad. His eyes widened, tearing up a bit. Needless to say, I was astonished but I tried my best not to show it. Anyway, only God knows how he truly feels. I shook it off and continued to talk,

"I know, it's forbidden in Sorah to celebrate any occasion that is related to a deceased person. Moreover, only the royal family can celebrate him. But, I just can't not celebrate. King Jethro has done so much, especially for people like me and my family. For a man like that, the least I can do is remember him and remind myself that on this day, a he was born." I explained.

King Jethro was a very special man.

He was kind to all and was very wise.

I adored him ever since..

Ever since he helped a certain little girl get home.

(FLASHBACK)

sniffs

"What was that?" A young King Jethro asked his guard.

"I don't know, your Majesty. It's very late and we must go home now."

"Shhh." The king shushed.

sniffs

"There is it again. I wonder what could it be?"

The king searched every dark place. He won't rest until he finds out where that sound is emanating from. Finally, in a small nearby cart, she found a precious little girl, shaking and scared. Tears were falling from her chubby cheeks.

The king's heart softened, "Little girl, are you lost?"

The girl looked up and saw the face of a stranger. She was unable to speak.

"Why are you hiding in this cart? Where are your parents?"

Still, the girl didn't respond.

"Do you want to get home?" He asked.

The girl nodded. Of course. Who wouldn't want to get home?

"Do you know where you live, dear?"

"Yes." She softly muttered

The king smiled, "So you speak. For a second there, I thought you were mute, or you didn't like me."

They both laughed. The guard smiled at the two.

King Jethro then handed his handkerchief to help her wipe her tears. After she did, the king asked, "There, there. Now, will you tell me where you live?"

"Promise you won't rob our home once you know where?" The little girl said.

The king heartily chuckled, surprised by the girl's words, "Little miss, you are a poor judge of character. I promise you, I'm not like that." The king raised his hand as if swearing. Not that bad kind of swear.

Who knew such big words could come from something so small?

The girl smiled, "Okay. I'll let you prove your character and virtue by walking me home. Only then will I say that I was wrong by judging you."

The king grinned at the smart girl, "Alright. Me and my trusty guard will prove our character and virtue by taking you home safe and sound, milady." Then he held out his hand, as if asking her to dance.

The girl grabbed his hand. The king lifted her up and out of the cart and held her hand as they walked.

"By the way, what are you doing in that cart when you knew your way home?" The king asked, obviously wanting to start a conversation with the girl to keep him amused.

"I got lost and night fell. I wanted to go home but it was night and if children travel without a companion during night, bad things may happen. You look like a scholar, sir. I take it you know that." She explained, looking at the king with eyes as bright as her mind.

He coughed nervously, astonished with the girl, "W-well. Of course I know that. It's just that my first impression was that-"

"I was afraid? Is that it, sir?"

"Why, yes indeed."

"You are a poor judge of character, sir." She smiled while the king tried so hard not to laugh in amusement. The little one continued,

"Just because I'm small and young doesn't mean I'm a baby. My mom and dad taught me how to be brave and tough so that I won't be like the other women when I grow up." She bubbly said.

"Like other women? You mean those damsels-in-distress kind of women?" The king arched a brow.

"Yes."

They walked like that, hand in hand, conversing for about an hour or so, until they reached the little girl's home.

"This place..." The king uttered at the sight of her house. He cleared his throat, then knelt down in front of the girl to level with her face.

"Well, this is it, good sirs. You have proven your character and virtue by keeping me safe and sound. Thank you." The girl curtsied, stumbling a little bit.

The king smiled, amazed, "Wow. You know, I've come across people- nobles and royals- but I've never met a girl like you, young miss. I think you're going to be a great woman once you grow up."

The girl gratefully smiled as the king continued,

"You know what, if my son was a girl, I bet he's going to be like you. But, he's a boy. Still, the two of you-"

The king's eyes widened. He paused for a bit. He looked at the guard, then the girl, then he smiled to himself as he reached out to get something out of his pocket. He took out a small box, took the girl's hand and gave it to her.

"Little miss, please do me a favor. I'm giving this to you as a gift. Open it once and only once you have married." The king said.

The girl tilted her head and pouted, "What if I don't want to get married?"

"Well, maybe someday, or just maybe, that can change. Until then, please hold on to this box and do as I have asked. Please."

The little girl paused for a while to think, until she finally made up her mind, "Okay then. As thanks, I will do as you say. "

"I'll never forget you, young miss." The king said, touching her scrunchy little nose.

They smiled at each other as they bid their farewells and got home.

(END OF FLASHBACK)

I'll never forget that man.

Only then that I realized that he was the king when I got a closer look at him during a festival years ago. And the moment I realized it, the more I couldn't believe that there is such a king; a ruler so great that you just have to do this for him.

When he is with the commoners, he forgets that he is king and becomes one with us. For me, that's what a true king looks like.

I looked back at Aspen and saw that he still had the same expression as before, only softer.

"B-but, it's forbidden. If someone sees you or if someone learns this, your life may be in put in danger. You could die. Don't you care about that?" He asked. The way he spoke clearly stated that he couldn't believe what I was doing.

I smiled at him, softly shaking my head all the while, "I'd rather die knowing I brought honor to my king, than to live not acknowledging him. If I didn't do this for him, it's like bringing shame upon myself."

"Even if it's forbidden?"

"Even if it's treason." I firmly stated, "Yes. I know that they're gone and what I'm doing now won't even matter to him. But, it matters to me. Just like what Master Im-Kein said in the Book of Masters-"

"The pain of the loss is not felt by the one lost, but by the living." He recited, his gaze not leaving my eyes.

I nodded, "To ease the wounds of the pain, people always try to relive everything for at least one moment. They want to make sure that the ones they lost will always live with them. Still, the pain of reality stays there, the reality that they're gone. So, they celebrate again and again to escape from that reality. That's one thing you can't take away from a person. Heck, even bad people do this. We can't take it out of our system. So, don't be surprised if we see another one do what I did."

He leaned his back against a the wall and looked at me softly. He looked weak and pale, like all the strength he has left was taken away from him.

I crawled forward to check if he's alright. He really looked sick, as if he has a fever, "Aspen, are you- woah!"

I was not expecting that at all.

I felt warm, with butterflies inside.

Why?

Aspen suddenly pulled me by my hand, making me lunge forward and wrapped his arms around my arms and my waist, his head on my shoulder. The way he's hugging me, it's very endearing, like he's asking for comfort. I didn't know how to react, exactly. My first instinct was to talk to him.

"Aspen..." I struggled to break free, wanting to ask him what's going on, but I only managed a small push. Actually, I'd just call that a mere tap.

"Please... don't let go just yet." He softly pleaded.

I paused for a bit before I slowly moved my arms. All I wanted was to hug him back. I wanted to comfort him from whatever he's feeling right now but I didn't know how. My arms were trapped in his embrace so I only managed to rub his lower back. I waited for him to let go. Once he did, he leaned back again.

"What's wrong, Aspen?"

He smiled and looked at the ground weakly, "Nothing. I just... I remembered someone."

I looked at him, my eyes softening. He looks so vulnerable yet strong. His eyes were fixiated on the clouds above. He's missing someone and I know that kind of pain. So, being the good friend I am, I looked for a way to comfort him.

My eyes then turned to my bag. I just recalled that I brought a rebec with me. I took it out and tapped his shoulder, handing it to him.

"What's this for?" He chuckled, taking the instrument.

I smiled as I held my flute, "For them?"

He sighed at me and prepared to play the violin. We started playing music in honor of the ones we lost. We comforted each other through our tunes. I looked at him and he looked back at me, smiling. And, time just seemed to stop then and there; we even managed to ignore the beautiful sunrise.

Why?

We had something more beautiful. As of now, we had something better than the sight of a new day coming. And that is us, trying to visit and relive everything.

Fallon

"We're terribly sorry, your highness, but we found no sign of him anywhere." The soldiers admitted.

"Anywhere?"

The soldiers nodded, trying not to look sad and disappointed. I looked at them, "It's fine. You searched all day and night. You must've been tired."

"We deserve to be punished, your grace. We failed you." They said in chorus with their voice breaking.

I rolled my eyes and sighed, "Do you really want to be punished?"

"W-well.." he stuttered.

"As I thought. It's fine. Go and rest, before I change my mind." I chuckled lightly.

"Thank you so much, princess. Have a good night." Then they marched and left.

"I doubt that I'll be having that." I said to myself.

Where could Aspen be?

The moment we left, we never found him. It's almost morning, darn it.

As expected, he escaped again. What is with that king?! Why couldn't he marry?!

Does he wanna fall in love first?

I doubt that. He rarely interacts with any noblewomen during royalballs. He would mostly just speak with princes, and other important people from different kingdoms.

What if...

No, I don't think it's possible..

It would ruin him.

It would destroy the kingdom!

He wouldn't..

He couldn't be..

But it's not impossible with the rate he's going now...

Could it be...

HE'S GAY!

No! That's n-not.. Okay, now I'm hyperventilating

"Easy, easy, Fallon. Maybe not that kind of gay." I assured myself.

Maybe he's just really friendly with men. Well, rulers were mostly men and the greatest generals and soldiers are too. He's doing it for the kingdom. Now I get it!

I'm overreacting.

But...

If my theory is correct (please, let me be wrong for the first time.), that can be the only explanation why he wouldn't marry! But Aspen is not like that at all. He loves Sorah too much to bring shame upon it by having a king diverting from his own gender.

Oh dear.

I need to find him immediately.

I have to clear this up.

I'm literally going crazy!

With my mind set on finding him, I went to my room and grabbed the nearest coat I could find. I prepared to leave. I passed through the main ball room and the corridors. I was nearing the entrance before I remembered something. I don't have any gloves. I'm gonna freeze my joints out there.

Ugh.

So, I went back to my room, passing all the way from where I came from. I finally got my gloves while cursing the size of this castle.

I went through the corridors again but I stopped when I saw a black figure walk through a hall. I instantly felt shivers up my spine when I saw that.

Please, don't let it be a ghost.

Fearing more that it may not be a ghost but an intruder instead, I followed him closely and stealthily. I grabbed a sword from one of the displays and ornaments on the walls. It's really a good thing they had these. I heard his footsteps stop inside a room ,and I know that I got him. This room he entered had no other door besides this. Slowly, I opened the door, not even earning a creak from it

I quickly charged inside, only to stop myself after taking a long good look on who the figure was.

"Darn you, Aspen." I said as I dropped my sword and approached him, "Do you know how late it is? Where have you been? Almost all of the staff were looking for you! Don't you-"

But, I stopped in my tracks when I saw him touch the portrait he's been looking at since I've entered the room. I was immediately curious, especially when I saw a tear fell from his eye. I forgot all of my anger and anything that caused my head to burn and focused on him.

Aspen is crying?

"Aspen...?"

He wiped his tears and spoke, still not leaving his gaze from the portrait, "Some son I am." His voice broke.

"What?"

"How dare I forget?" He said softly.

"What are you talking about?"

He then faced me, "It's father's birthday, Fallon."

My eyes widened.

My heart broke.

My stupidity dawned on me for the first time. How could have I forgotten my own dad's birthday? Never have I forgotten that special day. It was always happy and fun, just like my dad.

A lot of thing has taken place, important matters, and other stuff. But, never have I forgotten my dad's birthday, until now.

What have I been doing?

I moved so that I was facing the portrait, and I saw the loving face of my father.

There were so many things going on, and there's that tradition not to do anything for the deceased.

"Oh, daddy." I said, as I also touched the portrait, "We're so sorry."

"I needed a commoner to remind me." Aspen shook his head in dismay.

"I miss him...so much." I stated as I started crying softly.

There was a long pause before my brother spoke firmly, "She's right."

"What was that?"

He faced me, "Later, I'm gonna have a new decree."

My eyebrows scrunched, trying to get hold of what he's thinking. When I did, I gasped, "A new decree? You don't mean-"

"No, I won't void the law of King Regulus. I'm only gonna bend it a little bit, only for a day, once a year."

"A day of the dead? You know that the ministers won't allow that. They are very supportive of King Regulus' decree."

"I'm the king now." He scoffed.

"Yeah, but still-" I was cut off by him.

"Listen, Fallon. They said not to do anything with the deceased. Look, they may be deceased but they don't have to be dead or gone, especially dad. They live in every Sorahian."

"I know. But bringing back the day of the dead?"

"Remembered." He said firmly, smiling.

"What?"

"The day of the remembered; that's what it's gonna be called. Like I said, they're not dead. They'll live for as long as we remember them. So, it's gonna be-"

"The day of the remembered... not dead." I said, smiling as I was grasping his idea.

"Yeah. We're celebrating life, Fallon! Just like Isabelle said." He said cheerfully, whereas I was surprised by his quick change of mood.

Wait a minute.

"Isabelle?" I mused.

"W-what? I-I didn't say that! Who's that girl?! I don't know what you're talking about." He quickly said, trying to cover up.

I raised a brow at him. You know, he may be a prodigy, but he's bad at making excuses. He continued to bite his lip. I rolled my eyes and decided to let it go. But, I'm still gonna be alert.

He coughed, trying to calm his obvious out-of-control heartbeat, "Anyway, as I was saying, we're celebrating life. So, there will be no relation to the dead at all. No candles, no dull clothing, no mourning or tears. We're going to have a festival! It will be fun, colorful, just like the life of the Sorahians we're going to celebrate. It's gonna be a week long festival!"

I smiled, marveling at his idea, "I think it's gonna be awesome, your majesty."

"Oh it will be. The festival will start today."

"Today? But it's too early! And you haven't even made the decree yet."

"I'm gonna make it now." He grinned.

"How 'bout the people? They wouldn't have time to prepare. It's gonna be a big festival, and we still have to pass the decree to the other cities."

"Please, they're gonna be so excited, everything's gonna be done before you can say 'Darn you, Aspen'."

I chuckled as he said my favorite catchphrase.

He smiled at me and hurried to change into his main outfit and announce the new royal edict.

Oh, I almost forgot!

"Aspen!"

"Yeah?" He said, stopping from his steps to turn to me.

I gulped before I asked him. How am I going to explain this.

"Please, don't be mad, okay? I'm not saying that you are. Well, it's actually pretty funny how I came up with this theory because I was overthinking why you left earlier and I don't know where my mind flew off to and I came up with this-"

"Fallon, just spill." He narrowed his eyes boringly.

I folded my hands in nervousness, hoping he won't be furious, "But please don't be mad."

"We'll see, after you say it." He folded his arms in a suspecting manner. "Will you please make it quick, I still have a decree to announce."

I closed my eyes and gulped, "A-a-are you..."

"Am I what?"

I took a deep breath, "ARE YOU GAY?"

After I said it, I opened my eyes to see his reaction. I caught him frozen as a statue with a plain look plastered on his face, before he yelled.

"IN WHAT PART OF YOUR BRILLIANT MIND DID YOU GET THAT?!" He berated, visible veins popping on his forehead.

"N-nowhere. I just-"

"Me?! Gay?! You better mean happy!"

"W-well..."

"Either way, I AM NOT!"

I sighed, "I know. It's just that, you know, you avoiding marriage was giving me this crazy ideas-"

"Okay. How bout we celebrate their life, and your death. That way you'll be remembered." He said sarcastically.

I feared for my life. I know I'm his older sister but he is the king, and you would never dare anger a king like him, or any king at that.

"I-I take it back. Of course you are a man."

"THE HECK I AM! A VERY MAD MAN!"

"I understand. Sorry." I said, slowly backing up towards the door.

He widened his eyes, imaginary smoke coming out of his nose as his nostrils expand in anger.

"I'm sorry." I said, leaving the room in fear. I stopped at one corner, trying to catch my breath.

Well, that went well.

"Calling me gay." I heard him mutter as he was leaving the room.

I shouldn't have done that. My curiosity's gonna kill me, literally.

8

— • —

CHAPTER 8

Isabelle

"...And it shall be called the Day Of The Remembered. Henceforth, it shall be annual, taking place every 5th day of the 3rd month. We shall celebrate the life of the Sorahians! It shall be a festival of color and parade, exhibiting the life of Sorah. Now, let us not wait any longer; prepare for the ceremony, ready the booths, prepare yourself, for this is our day. We shall begin the Day of the Remembered!" The public orator finished.

And the crowd erupts into cheers, laughter, and excitement. Immediately, they dissolved into their own homes, taking supplies and equipment for the festivals. It was only a matter of minutes until most of the booths, stores, flags, and decors were ready.

It was a very happy day. Everyone was helping each other in preparation. Me? I couldn't be more happier. I can't believe that the king made a new law like that, and today!? It was such a perfect occasion. It really turns things around.

I was currently running. After the announcement, I quickly rushed to our home to tell my parents the good news, only to find out that they've been busy attending to the people.

As soon as I entered our house, there were baskets everywhere, crops, spilled milk.

"Dear, you're home! Come help us. Quickly!", mother said while she peeked her head from a corner. I followed her to where she was and I was surprised with what I saw; people were on our windows, racing to buy our freshest supplies! Mom, together with our helper, Luella, was getting crazy with bags of coins dangling from their faces.

"One at a time! One at a time!" They both yelled.

"M-mom! What's going on?"

She tried to catch her breath from serving, "These people are too excited! We're running out of supplies!"

"Isn't that good?" I asked.

"Yes, it is. But our lives are being taken with every serve!" She complained.

"It's like milking 1000 cows, miss." Luella added while handing some eggs to a buyer.

I laughed, "I guess this really is a day to remember. Here, let me help." Mom turned to me and held my shoulders, "If you want to help, go help your father. Poor old man, alone getting all the supplies. Help him for me." Then she turned to serve the people again, "Hold your horses! You'll get your eggs!"

I shrugged, "Okay."

I escaped the chaos through the back door and I set my destination to the field. Once I reached it, I saw some unattended wagons full of rice and corns. We are really understaffed today. Running a farm isn't very easy, especially when there are special occasions, since most workers are out with their families.

"Father!" I called out to him. He was currently milking a cow rather harshly inside the barn. Poor cow.

"Isabelle!" He greeted back, wiping the sweat off his forehead. Father isn't really used to helping in the field. He would mostly watch people work, direct the farmers, and manage the field during the harvest, calculating the earnings. He used to work at the palace, although I don't really know that specific job he had there. One thing's for sure: it's not milking cows.

"Father, don't you think the cows could take a little break. Blood might come out instead of milk." I chuckled, getting closer.

"I'm not cut out to be a milkmaid, for your information." He glared at me, standing up to stretch his back. I went in to hug him and laughed.

"I know."

He smiled and sat down once again to milk the cow, "So, the Day of the Remembered, huh?"

I nodded, "Yeah. Isn't the king amazing to come up with that? I guess it's part of their celebration for the late King Jethro."

"Indeed. What a loving family, letting the whole kingdom celebrate for the late king." He chuckled.

"Speaking of family, as your loving daughter, what can I help you with?" I offered.

He rolled his eyes at my words, "Why don't you kill this cow by squeezing the milk out of it. I'll just go get another pail." Then he turned to me once more, "But, please don't really kill the cow."

I laughed, "Okay, sir."

I grabbed the pail, sat on the stool, and prepared to milk the cow. Suddenly, I heard a crashing sound from the back of the barn. I hurried to where the noise was and found my dad trying to get up, holding on to a fence.

"Father! What happened?! Are you alright?" I asked in worry, rushing to him.

"Something's wrong." He muttered.

"Father, what is it?"

"Something's gonna happen." He muttered once more, his widened eyes focused on the ground.

"Father?"

He didn't respond. He touched the side his head, as if thinking, "Isa, can you go to the town to buy some bread? I'm afraid there will be nothing left for us later."

I blinked, "That's the thing that's gonna go wrong? We're gonna run out of bread?"

He shrugged, "I wish it was just that and not something big. Here I am having premonitions again."

I assisted my father, "Here. Let's go get you some rest and I'll buy some bread. Maybe, you're just tired."

"I hope so. I am feeling a bit drowsy earlier." He said as we walked to the house.

"I bet you'll get a good premonition once you've rested." I encouraged.

"Maybe I will." He smiled.

I opened the door for him and my mother greeted him, leading him to his room. Once she did, I told her about what happened.

"We should let your father rest, darling. Now, go and buy that bread. He's right. There might be nothing left if we buy later." She stated, handing me some money.

I threw the money in the air and caught it, "I'll be on my way then. I'll be back soon, mom."

Then, I went out.

As I was walking, I can't stop thinking about earlier; dad having premonitions again. Usually, his words were always right, one way or another. He was a scholar in the old days, that's why many people seek his advice. So, when he says something bad is gonna happen, it always gives me the jitters because it's likely to come true. It happened once. It was also this day, and I never forgot it. I was only 10 years old and it was the worst day of my life.

"Lio, are you alright?" My mother asks in worry, assisting my father who stumbled earlier.

"Lou..." my father muttered.

"Lio, dear. What is it?" She asks in concern. But he kept saying it...

"Lou."

My mother kept her hold on my father, and she guided her to his room to rest.

"Isabelle, come."

But I didn't follow, because I knew the meaning of what father said.

And no, I can't let that happen.

I won't.

In small swift steps, I grabbed my coat and I was out the door.

And the moment I stepped out of the door became my greatest regret. I should have stayed. I shouldn't have went. If only I never left...

So now, when my father has those kind of happenings, I become afraid. And this day again?

What could it mean?

"What's it for you today, Isabelle?" Mr. Po-Chu asked. He was the best baker in town. He was originally a citizen from Sui-Chong, a kingdom from the east.

"Good morning, Mr. Po. I would like to have some rolls please." I requested.

"Ah, good choice. It's our specialty for the food festival later." He added as he was filling my bag.

"Is that so?" I asked, to which he nodded. He gave me my order and I gave him the money. I thanked him and went on my way.

As I was walking, all I saw were busy people; setting tents, arranging the booths and practicing for some performances. I gotta tell, Sorah has never been this lively. Everyone's so happy and excited. What could possibly ruin this?

"Isabelle?"

I turned around when I heard my name, and I saw him.

I smiled instantly, "Aspen!" I ran to him and hugged him.

His body flinched when I embraced him and that's when I realized...

Why the heck did I hug him?

I didn't know what I was thinking when I hugged him. I was about to let go and say sorry for my sudden action but what surprised me more is that he hugged me back. After that, we let go and gave a chuckle and a smile.

"We missed each other that much, huh?" I snickered.

"So, should we always be like that when we meet?", he coughed and grinned.

"Uhh... I don't know. What do you think? " I shrugged.

"W-well... it's a good way to start a day together." He admitted, scratching the back of his head, which was kinda cute, by the way.

Come to think of it, we haven't been apart since the day we met, which was only 2 yesterday's ago. The thought of it was more than enough to make my heart, and all my other internal organs flutter.

But I wouldn't say that to him.

I turned my head to the side to hide my blush, "If you say so."

"Were you able to sleep that night?" He asked me.

"Not really. But I was able to take a short nap. You?"

He rolled his eyes, "Ugh, I was up all night doing the decree. But, it was worth it." When he finished that, he instantly covered his mouth and looked at me.

Did he just said that he worked on the decree? What was that supposed to mean?

"What? You lost me there."

"Let's just say I wasn't able to sleep." He quickly said without missing a beat.

I pouted, "Fine. Fair enough."- I paused for a bit- "I heard there's gonna be an opening ceremony at the palace grounds."

He nodded, "Yes. Everyone's invited. Are you coming?"

"If everyone's invited, then, yes. I would come. Would you watch with me?" I asked, hoping he'd say yes.

He smiled, but then his expression turned into a sad and disappointed one, "I want to. I really want to, but... I'm an officer and we have to-"

"Duties for the event, huh?"

"Sadly." He bowed his head.

I smiled politely, "I understand. But, will you come to the food festival after?"

At this, he grinned widely, "As long as you'll be there."

"I will. I surely will."

Then, we heard the trumpets. The people cheered at that. They knew that it was starting. Quickly, the people grabbed their things and headed for the palace grounds. Aspen and I got separated in the crowd.

"Aspen?" I shouted, looking for him.

"Isabelle!" He waved his hand. Luckily, I found his face in the crowd. How can you not notice a face like that?

He mouthed the words, "I'll see you later."

I smiled, nodded, and headed towards the palace with the others. I turned around to get one last glance at him, but he was long gone, maybe to attend to his duties.

"Don't worry, Isabelle. You'll see him later anyway." I said to myself, making me smile.

It's a good day indeed.

Scarlett

"Come back here, you stupid prince!" I shouted, chasing him with the finest and sharpest sword in my hand. I wanted to make sure that the blade that would strike his heart would be suitable for a prince.

"And die?! No way!" He said as he ran through across the room.

"Well, you shouldn't have lived in the first place!" I said, as I threw anything I could find, while swishing my sword every time I get close enough to his head.

The moment I get wind of the name of his chosen bride, I wasn't able to sleep, thinking of a thousand plans to kill him a thousand times.

Why me?!

When did this stupid and annoying prince grow the guts and the balls to pick me?!

Now, I can't escape.

I'm gonna be turned into a princess, damn it... a-and his wi- wif... Ugh! I'm too disgusted to say it!

I can't even stand the thought of being a princess, what more the thought of being the bride of my childhood enemy?! At first, I said I'd rather die, but then I changed my mind; I'd rather kill him.

So, here I am trying to do so in his room. So far so good. I made him scrape his knee and came pretty close to pushing him out the window to his demise.

I paused for a bit, feeling exhausted, "Why me? Are you kidding me?! You really know how to make my life a living he-"

"I'm sorry. I didn't want this as much as you do but I didn't have any other choice. You were the safest choice I could make." He admitted,

"Safest choice?!" I exclaimed incredulously.

"Well, you're the only candidate I knew ever since I was a kid. And I thought that.."- He gulped as I walked slowly towards him dangerously - "because of t-that... it would be easier for me if you became my bride instead of someone else."

He quivered, his voice getting smaller as I glared at him.

"You thought wrong." And I swished my blade, which he dodged, unfortunately.

"Easy on the sword, Scarlett!"

"Safest choice your ass, because you're not safe with me!"

I began throwing the daggers on display at him, anything I could throw just to make me feel better. But, I never will be. I'm gonna be stuck as this idiot's bride.

Suddenly, a door swinging open interrupted us. Out came a hurrying Aspen, trying to wear his ceremonial coat. He looked at the scenario inside the room. He blinked once, twice.

"Aspen, you're my hero!" Daniel cried.

Aspen looked at Daniel with remorse," Sorry, buddy. I know what's best for me. Good luck wih her, though."

Then I gave him one last glare before he turned around and ran out. Daniel was left hopeless and with a speechless, horrified face.

"So, where were we?" I coughed.

"You were trying to kill me?" He said emotionlessly.

"Fine then." I smiled sarcastically. I was about to strike him with the hilt of my sword but someone came in.

"Ugh! What is it now!?" I roared.

I looked at the door and I saw a shaken, skinny messenger holding a scroll. He tried to deliver his message properly, "D-dear prince Daniel, and dear f-future princess" -I glared at him at this and he gulped-" Miss Scarlett de Beville, the king requests your presence f-for the opening ce-ceremony."

I scoffed, "Look, messenger. Tell that ugly king that there is no way I'll-"

"Thank you, messenger! Thank you! I am forever in your debt! Now, let me return the favor." Daniel smiled at him, giving me one last look before grabbing the guy's hand and running out the door.

"Hey! No fair!" I yelled. But, they were long gone.

That prince! Using the guy as a shield!

I sighed, stabbing my sword at his table and leaving it there. It will serve as a reminder that he'll be dead soon. I brushed the dust of my dress and walked out the door, heading for my father's office at the palace grounds. There's no way I'm going to the ceremony with a dress. I'll wear my armor to carry my swords and other daggers in case Daniel asks for another round.

After passing through halls, I finally arrived at my father's office. I have an area located on the east wing. There, I have all my goods: my swords, my figurines (I use them for strategies), dummies, my small training center, my clothes. It's actually like a miniature de Beville home. Our house is kinda like this.

I used to work alongside my father when I was a little girl, trying to learn his ways. I was fascinated with weaponry, armors, and strategizing that I studied it and eventually, became a strategist myself, being a captain in the process. The very first female captain. I plan the distribution of the soldiers, and I'm also responsible for positioning guards during festivals and other big events in Sorah. You never know when, how, and where can trouble strike.

That's maybe the reason why me and that prince won't get along; he's trouble and I'm... uh.. whatever the opposite of trouble is.

My dream is to become the first female general and go outside the country as a representative. So, I still have a long way to go. Obviously, I have a very short temper, which was enhanced thanks to people who keep calling me pretty. I don't actually like being called like that. It makes me feel weak, when in reality, I'm not and I refuse to be.

"Let the ceremony begin!"

I heard the host shout as the trumpets blast, marking the start of our new celebration.

I finished my armor's final touches and I tied my hair up into a bun so that it'll be easy for me to move. I grabbed my sword and was about to leave when I heard glass shattering.

I must've bumped it.

I rushed to pick up the broken pieces of the object. Turns out a framed portrait fell with it. I turned it around and saw that it was a portrait of me and my dad. He has been away for a week because he had royal businesses to attend to in Bethany.

"What the?"

My heart started to pound, like a thousand marching soldiers in my body. I felt fear through my veins, creeping into my head.

In the portrait, dad's lips were scratched. His head was torn, and red ink stained the part of the picture where his heart was. In my side of the picture, my hands also had red ink.

"Dad." I gasped.

No, I'm overthinking. He's in Bethany. A really far away place... where anything could-

NO!

Whatever danger may come, dad can handle it. He's the highest ranking general in Sorah for crying out loud! I have absolutely nothing to worry about. Right.

I started taking deep breaths, slowly.

"Don't worry, Scarlett. Nothing's gonna happen. You have things to do. You have a kingdom to guard and you're going to have fun along with the people in Sorah because today's the Day of the Remembered." I mused, trying to calm myself.

I heard another trumpet sound and I knew that was my cue. So, I stood up and headed for the palace grounds, repeating to myself,

"Everything's gonna be alright."

Aspen

Everything was perfect.

The people were now at the palace grounds where the stage was set for the opening ceremony. I'm currently at my room, looking through a window. I was looking at the people from down below. Okay, but to be specific, I was looking for her. I felt really bad when I said that I couldn't watch the ceremony with her. Technically, I will watch the ceremony with her but we're just not together.

There's the musicians, the dancers, and the whole parade. Our officials were already on their places at the balcony and at the ground. Everybody had smiles on their faces. This could be the greatest decree made in history!

I turned around to face my mirror. Well, I look ceremonial. I just need to have the final touch. So, I grabbed my stubble. Yes, it was made and sewn using clean goat hairs by yours truly for I am now a king who's trying to hide his identity for a girl just so that she wouldn't know he's the king. Why? Because, he doesn't want her to be scared and he doesn't want her to avoid him.

Why? I don't really know.

What better way to do that than attaching fake hairs on your face! Brilliant, isn't it?

I did exactly that by using some light adhesive. I made sure that it won't fall out easily. Once I was done, I checked myself in the mirror again.

I looked alright. It looks natural. Not bad at all.

All done, I equipped myself with my sword and prepared to head out. I was only a few steps out the door when I felt a sudden headache. My sight became blurred for a minute and I couldn't stand properly.

"Aspen, everyone's- hey, are you all right?" Daniel exclaimed, rushing to me. He held my shoulders as he assisted me.

"I-I'm fine." I stuttered, feeling better.

What just happened?

That's right. I forgot to eat breakfast. Maybe that's what it is.

"Did you put fertilizer on your face?" He blinked, looking at me.

"What?" I asked, breaking from my daze.

"How on earth did you grow hair like THAT!?" He marveled, his eyes examining my face, getting all excited about my fake manly hair. He slowly poked my stubble and imitated the squeal of a girl. "Eeek! I want that! I want that! I want that!"

Then, he backed a few steps away and bowed with his knees on the ground, "Teach me, O hairy master."

I rolled my eyes and sneered at him, "Get up, Daniel."

He smiled before standing, "Sorry. But seriously, how did you-"

"It's none of your business. Now, come on."

I went ahead of him and he quickly caught up. He chuckled, "By the way, we hired a new messenger earlier this morning.

"Well, hope you hired the right guy." I muttered.

He suddenly spoke, "You know, breaking-"

"Bending." I corrected.

"-bending a king's rule is not really favored by the government. But, it really made the people happy. You sure you know where you're going with this? This is not a joking matter."

I smirked, "Says the guy who treats everything like one. And when did you become so smart?"

"Just saying, your majesty."

I sighed, "I know where I'm going with this. Besides, it's only for one day. Don't the people deserve at least that? To celebrate, to be celebrated?"

"I hope this goes well." He added.

"Speaking of things going well, how's your fiancee?" I asked.

"You mean my nightmare! She's been trying to kill me all day!"

"Please, she won't really kill you." I pointed out.

"Yeah, but she can kick my ass! I'd rather die than be at her mercy. Wait, she doesn't have that." He complained.

"Yeah, right. Now, enough about that. We don't wanna be late for the ceremony."

We nodded at this as we quickly picked up our pace, rushing towards the balcony.

We don't want to keep Sorah waiting.

Finally, the wait was over. The pope began the ceremony with a benediction. After that, he sat with the royal family. Then, the public orator proceeded, "Now, let's not wait furthermore; Let the first Day of the Remembered commence!"

The crowd bursts into fits of cheers, laughter, and excitement. I've never seen our kingdom this lively.

"Aspen? What's with the hai-"

"Don't ask." I said sternly, cutting Blair off. I also tried to ignore the looks that Fallon, Genevieve, and my own mother gave me.

"How did you-" Genevieve began, but I growled at her.

"Sorry." She whispered.

Not a moment too soon, a messenger came out the balcony. He was unfamiliar. I think he's the new messenger the court has hired, the one Daniel has been talking about.

"Your Majesty, here's the- King Aspen?" He looked sidewards, probably looking for a hairless king. I sighed and facepalmed, but I raised my hand to show him that I was here.

"O-oh! Your majesty, please forgive me! I didn't... Oh dear!" -he bowed down in remorse and guilt- "I deserve death, your majesty."

"Why do you people keep saying you deserve death? Tsk. Just get up and say what you were going to say." I replied, slightly annoyed.

"Thank you for your mercy, King Aspen."

"Whatever." I muttered.

"But, what's with the-"

"I'm running out of mercy." I warned.

"Forgive me, my king. I would like to inform you that General Aris de Beville has arrived and will be joining the ceremony shortly."

I smiled, "Perfect. Please tell him that we will expecting him."

"Yes, King Aspen." He bowed and marched towards the exit.

General Aris has arrived, huh? Does Scarlett know?

Well, looks like things will be turning out fine. Now that the general has arrived, nothing can happen.

I was observing the crowd and I saw her sitting on a tree, waiting for the show. I sighed in relief knowing that I was far away and that she won't be able to recognize me. She looks so happy, though.

Back to the ceremony, the musicians were now onstage and so are dancers. They had drums, lyres, flutes, cymabals, and others. They all wore big smiles upon stepping unto the stage. They got into their positions and prepared to play. First, the drums sounded. It started with small beats to which the dancers moved to. I can't help but smile as they were dancing. The crowd also appears to enjoy the show.

Then, the flutes played along with them. The clashing cymbals synchronized with the beat along with other percussion instruments. I was really looking forward to the string instruments. For me, they produce the most wonderful sounds. Finally, the others started to play.

Harps joined in along with low sounding trumpets, then the lyres. The music was glorious and definitely worthy for a grand ceremony such as this. Other musicians were still waiting for their cue. But,

I think the music was already good as it is. Then again, we are Sorahians. We never stop at good. What we do will always be at its best.

Now, it was the turn of the rebecs. They prepared their bow and started to put the first tunes into play. I was waiting for lovely and relaxing music to echo but what I heard next scarred my ears.

The rebecs made a loud screech, making the other instruments lose their cue and their rhythym.

Discord.

The crowd gasped. The musicians onstage didn't know what's going on. The once ecstatic faces of the people turned horrified expressions. One after the other, including the officials, started stating reasons.

"What happened?"

"Did something go wrong?"

"The other instruments were perfect! What's happening?!"

"Oh no, I think it's because we celebrated the dead."

"That's not possible."

"The omens. The omens! They're happening!"

"This is terrible! Sorah is doomed!"

The people erupted into gasps, then into screams of horror. The guards were doing their best in controlling the crowd but soon, there were people running around in fear. Heavy footsteps and people in panic made the decorations and the booths fall apart. The stage keeled over. The floats, the tents for the festival were destroyed. The officials and ministers went back inside the palace.

I remembered something suddenly. I glanced at the tree where she sat earlier, and she wasn't there anymore. Was she hurt? Did she fall? I hope she didn't.

I cannot believe that this is actually happening. The chaos that I'm seeing from the balcony made my heart pound in fear and anguish. There has never been a scene like this.

It was impossible. The omens, they say? Just because of the decree that this is happening?!

It's not true. This is not Sorah at all. I won't let this happen. I have to get to the bottom of this.

"Aspen?" Fallon asked in worry, holding my shoulders.

I turned to her with a stern look, my robe swinging with my sudden movement, "Gather the court immediately."

She nodded and went to do so. I took one last long look at the palace grounds and at the people before I stormed to the court.

"It's because we broke the law of Regulus."

"This is what he wanted to avoid. Now, it's happening." The other minister added.

"Shut up." I warned them. And this is another kind of Discord that I loathe most.

The moment I sat on the table, I immediately heard complaints, mostly about the the decree and what happened earlier. The hair that I glued to my face was long gone.

They looked at me with concern, "Your highness, it might be because of the decree! Bad luck has happened because of that. Sorah is now undergoing the omens! The first one has already-"

I rolled my eyes, "I know the three omens, alright. Discord, Demise, then Downfall. Just because of what happened, you concluded that we are already going through Discord?"

One blinked, "What else could it be, my king? It was very clear. What happened was certainly chaos, discord! It's all because of the new decree!" He blamed.

My eyes narrowed at him.

One replied, "Maybe the instruments weren't tuned. We're over-reacting."

"I agree with him." I said, agreeing with a few. But, another argued,

"What if it's not? Our musicians are well-trained and they should know how to tune their own instruments. What took place was certainly discord." At this, many agreed and nodded.

"Sorah might end up like the Five fallen kingdoms if this goes on. I suggest we void the decree and prepare for war." The minister of defense said.

"That will not happen to Sorah!" Others rambled. Then it started. The noise of their dispute increased. They debated endlessly, making my head ache.

The omens they were saying, if anyone would ask, were the greatest fears of every kingdom:

Discord.

Demise

Downfall.

This became a trend because of the Five Fallen Kingdoms:

Abbadon, Venadar, Rave, Ectal, and Seira.

The omens occurred a very, very long time ago in these kingdoms before falling into civil wars, being easily conquered because of that, and then came the end of their glory and reign. People thought it was just a mere coincidence but as soon as they realize the pattern of having the 3 omens, they believed that the kingdoms' fall was actually because of those.

For that reason, every kingdom watches out for the three said portents and what would happen to them. As much as possible, they form alliances and laws to avoid such situations, to avoid the devastation of their kingdom.

Now, they think that Discord has happened to us and it's all because of the law I made. I implemented that to celebrate life, and it has brought destruction upon our kingdom.

No, it cannot be. We are not under those omens.

There must be an explanation for this.

Discord is not the answer. There will be no Discord, no Demise, and absolutely no Downfall. I won't let that happen. Not to Sorah!

"Your Majesty, what if Demise happens next? Will you believe us then?"

I slammed my hands on the table and stood up, "I WON'T LET THAT HAPPEN! Those stupid omens have no place in Sorah. Now, why don't you get that lunacy out of your heads or else get out of my court!"

My sudden outburst silenced the whole room for a second. The said silence was annoyingly shattered by the doors flinging open.

"What is it now?!"

A guard revealed himself, trying to catch his breath. He bowed and stayed with his head down as he spoke, "Y-your Majesty..", he quivered, finding difficulty in bringing the message.

"What?"

"It's General de Beville..."

I faced him, "What about General Aris?"

He looked at the court with much worry and remorse before saying the words. And, when he did,

His message fell like a thousand thunderstorms upon our ears.

I felt heavier. I was trying hard not to lose my balance from the news. I had to hold on to the rim of the table just to stand properly, which I am currently finding hard to do. But, the worst thing was, I had this stupid feeling in my gut that things are gonna go downhill from here on out.

Oh no...

"My king, General de Beville is dead."

Demise.

I fell upon my chair in distress, "W-what?", Daniel, along with the ministers surrounded me as I fell. I felt numb. Is this really true?

"That's preposterous!"

"It's a lie!"

"Outrage! That is impossible! Our greatest general?!" One roared after the other.

"He has just returned from Bethany. Was it an ambush?" They asked, but the guard couldn't say a thing.

Daniel looked at me with much concern, "Aspen..."

But I wasn't able to utter a word.

Demise. Is this really it? Is it really happening to Sorah?

"Who's behind this?" Daniel gritted between his teeth.

"If it was an ambush, I doubt that de Beville would let his guard down. He could've easily escaped." One mentioned.

"I'm afraid...", the guard managed to speak, "he wasn't able to escape because..."

"Because?" Daniel asked.

"The murderer was...his own daughter, Miss Scarlett de Beville.

9

—— ◦ ——

CHAPTER 9

D aniel

"Scarlett!" My voice echoed through the halls as I ran towards the room where the said crime scene was.

"Daniel!" Aspen's voice said behind me.

"It can't be." I kept repeating in my head as I almost tripped, racing towards that room. I won't believe it. Never. Scarlett, as dangerous and life-threatening as she is, will not be able to do what she's accused of.

I know her and she is not a murderer. Anyone who accuses her one shall go through me. I'll send them from the living world to Hades' platter.

"The murderer was.... his own daughter, Miss Scarlett de Beville."

Without missing a beat, I charged at the guard and held him by his collar, lifting him off the ground. I growled, "How dare you accuse the future princess a killer!"

"Daniel." Aspen warned, but my ears were covered with anger rushing through my veins, popping unto my forehead.

He helplessly held on to my fists for his dear life as he quivered, "I-it's true, your highness. I saw it with my own eyes! In his office, miss Scarlett was pulling out her dagger, pierced in the flesh of her father."

I shook him, "Liar!"

"Your highness, please..." he pleaded in fear.

I glared daggers at him, sharper than the dagger in my belt and in my pranking tools.

"Daniel!" Aspen roared once again in warning. Forcefully, I threw the guy down and stormed towards General Aris' office with Aspen following me.

"Scarlett!" I shouted once again. Finally, I arrived at the general's office. I wasted no time in pushing the door open. Aspen followed right behind me. I raced through the office and there, to my horror, I found a scene which I initially said was impossible to happen. Still, I refused to believe it.

Scarlett was holding her blood-stained dagger and was stunned, unable to speak or move in front of her father's corpse. He was wearing his armor and was facing down. It was General Aris. Scarlett's back was facing us, but we clearly saw how she was shaking.

"Scar..." Aspen and I said in disbelief.

She turned around, revealing her face in shock and tears. "I-I- I don't.." she stuttered.

We heard footsteps coming right at us. Some ministers followed us in the office to see the scene for themselves. And it all took one look for the stupid courtiers to actually believe that what the guard said was true, that Scarlett was the murderer.

"Behold, demise, king Aspen." One uttered, facing Aspen, making him look at the man in disbelief.

"So, it is true." The other gasped, "Miss de Beville, how could you?"

My instincts took over me and I quickly grabbed my sword and pointed it at the minister's neck, "How dare you question her? How dare you believe that she was the one who did this?!"

"Daniel." Aspen warned again.

The minister remained calm, "Prince Daniel, what better proof could we have? We have seen the scene for ourselves and there is no other explanation for this except for the one we're told. Her daughter is the murd-.

I pressed the sword against his flesh and I growled, cutting him off, "Well, you're all blind and deaf. And I'm gonna prove you wrong."

"Daniel, that's enough." Aspen said.

I gave one last glare at him before I finally put down my sword. I turned to Scarlett who was still paralyzed in shock. I slowly held her shoulders as I tried to comfort her.

"D-dad..." she quivered. "I-It wasn't..."

I shushed her in a gentle manner, "I know. I know. We're gonna solve all this, okay. I don't and I'll never believe them, Scar."

"My father. Daniel, he's...", she sobbed.

"I'm sorry. But, I promise you, we're gonna solve this." I assured her.

"No." She whispered in regret, "No!"

Shaking, she went to sob over her father's corpse. "Dad!" She held his pale and lifeless hand. "Please! Oh dear God! No.."

I bowed my head. I can't take it seeing her like this. She is not like this.

"I'm gonna prove them wrong. I'm going to find the real assholes behind this. " I said to myself, clenching my fists.

One minister behind us started, "Do you believe us now, your majesty? This is not yet the worst. Discord took place and Demise has happened in front of our very eyes. What happens in Downfall?"

"There will be none of that." Aspen assured, "Make sure that what happened stays here and no one else will know about the death of the general. We'll get to the bottom of this. There will be no Downfall in Sorah. Not on my watch!" Then he raged out the office.

The minister sighed at his stubbornness, "I say we must prepare for the-"

I glared, "Get out of here before I have you arrested."

He sighed and rolled his eyes but went out anyway.

Not a moment too soon, two guards came marching in, "Prince Daniel, we are her to take Miss Scarlett into custody and-"

I quickly unsheathed my sword and pointed it at them, "If you value your manhood, you better get your metal-covered rears out of my sight." I finished with a glare sharper than their swords.

"But-"

"You want me to take off your ass?"

He shook his head, "No, sir. Forgive us. We were only doing our job, following orders."

"Well, follow this order. Turn around and get out that door." I demanded, pointing my sword towards the exit.

First, they looked at each other, refusing to move. Annoyed, I touched the tip of my sword and narrowed my eyes at them, "While you still can."

Finally, they nodded, "Y-yes, your highness.", and went out the door.

I rolled my eyes before turning around to glance at Scarlett. "Scar?"

She didn't move. She was still sobbing over her father. Actually, she's not moving at all. What the?

"Scar? Scar!" I said as I rushed to her and held her shoulders. I felt her breathe and I sighed in relief. It looks like she has collapsed from too much crying.

As for General Aris...damn it.

I couldn't do anything but watch his corpse bleed and his daughter lament over him. Everything happened so fast, there wasn't enough time to act.

Scarlett. She must be devastated and I can't believe that they would accuse her of murdering her own father! They actually concluded in that sick theory?!

Okay. I need to calm down. In the meantime, I'll take Scarlett to her room and have the general's corpse be taken to the morgue. I carried Scar gently as I walked out of the office. I took one long look at the general before completely walking away. He was one of my mentors too. He taught me how to handle swords and stuff along with Aspen and Scar on few occasions. I can't believe that this has happened.

In depression, I stepped out the door, carrying my fiancee. I passed the medics as they headed towards the office to get the dead body of the general. As for me, I went straight ahead to her room in the east wing of the defense office. I rested her on her bed and tuck her in. She must be in so much pain right now that I can't even imagine.

"I'll be back, Scarlett." I whispered in her ear as I touched her forehead to check if she has a fever, and she does. The nurses must be busy tending to the people hurt during the whole mess back there. I guess I better tell Aspen where I'll be for the next few hours.

I left her there for a minute to go to Aspen's room. I opened the door and saw him putting on his inspection coat.

"Where are you off to?" I asked.

He shrugged his head, "Anywhere but here. I need to think. I have to find a way to get around all this bull-"

"Before you finish that, if you need me, I'll be in Scarlett's room. She has a fever and I need to tend to her."

His eyes narrowed in curiosity, "Why you?"

"Well, the nurses will be busy attending to the people." I explained.

He chuckled,"So? We have a thousand nurses. Since when did you become one of them?"

"Well I-"

Why does he always have to have a point? A very sharp one at that. I scratched the back of my head as I tried to think of a reason, "I have nothing better to do anyway. And, I need to be there when she wakes up."

"Why?"

"Seriously, can't a prince take care of his bride?!" I snapped, only to cover my mouth with my hand and try not to turn too red. Why the heck did I say that.

He smirked, "And the truth comes out. You should've said that in the first place."

"Whatever." I muttered, sighing in defeat. Tsk, bully.

He walked to me and punched my shoulder, "Well, I'm off."

Before he walks away I asked him, "Aspen, what do you think of all of this?" -I faced him- "What do you think will happen to Sorah with all these omens and stuff?"

"Here is what I know and what I will always believe in. As far as the omens are concerned, Sorah will never fall. This is our kingdom and we're not gonna lose it to some premonition. Not on our watch."

Then, he went outside. He's a king who won't really give up. Despite what the people think, despite what others believe in, he stands firm and believes in one thing: That Sorah will stand forever.

This is Discord, this is Demise, they say. Well, I don't believe it. Aspen's right. We have to get to the bottom of this.

Omens, my ass.

10

—— • ——

CHAPTER 10

Isabelle

"Oh dear, the people must be dismayed with the events."

"If the people are, what more the king?"

"Yeah."

"Why does this have to happen to Sorah?"

As I went home, I passed a couple of people who were talking about the chaos earlier, about the Discord. They say that the 3 omens are taking place. Discord, then Demise, then Downfall, just like the 5 Fallen Kingdoms.

So, this is what father's premonition meant. I can't believe that it's this disastrous. As for me, I'm not really sure if what took place at the ceremony earlier was really a sign of the omens. I think it was just an accident. Instruments can't go wrong that fast. There has to be an explanation for that, a logical one.

I'm not that kind of girl to believe in bad luck and curses, unless there's proof.

"Mom, Dad?" I said, as I entered the house. I saw that everything was still a mess. Gertrude, my mom and dad were cleaning the floor and the tables.

"Let me help you guys." I offered as I grabbed the broom.

"Thank you, Isabelle." Mom smiled.

There were a lot of vegetables lying around and the smell of egg yolks overthrew the fragrance our flowers gave. Looks like I have to clean really hard if I want these removed.

I was sweeping near dad's room when I noticed that his prized lute had broken strings.

Wow, the chaos really reached as far as his room.

I sighed as I looked at it. I loved it whenever dad played that for me when I was little. He made it himself and he also taught me how to change its strings and polish it til' it shines like a noble's forehead.

I dropped the broom and went inside to grab the lute. Dad came in and saw me holding it as I was sitting on the chair.

He chuckled, "Poor lute."

I grinned, "Yeah, I know. Poor, unsuspecting lute."

Dad sighed, "It really takes me back. I missed those days when you were just a little girl, Isabelle."

I chuckled, "Yeah, I missed those too, when you used to sing me to sleep."

Dad leaned against the doorframe as he was scratching his beard, "You know, it's never too late, especially now that you really need some cheering up."

My eyes brightened, "Can I change the strings?"

He laughed softly, "Sure, dear. Get some from the drawers."

I excitedly edged from my seat to get the strings from the drawer beside me. As soon as I got it, I quickly sat properly and placed the strings in place one-by-one. In the middle of placing the last one, I noticed that one string was missing.

"Dad, you're missing a string."

He took the lute, "You're right. We need to find another string or else it's gonna sound different."

"Yeah, it's gonna sound-"

I paused for a minute.

"Say that again."

He blinked, "Say what, dear?"

"What you said, dad."

He scratched his beard, "Uh, it's gonna sound different."

My eyes widened.

It's gonna sound different. Of course it will. And, if it sounds different, that would mean, it's untuned. What if...

"Wait here, Dad." I said, dropping the lute and rushing to my room. I grabbed my rebec and took a string from it. I grabbed my bow and started playing it. And it sounded like the rebecs in the ceremony.

It sounded like Discord.

Discord.

I tried to recall what happened at the ceremony earlier...

What if it wasn't Discord at all?

What if it wasn't an omen?

What if it was an accident? A planned accident.

Discord can't just happen instantly. Instruments can't just go wrong. Not without a reasonable cause.

With that, I grabbed my coat and my shoes, and headed for the music hall. It was also a school for musicians. The one and only school for them. So, it was big, making it hard to sneak in.

Well, I'm smart and tricky.

I'm gonna find my way in. Then, I'm gonna solve all of this.

I was already beside the gate of the music hall. Getting in wasn't as hard as I thought it was. Depressed, the other musicians were at their homes, or so I heard, whilst some are here, trying to practice, especially the masters who wanted to give a concert for the king as atonement for their failure, or so I heard.

Their failure. That's what they thought it was.

Bad luck. That's what the people thought it was.

Goat's crap. That's what I think it is, and I'm gonna prove all of them wrong, that this is all what I think it is.

So, using my greatest weapon, which is dressing up, I easily went past the guards. I entered the storehouse for instruments dressed as a musician. I saw the rebecs and lyres that they used earlier. I locked the door and went closer to examine it.

"This is it." I whispered.

I held the rebec in my hand. Usually, it would have 1-5 strings. But, not one was missing. I tried to examine more of it, the ones they used. But, the strings were all there!

"What? I'm pretty sure that this would be the reason for the discord."

I tried to think. What else could be the reason behind all of this? Maybe it's the type of strings used. Denser or lighter strings tend to sound different. So, I examined those.

But, it all had the same material. Even my own rebec had this standard material for the strings. I don't understand. Why would ordinary rebecs go off just like that?! As far as I remember, these instruments were the only ones that went off tune and caused the others to lose the beat. So, these are the only instruments I have to study.

But, why rebecs?

Great. Now I have to think like the criminal or criminals that caused this. I'm no criminal but I am smart. I think I can tinker this out.

Why, rebecs?

They could've used the flutes and the drums. So, why rebe-

"Hold on."

Rebecs.

Rebecs are bowed instruments.

Of course. The bows!

It is composed of more strings than the rebec itself. That's why, if ever one or two strings were missing in the bow, it would go unnoticed. Still, having the right or wrong number of strings would affect the tune. Musicians tend to miss that crucial part. So, the bastards must've went for the bows.

And also, if they used the drums or the flute to cause the chaos, they wouldn't have time to mess with it because those instruments were prepared and polished first because they make the main tones in the ensemble.

With that, I went to the bows. And, my theory was right. The bows had missing strings and some had different textures and compositions. I think they made it rough by using rock salt.

So, this is it! I solved it. I know what the problem is. I just need to take some evidence.

Problem is, who would I tell? Who would believe me besides my supportive parents? Who would help me with my discovery.

I need someone with power, with a little bit of influence, and authority. Someone close yet not too close to the main royal family and highest authority.

Maybe a guard, a soldier, an inspector or an officer.

An officer.

Aspen!

Aspen is the right guy to tell this. I know he'll believe me. I just know it. But, where would I find him? Being an officer, he must be busy with this case and must be going to places to inspect. If I go now, maybe I'll catch him at the inspection tribunal.

"It's in the storehouse." I heard someone conversing.

"Thanks."

Oh boy. I need to get out of here fast. Someone's coming. I quickly ran to the door, but it would be risky to go out now because the footsteps were getting closer. So, in the last minute, I got behind the door, and as it opened, it hid me.

As the guy entered the room, looking for something, I took the chance to tiptoe my way outside. I was biting my lip in nervousness. As I took my last step away from the door, I was long gone because I started running away.

"I need to find him."

And that's the only thing replaying in my mind as I made my way to the inspection tribunal.

Big, fast, and determined steps led me to my destination. It was not that far away if you run, actually. How convenient. Plus, I know the city like it's permanently written on the palm of my hand.

Taking deep breaths, I skipped towards the gates and used the ring to knock.

After a few knocks, I still got no answer from those stup-

"What is it?!" A middle-aged guard angrily yelled as he opened the door.

I sighed in relief that someone in this world knows how to answer a knock, though not politely, "Good day, sir. I was wondering whether you would know officer Aspen's whereabouts."

He narrowed his eyes, "Young lady, we are in the middle of a case here and you disturbed us just to ask for a man's location? A man I don't even know."

I blinked, "What do you mean? You're a tribunal guard, sir. It's impossible for you to not know of officer Aspen, who is an inspection officer."

"Are you questioning my words?! Listen, if there ever was a man, I would know because I would live my days kissing up to their asses."

"Gross." I cringed.

He facepalmed,"Not literally, young lady."

I bit my lip in embarrassment, "Sorry."

He exasperatedly sighed, "Look miss, you better get out of here before I send guards to send you home."

"You're a guard. Why can't you just do it yourself?"

"I'm too lazy." He replied.

"Wow. I wonder whose ass did he kiss to hire him." I muttered under my breath.

"What was that?"

"Nothing, sir." I straightened myself, "Thank you for your help."

He snorted and closed the door forcefully.

"Your useless help. Tsk."

I walked away, dismayed. He doesn't know Aspen? What does that mean? This is the only inspection tribunal in this kingdom. Aspen has to be here. What is going on?

"Isabelle?"

And just like that, I felt butterflies inside at the mention of my name.

What on earth is happening to me?!

"Aspen?" I turned around. And, I was right. It was him!

He smiled widely and walked towards me. I approached him slowly and I was about to stop so that I would be positioned just in front of him. But, I was taken by surprise. My heart leaped inside of me suddenly.

When I approached him, he took my hand, covered by my long coat, and he pulled me into a warm, quick hug.

"Boy, am I glad to see you." He whispered.

I wasn't able to speak for a while and I wasn't able to hug him back. He let go of me and smiled. His eyes examined me, "Are you hurt? Were you safe during the chaos? I was worried sick when I didn't see you sitting on the tree anymore."

Again, I wasn't able to speak. Was he really worried about me? Was he thinking about me all this time? How I was?

Suddenly, I felt ashamed.

He even knew where I was sitting during the ceremony. So, he was looking out for me. I actually sat at the tree to get a view of him. But, I didn't.

Good Lord, here I am thinking about a case that he and the other officers are supposed to solve, but here he is, thinking about me, someone he isn't suppose to consider at a time like this. Man, I'm a terrible friend.

"I'm fine, Aspen. Thanks. You?" I nervously said.

"Better as of now." He smiled.

I smiled back at him. What was I supposed to think about again?

"Where have you been?" He asked.

"What?" -I was caught off guard- "Oh. I went to the inspection tribunal looking for you."

He blinked, "Why?"

"Well, you're an inspection officer, right? You wear inspector's clothes. So, I assumed that you'd be there. But, they said they didn't know you."

He coughed suddenly and looked sideways, "Uh...Well, I am an inspection officer. But I-I... uh... I'm the royal inspection officer! Yeah. I work at the palace and not here. So, they really wouldn't know me. Plus, I'm not based at this tribunal."

"Oh." I said, getting it. For a second there, I thought something was wrong.

I glanced at him and saw him pumping his fist in the air and sighing in relief.

"Aspen?"

He suddenly straightened himself up and looked at me, surprised.

What's wrong with him?

"Are you alr-"

"Why did you look for me?" He said, changing the topic.

I looked at him suspiciously but I answered him anyway, "Well, I had something to tell you."

"What is it?" He whispered.

I observed our surroundings. It's not safe to tell him here, "Come."

I dragged him to a narrow alley where there was a lesser crowd. Actually, no crowd at all. Seeing that it was safe, I took the evidence out. It was a bow. It's the only thing I can fit in the pocket of my coat.

His eyes widened, "Is that...?"

I nodded, "I think I know the cause for the Discord."

He took the bow and examined it himself. His eyes turned as big as saucers as he discovered the broken strings on the bows and touched it, feeling the change in texture.

"I think someone cut off the strings and changed its texture. It could easily go unnoticed, that's why no one easily found out about it. They went for the bows. That's why-"

"Discord happened." He finished, still in awe.

I held his arm, "Aspen, we can still fix all this. You're an inspection officer, the royal inspection officer. You're the only man that can relay this to the ministers, better, the king. And, they could stop all of this from happening. Sorah won't have to fear anymore."

"Isabelle, how did you-"

"It doesn't matter." I shrugged, "Now, we can prove that what happened was just some sort of accident, and they won't think that it's the omens anymore. We have to do this before it gets rampant. Good thing is that it was only Discord, right?"

At this, he bowed his head and his face turned uneasy, as if he was worried, or hiding something.

"Aspen, is something wrong?"

He sighed, "I'm sorry. It's just that though I know the reason for what happened earlier, I'm still not sure what to believe in."

I blinked and examined his face, "What? Aspen, it's only an accidental Discord. No need to fuss about it. It's not the omen, okay. It's only-"

"Demise." He suddenly whispered. He then grabbed me by my shoulders. He held them tightly as his worried eyes pierced mine, "Demise. It already happened, Isabelle."

"What?"

He was about to speak when we heard shouting in the streets.

"IT REALLY IS THE OMEN!"

"The general's death is the sign!" Several wailed.

"Sorah is going to fall. We have to get out of here. We must protect our families!"

"We have to move!" One said, encouraging the others.

"Yeah!" They all agreed.

We got out of that narrow alley to take a look at what's happening. Sadly, what we saw was like a repeat of what happened before at the ceremony. The people were running in fear, getting their bags and family members. Carriages and shops were also destroyed. Some animals were let loose because of destroyed pens and fences.

"It leaked out." I heard Aspen curse under his breath, "Those imbeciles!"

"Aspen?" I whispered as I reached for his shoulder.

"Come with me." He said, taking my hand as we ran together. He whistled loudly, to which a horse appeared. He climbed up first then he helped me up. I braced my arms around him as the horse ran.

We kept running until we stopped near the palace grounds, where he met with an unfamiliar noble with a horse. He came down from the horse and helped me down too. He walked towards the man while I waited for him. Luckily, I was near enough to hear the conversation.

"Daniel, how did the-"

"I'm sorry, Aspen. It was minister Laurent. He told a messenger to spread the news." The man said, trying to catch his breath all the while.

"Where is that stupid minister?!" Aspen growled. I've never heard him sound so dangerous.

And that scared me... a lot.

Then, I saw another noble come out, an older man, "Your maje-" I heard him say but he was cut off. I took a peek and realized that Aspen has took him by the collar and dragged him to a far corner. I can no longer see them but I can feel that things are getting intense. I glanced at them once more and I saw Aspen let go of the man.

"You scared the people!" Aspen exclaimed.

"It has to be done. Can't you see that we are protecting our people? The faster they move out, the better. That way, they can all be safe from the coming Downfall." The man answered.

"I told you that we're gonna get to the bottom of this. But, now you've told them about the general's death?! What are the people going to think?!"

The general's death?

"Demise. It already happened, Isabelle."

Is this what he was trying to tell me? That...it wasn't only Discord, but Demise as well that has happened?

Oh dear. Then, things were getting worse by the minute!

"They're gonna take it as what it is- Demise. Don't be blind. You know what these all mean, and you intend to hide it from the people? Let's face it. The omens are-"

"No! Never in Sorah!" Aspen interrupted, "Look, we are investigating the case. So, you better get out of the way. I don't want anyone making a move." He turned around and headed towards my direction.

I guess he really had some kind of authority to speak and command like that. Even a man dressed as a court member he can command.

"Daniel, take your steed." He said firmly to the noble he first talked to. That noble obeyed, nonetheless, by taking his horse.

I immediately rode the horse on my own as I felt his footsteps near. He looked at me, "Please tell me you didn't hear any of that."

I gave a reassuring smile, "I heard nothing."

"Sorry bout that. I wish you didn't see that. I hate myself mad."

"I told you, I heard, smelled, and saw nothing at all. And besides, that will teach me not to mess with you." I grinned.

He gave a sigh of relief, knowing that my lips are sealed, and proceeded to climb onto the horse. I scooted a bit to give him space.

"What are we gonna do, Aspen?" The noble asked.

"Let's talk someplace else." Aspen said, then he held the reins and ran the horse towards a secluded area. The noble followed right behind.

We arrived at an abandoned pavilion near the lake. It was really secluded, secluded enough to tell secrets. We went down from our steeds and went to discuss at the pavilion. Aspen took out the evidence I got him, but before he could explain, the noble asked him,

"Who's this?" He pointed at me.

"I think you mean, 'who is she?'", is what I wanted to say to his face but I didn't.

"Oh. This is Isabelle. A friend." Aspen answered.

"Since when? I've never heard about an Isabelle." He raised his brows suspiciously.

"Since yesterday, sir." I answered for Aspen.

"She will be helping us with the case. She was the one who discovered-"

"I'm Daniel. Prince Daniel." He said, handing out his hand to mine, to which Aspen got annoyed with, smacking his own face with his palm.

Wait.

Prince?

Prince Daniel.

He's Prince Daniel?!

The guy I was supposed to be a bridal candidate for?!

Oh, damn.

I was stuck, unable to shake his hand. Literally, frozen.

I was horrified. I put aside the fact that, if ever, he was supposed to be my husband. I wonder how Scarlett took all of this. I hope she didn't go killer on him. I, for one, know how she can be with boys. I haven't seen her since the Selection and the announcement of her engagement.

But, besides that, I was alarmed that I made contact with a royal.

A real royal!

Royalty means politics, my family's number one enemy. The thought of it would scar their ears. The thought of me with it would scar their heart and all other internal organs that they have, or so I heard them say.

As I stood there in shock, Aspen dragged the prince by his ears and pulled him into a corner.

Is he mad?!

He was just an officer?! Pulling a prince by the ear?! Does he wanna die?!

"She doesn't know what?!" I heard prince Daniel exclaim as he stepped back in surprise supposedly from what Aspen said. They both looked at me, smiled nervously, and went back to talking.

What am I supposed to do?

I can run and escape this. But, how can I help if I do that? And if I do help, how would my parents feel? It would mean having a connection with a prince. I don't want that to happen.

"I don't care. Just say what you have to say." I heard Aspen mutter under his breath. After that, they both turned and walked towards me. I gulped and my heart pounded in nervousness.

Oh dear mother of-

"Umm, Isabelle. I'm sorry I didn't tell you." Aspen said.

"What?" I asked, brought back out of shock.

"The prince is a dear friend of mine. He's here because he wants to help with the investigation. Don't worry. He knows how to keep secrets." He finished.

"Miss Isabelle, I'm sorry for startling you by making known of my royal stance. But please, treat me as a friend and don't be too uncomfortable. I'm not as regal as you think I am." - Aspen nodded knowingly at this- " And it's just gonna be the three of us. So, don't worry." The prince assured.

I was still unable to speak. How can I treat a royal so familiar? It's like treating a king as a footstool. I can't do that.

"Oh, and don't worry about the things Aspen does to me. When it's just us, we're like brothers. Feel free to do that too whenever I would seem not myself, Isabelle. I can call you that, right?" The prince smiled.

"Okay, don't get too familiar." Aspen said, pushing the prince a little bit farther.

"The prince..." I whispered.

"Oh, come on. Just call me Daniel."

"The prince Daniel..."

He chuckled, "No. Just Daniel is fine."

"Just the prince Daniel..."

"Okay. I think it's a lot for her to take in, Aspen." He told him.

"Isabelle. Are you-"

I don't know what took over me. But it's probably mostly fear, because despite their assurances, I still don't know how to act in front of such a powerful person. Will I get killed if I say a word? Will I be imprisoned if I didn't curtsey?

Things like that circulated my mind.

"Oh dear! " I then bowed with my face close to the ground and my back bent slightly. "I am sorry for not recognizing you, your grace. I was face to face with a royal, and yet, I acted so ignorant. Please forgive me, I deserve to be-"

"Come on. Don't do that. Man, you sure have high ideals of honor. Me? I just say sorry. I don't even mean it, then poof, honor." He chuckled.

Funny as it is, I didn't have the guts to laugh.

I feel so fragile in front of powerful people.

"Alright. Enough with that. So, Isabelle, meet Daniel and don't pay any attention to him."

"Ouch! Aspen, you hurt me here." The prince said, pointing to his heart.

"Do you want blood and gore with it?" Aspen asked, annoyed.

He swallowed, "No thanks. I'm good. In fact, I wasn't hurt at all."

Aspen rolled his eyes, "Daniel, meet Isabelle, my friend and the girl we'll need to solve all this."

"Aww, why did she get a good introduction? No fair!" He said, mimicking a child.

Is it me or these two really resemble two 5-year olds?

"Shut up. You don't deserve a good introduction. Besides, what would I say?" Aspen retorted.

"I hate you."

I laughed lightly, interrupting the two of them from their squabble. They glanced at me and they too, smiled.

Aspen smiled at me, "See. We're just like normal people, argue like normal people, and talk like normal people. Don't be afraid, Isabelle."

"Yeah, what he said." Daniel added.

I took a deep breath and exhaled as if I was exhaling all my fears. They do seem like normal people. Without the crown and the fancy clothes, they do look like us. They were both smiling at me as I was reeling from the shock that I had earlier.

"Okay then. If you say so-"

"Daniel. Call me Daniel. The prince part isn't really necessary."

I nodded. "Daniel."

I see now that there is nothing to be afraid of.

These two, though nobles, weren't like the rest. They kinda remind me of King Jehro. Nobles by birth, but commoners at heart. I wonder why my parents hate these people so much. They seem like good people. But come to think of it, it's not specifically the people they hate.

Aspen coughed, "Okay. Now let's go back to the matter at hand. As I was saying, Isabelle found the cause for the Discord at the ceremony." Then, he handed out he bow to Daniel.

Daniel got the bow and he wore the same face Aspen had when I gave him the evidence.

"Those half-assed, son of a-"

"I know right. But, I can't deny that they were smart too going for the bows. Who would've thought of that?" Aspen said.

I smirked, "Who would've thought that they would use our negligence on the little stuff as a strategy?"

"Smart bastards indeed." Daniel scoffed.

I turned to Aspen, "Aspen, what you said before, that demise has already happened, is it true?"

He bowed his head, "Sadly."

"What?! Who then? Who died?" I asked.

I saw Daniel tighten his hold on the bow, almost breaking the bow, "General de Beville." He gritted.

I staggered, "De Beville? Scarlett's father?"

Daniel looked at me, "You know her?"

I looked at him sadly, "Yes. She's my friend. A very dear friend of mine. She was my ally. The first one who saw me among all the people who pretended I was invisible back at the academy." -I sighed deeply- "How is she?"

But he didn't answer. Instead, he turned away, maybe to hide the anger in his face. He looked to the far clouds above, maybe to calm himself.

"They accused her." Aspen said.

"Accused?"

"They accused her of killing her own father. She was found holding the dagger that killed the general, and they foolishly jumped to conclusions." He said.

"It's not true!" Daniel suddenly exclaimed.

"We know that, Daniel." -Aspen said without missing a beat- "Calm down."

Daniel raised his hands in a form of apology and pardon then looked away once more.

"That is disturbingly impossible. Scarlett will never do that." I appealed.

"Yes. And that's what we're gonna try to solve next. Scarlett surely didn't do it. Then who did? Even though they say that the crime scene explained it all, I won't believe it. Some even said that she killed him to take his place! What kind of person in a right mind will think of that?!" Aspen said.

"Idiots." I muttered, referring to the ones who accused Scar.

Everything was dead silent for a while. Until Daniel spoke up, his back still facing us.

"When I saw Scarlett at the office, beside the corpse of her father, she didn't seem herself. Her eyes were droopy. She was very shocked, as if she didn't know what exactly happened. She looked frightened. I carried her to her room. She woke up soon after, shaking. She said that..."

"She said what?"

"She said that she did kill her own father. She saw it before she collapsed. She remembers that she did. But, I still don't believe her. Even if she said it herself, I know in my heart that she isn't capable of that. But she keeps on insisting. She even wanted to go to exile, kill herself even. But I put her to sleep before she panics and do something crazy."

Aspen and I looked at him then at each other.

Daniel finally faced us and pulled out something from his pocket, "I found this when I returned to the crime scene, after it was cleaned up."

He dangled a talisman in front of us. It was a creepy-looking one. It had a black lace and the pendant resembles the mask in one of our folklores. It symbolizes a killer.

Hold on a second.

"Daniel, let me see that." I said, grabbing the object, "This looks familiar..."

"What is it, Isabelle?"

I know this one!

I gasped, "This is the kind of talisman gypsies use! Of course, being logical and smart, I don't really believe in that kind of magic. But, most of the time it works. It has something to do with the brain. But-"

"What do you mean? Gypsies? Magic? Brain? I don't really understand." Daniel admitted.

"Trance." Aspen answered for me. "They might have tranced Scarlett, Daniel."

Daniel widened his eyes, getting it,"So that means... they used her." He growled in a low and dangerous tone, "They used Scarlett."

Aspen shook his head angrily, "Those shameless... Agh!" Then he hammered a fist on a column of the pavilion, cracking it a little.

"They're dead." They both said in a low tone.

I gulped, "I'm sure they'll be." I whispered to myself.

I took a deep breath before speaking, "But, we need more evidence than this."

They both turned to me, trying to calm down.

"This talisman is merely used for putting a victim in a trance or sleep. They must've used something else to get Scarlett to do-" I looked at Daniel and changed my words, "-to think that she killed her own father."

"There's more to it." Aspen added, "We need to go back to the office and investigate the place."

"Let's." Daniel nodded.

"Wait!" I stopped them, "I can't go with you. That's in the palace and I can't go in there."

Having contact with a prince was more than enough for my parents to faint and yell at me, and faint again. What more going to a palace?! One filled with nobles and royals?!

I don't want that as much as my parents don't.

"She's right. Commoners aren't allowed there for no urgent reason."

"No, Aspen. I meant that I-"

"Well, we can't say that she's with us, or she's a witness of some sort. They'll question her." Daniel added.

"You don't understand, guys. I really don't-"

"I know a way we can get her in." Aspen replied.

"What?" I blinked.

"You can sign up for a lady investigator. Being an apprentice is more than enough reason for you to enter and come with us." He explained.

I groaned, "Please, just let me-"

"It's set then. We'll help you sign up and you can enter the palace with us."

"Aspen, I really can't-"

"Don't worry. It's just gonna be temporary. There's gonna be a test for novices at the end to choose those who'll be full-fledged lady investigators. If you want, you can fail that, or simply don't show up at the day of the test. That way, you're apprenticeship will be invalid. That is if you want it to be temporary." Aspen said.

I lowered my head, trying to decide. Only temporary, huh?

But, still, it's in the palace. It would be against my parent's to interact with other royal people. Come to think of it, I already broke that rule, interacting with a prince.

Some daughter I am.

However, lady investigators are not really royal or anything. They just work for the palace, and are not really that connected to politics. Plus, lady investigators are also commoners. They work for the politicians, but have nothing to do with politics.

Okay, I just made it worse. Now, I really can't decide.

"Please, Isabelle. I promised Scarlett that we would solve all this. Please do it for her. Please. I can't stand it anymore seeing her like this." Daniel pleaded.

Oh, God. Why me?

It's only gonna be temporary. Anything temporary won't last forever. So, I guess it wouldn't really leave that much of a mark in my life. I suppose I don't really have to tell my parents so...

Ugh. I must be out of my mind.

"Only temporary, alright." I sighed.

"Yes!" Daniel cheered, hugging me. I smiled at him. It was short friendly hug.

"We're wasting time. Let's go." Aspen took my hand and grabbed my waist, putting me onto his horse.

My heart beat sped up.

Easy, girl. That was just a grab on the waist. That was absolutely nothing compared to a hug. But, why did I feel different?

Is it because of...

"Isabelle."

"No, it's not because of you!"

I officially lost my mind. I gaped and covered my mouth quickly after.

Why on earth did I say that?!

"What?" Aspen blinked.

"Nothing." I shook my head.

"Are you sure? You look really red." He asked.

"No. I'm fine." I assured him, trying to hide my blush all the while

He gave me a smile, "If you say so. Just tell me if you're not feeling well." Then he climbed onto the horse too.

"Let's go." Daniel said, climbing onto his own horse.

They both held the reins of their stallion, and we went off.

As we neared the palace, all I could think about...

Is how crazy things are going to be from this day onwards.

11

— ◇ —

CHAPTER 11

Daniel

"Do you really have to?" I asked, face-palming at Aspen.

"What do you expect? People might recognize me and fall on their faces flat saying 'Your majesty'. And then what? She'll know I lied to her about my true identity." He said as he was putting his mask on. It covered every part on his face except for his eyes.

He really looked like a criminal, but he kept on insisting that it was badly needed. Well, he's the king. So be it. I'm just saying he looks crazy.

"This Isabelle, are you really that close?" I asked him out of curiosity.

You can't blame me. He had no interest in girls ever since we were kids. Whenever he would interact with them, it would always be because of royal matters. Then suddenly, out of nowhere came this girl that he was immediately so attached to?

I seriously have to know.

"What's it to you?" He narrowed his eyes at me.

"Just asking. I thought you'd never be with a girl. You can't even stand being with one before. Now, look at you, all grown up." I said, wiping imaginary tears off my face.

"Speak for yourself, as if you're a prodigy in this." He smirked, "As far as I know, you've never been with any girl because of a certain red haired-"

"That is just as far as you know," I glared.

"And that's all there is to it."

"Tsk," I mumbled.

Growing up with him has a lot of disadvantages. One of the worst was he could bully you all the time. So what if I don't have any experience when it comes to courtship, chivalry, being a gentleman or a romantic, and stuff? I'm not that kind of guy.

Mischief is my first love and that won't change.

I don't need to have any girl to make my life complete. Just hand me my tools and a victim, then I'm in heaven.

But....

Here I am now, trying to solve a mystery for a girl, for a promise I made to her.

As always, Aspen's right.

Suddenly, I become something I'm not when I'm with Scarlett. I suddenly take interest in how to make girls happy, I also try to learn to be that romantic guy, a lot of stuff which used to disgust me.

I guess this was just some sort of aftermath due to the past crush I used to have on her. Yes, I did have a crush on her, far more worse than that. And Aspen keeps parading it like an official decree. She and I were really really really so close back then. Too close.

As for him, he never had any flings as far as I know. Maybe it's because of our fathers. Both uncle Jethro and my dad hold this belief of one true love, marrying for love and stuff. And we, being obedient sons, applied that to our life, and now we're infected.

But, truth is, it's not really because of that that we can't seem to like any damsels.

Damsels bring us distress. Take my position for example.

Somehow, we grew to find girls annoying. Big dresses, hair as high as towers, clown-like faces. It's sickens men of our kind.

But something's different about these girls. They don't sicken us one bit. Threatened, yes, most of the time on my side. Yet, the point is, instead of sickening us and staying away from them, we can't stand to be apart from them.

What the hell is wrong with us?!

"Is Isabelle already outside?" He asked.

I peeked out the window and saw her fixing her lady investigator uniform.

"Yeah," I replied. Suddenly, I turned to him with a serious face on.

"Aspen, do you think we can really solve all this?"

He sighed, "We'll try. We won't let Sorah go crazy like this."

"You really are king, aren't you?" I snickered, "All I'm thinking about is how Scar will be after all this. I'm not used to seeing her miserable. It doesn't feel right."

He smirked, "Because you still have a cru-"

"Shut up or I'll blow my cover," I grunted.

"If you say so," he said, raising his eyebrows knowingly.

If he wasn't my cousin and the king, he would have a fist mark right now on his face.

"Let's go."

And we went out the cottage. We ran there after we got Isabelle signed up.

She turned around, facing us. Her uniform consists of a black custom dress topped with a long purple coat with long loose sleeves

, a color worn by the beginners; blue for the mid-ranks and red for the superintendents. The said coat also had a hood at the back, but most of the time, it couldn't be seen. She also had her hair braided, a custom for all lady investigators, with a headband matching the color of her coat.

She looked beautiful, I'll admit.

Now I see why Aspen is so whipped. Not sure if he is, but I'll take my chances.

"Aspen? You still there, buddy?" I waved my hand in front of him. He was standing there, eyes wide and speechless.

"I'm really nervous, guys." Isabelle said, walking towards us, then she stopped and gaped at Aspen.

"What's with the mask, Aspen?" She asked, but the idiot was still unable to speak and was dazed.

"Aspen... uh... feels cold. So, he had to put the mask on to warm his face, which feels cold." I cracked.

I'm really bad at making excuses.

"Okay." She smiled, falling for it. Then she shivered and sighed heavily.

"Don't worry. Like we said, it's only temporary. Right, Aspen?"

"Y-yes. Tem-temporary." He stuttered.

On a scale of 1 to 10, I'd say this girl hit him by 11.

"So, what are we gonna do?" Isabelle tilted her head.

Aspen shook his head to break himself from his own daze, "We'll go with the plan. You said that the criminals used more than a talisman, right? So, all we have to do is to find out more. Let's go back to the office and do exactly that."

"Let's go." She said.

And we went.

Upon arriving at the office, we quickly got into searching for some clues or any damn hints.

"Anything?"

"Darn it." I grunted.

"I'll take that as a no." Isabelle shook her head. "Any luck there, officer?" She glanced at Aspen.

"None." Aspen sighed, taking his mask off.

I shook my head in dismay. We can't move forward if we can't find more. If we can't find more, what about Scar? I promised her that everything's gonna be alright. Now, I'm not even sure about my promise. We searched every shelf, every chest, every drawer. Still, nothing.

"How is she doing?" Isabelle suddenly asked, referring to Scar.

I sighed, remembering her state, "You won't even recognize her."

She gasped, horrified, "Did they do something to her face?! Those descendants of Grendel!! If I find those shi-"

"Woah, easy there. It's not like that." I laughed lightly at her reaction, "I meant that... she's so miserable and damaged now, you won't even see any hint of the strong de Beville heiress we all know. What happened was... it really..." I stopped, unable to finish. Nothing can describe what she must be going through right now.

She reached out for my hand, "Don't worry. I'll do everything I can to help her so you don't have to carry that promise on your own. I'll do everything. You have my word on that."

"Thanks. I'll count on it." I smiled at her.

"I won't let you down." She smiled back.

No wonder Scarlett became her friend. She was approachable, friendly, easy to talk to. I just met her today but look at her. It seems like I've already known her forever. She was already doing something for me.

She's an angel.

I guess this was another reason why she and Aspen seemed so attached. Aspen's kinda like a devil. Opposites attract, right?

"Guys, I found something."

We rushed to Aspen and saw that he was holding some sort of card. We all examined what he was holding closely. As for me, I really can't understand what's on the stupid card. Ugh, I feel so useless.

"I think this is..." Isabelle muttered, grabbing the card and looking at it closely.

"What is it?" We asked in unison.

"It's another instrument gypsies use! Of course. The talisman was used to trance Scarlett but to mess with her memory, they would need a picture or something to torture her brain, to make her think that she murdered her father. False memories of murder! This card..."

We examined the card once more after her explanation. I took notice of the picture of a man with a creepy mask on. He was dressed in all black. He had blood in his right hand, and in the other, he beheld a bloody sword. It was indeed a picture depicting a murderer.

"It's a killer," Aspen uttered while Isabelle nodded at him.

"So, to put a false memory of her murdering the general in her mind, they must've used this card with the talisman. Is that what you're saying Isabelle?" I asked.

"Exactly."

I staggered. I'm not really good at controlling my anger or my temper. What they did to Scarlett... IT'S UNFORGIVABLE! I was gritting my teeth in anger. Smoke was literally coming out of my nose as I thought of a lot of ways to hunt those criminals down, and another variety of ways to kill them.

Suddenly, I felt something under my foot. It felt like a paper. I looked down and saw a picture of the general. I picked it up and gestured for the two to look at it.

"Hey. Look at this."

"General de Beville," Aspen sighed.

I noticed the red ink staining the portrait. I could barely make out the face of the general. Maybe they used this too to make Scar miserable. Those little fu-

"It's confirmed. They did trance Scarlett and put false memories of her killing her father," Isabelle added.

"Who in this damn world would do this?" Aspen said in a low growl.

"I don't know. But if we find out who, we can save Sorah from all of this."

"And then we'll bring those rats to their doom," I added.

"Is that necessary?" Isabelle asked.

"For justice," Me and Aspen said in unison.

"For Sorah," Aspen said seriously.

"For Scar," I said in the same tone.

"For mankind." Isabelle muttered, making us tilt our heads.

"All of you got to say something," she complained.

We went silent for a while, looking at each other, then gave in and laughed lightly.

"Why can't you be more like her. She's fun to be with unlike some annoying king I know," I teased.

Then I quickly covered my mouth after I realized what I just said. Aspen eyes turned as wide as an elephant's sole.

"King?" Isabelle asked.

Shoot.

Aspen glared at me, pressuring me to make an excuse for the slip, "D-did I say king? I-I meant bing."

Ugh.

Isabelle looked at me emotionlessly, "I hope you wouldn't arrest me for this, Prince Daniel, but that's the poorest justification I have ever heard."

And I just got burned.

"Stupid," Aspen coughed.

I rolled my eyes then began to laugh nervously, "Hahaha. I was just testing you. I did say king. But I meant king....of annoyance! Hehe.

Isabelle chuckled with a hint of doubt in her voice, "Ooookay."

Aspen interrupted us before it gets any worse, "So, back to the case. How will we find out the identity of the asses who did this?"

"That's gonna be hard. I know a lot of asses in this territory. Some are obvious, some are just too good at covering up," I sighed. "I thought we'll get close to the culprits once we solved this."

"You know, I heard a lot of cases about jealousy in position, and the general had a stance worth killing for. It could be possible that it may be one of the nobles. And, the culprit from the Discord could also be a different person. What if all was just a mere accident or coincidence happening in one day? What if someone really planned on killing the general?" Aspen suggested, "and we mistook it for the omens."

"That could be an explanation. Two different culprits for two different cases or coincidences; Demise and Discord." I took a step back, "But, why would they do that? Why would they want to mess with the ceremony? Why would they choose to kill the general? Especially after Discord has happened? Of all the times they could've executed their plans. And why did they have to include Scarlett?" I questioned.

"That's one of the things that makes this case harder," Aspen placed a hand on his nape.

"But come to think of it there's a chance that..." Isabelle started, making our heads turn to her, "If these culprits that we're looking for are responsible for the death of general, then they could be responsible for the Discord too. They must be the ones who messed up with the bows. So, it is possible that the criminal who caused both Discord and Demise could also be one man."

"That could be possible. But, as Aspen said, it could just be a coincidence."

She walked towards us, "All in one day?! No, think of it. All of the things they did were in accordance to the omens. They messed with the instruments to make Discord come true, and killed the general while using Scarlett to make it look like it was really Demise that came true. They knew that Sorah is very superstitious. They made it all look like coincidences of bad luck... so we would think that they were the omens! So, it would be a greater possibility that the one responsible for Discord and the one responsible for Demise is just the same person."

Damn. She's smart.

Aspen and I looked at each other, realizing the sense in her words,

"They're trying to scare Sorah to bring it to it's downfall. And they're using the pattern of the omens to do that," she added.

"So, if we follow the omens, then we will be able to trace their steps, and figure out who the culprits are," Aspen stated.

She nodded, "The next omen is Downfall. In the case of the five kingdoms, their downfall would be caused by another kingdom conquering them, or mostly a civil war."

"So, it could be possible that it is a noble because only someone with a reasonable authority can rally the people and start a civil war," I exclaimed. I turned to Aspen and we nodded.

"I'll handle that part." Aspen assured.

"You can?" She tilted her head.

"He can," I smiled.

"Okay then. I'll just be here if you need me... But, before I leave, can I visit Scarlett?" she asked, worry in her eyes.

I looked at her, "Of course you can. Come on."

12

— ◆ —

CHAPTER 12

A spen

We carefully passed some guards as we made our way to Scarlett's room in the east wing of the defense office. I put on my mask to avoid recognition.

My heart pounded every time I see a guard coming, but we managed to avoid them anyway. Finally, we reached Scarlett's room. Isabelle, upon seeing her lying on her bed, rushed to her. My heart sank as I saw my friend unconscious. It felt very different in a bad way because I'm not used to seeing Scar like this.

I removed my mask, then Daniel and I walked towards them and sat on the chairs beside her bed.

"Scarlett? Scar? It's me." Isabelle whispered, trying to talk to her, but she got nothing. Scarlett didn't even move.

Isabelle sighed. I can sense the worry and sadness in her. Her face was grief-stricken as she looked upon her friend.

She caressed Scar's head lightly, "Don't worry, Scar. We're gonna solve all of this. We're gonna avenge your father. We're gonna give those bastards the punishment they deserve, the kind you'll give them if you see their faces, you know, with the swords, torture,

torture, and stuff. We're gonna treat them so bad, you'll be proud of us."

We smirked at her words. If only Scarlett could hear her, she would be cheered up too. Isabelle had this kind of warmth that could immediately comfort a friend. It's like a power of some sort.

"I'm sorry, Scarlett. I'm sorry I wasn't able to do anything. I'm sorry about every-"

"It's not your fault, Isabelle." I assured her as I held her wrist. She was crying as she said her apologies.

"I know, but it feels like it is. You feel it too, right? Seeing her like this makes you think that you should've done something but you weren't able to, and you feel guilty. " She muttered.

"She's our friend. It's normal." I added.

"I guess." She sighed.

She went back to Scarlet and continued to talk to her as if she was listening, "We're here for you, Scar. Always. Anytime you need us and even if you don't need us, we'll be there."

As she finished that, we saw a tear fall from Scarlett's closed eyes. Isabelle shed a tear too as she wiped that away from our friend's face.

She's listening.

Daniel moved to the edge of Scarlett's bed as they continued to talk to her in her sleep. As for me, I have some things to attend to.

"Guys?"

They turned to me.

"I'll just be in the royal library if you need me." I said.

They nodded at me and went back to talking to Scar. I gave them one last look, then I went out.

(4 hours later)

Pain.

Yeah, that's the word I'm looking for right now.

From the books I've been reading for hours, to my back that's been tortured from sitting for so long, I couldn't feel anything but damn pain.

As Isabelle said, we need to look for more information about this chaos. So, being logical, I consulted our library's books. But, the only thing I forgot is to estimate how big this library was. My eyes hurt from reading hundreds- scratch that- thousands of books, and yet I still couldn't find anything crucial.

I've literally turned the royal library upside down, and I don't think I have any blood left to spare for later. Maybe, I really wouldn't find anything here.

I stood up, feeling the surge of pain on my back, and the pleasure I felt as I stretched it, and another surge of pain as I heard a crack.

I was about to leave the room, but then Sorah came into my mind, Sorah in chaos, my family, my friends, and everything I love vanishing before my eyes. My head ached.

I can't have that.

I can't give up now that we've found so much and now that I have the most brilliant girl on my side, working this case with me. I can't give up, even if it takes the destruction of my library.

I cracked my knuckles," Okay royal library, prepare to be- OWW!"

That hurts! I think something just felt on my head. I looked up to see what it was but I found nothing. I averted my gaze and looked down at the floor and saw what hit me.

I picked it up. It was some small, old notebook, and it had a picture of some sort of abstract shape on it. I think it's a boat or something.

Whatever it was, I didn't hesitate to open it, and feast my eyes on the pages.

My heart pounded at the sight of what's inside. I feel this is gonna be something big.

I scanned the pages and I saw a lot of information, I might I say, about the fallen kingdom. It's geography, it's weaknesses, the rulers of the land, the places and landmarks, everything about it. The first one I read about was Ectal, the first fallen kingdom. Also, the handwriting looked like this notebook belonged to a scribe.

Ectal, Land Of Spices

Ruler: King Rajin Tagore

Weaknesses:

-Superstitious people; gullible; weak in combat; too dependent

-Weak structures

-Naive and Vain king

Domination: 5th day of the 9th month; Avi

Place: Shrine of Hagriv

Speaking of crucial... What the hell!?

I don't know if I should be happy or terrified, or if this detail is a blessing or a curse to the case.

But, if one thing's for sure... This is scary and alarming.

Almost every necessary information of Ectal are here in this book. Only a citizen of their own could've known these. Whoever would know this could've easily taken over Ectal.

Who got this dangerous information? It even had a map with an 'x' drawn it, as if that location was a target.

I examined the pages and it looked like these pages I'm reading now were written about 100 years ago.

The fall of Ectal occurred 100 years ago.

And Domination?

I searched for one of the books I was reading earlier among the other books discarded on the floor. Luckily, I found it and I read it again. It was a book about Ectal. Coincidentally, it is said there that its fall was the 5th day of the 9th month. It was the day of Avi. It was considered a holy festive back then, but after the fall, it was now considered a day of curses.

These books I'm holding had similar information. But, the notebook that hit me looks older than the book I grabbed. So, the notebook was written earlier, possibly before of the fall of Ectal.

Could this mean... No.

My guess is that this notebook was written by a prophet of some sort. But, for a prophecy, this was too detailed. Even the day of the fall, the place, not to mention the weak points of Ectal are written here.

This information could not just be listed down in a vision or a glimpse of the future.

So, I doubt that this was written by a prophet or a monk.

From the looks of it, this seemed like some sort of plan, a plan to... conquer a kingdom.

A plan to conquer a kingdom.. written before or during the fall of Ectal.

Does this mean... that the fall of that kingdom, which started the omens, was not an omen at all?

No. I can't jump to conclusions. I have to look deeper into this.

I looked at the book again and examined its content. I keep comparing it to the book I grabbed earlier. It had the same information, the day of the fall, the location of the chaos, the events. And there was also a name written on both books that didn't really sound unfamiliar to me.

Pia Ashanti

I quickly searched for that name in another book. Luckily, I found it.

Pia Ashanti

- last queen of Ectal

-Pirean candidate

It says here that she was a Pirean candidate. Back in the days, it was considered bad luck if the king didn't marry a woman from their country. King Rajin Tagore was the only king of Ectal who married a foreigner. He was also the king during the fall. His marriage caused uproar in the kingdom.

Hmm. Uproar?

Chaos. It caused chaos. So it can also be related with Discord.

This was their kingdom's Discord: His marriage.

I scanned the old notebook once more. All of the information about the fallen kingdoms are here, except for Seira, the last one to fall about 20 years ago.

If my hutch is correct, and these kingdoms underwent the 'omens', then they must have Demise as well.

I examined the other book. It said here that the day of their fall was also the day of the king's death. He was poisoned for some unknown reason.

That is their Demise.

After that, some ministers led a civil war and a lot were found dead. Another kingdom entered the scene and took the remaining people as captives. Everyone was left either dead or a slave to the kingdom that conquered them. But, it is also said here that the queen was never found.

Now, that sounds suspicious.

Her state remained unknown, even after the kingdom's fall. If my stock knowledge from my studies serves me right, she was the last person with the king. It was the night 2 days after their marriage.

Thank god I studied history.

So, it may be possible that she may know something about the king's death. But, if she did, she would've screamed or something, alerting the guards. But, it is said here in the book that the king was found dead and blue, meaning that the poison has spread and the king was dead for quite some time. Still, the queen, who was the last person with him, was never found.

It doesn't sound right.

But, with the surprising information I'm getting, it wouldn't sound wrong either.

What if... Queen Pia was the one who poisoned the king?

Woah. I feel like I'm uncovering historical secrets!

It's not impossible, actually. If another one was responsible for the king's death, Queen Pia should've been dead too. But, she was mysteriously never found. And, her name was written in this old notebook.

What did she have to do with all these?

I have to know more.

Turning to the next pages, I saw the same kind of information about Venadar, the second kingdom to fall. Their weaknesses were here too.

- Stubborn rulers
- Values strength above all

-weak people

Domination: Festival of the Mane; Chain Dare

Of course. Venadar was a country made for battle. Their country was titled 'anchor of battle', for the reason that no one could defeat them in battle and for their weapons. They had strict security and wouldn't allow anyone in their kingdom unless they are a citizen. That's why it would take almost a miracle for them to fall. If I was going to conquer them long ago, I would've destroyed them from the inside because no one can wage a war with them and win.

Hold on.

Destroy them from the inside.

That's it.

From the inside!

I grabbed another book; this time it was about Venadar. It is said here that it was indeed the day of the festival that their kingdom. It all happened in one day, same as Ectal. Discord, Demise, and Downfall, all in one day, almost instantly. They were conquered by an unknown kingdom too.

If I have to figure out all of this, I have to think the same way the one who caused the omens did. I have to think like I'm going to conquer them using the pattern.

Discord was too easy. Their rulers, generals and officers, were always in arguing. Because they valued strength, they wanted to know which one of them was the strongest. The arguments came in naturally, given that they were braggarts, at least that's what history tells.

Now, for Demise. As far as I can remember for the thousands of books that I've read, they've played this certain game; a game that would prove who's the strongest. It was this stupid game played during the festival of Mane. It caused the death of their generals

It was the Chain Dare.

The participants lock themselves up in a chain and try to escape using nothing but pure physical strength and bare hands. All the generals joined the last game of it. It used to be popular but now it's forbidden. The last game of it caused the demise of the generals, and as well as the kingdom.

Something went wrong in that game. The chains were too strong the generals couldn't escape. But thanks to their pride, instead of asking for the key, they died trying, literally. The force they exerted caused the columns, which they were tied to, to fall apart and the debris fell on them. It killed them instantly. After a few moments, the unknown kingdom attacked and the rest was history.

The generals of Venadar were the strongest of all, so I still can't believe they weren't able to escape. The thing is, why weren't they able to?

I searched the notebook for clues, but all I found was another name.

Alistair Dakar

I don't know this man, but his surname seemed familiar. The Dakars were famed because of their profession. They were black-smiths, and their weapons and forgeries were the strongest of all. They were located in different kingdoms though. We even have a royal blacksmith from their clan. I'm pretty sure that Venadar had one too.

If Venadar did have a Dakar in their midst, that would explain their magnificent weapons, and also the strength of their swords.

Strength of their swords...

Could it be that they weren't able to escape.. because the chains were too strong?

I smiled, finally being able to piece things together, "Only a Dakar can make that happen."

It all makes sense now!

After all of these, the conquerors came in, bringing their Downfall.

I turned to the other pages and it was all the same; some information about the kingdom, date of domination, and an unknown name at the bottom of it all. All kingdoms were conquered by an unknown group. Only Seira was left out.

Right now, what I have is this:

First, this notebook was written by a strategist, like Scarlett- one who makes plans to conquer a an enemy or a kingdom. Obviously, the writer of this book belonged to that unknown kingdom that conquered everything. For now, I still have to figure out who they are.

Next, the omens are fake, just like Isabelle said. The conquerors somehow came up with a pattern and sold it as omens when in reality, they caused every single event. They used the omens to cover up their ways, and to attack the kingdoms from the inside. It was used like a Trojan Horse!

And the most surprising of them all, the spies.

For Ectal, it was Queen Pia.

For Venadar, it was Alistair Dakar

For Rave, it was a soldier named Luka.

For Abbadon, it was their own prince.

For Seira... it wasn't written here.

I understand it all now. We've all been under the influence of something false. I can't believe that they are intending to mess with Sorah.

I clenched my fists and gritted my teeth, "They messed with the wrong king."

Whoever this kingdom was, I'm gonna make sure they get it hard.

If they still move in accordance to the pattern of the omens, that means Downfall will be coming to us soon. But, of course, I won't let that happen. I'm now ahead of them all.

They're planning to make Sorah fall, huh?

I'm gonna make sure they won't be able to.

I'll get them first.

I took the notebook with me and I proceeded to share everything I discovered to Isabelle and Daniel.

"I'm not gonna let this kingdom fall."

I hurried back to Scarlett's room. I opened the door shut it after. I saw Daniel still looking after a sleeping Scarlett. My eyes searched for Isabelle but I didn't see her.

"Where have you been, Aspen? It's been hours." Daniel asked upon seeing me.

I shrugged, "I've been busy. Anyway, I have something big to tell you guys. Where's Isabelle?"

"She left a few minutes after you did."

She left? Oh.

"Sad much?" He looked at me in the most annoying way.

I glared at him," This is a very crucial information and she needs to know."

He scoffed, "Whatever you say, your highness."

I walked towards the bed but not a moment too soon, Scarlett woke up.

I stepped back and waited for what's gonna happen. I know she's depressed and all, and so are we, but you never know what's waiting for you with her. She might throw a spear or something me. Unlike me, Daniel rushed to her and held her hands. He looked at her with worry distinct in his eyes.

"Scar? Are you alright?"

I saw her calm and she was breathing heavily. But, her hands started shaking after. I walked closer to the both of them, worried. She tried to speak, but her voice was kinda shaky too.

"I h-had the most scary d-dream. M-my dad. He was...and I-"

Daniel and I bowed our heads in sadness. We knew that we have to find the words once she wakes up. But we were unprepared. We didn't know how to explain a father's death to her daughter.

She looked at us, scared, with tears welling up her eyes, "I k-killed him."- then she looked at us, her eyes widened at our expression of sadness. Darn it. I should've smiled-" It wasn't a dream isn't it? I really did-"

"No. No, no, no, no. Scar, listen to me. You didn't, okay. Someone-"

"I KILLED HIM DANIEL! IT WAS MY FAULT!"she wailed.

This time, I went to her and tried to explain everything," Scarlett, it wasn't you. There were these criminals. They put in a trance and made you think that it was you who did it. They used this talisman and a-"

"JUST KILL ME, ASPEN. PLEASE! I'M BEGGING YOU, PLEASE KILL ME!" she cried as she held on to my torso.

Daniel and I looked at her in pain,"Scar, please.... let him explain. It wasn't you who killed your father. We had Isabelle on this. Even she believes that it wasn't-"

"How do even know that?! I was there. I had memories of how I did it, Daniel. I'm a traitor to this country. Just please kill me.... kill me now." She whispered as tears fell from her eyes. She handed me a sword, insisting I kill her. But, I threw it away and I held her shoulders.

"Scarlett, you have to believe us. It wasn't you. We're gonna get to the bottom of this and avenge General Aris." I tried to explain more but she pushed me away. She was already out of her mind and I knew that. She can't think properly for now, thinking that she murdered her father. I glanced at Daniel and he was as pained as I was for seeing her like this. He was gritting his teeth and I'm sure that he was angry at himself, for everything that's happened.

She then grabbed another sword beside her, " If you won't kill me, then I'll do so myself. By that way, I no longer have to suffer this guilt." I widened my eyes as she whispered the words without emotion, " I'm sorry, father."

Then she pointed her sword towards her body. I tried to get up in time to stop her, but I wasn't able to. Luckily, Daniel stopped her in my place. He angrily threw the sword away and held her shoulders.

He shook her angrily as she looked up to him in fear," What the heck is wrong with you?!"

"I-I-"

Daniel looked her intensely as she moved his hands to her face, and his head closer to hers," Look at me, Scar. Do you think you can really kill your father? Even Aspen and I won't believe it. Do you really believe that you're a murderer? Since when did you become this stupid?!"

"Daniel." I tried to calm him down because he looked too serious. I'm not used to it. But, he went on anyway.

"Scarlett, I need you to believe us. We are going to explain everything, and I promise you that everything will be resolved.I just need you to please calm down and listen to us. I'm going to ask you one more time, de Beville. Do you believe us?"

Scarlett stuttered, "I-I'll try."

"No." Daniel tightened his hold, "I don't want you to try. I need you to believe us for real. You know we can never lie to you. I'll ask you again to put your faith in us , Scar. Will you believe us?"

It took Scarlett for almost a minute to say something, but she answered, "Yes. I do.I will."

"Thank you." Daniel sighed. He then took notice of how close their faces were and he instantly backed away, hiding the redness in their cheeks.

He seemed too attached to her face though.

After Scarlett calmed down, we explained everything to her. We showed her the card, the talisman, everything. It took her a minute to process everything. Her expression darkened. Sadness didn't overwhelm her face anymore. Her bedsheet was getting wrinkled in her fists and her head was twitching. She was mad.

And that was a warning sign for us. Daniel and I stepped back. It was fortunate that we did because the next thing we know was that a spear came flying through the air and towards the wall. How many weapons does she have on her bed?

"And she's back." Daniel muttered.

"Honestly, I liked her better sad now,"

"Yeah. Me too. I was even able to hold her face without getting my butt whipped."

I felt something warm against me suddenly. Only then did I realize that I was hugging Daniel and he was hugging me out of fear. I quickly pushed him away and we glared at each other.

"I'm in." Scar suddenly said.

"What?"

She stood up," You promised me that you're going to avenge my father. I want in. I want those criminals alive. I'll be their death."

We gulped, unable to say anything. We nodded our heads instead.

"What's your next step, Aspen?" She asked as she walked towards us with 'death' evident on her face.

"Well, I found out couple of crucial things. But we need-"

"Hey, guys."

We turned around and looked at the door, and there she was. She came back!

"Isabelle!" I ran to her, "Where have you been?"

She let out a breath, "Never mind that. Where's- Scarlett!"

Then she ran and embraced Scarlett. Her eyes softened as she hugged Isabelle, as if she was comforted. Our jaws dropped. Really, what kind of magic does this girl have?

We gathered together near them, "Now that we are all here," Isabelle started, "I have something big to tell you."

I nodded,"Me too. But, ladies first."

Who knows, hers might be bigger news.

"Scarlett, I think your father's still alive."

And it was.

13

CHAPTER 13

Isabelle

(4 hours earlier)

After leaving the palace grounds, I wandered around, but not before removing my Lady Investigator uniform, of course.

I still can't get a hold of what I've gotten myself into.

What am I going to tell my parents?

I honestly don't know what to do. I don't think I can even face them. But, I had to go home.

So, after some time, I finally got just the right amount of guts to go home and tell what I have to tell.

I arrived at our doorstep not a moment too soon. I took a deep breath, "You can do this, Isabelle."

Wait.

What am I gonna say?

"Hey, mom, dad. Guess what? I'm a Lady Investigator! Woohoo! You can disown me now if you want."

Yikes. What am I? A martyr?!

"Mom, Dad. I'm really sorry. I've disobeyed you. I went to the palace, and talked with a royal. I accidentally signed myself up to be a Lady-"

No. They'll have a heart attack even before I finish a sentence. Ugh..

They'll be furious! I'm gonna be a disgraceful daughter in their eyes. I've disobeyed them. It being temporary is not an exception they'll accept. They're not gonna like this one bit.

But, I have to face this. I'm not one to hide these kind of secrets from them. I have never lied to my parents.

If I choose to tell the truth, It'll lift this heavy feeling off my chest, but I'll be punished for my actions twice as heavy as the guilt.

However, if I choose to hide this, it'll spare their lives and save them from having a heart attack, but I'm gonna have to drag like what, 2 anchors, everyday for hiding this.

But, either way, the worst thing is that, I'm gonna hurt them.

Well then, here goes.

I opened the door and saw my mother sweeping the floors, doing what she does best.

"Dear, you're here." She smiled lovingly.

I can't believe I'm about to take that smile off her face.

"Hi mom. I'm sorry for leaving for too long. Where's dad?" I asked as I sat in the couch.

"Oh, he's taking a rest in his room. Let's just let him be for the time being." She chuckled.

"Okay." I sighed.

I can't stop thinking about the whole Lady Investigator thing, and the case I'm working on with the prince and Aspen. My heart pounded inside me and my brain is about to malfunction from over thinking this. The weight in my chest was getting heavier by the second.

"Honey, are you alright? You seem troubled."

I looked up to her, "Me?"

"Who else do you think I might be referring to? The vase?" She quirked a brow.

I sighed," No. I'm fine."

She rolled her eyes,"Isa, when you see a person with bruises, bumps, cuts, and injuries, do you think he's fine?"

I chuckled. She is really observant when it comes to these stuff. No matter how hard we try to hide, she would always imply that it was too obvious that we're troubled. How keen is her sight anyway that she can see right through us?

I closed my eyes for a second and sighed, "Mom, I need to tell you something."

She nodded and sat down, "I'm all ears."

This is it.

Will I tell the truth?

"Mom I-"

Wait.

If I tell the truth, I'll be forbidden to even go near the palace grounds. I won't be able to help Daniel and Aspen.

I won't be able to fulfill my promise to Scarlett.

If I don't tell the truth, I'll be spared, I can continue to work with my friends, and my parents will be saved from possible stress for life.

Prolonging the truth may seem to have more advantages, but it's gonna have the biggest consequence. Telling the truth, I'm gonna lose a lot of things, including the ability to help my friends, and possibly Sorah.

Either way, I'm gonna lose my parent's trust and I'm gonna hurt their feelings.

"What is it, Isabelle?"

I still got nothing. So, I sighed and...

"Mom, what if one wants to tell the truth, but she'll lose a lot of things with it; a lot of important things. What would be the best choice then?" I asked.

She placed her head on her palm and started to think,"I see. You want to tell the truth, but at the same time you don't want to. Is it because of fear, darling?"

I lowered my head," No, not really. I just don't know what would be worth saving."

She stood up," Well, if I were you, I suggest you weigh it out."

I looked up,"Weigh it out?"

"Well, what is more important to you? The things you'll lose telling the truth, or the things you'll lose if you choose to hide it?"

That had me thinking.

My family is more important to me. There's no question there.

But, I made a promise to Scar, Aspen, and Daniel. They need me.

"I'll just leave things to you, Isa. If you need me, I'll be in the kitchen."

"Thanks, mom." I smiled. Then, she went on her way to the kitchen.

Me?

I sat there trying to come up with a decision.

To tell the truth, or not to tell the truth?

My family or my friends?

Honestly, now that I think of it, if I choose to help my friends, I might help in saving the kingdom. I don't wanna get credit for it, but bottom line is... If Sorah is saved, so will my family.

But if Sorah gets into trouble, what will become of my family?

Will hiding the truth save them? Hurt them?

After all, they are more important to me. They have to be my top priority.

The thing is... what should I choose?

I sighed, tired of thinking and fighting for what I should've let go earlier.

Signing up to be a lady investigator was wrong in the first place.

And at the end of the day, it would always be the truth. So, why not today?

I can't afford to lose my parents, or them losing their trust in me. If I tell the truth as early as possible, I won't have to walk everyday with cannons on my back, and I'll be able to spare all of us the heaviness and pain while the lie is still short-lived.

I'm sorry, Aspen, Scarlett, Daniel. I can't lie, not to my family, not to myself.

I hope they'll understand.

I stood up, my feet pointing towards the kitchen. But, before I could even take a step, the door opened without warning.

"Isabelle!" The person , who was standing at the door, exclaimed.

"Edith!?" I whisper-shouted. "What are you do-"

"Not here. I have something to tell you. Come on." Then, she grabbed my hand and dragged me outside.

"Where are we-"

"Hush! Wait til' we get there."

I rolled my eyes and let her drag me towards our destination, which was in the middle of our field.

I let out a breath, "This better be good. I was in the middle of something there."

She looked around,"I need to tell you something."

"Yeah, you mentioned that earlier. It better be worth standing in the middle of a field, Edith."

"Okay, okay, fine. I brought-"

"Try drag." I smirked.

"Ugh...okay. The reason why I DRAGGED you here was to tell you..." -then she whispered it in my ear-" Lione's still in Bethany."

My eye twitched," You brought me-"

"Dragged."

"-all the way here... just to tell me that your husband's still on vacation?! What the heck, Edith?!"

Then, this girl suddenly slapped my head.

"Ow! What was that for?!"

"It's not that, you idiot!" She exclaimed, "My husband's still in Bethany...with General Aris."

My eyes widened," Say what?"

She took something from her pocket, it was a piece of paper.

"My husband sent me this letter just today. He said that he's still with the general, along with a couple of soldiers. Their arrival was supposed to be today but something happened. He told me that there was a landslide along the way, and it's gonna take a few days for the road to clear up."

She handed the letter to me. I scanned the words, the date, and true enough, what she said was right. Her husband is with General Aris, and they weren't able to return today. They're still in Bethany as of now. So, that means...

"But, the death of the General was reported earlier and-"

"My husband never lies. If he's home by now, I would be the first one he'll see. He's still with General Aris in Bethany, Isa. I'm sure of that."

"So, that would mean that...the general may be alive." I uttered.

She nodded," I didn't tell anyone. I know that you're the only person I can share this with. So, what are you gonna do about it?"

My eyes focused on the letter,"Mind if I borrow this for a while?"

She shrugged,"Not at all." Then she smiled, "Good luck, Isabelle."

I chuckled, "Thanks. Oh, if you need me-"

"I'll know where to find you."

I looked at her incredulously," You do?"

"No, I actually don't. But wherever it is, I'm sure you'll be doing just fine."

"Well, I'm off. Thanks, Edith." I hugged her.

"Bye!" She waved as I ran to the house to get my uniform and get dressed.

I'm sorry, mom. I'm sorry, dad. But, I can't just shut up about this. The truth will have to wait.

(PRESENT TIME)

"Isabelle, that's ridiculous!" Aspen insisted.

"Yeah, we all saw him dead." Daniel added.

"Isabelle, this is not funny at all." Scarlett choked.

After I relayed to them about the chance that Scar's dad is still alive, they kept bombarding me with protests, saying that it is way too impossible.

I rolled my eyes, "See for yourselves."

I handed them Edith's letter. They read it from top to bottom as their eyes turned as wide as discuses.

"Isabelle... this is-"

"I know it's hard to believe, okay. But, trust me on this. My friend has no reason to lie. There is a possibility that the general is still alive." I explained.

"Isabelle, we're not sure about this. All of us saw what happened, even the ministers. " Aspen said.

"Yeah, it's very hard to believe." Daniel joined in.

Scarlett averted her gaze towards the floor, not knowing how to take in all of this.

I became worried about her, but now I'm giving her hope that her father is still alive. I want her know that she's not alone.

I went closer to her and held her hands, "Scarlett, I know this is a lot to take in, especially after what you've witnessed earlier. But, I need you to trust me on this."

But she remained silent.

"Isabelle, we all saw him. A corpse, cold on the floor. It's-"

"Did you?" I cut off Daniel. "Look, he may might have worn the general's armor and may have resembled him too. We're not sure about that. If the general's still alive, it might have been a decoy or an imposter that died."

The three looked at each other, then at me.

"Now that I've thought of it, the general's corpse was down with his back facing us. I didn't even see his face clearly because of the blood. He had the hair, look, and suit of the general. That's why I didn't do any second thinking." Aspen admitted.

"Besides that fact, he was also in the defense hall where Scarlett was. That's why no one would ever hesitate to think that it wasn't General Aris." Daniel added whilst scratching the back of his head.

What they said had me thinking.

So they weren't really sure if it was the general. But, Scarlett was convinced that it was him.

Hold on.

General Aris went to Bethany, and everyone thought that he was already home, including Scarlett, Aspen, and Daniel. By any chance, did they have an encounter with him before his said 'Demise'?

I faced Scar, "If you don't mind me asking, Scarlett, were you, by any chance, able to talk to your father between the time that he arrived from Bethany and before his death?"

Scarlett's eyes widened, "N-no."

Just as I suspected. I looked at the two boys, and I have a hunch that they know what this means.

It just became all the more suspicious.

No one was able to talk to the general between the time of his arrival and death. So, in other words, we're not really sure that it was the general who died because no one was able to see him before his death. No one would have any proof that the general was in Sorah that time.

When the news came that he arrived, without seeing him, we immediately believed that he really was home. Because of that, we didn't do any second thinking, as Aspen said, and believed that it was really Scarlett's father that was murdered.

I began to speak, "He was home, he was here, he was murdered in Sorah because he is in Sorah. That's what everyone believed, not having any proof that the general was even home. They didn't even see him."

"But, what if we knew he still wasn't home, what if we knew that he wasn't in Sorah? Then we would have doubted about his 'Demise'." Aspen added.

"Okay, now I'm a believer." Daniel uttered.

Scarlett was looking at the floor, stitching all the pieces together.

"But, these are just suspicions. How do we really know that it wasn't him who died?" Daniel asked.

"There's only one way to find out. And we're gonna do exactly that." Aspen said while grabbing his coat, and a cloth to cover his nose.

Daniel grunted, "I have a feeling that this is gonna be a bloody darn place. Literally bloody."

"It's just gonna be like a tour on a memorial park." Aspen said, trying to encourage him to go.

"With people NOT buried! Do you know how sick and disgusting that will be!?"

"No one's asking you to go, but you promised to help someone." Aspen said, pointing his lips at Scar, whose gaze was still on the floor.

"W-well then," -he coughed- "What are we waiting for? Are we gonna solve this case or not? Come on, people. You're too slow. Don't be afraid. It's just gonna be like a walk in the valley of Fallen Sorahians."

"Yeah, with people not buried yet." Aspen teased, throwing his words back at him.

Daniel gritted his teeth, "Idiot! Can't you see I'm trying to be brave?"

"Try a little harder... you know, without contorting your face in disgust." Aspen said, walking pass by him and out the door, "Come on, Isabelle."

"Coming." I said as I stood up.

"Why that little-" Daniel growled as he too, went out the door.

I chuckled at the two. They may look like adults, but they have the spirit of 8 year olds.

I turned my head to Scar,"You coming with us?"

She looked at me, gave a slight smile, nodded, and stood up.

"Let's go." I said, walking ahead.

"Isabelle.." Her voice sounded soft, weak, desperate yet hopeful," Do you really think that my father may be.."

I smiled at her softly,"We're about to find out. But, based on what we've just found out, yes. I believe that he is still out there. You'll be able to see him again. So, don't worry. We promised you, didn't we?"

She finally gave a sincere smile. You could barely make it out on her face, but you can feel she's smiling, "I guess so. I just don't want to hope for an uncertainty yet, a false hope."

"Do you trust us?" I asked out of the blue.

She looked at me in a confused manner," I-I, well, of course I do."

"That's all we need, Scarlett. We won't let you down. We're not asking you to hope for something. That's up to you. But, all we need for now, is for you to trust us, because we made a promise to you and we won't go back on our words. " I said to her.

She sighed for a moment; a calm, soothed, and hopeful sigh,"I trust you, guys. With all my heart."

I nodded and smiled, "Everything 's gonna be alright, I promise. Now, let's go."

She smiled, took my hand, and I assisted her as we went to our destination. Her knees were still weak, but she was getting better. I felt the heaviness as I held her, not the weight of her physique, but the burden she carried.

To lose someone is really painful, and it's gonna take years for it to heal. I know that kind of pain. I just hope what Scarlett's feeling right now is temporary. We don't want to lose the brave girl we all know.

He's alive, Scar. And we're gonna prove that.

14

CHAPTER 14

Isabelle

"This stinks," Daniel complained.

"I'll give you a million pieces of silver if you can give me a fragrant corpse, Daniel," Aspen shook his head.

"I know that. I'm just pointing out that it's down right foul and disgusting," Daniel retorted.

"Be careful. You just stepped on the lungs." Aspen teased as we were walking forward with our hands on our nose.

"Gah! I hate this place!" Daniel exclaimed.

"Actually, no one would really love this place," Aspen emphasized.

"Quiet now. You might wake them."

"Isabelle!" Daniel screamed.

"Good one," Aspen said, giving me a high five. Then, we all piped down, reminding ourselves that we were at the Cadaver's Chambers.

We came here for one thing only: to examine the corpse of the general.

It was secluded at the end of the hospital. Only investigators, officers, and royals can come here. With Daniel alone, we were granted passage. Then, we took the opportunity to look for the corpse. It was dark and no one assisted us through that maze of a place. Most of the people already evacuated to the other far cities of Sorah and to their own provinces because of fear.

We need to fix this soon and fast.

"Found him?"

"Nothing here." Aspen replied.

"Just corpses.. ugh..", Daniel groaned.

"Father..."

Then, we turned our heads to Scarlett. She was looking at a corpse, the only one who wore an armor, specifically speaking.

We walked closer towards him, or it, since he's already dead. He was inside a special room inside the large chamber.

"It is him. This is the armor he wore." Scarlett informed.

"Scar, with your permission, we will-"

"It's fine, Isabelle. Like you said, we're not really sure if it is dad. So, there's no point in asking for permission, really." Scarlett gave a smile.

"Okay then. Let's find out if it really is our beloved general." Aspen started.

We nodded our heads and wore the gloves provided beside the body's table. We didn't let Scarlett examine the corpse. How would anyone feel about touching and doing tests on a cadaver of a possible loved one?

We thought about that. Daniel and Aspen found it hard too. They were barely able to touch it, so I insisted that I go first.

They helped me remove the heavy, stained armor on the body and I proceeded to do my work after.

I examined first the wound. Mother, being a nurse, taught me how to do it. The wound at the side of the waist was deep; it was certainly caused by the dagger. That's the only wound I saw so far. Everything else was pale and blue, given that it was a corpse, but other than that, the flesh seemed normal; not bitten, not scraped. It was just that one wound at the waist.

I took a step back in confusion.

How strange. How could he possibly...

"What is it?" Aspen asked, stepping forward.

"It's nothing. It's just that..."

"What?"

One wound? And it's just at the waist. Could he really suffer death just from that? I mean, for someone with a trained, fit, and strong body, belonging to a general at that, this would just be a minor injury.

"Aspen, tell me, could someone possibly die from just one wound? What if he's a soldier or something?"

Aspen stooped to think, "Well, it depends if a critical area of the body was wounded, but other than that, no. No one, especially a trained soldier, could've easily died at that."

"Huh."

"Why?" Daniel asked.

"The general only had one wound. And it's just at his waist. The waist is not a critical part of the body, isn't it?"

"Yeah, you do have a point. But he may have lost a lot of blood. Maybe that's the reason why." Daniel reasoned.

"If you were stabbed, would you really let the blood flow out?" I quirked a brow.

He scratched his head at his careless thinking, "Hehe. Of course he might have covered it, being a sane and logical thinker that he is."

Yes. If he was wounded really bad, no matter who his enemy was, he would've created an opportunity to at least cover it.

So, the wound was at the waist, a very minor injury if you'd ask me. I also doubt the theory he died of blood loss. He would only lose blood if he wasn't able to cover his flesh wound because he couldn't move. But, he could've easily moved because of the damage to his body wasn't as fatal.

So, what really caused his death?

If it wasn't the dagger that killed him, then it wasn't Scar at all.

I observed his hands and his skin. It was blue. Blue...

Could it be?

"Isabelle, look at his face." Aspen said, pointing at it.

I picked up my feet and went to his face. It was blue as well. But, my attention was quickly drawn to his lips, which were unusually in a very dark shade of blue than his skin.

I touched his cold lips and opened it. To my shock... and disgust, to be honest, his teeth were also blue.

Blue.

He was-

"Poisoned." Aspen uttered while he looked at me with eyes as wide as mine.

"He was poisoned! It wasn't the dagger or the wound that killed him. It was poison." Aspen exclaimed.

"His teeth was in a very dark shade of blue, meaning that the poison took effect and has been in his body for quite some time now. The wound was fresher than the hue of his skin and teeth too.

That means that he was already poisoned by the time the dagger stabbed him." I explained.

"So it wasn't Scarlett who killed him." Aspen added.

"Obviously." Daniel scoffed.

"Just saying."

I shrugged as the two boys bickered. I then turned to Scarlett who looked at the corpse with confusion and relief. She let out a sigh an smiled,"So I'm not-"

"You never were, Scar." I finished," And you never will be a murderer."

She looked at me with gratitude in her eyes, expressing her thankfulness for finding out that she was wrong about herself; she was wrong to think herself as a killer. We have proof that she isn't to anyone who wronged her.

Then she scrunched her face and turned his attention towards the back of the corpse's hand. The two guys stopped bickering to look at her too. She went closer and closer until she was close enough to touch the hand of the corpse.

"It's not him. It's not my father." She muttered.

"What?"

"He had a mark at the back of his hand. He had the crest of Sorah on the back of his right hand. This one doesn't." She stated.

"A crest of Sorah on the back of his hand?"

"Yes." She insured.

The two walked closer to us to observe the dead body and ask the question we've all been wanting an answer on," Then who is this?"

Yeah.

Who exactly is this dead man?

"Hold on." Aspen said as he touched the beard of the man," Is this...goat hair?"

"Like the one you put on your- ugh!" Daniel said, before Aspen elbowed him on his gut.

"Shut up."

"Aspen did you say goat hair?" I asked.

"Mhm. I think it's fake." He said.

Fake?

Only one way to find out.

I peeled the said fake hair off his face. And, to our surprise, it was as Aspen said.

Fake hairs.

"It's-"

"What is it, Daniel?"

"It's the messenger!"

"Messenger?" We tilted our heads, trying to figure out what he was talking about.

He tapped Aspen's shoulder, "Remember? Back before the ceremony began, I told you that we hired a new messenger? It was this guy." He said, pointing at the corpse.

Aspen's eyes widened," But a different messenger came to me and told me about the arrival of... Oh damn."

"What is it Aspen?" We asked in unison."

"The messenger. Back at the balcony, he was the one who told us about the arrival of general Aris, the one who made us think that the general was home." He relayed.

We were now able to piece things together.

"So that guy-"

"Killed the messenger and replaced him... to give us the news that the general was home, even though he wasn't." Daniel finished.

"He's the spy. He's the mole that's gonna lead their kingdom in conquering Sorah, just like in the notebook!" Aspen exclaimed.

I got nothing.

The part that the messenger killed this guy to take his place I got, but what the heck did Aspen say?

Mole?

Spies?

Conquering Sorah?

"Aspen, if you have a problem, talk to us, okay." Then Daniel moves his mouth to my ear and whispered,"Poor guy. The case must've driven him nuts."

Then, the horrific unexpected happened.

Aspen laughed.

"I think you're right." I whispered back in dismay.

"Stupid." Aspen suddenly shook his head at us and glared," I forgot. I haven't told you yet."

"Tell us what?" I asked.

"Well, now that our business here is done, let's go to a safer place, like the library. This is definitely not the place to speak about it. Let's go." He said, leading the way out.

I wonder what it is.

We were about to leave but then we suddenly heard someone crying. We turned around to see that it was Scarlett; she was sitting down with her hands covering her eyes.

"Scar! Are you alright?" Daniel rushed to her, helping her stand.

She tried to speak between sobs,"He-he's alive, isn't he?"

We smiled. Her voice sounded hopeful, but this time with relief and joy. No more signs of desperation. She now believes.

"Yes, Scar."

"My father's alive!" She exclaimed, as she, unexpectedly, hugged Daniel, "Thank you, guys. Thank you so much."

Ooooo.

Aspen and I looked at each other knowingly as we laughed at Daniel trying to hide his evident blush.

We smirked at the two. Daniel was shaking, but then Scar let him go to hug us too.

"We promised you, didn't we? Now, let's go find out the rest." I cheered her up.

"Let's go."She said. Then we went out the room, letting Scar go ahead of us.

Daniel was unable to erase the redness in his face the same way Aspen can't remove the smug in his face.

"Well, somebody's happy." I smirked.

"Yeah, really happy." Aspen agreed.

"She just h-hugged-"

"Let's go now." I said, walking past them and out the door," There are a lot of important things to put first."

Going back to the case; we solved Discord, Demise as well. We find out that everything was planned, and the omens were just as I said... Crap. A whole buttload of it.

And now, for the rest.

"-see? It's all the same for the other kingdoms. Whoever the writer was, he must've been the strategist of the ones who created the omens." Aspen finished explaining.

What he just said literally blew our minds. I've studied about the omens and the fallen kingdoms, but I didn't think that there was more to it. He showed us the notebook and explained every detail. I can't believe how clever this kingdom was.

Imagine, deceiving the whole world with the omens, but actually using them as a weapon to conquer.

Wow.

I was impressed, but terrified at the same time.

"So, you're saying that another kingdom will come and conquer Sorah just like what happened before, and that same kingdom caused the Downfall of the five fallen kingdoms?" I asked.

"Yes. And we need to find a way to prevent that." He said firmly.

"Whoever these guys are, they're gonna die." Scarlett said, stabbing a dagger at the table. We were currently in the library working our on some plans. We were all relieved that she turned back to normal, but at the same time scared.

"Easy on the table, Scar."

"What was that, you prince!?"

"N-nothing!"

Aspen cut them off before things get dangerous,"Hey! Guys, focus. We need to act while it's not yet happening."

"How? We don't have a lead." Daniel reasoned.

"The messenger's our lead, remember? He's the key to everything. If we catch him, we can stop all this."

"And what's our lead in finding that spy?" Daniel quirked a brow.

And all fell silent.

"See? We don't have a lead."

I looked at them in a knowing way," Actually, we might have a lead." I said as I grabbed a nearby book. It was about the omens.

"What do you mean?"

I opened the book, trying to find that certain page,"You said that there were always moles everytime that kingdom uses their omens to destroy another kingdom; one mole. And, for one person, fulfilling an omen may take days, or even weeks. So, how will the kingdom know when to attack?"

"The mole signals them." Scar answered.

"Exactly. The same mole signals them. And how do they do it?"

"No idea." They admitted.

I chuckled," We missed something." I kept on turning the pages as they stood closer to me," There was another thing that always happens in the omens, between Demise and Downfall."

"What?" They asked.

"The cannon." I said, pointing at a specific phrase of the page. They moved their heads closer,"A survivor reported here that before the 'terrorists' came, a cannon fired at their highest mountain. Every survivor said the same thing; there was always a sounding of the cannon before the Downfall. This is what signals them to attack."

They smiled," So, all we have to do is catch the mole before he fires the cannon, and that would be-"

"At the highest mountain in Sorah." I finished for Aspen.

"Mount Harmel."

Suddenly, we heard Scarlett smirk, "How do you plan on getting there? The spy must be halfway towards the summit by now."

"Oh darn." Aspen said in discouragement.

"I'm just pulling your leg. Luckily, that mountain happens to be my training ground. I have my own secret tunnel towards the summit. If we go now, we can catch up to him." She explained.

Aspen laughed,"Then what are we waiting for? Let's go kick some spy-ass!"

"Yeah!" We agreed.

"Why don't we send soldiers too?" Scarlett suggested.

That's a good idea. That way, the spy will think twice about doing anything funny.

"We can't do that." Aspen shook his head.

"Of course we can, especially you. You're the ki-"

"Woah!" Aspen and Daniel grabbed Scarlett and held her mouth. They whispered something in her ear. After that, her eyes widened,"Oh."

What's going on?

"Maybe some other time. It's better if we keep this thing between the four of us first. We can take him down." Scarlett said, changing her words.

"O-okay. If you say so." I shrugged.

"Now, let's move out."

We nodded, and followed her lead towards the tunnel that she told us about. We ran to the stable to borrow some horses, then we set off towards Mount Harmel.

Daniel

We were quickly climbing up the stone stairs inside the secret tunnel of Mount Harmel using our horses. We were getting closer to the summit, and I can already feel the coldness of the atmosphere inside the tunnel.

"We're almost there. Ready your swords." Scarlett commanded.

"Yeah!"

It's gonna be over after this. There's no way he'll be able to escape now.

I saw a light and a gust of cold wind coming inside, and I knew that we were already at the summit. We wasted no time. We climbed down from our steeds and proceeded towards the cold.

True to our calculations, the messenger was there, about to fire the cannon.

Before we could attack secretly, Scar charged towards him violently, giving him no time to fight back. He dropped the cannon and attempted to run away but she slashed his legs, wounding him severely. He screamed in pain, holding his legs.

"Now, we have you." Scarlett lifted him by his neck with one hand.

Aspen intervened before the man can choke to death,"Scarlett! We need him alive."

"Just a second." Scarlett said, as she tightened her hold on his neck. The man struggled for air, but she wouldn't let him.

I held my neck, feeling what the man felt. That must hurt a lot.

"Scarlett!"

"Okay, fine! I'm done." Then she forcefully dropped him on the floor.

The man held his neck, feeling weak from the strangling.

"Thank you for leaving him alive." Aspen rolled his eyes.

"Fine. But when the time comes, I get to kill him okay." She groaned.

"Yeah, sure. Just not now."

Isabelle and I walked to them," That was a close call. The cannon would've fired if we weren't fast enough."

I smiled at our victory. But then, I saw the man grabbing some kind of dagger, preparing to stab his own heart.

"You'll never get me alive." He stated. Then, he was about to stab his own heart, but I stopped him.

I rushed to him and grabbed his dagger as I did a roundhouse kick on his face, knocking him out with his face buried on the snow.

"Good call, Daniel." They said, running to me.

"Yeah, that was awesome." Isabelle said.

"Thanks, Isabelle." I smiled. I looked at Scar, waiting for her to say something, but she just walked past me and grabbed the criminal.

"Let's go." Then she dragged the man and put him on her horse.

I sighed. Of course. She could've done better than what I just did. I could never impress her with that.

We rode on our own horses and climbed down the stairs of the tunnel. Aspen and Isabelle went ahead, followed by Scarlett, then me.

As we were climbing down, Scar stopped for a while and turned to me,"Nice job, Daniel. I glad you were there."

"N-no problem." I stammered. We looked at each other and time seemed to stop for a moment. My heart beats the fastest when it comes to moments like this with her.

Unfortunately, she quickly averted her gaze and climbed down the stairs in a faster pace.

I smirked,"So, she was actually impressed huh?"

And that's what kept running in my head as we went down the mountain.

The bad guy was caught, I was able to beat him up with one kick, Scar just complimented me, and Sorah is now saved.

This day rocks.

"Speak! Who sent you!?"

"Never!"

Scarlett kept slapping the guy to his senses; and it wasn't just some normal slaps. They were hard ones, harder than stones.

We were back at the court. We've already revealed the matter, and what we've found out to the ministers of the court and as well as the royal family.

Fallon, Blair, Genevieve, and Queen Leah.

Isabelle wasn't allowed in here, and she mustn't know about Aspen's true stance in this kingdom. She was left outside, back at the Investigators' office. She was a temporary apprentice there after all.

Aspen, now dressed in his royal robes, faced the spy in the court. The ministers were also here. Scarlett happily volunteered to be the one to have the man confess.

No luck, so far. He haven't spilled a word about who sent him, and why was Sorah their target.

Accidentally, Scarlett hit the guy too hard, so his cheek bled. All of us looked away in disgust. Even the ministers thought it was too much. Aspen, didn't look away, however. Instead, he narrowed his eyes even more. He'll do anything for Sorah. He lives for this. That's why anyone who messes with it deserves death, and he'll be ruthless just to give them what they deserve.

Earlier, after a lot of people went back from their planned evacuation. They came to their senses and decided that if Sorah was gonna face Downfall, they'll be there to fight beside their king and their heroes. They stood at the palace grounds shouting their war cries.

Apsen, being the king, became worried and yet touched by the scene. Worried that, if Downfall should come, his people would get hurt. But, he was touched that the people earned the courage of a thousand soldiers to fight for Sorah, even if it costs them their lives.

I'll never forget what he said when he saw all of it.

"If we weren't fast enough, imagine what great people we would've lost. These people are not trained for battle, yet their hearts are set on it, for their home. I was actually relieved that they left Sorah, so that if we weren't able to stop this, still no one would get hurt. But, they're all here. They came back. I'm so thankful we're able to stop Downfall. I won't be able to forgive myself if I wasn't fast enough."

"Well, it's too late now. The war's never gonna happen. Still, these people truly are amazing, willing to stand to for their kingdom." I added.

"What kind of sick bastard would try to mess with Sorah? Whoever he is, I bet he's suicidal, because he just messed with the wrong king. Come on, we still have things to do and a lot of people to pay us back....with their lives."

And that's why we're here at the court, with the ministers and the royal family serving as witnesses, and Aspen having Scarlett beat up the man.

"That's enough, Scarlett. He won't speak here." Aspen intervened.

"Let's not give up. A few more punches will do." Scarlett insisted, preparing for another punch.

"Enough!" Aspen barked, loud enough to scar our ears.

Scarlett rolled her eyes at the king, but she was compliant anyway.

"I'll handle this." Aspen said as he stood up from his chair and ordered the guards to take the spy to the dungeon.

"Don't kill him yet alright." Scar reminded.

"Daniel, come with me." Aspen demanded. I shrugged and went with him.

"Why does he get to go?" She complained.

"Guess I'm just that lucky." I smirked, but I was soon shut up with a glare from her.

Trust me, that glare can kill.

Before we left the court, the ministers lined up before us.

"Your majesty.." They started.

Aspen and I turned to them.

"Please forgive us for our imbecility. We almost lost faith. But you, our king, did not. Instead, you faced this problem and saved Sorah. From now, we will respect you with our utmost, your highness. Thank you." They bowed.

Aspen smiled at their words, "There are a lot of people to thank. But, I'm grateful because even so, you didn't leave Sorah."

"Of course, your majesty. This is our home and you are our king." They smiled.

Huh. Well, aren't they starting to get along.

"Aspen?" His sisters spoke.

"What is-ugh!"

His sisters hugged him with smiles in their faces, "Thank you too."

"Okay. You're welcome. Please let go. I can't breathe." Aspen said, trying to catch his breath.

Everyone laughed at the scene. After that, queen Leah went to him," My son, your father will be truly proud."

"Thanks, mother. Now, if you'll excuse us."

We bowed and then we left the room. We made our way towards the dungeon.

"Well, someone's a hero." I bumped him.

He gave me a smirk,"It wasn't just me. I wish Isabelle was there too. She should be thanked."

"Why can't you just tell her your the king?"

He looked at me incredulously, "No! Anything but that! I don't want her to avoid me. If she finds out who I truly am, she'll leave me."

Hmm. I that seems true enough. Being friends with a king can be messy. But I'm his cousin so I get twice the tragedy.

"What if you're married? Will you still be-"

"I won't marry." He said sternly," I can do fine without a queen."

"Come on. Why not? I'm getting married." I reasoned.

He gave a smug, "Ha. Goodluck with that."

If he wasn't the king, I would've punched him by now.

"Why wouldn't you marry anyway? Are you still waiting for the right girl?"

He rolled his eyes, "I don't need marriage. I'm married to Sorah. End of story."

I shook my head in dismay, "Fine, live with that."

After a few minutes, we finally reached the dungeon, to the strictest cell we had. We had the guards lock him up. After that, we asked to be left alone.

We faced the man inside the bars, "Now, talk."

He weakly looked at us, "You'll never win. They're too strong. They're ruthless."

Aspen and I looked at each other," Who are 'they'?"

He crawled to closer and held the bars," The Quiet Conquerors."

Quiet...conquerors?

Nah. Doesn't really ring a bell.

The man laughed, as if turning crazy. He repeated the words, "You'll never win."

I'm the kind of guy that gets irritated easily. And, I'm not asking for forgiveness for that.

So, I punched him.

"Daniel!"

"Sorry! I can't help it."

Now I know how Scar feels towards this guy.

"Let's just leave him for now. I need to address the people."

"Sure thing."

Then, we had two guards positioned at the dungeon just to ensure that he has nowhere to go.

After that, we proceeded to the court to gather the ministers, and put Sorah into place again.

"For years, we were deceived, tricked into believing falsity. We were terrorized by the things that happened in the past."

We were currently at the balcony. Aspen was explaining to the people. He kept the few informations to himself. Instead, he only told the citizens that they caught the spy, the general was alive, and that the kingdom used the omens to terrorize Sorah. But now, Sorah is saved.

And that's what he really wanted to emphasize,

Sorah is now safe. They can celebrate now.

"But now, Sorah, I tell you that never again will we be like this, for all of you have stayed strong. You didn't flee from your country, instead you came back ready to fight for it with your whole heart."

The people applauded themselves. Just think, they were all in chaos earlier. Now, look at them, all smiling as if nothing happened.

"Now, we shall continue the celebration of the Day of the Remembered, because this day, is the day the we saw the strength of Sorah in numbers, in power, and in heart. And we will remember this day. Prepare your booths and your tents, because the true festival is about to begin!"

The people erupts into fits of cheer and laughter. They quickly scrambled to their homes to set up the booths again in preparation for the festival.

Aspen smiled, knowing that his job was now done. "Fallon, take it from here."

She nodded," Sure. But, where are you going? The ceremony will soon start."

"I have some unfinished business. Daniel, come on. You too."

I tilted my head," Me? But I-"

Then he growled.

"Fine. I'm comin'."

I followed right behind him. I don't even know why I'm included in this. Anyway, he dressed in his officer's clothes again.

"So, this is your unfinished business?"

"Not quite. Now, let's go." He ran.

"Ugh."

We went out the palace grounds, making sure that no one saw us. We whistled for our horses and they quickly responded.

I followed Aspen's lead as he heads to the defense hall.

There, we saw Scarlett exiting from her room. We stopped our horses right in front of her.

"What the he-"

"Get on." Aspen demanded.

"What? Aspen, I have things to-"

"Just get on." Aspen shook his head.

Finally, she rolled her eyes and caved, "Fine. This better be good, you darn king."

Then, she climbed up MY horse.

I looked at him," Psst. Why on my horse?"

He was about to speak when I felt a glare piercing my soul.

"Got a problem with that?"

"No. Of course not. Welcome aboard." I gulped.

Then, Aspen went ahead once more with us behind him. We kept galloping until we reached the end of the city. We soon arrived at this hill outside gates of the kingdom.

Isabelle was there. She smiled as she saw us coming. We stopped where she was and climbed down.

Scarlett quickly went to Isabelle, "Isa, what are you doing here?"

"Waiting for you guys." She answered.

"What are we doing here, Aspen?" Scar asked.

"Waiting for someone."

"Who?" She demanded impatiently," This better be worth my-"

She stopped in her tracks as she had a good look on who we're expecting. He was still far from us, but Scarlett didn't need to think twice.

She ran to her father with tears in her eyes like a little girl, "Dad!!"

She stopped in front of him and saluted, so did her father to her.

General Aris was surprised by his daughter's actions. I guess he didn't know that the whole kingdom thought he was dead. We smiled at the scene. I almost cried too.

Almost.

But I didn't.

I tried not to.

I guess she has a lot to tell General Aris, but for now, I guess she would like to savor this moment first. Funny, it's like meeting her father for the first time. But I bet she felt more than that. She thought she lost him. But now he's come home, safe and sound. I'm so happy for her.

15

CHAPTER 15

Isabelle

"Breathe, Isabelle. Breathe. You can do this."

But I actually can't.

It's been a week since the case was solved. We stayed at a tavern last night and told the general about what happened. The experience was all fun for me. Aspen insisted on walking me home that night, but I didn't let him. We were all worn out, and I knew that he was tired as well. Besides, there was nothing to worry about anymore.

Sorah is now safe and celebrating. The celebration isn't over yet. In fact, the people refused to stop and are still making merry outside.

But the party's over for me. I was so focused on the case that I forgot my parents...

And the whole telling the truth thing.

My apprenticeship in the Lady Investigators is still valid because the exams aren't over yet. But, I have no plans on being a full fledged investigator. That would add weight to the sin I've already committed.

It was simple.

Never be close to a royal, or a noble.

Now, I got a full circle of friends composed of nobles and royals.

"Some daughter I am." I sighed.

Now that it's over, will they forgive me? Maybe if I tell them that what I did saved Sorah, maybe they would.

But I'm not sure of that. They loathed any relationship with politicians. The fact that I contributed in saving our kingdom won't make my punishment any less. I still betrayed them.

Ugh. Why does it have to be me?!

It could've been any scholar and anyone with the guts to be the hero. I have parents to obey and a 'good-daughter' reputation to live up to.

Why me?

"This is hopeless!" I exclaimed.

I don't know what to do, what to tell, what would happen. I hate myself. Why did I sign up for this in the first place?! I became too curious about the omens, which led me to discovering things, which led me to tell Aspen, which led him to drag me into this mess.

But then again, all these led into the salvation of our country.

Still....I'm toast.

I sighed. How am I going to face their wrath? I can already see images of dad with smoke coming out of their nostrils and mom pulling her hair out. And it's not that pretty.

"Isabelle? What are you doing? You're beating the eggs too hard!" Mom exclaimed.

"What?"

Only then did I notice that I destroyed what was supposed to be our delicious breakfast by beating it too hard. It started foaming because I lost myself in too much thought.

"Damn it," I shook my head as I wiped some droplets that went into my hands and my dress. "I'm sorry, ma."

Mom sighed,"Dear, if you're mad at the world or something, don't take your resentment out on our breakfast."

She takes the bowl away from me and wiped the table where I worked.

I can't help it. I need to tell the truth right now or else, I'll regret it forever. The longer I hide this, the worse it's gonna get. I just destroyed unsuspecting eggs, for crying out loud! I can't deal with this everyday. They're gonna find out at some point.

Now that it's over, there's no more reason for me to keep it anymore. I can't live with this inside my chest.

I need to tell them... now.

So, certain of my resolve, I inhaled all the air in my wake to ease my nerves," Mom, I need to te-"

"Save it for later, will you, dear? Those were the last eggs in our stock, and our hens aren't laying yet."

"But this is--"

"Isa, I need you to rush to the market and get us some eggs. You can say what you have to say once we have a stomach with eggs inside, okay. You know we can't have breakfast without eggs." She shrugged and pursed her lips upwards.

"Yes, we can." I scrunched my eyebrows.

"But we won't. Now run along and you might be able to get the fresh ones."

I sighed," Okay, mom. I'll be off then."

"Bye. And get those eggs." She waved goodbye.

As I stepped out the door, I felt it again; two anchors on my feet. I wasn't able to tell the truth and I have to walk with this again. I don't think I can even go on to buy some eggs.

"I can see your shadow under the door, dear. Are you gonna buy some or what?" She warned.

I staggered," Uh..yes. Bye, mother!"

I got up and ran towards the market. Mothers. You can never escape them. I bet it's easier to escape prison.

I breathed heavily. Looks like I ran too fast. I'm not an athlete. I shouldn't overexert myself.

Athlete?

I chuckled," That word feels nostalgic."

I remembered that time with Aspen. Our first time together was spent mostly running. That was the longest time I ran. Funnily, I didn't feel tired at all at that time. In fact, I wanted to run more.

Why do I feel tired now? It was only a short distance.

He held hands with me during that time. Was he giving off energy too as we ran?

AHH! I'm thinking of impossible things! How could he give me energy? It's not possible.

And more importantly...why am I feeling damned butterflies inside me?

.

.

.

.

.

The eggs!

"That's it. I must be hungry." I shrugged.

I need to go buy some immediately. So, I rushed to the store, but they told me that their eggs were sold out.

How can eggs be sold out anyway? How many people in this world badly need them?!

Ugh. Unfortunately, my family is one of those people.

So, I checked the other stores until I reached a small farm near the palace grounds.

"Excuse me, do you have some-"

"Eggs?" The owner smiled.

I nodded," Yes."

"Here." He said, handing me the eggs. "I reserved them for you, dear girl."

I was startled," W-what?"

"Well, I saw you coming from those shops asking for eggs, but they ran out, didn't they? So, before mine ran out as well, I reserved you some in case you pass here." He admitted.

This man's an angel.

"T-thank you so much! " I cheered crazily.

He chuckled," No need to thank me. You're still gonna pay for that though."

"Yes, of course." I grinned, getting the money and giving it to him, "Thanks again."

"You're welcome."

I nodded as I spun on my heels and proceeded to head home. I have to hurry and there were so many people blocking the way. I have to get home and fast.

So, I decided to use the narrow alley beside the houses close to the forest. It's the fastest way home. I quickly went there and luckily, there were no people lurking around. I took that path as I rushed home.

I wasn't even close to home when I heard....footsteps?

I turned around and saw that no one was there. It must be my imagination. So, I continued to walk in a faster pace.

Scarily, I heard it again. Footsteps.

This time, I felt it closing in on me.

What the heck?!

"W-who's there?" I asked with a shaky breath.

"Hello?" And still no answer.

This time I glanced at the wall on my left and saw worse than footsteps.

A shadow.

And what's worse than a shadow?

A shadow with a shadow of a spear in hand.

I looked up and saw the source of that shadow. A man with a spear was standing on a roof, looking at me as some sort of prey. He wore a mask that covered his face except for his eyes and he was dressed in all black. Without warning or reason, he said the words that made me regret taking this path...

"Die."

Then, he threw the spear at me. It whizzed through the air so fast and before I knew it...

I was caught in a possibility of immediate death.

I flinched as the spear went past me and into the wall. I took a glance at that said wall, now broken.

I looked back at him in horror. Who is he?!

He jumped from the roof and I knew that it was time for me to get away. Desperate to get out of his way, I didn't realize that I was running towards the palace grounds.

Come to think of it, he won't be able to attack me if we were in a crowded place.

Right.

I have to run faster.

I sped up my pace as I ran to get out of this alley. To my horror, he kept throwing lethal knives at me, but to my luck, I kept dodging it.

I could already see the end of the alley. After a few seconds, I was already out. I turned around, expecting that he already stopped chasing me. But, he was still on the run towards me, dangerously closing in. In turn, I continued running. I can't fight him now that I'm out. Everyone might see us and I don't want to create a scene.

I need help.

"Hel-"

I covered my mouth. I can't shout either. I'll be the center of attention. I just need to get close to someone who can help me.

Please.

Anyone?

I' m too young to die!

I kept looking for a savior as I ran because I could still hear footsteps getting closer towards me. I kept turning my heads to look for a stationed guard or an officer. But, there wasn't any. They were all close to the palace. I can't ask help from there.

Anyone?

I can't fight him. I don't have anything to go up against spears and knives.

I looked to my side and saw a couple of guards and an officer.

"There's my chance." I whispered to myself. I ran up to them and quickly took notice of a familiar face.

"A-aspen?"

I closed in to make sure. And I was right.

"Aspen!"

Yes! I'm saved.

"Aspen! Aspen!" I called out.

Thankfully, he seemed to hear me as he looked for the sound of my voice.

I called out again," Aspen! I'm here."

Finally, his eyes dawned on me, "Isabelle?"

"Aspen! Help me!" I yelled as I got closer.

"Isabelle!" But he didn't have any time to run to me when he was about to because I got to him first.

I felt such relief the moment that I was able to reach him. I grabbed his sleeves desperately as he held my hand," Aspen! Please! Someone's trying to ki-"

"You little brat! How dare you touch and address the king like that!" One soldier started blurting out at me.

My eyes widened at his outburst. They widened even more as the soldiers grabbed me for no reason and yelled. Aspen was startled too by their actions.

"You should be punished for your actions! What kind of stance do you have in this land to disrespect our king like that?!"

"W-what?" I said as I struggled to break away from their grasp.

What are they talking about? King? The king!? Who?

I disrespected the king?When!?

I was so lost in the event that I forgot about my life-threatening situation. I glanced to my side and saw, to my relief, that the killer was gone.

Now, back to the matter at hand...

WHAT ARE THEY TALKING ABOUT!?

"Aspen? Why are they like this?" I turned to him.

His eyes were so surprised, his lips were quivering too that he wasn't able to speak.

"Aspen?"

"How many times do I have to tell you to never disrespect the king?!" One soldier said as he violently shook my arms.

"Release her!" Aspen suddenly demanded.

"But, your majesty-"

"AT ONCE!" He roared," I know her."

Your majesty?

Why are they calling Aspen that? And why do they keep referring to him as our king?

As they released their hold me, my shoulders stiffened even more as I felt that this day is going to be so bad for me.

I swallowed a big lump in my throat as I asked," Aspen? What are they talking about?"

He wasn't able to answer, instead he looked at me with remorse.

"Why are they saying...that you're the king?" I gulped.

He sighed," Isabelle, I can explain."

Only then was I able to notice his appearance. He wore an officer's outfit, but not the same outfit he wore. It had the golden Sorahian crest printed on it's chest. Only royals wore the Sorahian crest, but in silver. For it to be gold.... you have to be the man with the highest authority.

The king.

I shivered in fear, "No. He can't be."

Is he really-

King Aspen?!

"Isabelle, please."

I covered my mouth with my hand in shock. I immediately bowed with my knees to the ground. My heart pounded wildly as if it was about to explode. My hands were shaking violently. All of my internal organs seemed to crumble inside me.

Fear.

Punishment.

Those were the words revolving in my head.

"Isabelle. Please stand."

I can't believe it! The king! He really is the king! I've been friends with the king. I've been talking to the king!

"Isabelle. Don't do this. Please, just listen." Then, I suddenly felt hands in my shoulders, trying to get me up.

I can't do this.

The more I looked at him, the more terrified I became. So, I stood up and immediately ran, turning a deaf ear to any call or distraction.

"Isabelle! Wait! Please!" He said as I heard his footsteps following me.

"King Aspen!"

"Your majesty!"

"Isabelle!" He called out.

But I can't bear to turn around because I was so scared. He hid it from me. He was the king all along and I befriended him!

How could I be so careless!

He was king Aspen!

He lied to me about his identity, but I can't feel mad right now. Instead, fear rushed through my veins. Pure fear, only fear.

I ran and ran, desperate to escape. I can't get over the fact that he was the king. I treated him like he was just a close friend of mine. I did disrespect him!

"What did I do to deserve this?" I said as I kept running.

Maybe it's because I disobeyed my parents. If I didn't go to the noble's academy, if only I'd stayed home instead of looking for bigger things, then I wouldn't meet Aspen.... I mean, the king. I wouldn't get in so much trouble.

Tears began welling up in my eyes," If only I'd listen. "

I'm was so foolish. I was naive. I was so careless. I was so stupid. I was so reckless.

"I even-"

Oh dear.

I didn't realize it sooner. All of the horrible things I did to the king.

I stepped on his back and broke it! I stepped on his royal back!

I even broke his sword!

I hugged him!

I dragged him around, I opposed some of his ideas.

Oh damn....

I'M GONNA DIE!

"Get it together, Isabelle. He's your friend. He won't let you die." I said to myself.

Agh! But, he's still the king. The soldiers are right. How dare I call him friend?!

I was getting closer to home. But, as I got closer, I started to feel heavy. I was literally having a silent heart attack. I need air. I can't breathe. I was crying so hard in fear.

I'm so dead. I want to die. I was about to die and I knew it. I couldn't take another step. I needed to get home and fast.

"Mom!" I called out as I sought for someone to help me.

"Mom! M-mom..."

My steps were turning heavy and slow, and before I knew it, my face was against the ground and I could no longer see anything, except for the short glimpse of my mom running towards me.

"Oh dear...Isa!"

Aspen

"Please Aspen! Save me!"

"I have no time to save your sorry ass, Daniel." I said as I kept walking.

"She's trying to kill me!"

"Get used to it! And stop pulling on my leg." I glared.

"Sorry." He apologized as he let go of my leg. He stood up from the floor where he was dragging himself as he held onto my leg.

"I have things to do Daniel. Go on a vacation or somethin'." I told him, walking away.

"I had no rest ever since she turned back to normal! She became more violent. She became a monster!"

"Yeah. Whatever." I shunned him, walking towards my destination.

He folded his arms, "Geez, you're one busy king, aren't you? Sorah's safe now. What is there to worry about?"

"A lot of things. Until we find out the kingdom behind all of this, we will never be safe." I said.

"You think too much."

"So I've been told." -I shrugged-" If you need me, which I hope you won't because I would really like some peace right now, I'll be in the library."

"Yes, your highness." He scoffed as he walked away.

I shook my head, then I proceeded to the library.

The moment I got there, I quickly got to my research. I took out the old notebook that I found, the one that came from that mysterious kingdom.

I opened the pages again and examined it. Truth to be told, there's nothing left to know. It's all-

"Wait a minute."

There's something written on the last page. It looked like a letter. I read it and I was astonished... and mostly, terrified.

They won't seize until the whole world is their under their command.

They're ruthless, they're cruel, they kill with their bare iron hands.

They attack in silence like a cold-blooded monster.

You'll never see them coming, you'll never hear them either.

The morality of its rulers was long gone before

Heartless, they drink the blood of the innocent

They take your family, your children, might you fail your purpose

They take delight in torture, as if loathing your existence.

Kingdom after kingdom has fallen in their trap

If you can, run now and don't look back

I'm warning you...

Beware, the Quiet Conquerors

I tried my best not to be shaken, but who can't be with these words?

Even as a king with firm faith, I was terrified for Sorah. If this was the kind of kingdom that would attack Sorah, I don't think I can handle the sight of my people being oppressed by them.

That is why I was so relieved we stopped them just in the nick of time.

But even so, this is so alarming. Even their own strategist wrote this thing about them.

Did he send this as a warning?

Speaking of, what really happened to that strategist and to this notebook? Why is it in Sorah? And more importantly....

Who is this ruthless kingdom? Who are the creators of the omens?

All I got from the letter was the description of this kingdom. They kill, they're dangerous, they suck blood, I guess, they're heartless, and scarily clever, given they created the omens and was able to keep that up for over 100 years.

No matter what, I need to know who these people are, what they do, and most importantly, what should I do to keep my kingdom safe.

I need to know the stories behind this letter, this warning, this book, and how it ended up here.

If I can figure that out , and why the strategist wrote this... then maybe I can found out who this kingdom is.

They've existed for more than a hundred years ago and they've been conquering kingdoms, so it would be accurate to say that this is a pretty big territory by now. But, there are so many, even as big as Sorah.

I need to find more clues. This won't be enough. I need to know more. I need to go further.

But how will I with only these and myself?

Myself....?

No, I think these details that I garnered would suffice. I just need someone who can work on these with me. I can't do this by myself.

I need her. I need Isabelle.

I just know it. She's the coolest girl I've ever met. She's kind, strong, brilliant, and beautiful. I can't deny that. No one can, and no one will. She's just amazing.

"What's wrong with me?" I said to myself as I held my chest.

My heart started pounding for some unknown reason. Maybe, it's because I'll be able to see her again.

I'm smiling and am excited like crazy just at the thought. Maybe I am turning insane. I need to fix myself. I am a king. Seeing a girl is such a petty joy that it's almost unnecessary to be happy

So why am I?

"Come on, Aspen!" I punched my own head," Calm yourself. It's just Isab-be-be..."

I covered my mouth instantly.

Damn it, I can't even say her name properly, and my lips are quivering.

What's happening to me?

I shook my head," I need to brush this off. How will I keep my cool when I face her?

I have to fix myself and find her. We have another case to solve.

So, with deep breaths, I grabbed my inspector's coat and my belt, staying with my disguise. I was about to walk out the door when I heard a knock.

"Your majesty?"

"Come in."

A soldier revealed himself, bowing before me," My king, your presence is requested at the Defense Hall."

"What? Why?"

He sighed with his head down," Forgive me, your majesty. They didn't tell me either. They only said that it was an urgent matter."

I shook my head and sighed," Fine. Tell them I'm on my way."

"Yes, your majesty. Me and my guards will be waiting for you outside." He gave one last bow before closing the door and leaving.

Looks like this case will have to wait. I can't see her today.

While trying to hide my disappointment, I slipped on my royal robes and went outside. I went to the palace gates where the guards were waiting for me.

"Your majesty." They bowed.

I nodded at them and went on our way to the defense hall, or at least we were about to when I heard a very familiar voice.

"Aspen! Aspen!" The voice said. At first, I thought I was imagining things because my guard didn't seem to hear. But, I doubted that it was just my imagination when they tilted their heads as I heard it again.

Her....calling out my name.

" Aspen! I'm here." She said again. I'm positive that it was her voice. I searched for her. I wanted to see her. The way her voice sounded....it sounded like she was in trouble.

Where is-

"Isabelle?"

Finally. It is her!

"Aspen! Help me!"

Everything went blank as I focused only on her sight and on her voice.

"Isabelle!"

I was about to run to her, but she beat me to it and got to me first. She held my sleeves and I held her cold hands. She was shaking.

Why was she shaking?

What's wrong with her?

Moreover...what's wrong with me?

My heart got heavier at the sight of her scared.

I forgot almost everything. The only thing that I wanted to know was what's going in with her; the only thing on my mind right now...was her.

"Aspen! Please! Someone's trying to ki-"

What is it, Isabelle?

"You little brat! How dare you touch and address the king like that!" One soldier started scolding her.

Time froze the moment she was grabbed by my soldier in front of me.

I froze. I didn't know what to do...

I was so stupid.

I forgot...

"You should be punished for your actions! What kind of stance do you have in this land to disrespect our king like that?!"

I stepped back.

"W-what?" She said, confused.

I was wearing my royal clothes and my guards were surrounding me.

I'm not dressed like the guy she knows as me.

My heart thumped...in fear. I know, being smart, she'd find it out sooner or later. But, I didn't expect it to be this soon.

I thought that I could've played it a little longer.

I thought it could just be casual, normal, and fun around her for a little longer, be with her a little longer as me and not as a king, just be like that for a little longer with her.

I guess I should've known all along that hopes like that are too high, too impossible for a king like me. These are the kind of hopes that are hopeless for someone as powerful as I am.

And I loathe that fact.

"Aspen? Why are they like this?" She asked.

But, I couldn't say a word.

All I thought about right now is her possible disappearance. There's no excuse for this now. I had to prepare myself because in a matter of seconds....she'll be gone.

She'll leave me.

How could I ever prepare for that?

"Aspen?"

Isabelle...

"How many times do I have to tell you to never disrespect the king?!" One of my soldiers said as he aggressively shook her arm.

My eyes burned as I saw her get hurt. What am I doing?!

"Release her!" I roared. I should've done it earlier but I was too occupied in my hopeless thoughts.

"But, your majesty-"

"AT ONCE!" I repeated, " I know her." I informed my soldier. They quickly released her at my words. She stumbled a bit at the release, but the shock and confusion on her face didn't wane.

I cursed under my breath.

How will I explain it all to her?

"Aspen? What are they talking about?"

I tried to speak, but nothing came out, out of fear. I didn't want her to leave. That's the last thing I'll ever want. I-I can't move now that it's all happening.

"Why are they saying...that you're the king?" She sounded so nervous...and terrified.

And I caused it.

I sighed, finally able to get some words out, but out of shame and guilt," Isabelle, I can explain."

Then it happened...

She stepped away from me.

I felt a sting as I saw her trust fading. She observed me from top to bottom. She took notice of my clothes.

Her eyes widened.

I can't undo this. I've done this to her. I hid things from her and terrified her.

"Isabelle, please," I begged her to say something.

She only covered her mouth and bowed down with her face close to the ground. I was so pained to see her like this. I never knew that I would hate to see someone bow out of respect for me one day.

It felt so ashamed of myself.

She was the most brilliant and amazing girl, but I made a fool out of her.

I can't stand it anymore, seeing her like this. I begged her.

"Isabelle. Please stand."

Still, she didn't budge. She stayed like that, shaking. I bent down and grabbed her arms and shoulders, pleading her to stand up.

"Isabelle. Don't do this. Please, just listen."

I begged her. I wanted her to listen to what I had to say. I was wishing for her to believe that I didn't say a thing for her sake, and also so that I could stay with her.

But then, to everyone's surprise, she suddenly took off. My hands slipped from her shoulders as she escaped my clutches.

"Isabelle! Wait! Please!" I ran after her. Call me desperate, but this is who I am around her. I still don't know why.

I don't want her to leave.

That's why I picked up my feet and ran after her. I didn't care if the people saw the king running on the streets.

I lied... because I wanted her to stay.

"King Aspen!"

"Your majesty!"

Now, she's leaving me because of that want. I knew it was too good to be true, to be friends with Isabelle without hurting her.

But, when I was with her, I had hope. In those times, I was happy.

That's why, even though I knew that things would never be the same again, I wanted to try. I don't want it to end like this. I don't want her to see me differently than the Aspen she saw. I don't want her to run away because of who I am.

I don't want to lose her.

"Isabelle!"

16

CHAPTER 16

Isabelle

A blurred face.

That was the first thing I saw as I opened my eyes.

"She's awake! Lio, she's awake!"

As I heard that voice, my vision cleared up. I was in my room, on my bed. My head was still throbbing but it's bearable. I got up the moment my parents came inside.

Mom placed a hand on mine,"Isa, are you okay?"

"We were so worried, darling," Dad said in a shaky voice.

"W-what happened?" I asked.

"You fainted outside," Mom replied.

"You've been out for 3 days. What happened?"

"I don't remember."

But, I really do. It was just to horrible that I wanted to forget it.

"Do you want something to eat? We have soup," Mom offered.

I nodded, "Yes, please."

After that, my mom left while dad stayed by my side. He looked at me with worried eyes. He sighed, "Is there something you're not telling us?"

I choked, "No, dad. Of course there isn't."

"Are you sure about that."

Biting my lip, I answered, "Yes." And there goes another lie.

Dad went closer and narrowed his eyes, "Then, why did you faint?"

Because of too much fear.

Because of too much anxiety.

I've committed some of the highest treasons ever known to Sorah.

I stepped on the king's back; I hugged him. Yes, I, a commoner, hugged the king, stepped on his back, and broke his sword. I'm gonna be punished and so will my family.

"Isa! Are you alright?!"

My normal breathing paced; my heart pounded with fear just like the last time. I started hyperventilating.

I'm terrified.

I'm so terrified.

"Gertrude, Bring us water! Quickly!"

My mom went in with some water. I quickly took it from her to calm myself. I even spilled some on my dress.

"Take it easy, dear."

"Sorry." I muttered as I gave the cup and wiped my mouth.

"What's wrong, Isabelle?" Dad asked.

I swallowed a lump down my throat, thinking of what to say, "M-maybe I overworked."

"Overworked? What did you do? I just told you to get some eggs." Mom argued.

"I went to almost 20 different stores, Ma. I was so tired. I guess that's why I passed out." I said, massaging my forehead as if dizzy.

"Is that all, Isa?" Father asked.

I nodded, "Yes."

"Well, that's a good thing to hear. I checked your temperature and your vitals. You have no signs of any disease whatsoever. I'm relieved." Mom sighed.

I smiled at them. For the meantime, I need to clear my head.

"Isa, where are you going?" Mom asked as I shifted to get up.

"I'm just going outside to get some fresh air. I think I need some." I explained.

"Are you sure, dear. You might wanna rest first."

I shook my head," I'll be fine, mom. I'll just be outside the house."

My mom sighed. Dad grabbed her shoulders to ease her worry, "Don't worry about her, Gertrude, dear. She'll be fine." My mom sighed but complied anyway.

"Just stay outside, near the house okay." Dad said.

I nodded and got up to go outside. I got out of my room and walked towards the door.

"We love you, dear." Mom suddenly said.

I flinched.

"Take care of yourself." Dad reminded.

I'm such a terrible daughter.

They've treated me with so much love and kindness. And I repaid them with trouble....and lies.

I haven't even given half of my life to them. I was so busy pursuing my own interests that I didn't notice what burden I'm forcing them to carry. Everyday, I worry them. They've already went through so much pain. Now, I'm making them go through all of it again.

I turned around and threw myself in their arms, "I'm sorry for causing you so much worry, mom, dad. I love you too."

They hugged me back an whispered, "Just be safe, okay."

I let go, nodded, and finally went outside.

That's when I realized...

I still wasn't able to tell the truth. And now, the truth is much more worse. It was only going to be the prince and Aspen, the officer. Now, it's the prince and Aspen, the king.

"Great, now I just have to meet the rest of the royal family.."

Ugh! What have I done!

I need to calm my nerves and think of a way out of this. Maybe, I can just beg him to leave my family out of it.

But if I was punished, they'd suffer too. Agh, what am I supposed to do?!

If I'm dead, we're all dead!

Why do I have to meet the king?!

"Isabelle Almere, what have you done?" I said to myself. I didn't notice that I was getting farther away from the house. Well, this part is a part of our field. I guess it's still home.

So, I didn't hesitate to walk a little bit further. I mean, it's not like anything bad could happen to-

Hold on.

I remembered.

Someone was trying to kill me. I wasn't able to find out his identity. What if he knows where I live? What if he's still out there looking for me?

"Oh no."

True to my nightmares, I sensed a shadow following me. He was swift. I took little steps back towards the house. I felt my body shaking. I can't call out for help. What if someone did come to help me? They would be hurt instead. I can't have that.

So, I'll continue this. But, every time I stepped forward, I hear his footsteps too, getting closer.

No, I'm gonna have to run.

So, I increased my pace. But, I wasn't even able to get close to the house because...

He caught me.

I felt the hem of my dress, along with my body, get pulled into a narrow corner near our barn. As I fell, I felt a hand catch my waist, which then sat me on his sturdy lap. The other hand, he used to cover my mouth. I didn't even try to scream for help because I know that it's no use. I was so helpless. I even felt tears streaming down my face.

This is it.

I'm gonna die.

My life's gonna end at the hands of this killer.

Goodbye, mom, dad, everyone.

Goodbye, Edith, Scar, and-

"Shhh. Please, be quiet, Isabelle."

T-that voice...

"I'm so sorry I wasn't able to see you sooner. I didn't want you to have anymore trouble."

This isn't a voice of a killer. It sounded calm, concerned and warm.

I know this welcoming voice, but I'm terrified to turn around and confirm now that I know who it really belongs to. I tried my best not to look at him. But, I was evidently shaking that anyone can feel it a meter away from me.

I can't turn around. But if I don't, that would mean I would be disrespecting the king because he's talking to me and I wouldn't face him.

Now, I don't know how to treat him....as a king? Or as...my friend?

"Isabelle?" He said in a remorseful voice as he finally removed the hand that was covering my mouth.

I was still trying not to look at him. It was getting harder by the second.

"Isabelle, please just talk to me." He pleaded. He sighed impatiently and forced me to face him. He grabbed my shoulders and turned me around so that I was facing him.

As he did, my heart pounded.

I was now facing him, well my body was, but my head was down low.

He then pulled back his arms and rested them on his lap. I took a quick glance at his face and saw him biting his lip. Unconsciously, I bit my lips too.

Neither of us knew what to do next.

"Isabelle, can you just-" then he inched his fingers to cup my chin, probably to make me look to him.

But, I acted beforehand. I positioned my knees and lowered my face to the ground. I literally didn't know how to act around him now.

"Y-your Majesty..." Were the words that came out of my mouth. It's just that fear overwhelmed me; fear that he was the king.

He gave a 'tsk' and sighed, "I knew it. I knew you would change." He muttered, sounding disappointed.

I won't be able to utter a word anyway, so I let him speak.

"Can you please just let me explain?"

I was just staring at him in silence. My heart paced as my eyes met his, sincere and worried.

I heard an audible swallow coming from him before speaking," Isabelle, I'm sorry I hid it from you. I swear I was going to tell you at some point. I just thought that..."

Thought what?

"I thought that things would change if I tell. I really, r-really, liked being around you as an officer, and I didn't want to sacrifice that. I honestly enjoyed your company and it was my first time being friends with someone outside the palace. It just felt...fun, new, and refreshing to meet you. I didn't want it to end and I didn't want to cause you trouble, so I didn't tell you." He explained with a few stutters here and there.

Finally, I was able to utter some words, "Why?"

"I'm sorry?"

I held back my tongue. Even though it was an honest talk, I was still talking to the king.

"Sorry. King Aspen-"

"Please." He said, "Don't ever call me that when it's just the two of us, or when we're with our friends. It's embarrassing and I won't be getting used to it."

I blinked, "Your majesty, I can't possibly just call you-"

"Aspen? Yes. Yes you can. Isabelle, you were my friend first before you knew I was king, and I want things to remain that way. Please.. .just treat me as you used to."

I choked," Your majesty-"

"It's Aspen." He demanded.

"Your majest-"

"Aspen." He groaned.

I paused for a while, "I can't..." I bowed my head.

"As king, I'm giving you the authority to do so."

My eyes widened at him,"W-what?!"

"No. I'm commanding you to do so.", he restated.

"But I-"

He sighed," Isabelle, please. This is why I didn't want to tell you. I was waiting for a right time in hopes that it wouldn't turn out like this. I know things could never go back to the way it was. So please, just give me this. Don't treat me as king."

"I-I-I..."

How could I do that?

Treat him as my friend?! Like before?!

I know now that he never wanted this. I didn't want this either. Who on earth would want to be in our position?

Why did I have to meet him anyway? How did I end up being friends with the king?!

He chuckled with a hint of sadness in his tone, "You must regret meeting me now, huh?"

I blinked. Once. Twice. Thrice. A couple more times after.

Yes. I was so terrified upon knowing that he was the king. But, never did I feel even a touch of regret meeting him. I felt no regret at all.

If anything, meeting him was one of the most memorable things I treasured in my heart. Meeting Aspen is where all the fun start ed...yeah...and the lies as well. But above all of that, meeting him, no matter who he'd turn out to be, would be one of the things I'll never erase and keep on repeating on this life and the next...if ever I'll have it.

There's something I feel that I can't explain when I'm with him. Like the time we jumped from a cliff and got stuck together, I felt that feeling too. The moment that I took his hand, something changed. It felt like I didn't care and I shouldn't care about a damn thing.

It felt free, yet secure at the same time. It was the good kind of free.

Aspen then sighed knowingly and sadly, "I knew it. I caused you more than enough trouble already."-he stood up and bowed his head-" I'm sorry, Isabelle. I never wanted this, especially for you. Don't worry. You'll never have anything to do with me again, I promise. I'll leave you for good."

I stayed silent as my eyes pierced his. I was still unable to get my mind straight.

Before he took another step, he said what was meant , I think, to be his final words, "I just wanted you to know that... I would never forget you, Isabelle. Goodbye."

As he turned around to walk away from me, Something meaningful finally came out of my mouth, "No."

Luckily, he heard it and stopped, "What?"

I stood up and looked at him intently, setting aside the fact that he is the king," Who said you can just say goodbye like that?"

"But you-"

I walked closer, "I never said anything about regrets in meeting you, didn't I ? Up to now, there was never a moment that I thought our meeting was regretful."

"You...didn't think that?" He asked as his eyes lit up.

"I'll admit that I was scared. Who wouldn't be?"

He laughed at this. I swallowed a huge one and gave a heavy breath before I said it, "Aspen?"

He smiled, with hope evident in his grin, "Yeah?"

Hope.

Despite what's happened, I felt it when I said his name; hope that it could be just like before, maybe even better.

I stuttered a bit and choked," I-I'm sorry, I'll try getting used to it. The shock's still here, ya know." I said as I pointed to my head.

He nodded, "I understand. I'm sorry, Isabelle."

"Don't be." My lips quivered as everything I did to him came back to me," I-I should be the one t-to apologi-"

He shook his head, "Don't think about it too much. I didn't mind it at all. Besides, it was my fault. You didn't know who I was because I hid it from you. Sorry bout that again."

"Still I-"

"Shh." He said as he put a finger on my lips... and pulled a string on my heart as well, " Isabelle, don't think about it, okay. It's fine, although using my back as a footstool did hurt a lot."

I grunted, "Ohh! I'm really, really, terribly, super, majorly, very sorry for that, your maje- I mean, Aspen. I wasn't-"

He smirked," Woah. I was just kidding. I'm not an old man. That part didn't hurt a bit. I didn't even feel a thing."

I looked at him, worried that he's lying, "I don't believe you. You said I was heavy and I heard that crack on your back."

"Y-you did?"

I smirked, "Yeah, the whole kingdom heard it."

The both of us fell silent, but laughed so hard when we weren't able to keep it in.

His laughter died a bit as he started speaking, "Oh. And also that sword. You know, I didn't tell you to offend you, but that sword was-"

I gasped, "No. No. No. Please don't tell me that it was worth my life."

He scrunched his face, "Unfortunately..."

I tried to catch my breath," Oh sweet mother of-"

"Gotcha!" He blurted out then laughed, "I was kidding again."

I looked at him in disbelief, "How dare you! I was having a heart attack."

Then, I punched his shoulder.

He looked at me incredulously with his eyes almost as big as the offense I just did.

Did I really just punch the king's shoulder?!

"Y-you..."

I quivered and shook in fear. My normal breathing paced along with the beating of my heart. I took my hand back to my sides.

For the millionth time...

What have you done, Isabelle!?

I got so used to him just being...just being Aspen.

I was waiting for his response because he was just staring at me like he just saw a ghost.

I tried to speak and apologize, "Your maje-"

But I was cut off by his sudden response. How did he respond? By taking me in his arms and hugging me tightly.

Unfortunately, I couldn't bring myself to hug back like before, so I just stood there.

"I missed you, Isabelle." He whispered in my ear.

I quirked a brow, "Wait. What?"

"Being hit never felt that good."

He finally let go, then he looked at me and smiled, "This is what I wanted. I want you to treat me like the Aspen you've known, and not the guy with the crown. I don't wanna be that guy and I'm not that guy when I'm with you or with our friends. I'm exactly the same guy you met during our escape."

I didn't know what to say.

I don't know if I'm gonna do it because he's king.... or because I wanted it too; to be with him just like before, without changing anything.

I wanted it too. I want it to be just like it was with Daniel, Scarlett, and Aspen. When we're together, we didn't care about our stance.

A daughter of a mighty general...

A prince...

A king...

An ambitious, common scholar girl...

It didn't matter at all when we're together.

"I want it too." I suddenly uttered.

He looked up, "What was that?"

"I want it to be like that too." I repeated.

He smiled," You do?"

I nodded in response. "But how will I do that? Do I have to hide the fact that I know you guys?"

"W-well.."

"You're the king. I already know that. Heck, I was passed out for three days because of that. But that's not the case anymore. My family doesn't want me being close to people like you. I don't wanna break that rule of theirs because that would break them too. I don't know what to do, Aspen." I explained.

He heaved a sigh, "We want to continue being friends with you without getting you in trouble."

I pursed my lips, "Same here."

He was silent for a second, then he spoke, "Isabelle, could you hide this for just a little bit longer?"

"What do you mean?"

"We'll help you tell everything to your parents. We can talk it out. We can explain everything. Maybe they'll understand."

I looked to my side, "I don't know, Aspen. Their resentment is a pretty serious one. They hate politics to the core of the core of their bones."

"But they're parents, Isabelle. Maybe if they'll know how happy we are together-"

"How happy we are...together?," I repeated.

Why do I feel light-headed all of a sudden?

For some unknown reason, I saw his ears get red. Was he alright?

He spoke once again, "I-I mean, maybe if they know how happy we are being friends along with Daniel and Scar, maybe they'll reconsider. There's always hope for that, right?"

Hope.

Yeah. I think that's more than enough for now. I really wanted to be friends with them, to be with them. So, I guess I'll hold on to it.

Hope.

But wait..

"You asked me if I could still hide this. Why?"

He swallowed a big lump in his throat before saying it,"Because, I'm gonna need you again for something."

I stepped back a bit. Something? Was there another case? What could be wrong?

"Isabelle, we need to figure out who that kingdom was, or else Sorah will never be safe. I also need to show you something which may be a clue." He explained.

I thought for a while. Should I go with him? Should I lie again?

But, this is for the kingdom; where my family lives. If I don't help, what would become of them?

"Fine. I'll go with you. But, let me go to my parents first." I complied.

"Okay. I'll wait for you at the village gate. Take your time."

"Alright." I nodded as I turned my foot to leave.

"B-but don't take your time TOO much." He added.

I chuckled, "Okay. okay."

But, before I leave completely I turned to him and did a curtsey. I looked up and saw a hint of worry and disappointment in his face.

I silently laughed as I got up, "See ya, officer."

He suddenly smiled at me as I addressed him as an officer, the way I know him.

"See ya, Belle."

I flinched, stopping in my tracks. Did he just say...

"What?"

His eyes widened, then he smirked as he looked sideways, "Is it alright if I call you that? I've been thinking of a nickname for you because saying three syllables when calling you can be tiring."

Belle, huh.

"It's fine." I bit my lip, trying to hide my red face which keeps showing up, "So, it's also okay if I call you As?"

He frowned and glared, "Not in this life, Belle."

It's beginning to sound like music in my ears! You mean I have to get used that, him calling me Belle?

I spoke again to avoid silence and him noticing my flushed face, "But it can be boring to say two common syllables when calling you. Now, I need to add 'king' too. So it's three now," I complained playfully.

"You don't need to. I told you that. Now, just please-"

"What about Assie?"

"What the-"

"Or Pen-pen. That's cute."

He glared again, "Now, that's just insulting."

"Penny?"

"No way." He face-palmed.

I fell silent for a while and then laughed, "I was just kidding." -I paused for a while and sighed, "I'll be back in a jiffy, As-as." Then I ran to my house

"Damn that cursed tongue of yours." He shook his head and smiled after, "I'll be waiting." Then he also left.

When he left, that's when I let the flutters out. I felt a slight pain in my jaw; I didn't even realize I was smiling all the time.

Hope.

I really do hope that everything will be okay because I don't want to be away from my friends.

Just one small lie and all of this will be over. Just another lie you have to make, Isabelle. Then, you can make that hope work.

As I got closer to our house, I saw my mom sweeping the front yard.

"Isabelle?" Mom mouthed as I got closer to our house.

I took a deep breath before rushing to them. They went to me before speaking one after another.

"Where have you been? Are you feeling better now?"

"Yes, ma. I'm fine now. But I need to go." I said.

My dad, who was getting some logs on the side of our house, overheard us and went to me.

"Go?! Where are you off to? You just got well." He complained.

I gulped. And here comes the lie.

"I have to go to the public library. I need to study. I can't lose my reputation as a scholar." I said, keeping my voice under control so that it wouldn't be shaky.

Dad scrunched his face, "You can study here, Isa. We have a lot of books you can-"

I laughed, "Dad. Don't worry. It's just the library. What could happen? Besides," I added, "There are a lot of things to discover. Not even this farm can hold it."

But dad scoffed, "And a small public library can?"

I shook my head, "Dad.."

Dad looked at me, then at mom, then at me, "Fine. But, be back soon."

I nodded, "And my curfew is.." I stated, waiting for Dad to give me a time limit as always.

"None. We trust you, Isa."

My spirit groaned from the inside and my heart flinched from my chest. Why does this have to be so hard?

I took a deep breath before I answered, "I-I'll be back before you know it."

With a worried look on their faces, they nodded, "Okay, dear. Take care."

I smiled, picked up my feet, then left. My heart felt heavier as I got closer to the village gate. But, as I saw Aspen's face, everything lit up. He really makes me feel like everything's gonna be okay. Well, I trust him. I'm sure it's gonna be.

"What took you so long?" He complained as he sat on his horse.

"Sorry, I still had to polish my nails." I joked.

He shook his head and smirked, "Hop on." He said as he stretched out his hand to help me climb his horse.

"Thanks."

I grabbed his hand and sat on the saddle. I grabbed the back part of the seat and the edges of it. I was waiting for him to giddy up and go. But we still weren't moving.

"What are we waiting for?" I asked.

He looked at me with his eyebrows raised. He sounded a 'tsk' and suddenly grabbed my arms, "The edges of the saddle aren't safe, Isabelle."

He rounded my arms and held it onto his waist, "This is safe. Now, isn't this more comfortable?" He teased.

My face flushed, but I didn't show it. I sneered at him, "For me or for you?"

He looked at me, unable to speak for a second , "Uh...giddy-up!"

Then he raised the reins, and the horse ran.

Fine. I'll just let it slide for now.

I tried to speak to him despite the shaky voice and the wind against my face, "Where are we going?"

He smirked, "You'll see."

I held onto him throughout the ride. I didn't mind it anymore, that he was the king. He was my friend first, just like he said. I don't wanna make him feel bad by showing him that I'm uncomfortable beside him.

I still really am inside, but I have to get used to it.

I want to get used to it...to bring back the way we used to be.

"You okay back there?"

"Yeah." I replied.

Finally, we stopped at a hill near the palace grounds. I was unable to get down by myself because my feet were numb just by looking at the palace.

Aspen held my waist, awaking me from my stupor, "Are you alright?"

I looked at him, "Yes."

His eyes then narrowed in worry, "Isabelle, are you scared?"

"What?"

He let go of my waist and shifted his hands to my hands, "I'm sorry for bringing you here. But this is where I need you to be. I can't do this without you. Don't worry, you won't get in trouble as long as I'm here."

I sighed, taken by his concern, "I'll be fine. It's just...how will you get in there?"

"Well, I'm the ki-"

I shook my head, "No. I don't wanna go in there as the king's favored commoner or as a guest. That'll put the both of us in a very tight situation."

He scrunched his face, "How tight of a situation?"

"It's a situation where people might see us, then talk about us, then gossips and rumors and that kind of stuff will go around." I sighed, "Darn. I thought you'll be smart enough to figure it out."

He pursed his lips funnily, "Well, I thought you'd be smart enough to know that I don't care."

I stuttered, "Wha-what?"

"I don't care what others think about me when I'm with people I like the most...and trust too. In other words, I don't care about anything about me as long as I'm with you." He smiled innocently.

Ahhhh! Those words make me feel so important and useful.

"Yochinvar V, Verse 76, A person neglects judgements that cometh out of the mouths of others when his ears are covered by truth, sensibility, dreams, happiness, and most of all, love." I suddenly uttered.

His eyes widened, then he chuckled, "Another verse from the Scholar's Creed? Really, Isabelle?" He said sarcastically, "Look. I already know how damn smart you are. You don't have to show off... But you are right. That's me. I don't care what other people say, as long as it's not about the people I care about."

I laughed, "And you care about me?"

It was only meant to be a joke or to tease him, but what I said was turned against me...in a good way.

Without hesitation, he spoke, "Of course I do. Why would you think I don't?"

My face flushed. I bowed my head, hoping he wouldn't see my Valentine-themed cheeks. What the heck's happening to me?

"Belle, are you okay?"

Oh! Why does he have to call me Belle at a time like this?

I coughed, trying to regain my sanity and normal cheek color, "I'm fine...As-As."

He rolled his eyes, "I think you can get yourself down from there." He said as he walked away.

I laughed as I saw him annoyed," Hey! I'm just joking. Aspen!"

I got down from the horse and walked to him, "Aspe- ugh!"

He suddenly stopped in front of me, so I bumped into his back.

I scrunched my nose as I observed him, wondering why he stopped. He was staring off into space, so I averted my eyes towards the direction he was looking at.

And I saw the most precious view of all- a full view of the kingdom.

"You really do love Sorah, don't you, your Majesty?" I uttered.

He sighed, "More than my life. They're everything to me. I live for them. That's why I'll do everything in my power to keep them safe and happy." -he turned to me-"That's why I need you Isabelle."

I nodded, "I'll do everything I can too."

He smiled at me and went towards the gate, "Let's go."

I stopped him, "Wait. How will I get in?"

He chuckled, "Oh yeah. I almost forgot about it." He went to his horse and grabbed something from the bag hanging on the saddle.

"What's this?" I asked as I received it from him.

"A lady investigator's uniform. But it's red."

My eyes widened, "But this is for the superintendents only."

"I know. I meant that. If you'll wear your purple one, you'll be questioned. No apprentice has ever worked beside the royal family. With that, they'll think you're a superintendent. That way, we won't have any problem."

I nodded, getting his point. I then went behind a nearby tree to change.

I glared at him before removing my clothes, "Hey! No peeking alright." I laughed inwardly. He already turned his back the moment I went to the tree.

With his back still facing me, he spoke, "Spare me some dignity, will ya? Of course I won't do that. I'm not a geezer, I'm a man....with chivalry."

I was changing my clothes when I answered him, "What does chivalry have to do with this?"

"Nah. Just thought of it."

I fixed my hair into a braid, carried my clothes and went out, "Done."

"Okay, so now we need to- woah." He suddenly said.

I tilted my head as I saw his reaction, "What?"

He continued staring at me, "I thought purple was your color. I was so wrong."

I smirked "Everything's my color. Now, what are we gonna do?"

He shook his head to break his daze, "R-right. We're gonna wait for Daniel at the palace grounds. I'm gonna dress up as king for now, okay with you?"

I raised my brows, "Uh, okay. You don't have to ask for my permission."

He started removing his officer's coat, revealing his royal coat inside, "I don't wanna make you uncomfortable. If you are, tell me immediately. I have a plan where I can dress as an officer too."

My eyes softened. He was that concerned? He even came up with a plan B.

"I'm fine now, Aspen. I'm getting used to it." I said to him.

He looked up at me with sparkling eyes, "You are?"

"Mhm. Don't worry. I won't feel different. You don't have to worry with making me uncomfortable. Like you said, treat you as I would treat anybody else."

He sighed, "Thanks, Isabelle. You don't know how much that means to me."

I smiled and nodded, "Let's go?"

"Let's."

DON'T FORGET TO VOTE! :)

17

—— ◦ ——

CHAPTER 17

D aniel

That king is without a doubt the most annoying one to take the throne.

He made me wait here out the palace gates. I have to go hide. I'm a man in danger. My life is always at risk of possible death when I'm out in the open. Scarlett has 360 degree vision when it comes to me. She can even smell my fear!

As some guards went by, I moved closer to a corner to avoid being seen.

"Damn it, Aspen. Where are you?"

I narrowed my eyes as I searched for Aspen and Isabelle in the Sorahian crowd. I can't see them. I shook my head and leaned against the wall. They're taking forever.

"Daniel..."

Oh no. Who is that?

I hesitated to turn my head at first to know where that creepy call is coming from. But, my head turned around by itself and I saw where all that creepiness emanated from.

Two grim reapers!

"Noooo! I knew it. Scarlett already had me! I'm already dead! Now, you two are going to take me to some horrible place bloodier than her hair! Whyyyy?!!!"

Suddenly, to my surprise, the disrespectful grim reaper slapped me.

"Be quiet, will ya?! It's us, stupid," he said.

"Hey! That hurt a lot." I said as I rubbed my cheek.

Finally, he removed the hood of his cloak and I saw a face worse than the grim reaper's.

"Oh. I thought I was going to finally rest in peace."

Aspen rolled his eyes, "Idiot! In hell?"

Aspen removed his cloak and so did Isabelle. He was already wearing his royal robes.

"Let's go, Daniel."

I nodded, "Fine. Let's take the west door. There are fewer soldiers there."

"And I'm here because...?"

"Because if Scar finds you, you'll be dead for sure."

I nodded, "Good call."

Aspen added, "You're lucky I'm letting you stay here with us at the library even though I can't afford distractions."

I rolled my eyes, "Please. As if I would distract you while you're flirting."

He perked up, "What was that?"

"I won't distract you, your majesty." I said as I did a curtsey.

"Good."

"But it's okay if you can't help yourself. I don't get distracted that easily," Isabelle said as she walked closer to me.

I almost cried at Isabelle's concern,"How do you stand hanging out with a devil? You're an angel."

She whispered, "Well, he does have half a halo around his head."

I scrunched my face in disbelief,"No he doesn't."

"Of course he has." She smiled.

I blinked, then I suddenly thought about it, "He paid you, didn't he?"

"What? Of course he didn't. Even if he did, I won't accept it." She said.

I gasped, "What kind of eyes do you have?"

She shrugged, "Maybe he just doesn't show that halo around you guys. But he does have one."

"I still don't-"

"If you're talking about me, I hope it's about good things." Aspen suddenly cut us off and raised a brow.

"We're talking about how good you are." Isabelle lied, saving us.

I don't know if the color appeared on his cheeks was red or pink, but I know that it was a blush.

"O-oh. Really?" He stuttered.

"No." She admitted.

I couldn't help but laugh my heart out. Isabelle has a great sense of humor, really.

Aspen glared at me as I laughed, "I can call Scar anytime, Daniel. I'm sure she's looking for an idiot to spar with."

"Sorry."

Isabelle smirked at me, "Don't worry. I'm sure the halo will appear anytime now."

"I've already given up at the chance of it existing."

We were at the royal library. Aspen had the door locked as he and Isa do a research on the secret kingdom.

Aspen was busy looking through books while Isabelle was just waiting for his signal.

After a few moments, Isabelle suggested, "Why don't you trace where the book fell and let's look there."

Aspen lit up,"Good idea."

I don't know if he's just playing dumb while Isabelle's around, but I really wanted to go to his ear and whisper, "Stupid."

Anyway, since I had nothing to do, I followed them and started to help them out. Aspen took the stairs to climb the next flight of stairs towards the next floor of shelves. The library had this spiral shelf of books where there is also a spiral staircase.

He climbed up to the highest shelf where he got the notebook he showed us the other day.

Somehow, that notebook got me curious. I guess this is gonna be interesting.

"Huh?"

Isabelle and I looked up, "What is it, Aspen?"

"Well, there's a box here."

"Can you bring it down?" she asked.

"Of course."

I don't wanna offer my help to him for the moment. I know how much he wants to look tough.

Not a moment too soon, Aspen has the box down. It was a small box, cute like a mini treasure chest. But, it had this small lock. It was rusty and old, I'm sure it can be easily broken.

"Let's open it," Aspen insisted. He grabbed his dagger and destroyed the arch of the lock, leaving the keyhole untouched.

But before they can even open it, we heard the door crashing down.

And I saw red.

I know what that means so I rushed behind a shelf.

"Scarlett, you have to be careful in bringing down a door. Be sure to not knock off the hinges so it can be repaired," Aspen warned her.

"Yeah, yeah. Sorry about that. I tried to knock but the door was locked. Anyway, have you seen Daniel?" She asked.

That was a first. Most of the time, if she was looking for me, her line would be, "Hey! Seen an idiot somewhere? " or "I'm gonna kill him." Or "I smell a prince's fear." And other scary things I don't wanna talk about.

But now, she said my name.

I tried to come out to show myself. Maybe it was safe after all.

"Why?" Aspen asked.

"I'm looking for an idiot to spar with," Scar said as she brought out a sword.

And that stupid king smirked, "Called it."

"You guys are the worst," I glared at them.

Before I realized my mistake, Scarlett knocked down the shelf where I was hiding, "Oh sweet turkey."

"Gotcha," She said in a murderous tone.

Before she can strike her sword down to plummet me to my death, Isabelle, our angel, intervened.

"Wait! Can everyone please take a pause?"

"Yes! Thank you," I exclaimed as I ran to her for safety.

"What is it, Belle?" Aspen asked.

"Belle?" Scar choked, then smirked, "You changed your name?"

Isabelle surprisingly stuttered, "N-no. Well he...I-"

"It's still her name," Aspen defended.

"Really, now?" Scarlett put a hand around Isabelle, "So, I can call you Belle now too?"

"No," Aspen suddenly said but then, his eyes widened, "I mean. ..ask her."

This guy is 2000 ft deep underground by now. Tsk. Possessive.

Isabelle's eyes softened as she smiled, "Is it okay if only him would call me that? He kinda gave it to me...so even though it's my name, it's technically his."

Scarlett and I were taken aback, "When did you two-"

"What did you find again, Isabelle?" Aspen cut is off. His head was bowed down. But I know that he's hiding his redness. I know because I do that too, but instead of red, pale blue in fear.

Scarlett and I smirked at the two. Then, she suddenly glared at me prompting me to avert my gaze. Damn.

Isabelle then spoke, "There are two letters in this box and a map."

"Can I see that?" Aspen said as he grabbed the other letter. I looked at the other letter and it had nothing but a bunch of num-bers.

I looked over his shoulder to see it while Scar went to Isabelle and examined the chest.

"What does it say, Aspen?" I asked.

"Here, I'll read it."

The three of us leaned over to listen.

"I'm sorry, Eleanor. I can't do this anymore. I can't serve for that monster anymore. He killed my family, he took everything away from me because my plan for Seira failed."

Seira? Isn't that one of the fallen kingdoms. As far as I know, they were the only kingdom to have more than half of the people survive. The impact of the omen was disastrous, killed almost all of the members of the royal family.But they were able to rebuild their kingdom from the ground up. Now, they are the New Seira.

"Plans? Aspen, I think it's from the strategist!" Isabelle said.

"Yeah, I think so too." He agreed.

"Wait, I just noticed." Scar suddenly spoke, "Aspen, you're wearing your royal robes."

That's right. Scar doesn't know yet. Those were the most hilarious moments I've ever had with Aspen. He was almost crying because Isabelle found out. His face looked like half of Sorah underwent a volcanic eruption...if we had volcanoes. His eyes had dark half moons because he wasn't able to sleep for almost three days! I know I should be pitying him, but I couldn't feel a pint of sympathy for him. All I had was self control....I needed to control myself from laughing.

Isabelle smiled," Yeah. I just recovered from the trauma of the discovery. It took me three days."

"Oh," Scarlett nodded, then she turned to Aspen, "Tsk. You're a horrible king. You made her suffer for three days."

To our horror, she brought out her sword, "You don't deserve to be king."

"Scar!" Isabelle ran to her to Aspen's relief, "You don't have to do that. I'm okay now."

Scar blinked, "You sure? Well, I can make you feel better." Then she was about to strike her sword again.

Isabelle, once again, stopped her, "Scar!"

Finally, she sighed, "Ugh. Fine." Then she withdrew her sword, "Continue reading...before I change my mind."

Aspen sighed, "I'm the king, ya know."

Scarlett pursed her lips, "And I should care because..?"

Aspen bowed his head, "Never mind. Anyway, let's continue."Then we leaned over once more.

"Eleanor, you have to run. Run away where they won't find you. If they find out that you're an assigned, if they find out you're with me, they'll take away your family and persecute them. They'll take away your child and destroy that kingdom. Please, I'm begging you. Start a new life. Leave their régime. Even for those as loyal as we are, they'll never hesitate to kill you. As your friend, I'm begging you, leave them. Leave them before it's too late. They can't do this to us anymore. They can't take the blood of the innocent no longer. I'm begging you."

Isabelle narrowed her eyes, trying to analyze the letter, "It looked like the strategist was warning someone."

Aspen agreed, "Based from this letter, I bet the one called Eleanor also worked for that kingdom too. And she was a mother."

I spoke as I grabbed the letter from Aspen, "Hold on. There's a part of the letter that says, 'If they find out that you're an assigned'. It's just odd. Assigned? Could it be that-"

"Hey, what if that 'Eleanor' is a mole?" Scarlett suddenly said. We all looked at her. Then she started explaining her suspicions.

"Well, it's just that, like you said, there were always moles in the kingdoms conquered. And I also remember Isabelle saying that it would take months even years for one mole to sabotage a whole kingdom. So, the moles are just waiting for their signal to carry out their plan. While they were waiting for that signal, they might have been collecting information to send to the strategist who will then polish their plans."

I knew she was perfect, she was smart, alright. But this smart?! I really feel left out,"How do you-"

"I'm a strategist too, stupid. I know their ways," She rolled her eyes.

Isabelle continued Scar's explanations, "So you're saying that Eleanor could be a mole. If she was...then okay. She's a mole. But what did it have to do with that letter and that box and that notebook being here?"

Yeah, I just realized that. She does have a point.

Aspen grabbed the letter once more, "It says here that the strategist failed their plans for Seira, the last fallen kingdom. So, that would mean that the kingdom where Eleanor's a mole was not yet conquered. It was supposed to be but, without the strategist, they can't carry out an attack."

"Aspen, could it be?" Isabelle gasped.

Oh man. If they're thinking what I'm thinking...

It's Sorah.

"Sorah. She was the first mole at Sorah before the man we caught," Aspen confirmed with a nervous tone, "That's the reason why the box is here."

We were all shaken by the discovery, even me. And that's a first because I usually don't care about stuff unless it's funny...or it's gonna turn out to be.

"So, Sorah was meant to be conquered," Aspen gritted. " But it never happened because the strategist turned his back against the kingdom. And I read the notebook. His plans were good. So, if he didn't quit, we would be-" Aspen stopped in his tracks because, from the looks of it, he was shaking in anger.

I understand him though. Any king would feel like his kingdom is being looked down on if he was in this situation.

Suddenly Isabelle sighed, "I don't really know if we should thank that strategist or not. I mean, he did indirectly save us."

"Yes, but he didn't mean to. It was just because he wanted to save his friend," Scar spoke.

But then I realized, "He didn't just save Sorah, but the other kingdoms as well."

"What do you mean, Daniel?" They asked.

"I just thought that maybe it wasn't just Sorah. Maybe a lot of kingdoms had moles too. When the strategist quit, the other moles no longer had the plans. The first ones attacked were the kingdoms which were already chaotic from the inside. I noticed that when Aspen read us the notebook before. Most of the fallen kingdoms had internal conflicts already. That's why it was easy for the strategist. "

Isabelle easily caught up, "And because Sorah was at peace and had less conflicts, we weren't one of the fallen kingdoms. It's because the strategist wasn't able to come up with a plan for the mole. Sorah never had a weakness.

"When we started believing in the omens, that became our weakness," I added.

Aspen sighed, "So Sorah was saved because we were at peace. But we can't deny the fact that there was a mole in our territory. Even our fellow trade partners have moles with them and they're not even aware of it."

"Yeah, you're right. How could we help all of them? I mean, we can't just keep this to ourselves." I added.

Isabelle then held out a finger and suggested,"What if we don't need to warn them all? What if we could just warn one kingdom?"

"Then they'll relay the message to others? Sorry, Isabelle. But if we only warn one kingdom about this I'm sure some will withhold the message because of competitiveness. Not all kings and rulers are like the ones we know and have." Scarlett countered.

But Aspen smiled knowingly, "No. Isabelle's right. We need to warn only one kingdom."

Scar and I blinked, "Which?"

There could be thousands of kingdoms out there that has a mole. We have thousands of friends out there. How could we warn only one?

Then Aspen, with a glint of secret awareness in his eyes, spoke, "We just need to find the right kingdom to send the message to."

"Yeah, but who? We have many fellow kingdo-"

"I didn't say that the kingdom is on our side." He stated while Isabelle smiled at his words.

These two are the only ones who could really understand each other because Scar and I got nothing.

But wait. So if that's the case, then the kingdom to warn is an enemy? There is no enemy kingdom that I know of. Except...

"The one who made an enemy out of Sorah." Aspen said firmly and he grabbed the strategist's notebook and held it out.

"But we don't even know which kingdom is that. If that exists today, it should be a big territory by now. We can't just accuse kingdoms with big territories especially when a lot of them are our trade partners. Besides that, we might make a bad impression on them. Sorah is also a big territory too. So basically, it's like looking for who ate the cookie among brothers. And we don't wanna act as the seeking guardian." Scar said, doubting their plan.

Aspen gave us a smirk, "That's why we need to find out who that kingdom is so that we can send them a warning. I'm sure they're still waiting for the mole to signal them. We'll send them the signal instead....the signal to stop screwing around with us." He narrowed his eyes as he said the last part.

"How are we gonna do that?" I asked.

"Simple." Aspen answered as he pointed at Isabelle, "We have her. This is gonna be a piece of cake."

Isabelle tucked a strand of hair behind her ears, "I'm not sure if it's gonna be a piece or a whole cake. But what I do know is... I need all of you with me."

All of us looked at each other an smiled, "Count us in." "What's the first step, Isabelle?," Aspen stepped forward.

She nodded, "Let's go find out about the strategist and this Eleanor.

Aspen

We started to rummage what's inside of the box. But that's all there is to it. The two letters and an old map.

"That's it. We have no more leads other than these." I sighed.

Isabelle didn't give up, however and kept searching for some clues as she examined the letter further. She really is an amazing girl. Who wouldn't be afraid to lose such a friend?

Ever since she found out I was the king three days ago, I wasn't able to sleep. I kept thinking and worrying. Every afternoon, I would dress as an officer and wait near her home. I've been so worried to the point that I hated myself. Talking to Daniel didn't help at all.

"Aspen, it's your fault. But don't worry. Starting now, she won't be bothered by you. Her life will be peaceful and she'll be happy."

"Why....?"

"Next time you meet a girl, tell the truth okay. That way, you won't hurt her or leave her traumatized."

That moron didn't make me feel better.

When I saw her come out earlier, I wasted no time. I was so desperate to see her and say sorry. I was so desperate to keep her. I wanted to tell her everything. I didn't want anything to change.

I thought she would regret it all. But...no.She surprised me.

I've never felt that much happiness in my entire life, when she said she also wanted what I wanted

It was too good to be true.

But I didn't care about that anymore. Now I have nothing to hide, although I'm fully aware that she's still uncomfortable on the inside. I'll try my best to help her with that. I want this to never end.

I want this for all of us.

Now, I'm just staring at them...okay...at her, just watching her work. I missed her. Yeah, it was just three days, but it felt longer. As they said, although I'm not really sure who, time flies slower when you're sad.

"Aspen look at this."

I stood up, "What is it, Belle?"

Yeah, I just wanted to call her with something special, to help her get used to me as king, to help us get closer. It's about time I came up with a shorter name for her. The ones she gave me are...really not that...ugh.

Let's just say I didn't like it.

I was really surprised when she said I was the only one who could call her that. Again, something stirred up in me. It wasn't bad. It was the total opposite of it. My heart literally left my chest and went to a small paradise.

Tsk. The only things I can't explain.

"Look at this."

And I did as I was told. I took a closer look at the area of the box where Isabelle was pointing out.

There I saw the full name of the woman the strategist was warning.

"Eleanor Maoris." I read aloud.

As I said it, we heard a very surprising gasp from a very surprised red haired girl. None of us could believe it. Scar actually let out something between a shriek and a gasp.

Daniel thought it was cute, as I've suspected from his blush. But Isabelle and I thought it was abnormal.

"What is it, Scar?" Isabelle asked.

Scarlett's eyes widened, "I-I know that name."

Belle and I looked at each other, shocked to learn and anxious to know.

"Really?"

Once again she gulped before speaking, "I think...she's my mother."

I almost fell back. Scarlett's mother...was the mole at Sorah?

Who would believe that?

"I was searching for dad's old daggers, then I found a picture of a woman that looked kinda familiar. Then, at the bottom, I saw the name and I've never forgotten it since.- 'My dearest and beloved, Eleanor Maoris.' Dad was never interested in women until my mother came, as he said. So, I think it was her." She shared.

We held our breaths as we tried to soak it up. General Aris and Scar are related to that Eleanor. If that's the case, then the general must know...even just a little bit.

Although, it's gonna take us a lot of moment to reel back from the revelation, we can't waste any time.

"Scarlett, do you know anything else about Eleanor Maoris...I mean...your mom?" I asked.

She shrugged, "Not a lot. My mother died when I was just a year old. All she left me was-"

"Your necklace." Daniel finished.

Scarlett quickly eyed him, "How did you know that?"

"You kidding me? You wear that everyday, ever since you were a kid. And I don't think the general's the kind to give you something like that." Daniel said.

"You're not a stalker, are you?" Scarlett glared as she touched the hilt of her sword.

Daniel put his hands up as if surrendering, "N-no. I've known you my whole life, ma'am! I know because-"

"Because what?" Scar raised a brow.

"Well, I've known you forever. How can I not know those things when I was always with you?" He put bluntly.

I'm not sure if my eyes were deceiving me or not, but did the almighty Scarlett de Beville...blush?

"Although those times would always be in times of danger.." Daniel muttered. He always screw things up.

But he was cut off when Scarlett swooshed her sword above his head. I grabbed Isabelle and placed her behind me.

"Scar, watch where you're killing him. I don't want any blood spilled here." I warned.

"Better get used to that, you prince!" Then Scar flung her sword again.

Daniel kept dodging in fear, "Scarlett, wait! -Gah!- Why are you so mad!?"

She's always like that.

"Because I still can't believe I'm your freakin fiance!" She roared, "I must be the most unfortunate woman alive."

Daniel paused for a while, "Oh. You know I almost forgot about that."

Scar then tightened her grip on her sword, took a turn and swung the sword hard. Because of that, her necklace came off and flew into Isabelle's hands.

"Guys, be careful." I reminded.

"Wait!" Isabelle suddenly exclaimed, making us stop in our tracks.

"What?"

Isabelle went to the table and grabbed the broken lock beside the small chest box. It was the lock of the chest.

She looked at Scar's necklace. I just realized that it had a very odd shape- a heart with a crooked tail.

We both observed her as she put the pendant inside the keyhole. And the arch moved.

"It's the key to the lock." Daniel uttered.

We looked at Scar as she put down her sword.

"Then that confirms it." She said, "The owner of the box is my mother." Then she bowed her head as she came to look remorseful and guilty.

And I know exactly what she's thinking.

I walked to her, "Scar, don't be-"

"I feel like the daughter of a criminal, Aspen." She admitted as she curled her hands into fists.

I looked at her sternly, "Look, I don't care if your mother's the mole. But Sorah is here, brave and still standing. It was her job to destroy it but somehow, she became a hero to all of us. Sorah's alive, Scar. Your mother had something to do with that."

"You're the daughter of a hero, Scar." Isabelle added, and we all agreed we her.

Yes, her mother was a mole. But, something, that we still don't know yet, happened. And that saved Sorah, that's why I need to find out what it is.

"I don't know what to say." She uttered.

We all smiled at her as I grabbed the chest, the notebook, and the lock. Scar wore the necklace."There's only one man who can help us with this." I stated.So, with our hearts set to find out the truth, we proceeded to the defense hall where we're hoping General Aris was.

Scarlett first spoke to her father to tell him what happened, what he needed to learn, and what we needed to know.

General Aris glanced at us in a curious way. Then he walked to us and invited us to sit down.

"So, your majesty," He started as he sat down, "What's all these stuff about moles and secret kingdoms, and why would it have something to do with my family?"

"Well, general, we've been trying to solve the identity of the secret kingdom, as Scar informed you. It's all in this notebook." Then I gave him the strategist's notebook. He took it and studied the pages.

I continued, "Where I found the notebook, I found this." Then Isabelle handed him the chest, along with what's inside. He read the letter carefully, his eyes widening as he reached the last part, "Where did you get this?" He asked.

"In the royal library." I answered, "Do you know anything about this, general?"

He sighed. Then Scarlett spoke, "Dad, if it's okay, can you tell us more about mom? If you can't-"

He raised his hand, "No, it's fine. But let me tell you this: I don't think I'll be that much of a help to you."

We looked at each other, "What do you mean, dad."

He ran his hands through his hair in distress, "The truth is...I don't know that much of Eleanor."

"W-what?" I exclaimed, "How can you not know anything about your wife?"

He sighed once more, "The thing is...we weren't together that long. Our story was almost just a second if you'd ask me. I wanted more time with her. But, I wasn't able to save her."

Scarlett touched his hand,"Dad, what's the story."

He straightened himself up and prepared himself to tell us everything, "I met Eleanor while I was going home from a mission. I was still young back then, when I saw her lying beside the riverbank of the Welch River. She was passed out and close to dying. So, I took her to my home and cared for her."

"Leave all the mushy parts, okay Dad." Scar smirked.

General Aris shook his head and smiled," Eleanor was very secretive. She was so shy, afraid, and spoke very few words to people. She had nothing when I found her. And every time she gets something, she hides it...even to the point of burning it to keep it hidden. They were mostly letters."

"Letters? She's been receiving them?" I repeated.

Those must be from the strategist.

"Yes." The general answered, "She was so mysterious that I couldn't help but keep an eye on her. I helped her every way I can. I was the one who got her a job as the royal librarian. Maybe that's why her stuff was there. Who would've thought."

"And you keep seeing her everyday, then you fell in love." Scarlett added, seemingly finishing the story.

"You're ruining the story." Daniel complained. Guess he forgot that he's gonna risk his life doing so.

Scar pulled out her sword again as expected, "What did you say?!"

"Children, please." The general intervened while snickering, "She's right."

"See?" Scar glared at Daniel.

"I quickly fell in love with her. I was never interested in women but there was something about Eleanor. Her rare smiles, laughs, and very scarce words brought me closer to her. We confessed our feelings to each other, then we got married and had Scar." He finished.

"That was fast." Daniel commented.

But the general smirked, "Not as fast as you, Prince Daniel. Imagine, because of you, my daughter's gonna be a princess."

Then we heard a sound of a shelf going down, "Don't even remind me." Scar mouthed.

We all gulped at that. But Daniel blushed when the general said that. "Umm, about that, General Aris..."

The general raised a brow, "What? The engagement? Please, prince Daniel. You don't have to feel guilty or something. If anything, I'm happy she fell into good hands. I didn't want to send her off to any man. I'm glad it's you." He smiled, then he inched closer to Daniel and whispered, "Good luck with her. Try your best to stay alive."

Daniel swallowed a lump in his throat, "Y-yeah. So far, so good."

I interrupted before we go way out of topic, "Sorry to break in." I chuckled, then I face the general, "General Aris, what happened after you guys had Scar?"

He straightened himself, "After quite some time, she changed. She went in and out of the city, and became all the more secretive than before. Because I didn't know anything about her, I respected her privacy. But, things took a turn for the worse when she decided to join the mission to sail to the Deep Cerulean."

Deep Cerulean?

"By any chance, is that the Cerulean tragedy that happened 17 years ago?"

He nodded, "None other than."

Isabelle gasped, "What happened? Why did she join?"

He touched his nape as he continued, "Like I said, everything changed. It was when she received a letter."

I thought about it and it must be possible that it was the letter we found in the chest.

"She said she was needed there as their navigator. She was good at reading maps. But I didn't want her to go because I had a bad feeling about it. It felt wrong and her actions...it felt like she was saying goodbye." He explained.

"Then?"

"It was raining when she left. I instantly knew there would a violent storm. I went to the port, hoping to catch her there but they already left. I was too late to stop her. Then, the storm came and the day after, everyone was reported...dead." He said sadly as he recalled what happened.

"That's it?" I asked.

"Yeah. That's all I know." He confirmed.

"That won't get us anywhere." I doubted.

Then, Isabelle suddenly asked him, "General Aris, you said she kept secrets. Is there any hobby of hers related to that?"

General Aris tried to think, "Well, she would always put codes and locks on her stuff."

"Codes and locks?" She repeated.

What does it have to do with this?

Isabelle whispered to me, "Aspen, do you think the second letter's-"

The second letter? It was just full of numbers. Wait.

Numbers?

Could it be?

"They're codes." She revealed.

My eyes widened. I wasted not time in grabbing the chest and the second letter. Isabelle's right. I think they are codes!

But codes for what?

"Another secret?" Isabelle said. Then her eyes widened and her brows raised, "Aspen, can I look at the box?"

I handed it to her as she examined it, "What is it, Isabelle?"

She handed me the second letter. The rest walked closer to us to observe, "Look at the symbol at the right side."

I did as she said, and I saw it. There was a a small symbol on the upper right side of the letter. It was similar to the lock and Scarlett's necklace. A heart with a crooked tail. Only this time, the crooked lines served as the wings of the heart, but without the feathers. So, it kinda looked like a heart with scary branches.

"It's the same as the key and the lock," I said.

Then he showed me the inside of the chest, "Not only the lock and the key."

I looked closer and saw that the chest also had the same symbol.

"What does it mean, Isa?" Scar asked.

"I think that the codes had something to do with this chest." She said to us as she was looking for something in the chest. She removed the two letters and the map too.

"Why do you say that?" Scar asked. The General went closer to listen.

"The lock of the chest, your necklace, and the chest itself all had the same mark. There may be a reason why your mother left this. There may be a reason why she left you that key. There is something she wanted you guys to know, and the right time is now." Isabelle suspected.

"Maybe she wanted us to know her identity and what she did." General Aris said.

Isabelle, still struggling with the box, spoke, "Not quite. We're missing something and it's in this box. It might not be her identity only, but also her story."

"Let me help you." I said as I took the box from her. I felt the inside of the cover and I touched an elevated area. I turned the box over so that everyone could see the inside of the cover. It had 5 adjacent knobs that can be turned individually.

Isabelle looked at me, nodded, and gave me the codes. I studied these kinds of locks once. So, I know how it works.

"3."I turned first knob three times."8."I turned the second one eight times and so on."5.""9."Then the last one."7."

After that, a secret compartment opened. It had another letter in it. I looked at the others and I quickly took the letter as I dropped the box.

I scanned the contents. My eyes softened at what I read. I stopped midway because it wasn't for me to read.

18

CHAPTER 18

A spen

"What is it, King Aspen?" The general asked.

I smiled and handed it to him, "It's a letter from a hero-" then I handed it to him and Scar, "To another heroes."

He took it and read it aloud , along with Scar.

My dearest Aris and Scarlett, my daughter. I wanted to thank you for bringing me so much happiness before I go. I'm sorry I wasn't able to tell you a lot of things.

I didn't want to put you in danger. Because I love you, I chose to push you away from my life. You see, my life was dangerous. I was a very dangerous woman before I met you, Aris. I was on a mission.

"Dangerous? Maybe it was her job as the mole." Scarlett said, then she continued reading the letter.

I was sent to collect information to bring down Sorah. My beloved, I used you to get closer to that information. I'm so sorry. My life and my family's life was on the line back then. My mission was to assassinate this nation.

That's all I was trained for. I was a citizen of a kingdom ruled by generations of ruthless kings. If I fail, they'll kill not only me, but also the ones I loved. I never wanted to do it, but I had no choice, my dear. This was my life.

"Oh Eleanor.." General Aris uttered.

But then, you changed everything. You changed me. I fell in love with you. I fell in love with Sorah. You introduced me to this kingdom.

For the first time, it felt like I had a family in Sorah. Everyone I met changed me, especially king Jethro. I've never known a king as kind as the one you have. I wanted to live there with you. I couldn't bring myself to destroy this kingdom.

That's why I decided to run away from it all by marrying you, Aris. You made me want to start a new life. I burned everything from my past to be with you; to be Eleanor de Beville and not Eleanor Maoris. Then Scarlett came. And that was it. I was never happier. Starting a family with you was too good to be true.

Honestly, I forgot who I was and the kingdom I originally worked for.

"Mom." Scar uttered as they read further.

I forgot that the kingdom I once reluctantly served never forgets those who sins against it. My friend warned me and wanted me to escape. Only then I realized that I never could escape them. I feared that when they find me...they'll hurt you too.

And that's what I cannot take. That's why I joined the sail to the Deep Cerulean.

I cannot let them take my family, or the kingdom I learned to love. I know that my death won't be in vain. It is going to be the greatest sacrifice I'll make.

"So, it was suicide." The general closed his eyes in agony, "She knew there'll be a storm. She knew she'll die there. But still..."

I took everything with me and left you this so that you'll know when the time comes. Don't worry about me. I couldn't ask for more anymore.

And don't worry yourself too, my love.

Don't worry about the pain of the water filling my lungs, nor the struggle as I lacked air. I was smiling, my dear.

"Eleanor." The general started tearing up and so did Scarlett.

You're safe now. They don't know about you or the kingdom I went to. You and Scarlett will live. That's more than enough for me.

Scarlett, I know that by the time you'll be reading this, you'll be a woman. Strong, beautiful, and smart. That's why I had that symbol in your necklace made.

A heart with a crooked tail. I had a dark past behind me but I didn't let that get in the way of me having a heart. And that's what I want for you. No matter what you go through, I want you to let it be a part of your beauty and of who you will be. I want you to be good, yet fierce. I want you to be elegant, yet brave. Because you are my daughter, as well as your father's.I'm sorry for leaving you too soon, my Scar.

"Oh mom.." Scar cried.

I wanted more time with the both of you. But, you've already brought me a lifetime of happiness. I wish you all the best, my dear daughter. And please, just in case, find a man like you're father. I won't approve any other man. Don't forget to learn a little bit of self defense okay.

Always keep your guard up and be careful not to fall in the wrong company. Stay loyal to that kingdom. It'll serve you well. I have so many things to say to you, Scarlett. But, time forbade it. I'll watch over you instead, in heaven. I'll always be with you. I love you. Always and forever.

-Eleanor de Beville

The general hugged Scar, crying as she held onto the letter.

"Mom." She whispered.

"I know, Scarlett. She has sacrificed this much for your future, my dear."

She nodded and smiled, "Thank you, mom. I love you too."Then she wiped her tears and kept the letter, "What now?" She asked turning to us.

"I'm proud of your mother, Scarlett. She was a hero." I stated, "But we still have nothing. She didn't even say the name of the kingdom. "

"You're right." She agreed, "But I-"

"I know." I said, "You got something."

She smiled, "I never knew my mom. But after reading this, I now feel like I've known her my whole life."

"Yeah." We agreed.

"But Aspen, this doesn't solve anything." Isabelle said behind me.

I nodded, "I'm aware of that, but I just don't know what to do next."

"Isabelle, right?" General Aris walked to her.

"Yes, sir." She answered.

"I have something from Eleanor that may help you." He said.

Our eyes widened, "What is it, general?"

He got a paper and a brush with an ink. He started drawing on the paper. After a few seconds, he revealed it to us.

It kinda looked familiar.

"I saw this symbol once from her dress from when I first saw her, before she burned it." He said.

I studied it and I remembered where I saw it."It's the symbol on the strategist's notebook." I grabbed it to show it to them. "See."

"What does it mean?" Daniel asked.

I took the paper from the general, "I don't know. The symbol is not clear and it only has one color. I've never encountered this mark before. We have to find out."

"How?"

Scarlett stepped forward, "There's one guy who might know something about it."

We all turned to her, curious, "Who?"

"We go to the dungeon." She said.

"Oh." Daniel said, getting it.

She's right. Only the mole might know something.

"So, let's beat it out of him?" Scar invited, feeling pumped up.

"Yeah." They cheered as they went out the door. I was the last one to go. Before I was able to step out the room, the general stopped me.

"Your Majesty?"

I turned to him, "Yes, general?"

"It's not that I'm assuming, but you're not gonna put my wife's name in the Scroll of Heroes, are you?" He said.

I chuckled, "Of course, I will. She's already considered a hero when she died serving the kingdom in that expedition. But, I think she deserves more than that because she has done more."

He sighed, "As honoring as it is, with all due respect, my king, I wish you wouldn't do that."

I blinked, "Why?"

"I think she'd be happier if we just keep this between us. She's not the type of woman who wants fame. And as her husband, it would please me very much if her story would remain as a family secret."

I nodded, "I understand. I just wanted you to know that you're wife's a hero, and Sorah owes her. I owe her."

He bowed, "Thank you, King Aspen."

I smiled, "Thank you for your help, General Aris. I'll be taking my leave now." Then I did a playful salutation.

The general smirked and did a salutation himself. Then, I left.

The others were standing by, waiting for me at the gates of the defense hall.

"What took you so long, man?"

I shrugged, "Just...stuff."

Scar complained, "We should've left him. Then at least we could've beat that guy up first. We wasted precious time."

Isabelle stayed quiet. It looks like she's in deep thought. Is something wrong?

"Let's go." Scar lead the way with Daniel following her.

I walked to Isabelle, "Are you alright?"She looked up, "Well, I-"

"You can tell me. Is something bothering you?"

But she stayed silent.

"You're still uncomfortable with me, aren't you?"

Then she raised her hands, "No. It's not that."

"Then what is it?"

"It's just that...three days ago, remember when I found out that you were the king?"

I just remembered, "Yeah, you were about to tell me something. What was it again?"

"Someone, I don't know who, attacked-" She suddenly stopped.

"What? Attacked? Who?"

Then, she shrugged, "It's nothing." Nothing?

From the way she was telling it, I know it's a serious matter. I held her shoulders, "Isabelle, what is it? Tell me."

Then, she flinched and started taking deep breaths, "Aspen, I don't wanna do this anymore."

I stepped back, "W-what? You don't actually mean that, right?"

Is she...giving up on us now?

She sighed, obviously depressed, "Aspen, I can't do this anymore. The longer this goes, the worse I feel. I can't lie to my parents anymore."

"I told you. We'll help you with that." I reminded.

"When? We don't even know if that mole's gonna speak. For all we know, he'd stake his life on it. We don't know how long this case may last. Aspen, I have to leave now before the lies and the secrets I'm keeping kill them." She stated.

It took me time to realize, but now I know that...I've been so selfish. She must've been suffering this whole time. She must've been thinking about her parents. I brought this upon her. I made her lie.

Why do I bring her nothing but pain?! I hate myself.

I know that we're still gonna need her. But, I can't do this to her anymore. I can't bear to see her like this. I'm gonna have to let her go for now. We need to manage without her.

"I understand, Isabelle. You can leave your clothes with me. I'm allowing you to leave." I reluctantly said.

She sighed in relief, "Thank you for understanding."

I see it in her eyes; she didn't wanna leave yet. But she has to. I have to understand that.

"You can change at the shed behind the hall, I'll get it later." Then I looked at her, "Thank you for everything."

She nodded, "You're welcome and thank you too, Aspen."

"Good luck, Belle. We're gonna miss you on this case. You sure you don't wanna-"

She shook her head, "I'm sorry, but I have to leave now."

"Alright."

She did a curtsey to tease me before going, "Goodbye, your majesty."

I frowned, "Only for now, okay."

She chuckled, "Yes."

"Goodbye then, for now." I waved as she walked away from me, "Just come to us if you need any help, okay. We're here for you."

She turned around and nodded, "Thanks."

Then I watched as she faded from my sight. It was never easy to watch her leave. I don't know why, but it always annoys me when she leaves...no, not annoy. More like, 'it pains me'.Well, she promised me it wasn't really goodbye. I'll see her later. I need to focus on the case first. This is gonna be harder without her.

I ran to catch up with Scar and Daniel. Then, together, we went for the dungeon. We used our horses to get there.

"Where's Isabelle?" They asked.

"We're on our own for now." I said shortly.

"Dang it." Scarlett muttered under her breath

."What happened?" Daniel asked.

"She had to go home."

That's right. We need to do this without Isabelle. We need to try.

"The dungeon's close ahead."

After a few minutes, we arrived.

"But I'll get to beat him up, right?"

I groaned, "Scar, that will not be necessary."

"Then, let's make it necessary!" She complained.

"Can we just get this over with? I haven't even had my lunch because of this." Daniel butted in.

Scarlett glared, "You're always hungry."

"Actually, both of us." I added.

"Aww, come on!"

"Let's-" I pleaded, "Let's just get this done."

"Fine." They groaned.

I faced the guards, whom we are disturbing with our arguments, "Open it."

"Yes, your majesty." Then they grabbed the bars and opened the cell.

The three of us walked quietly to where the mole was. He was still there with hands tied, outfit messed up, face covered with bruises and dirt, courtesy of Scarlett.

"Hi." Daniel greeted.

Scarlett looked at him, "What a great way to start a talk with a criminal." She said sarcastically.

"Well, I've never talked to one before. Princes would usually be in the dining room....eating lunch." Daniel retorted.

"Stop that." I warned them.

Then the guy looked at us and grimaced, "No, please. I'm enjoying the show. I love watching a lovers' quarrel."

Scarlett brought out her sword out and snarled, "I'll make sure to pluck your eyes out so that you won't be able to."

"And who said that this was a lovers' quarrel?!" Daniel added.

The guy lowered his head, "Well, it looks like it."

"If you're gonna say something, SAY IT TO THIS BEAUTIFUL FACE, BASTARD!", Scarlett pointed at her face with her sword.

"Enough!" I exclaimed, "We're here to question him, not entertain him."

These guys are annoying. Why did Isabelle have to leave anyway?

I took a deep breath and I glared daggers at the man, "Speak."

He held his head high, "What do you wanna know?" He asked as if innocent of what information we needed.

I took hold of the bars, "Where did you come from? We know a lot already, you can't hide it anymore."

"Then you shouldn't be asking me if you already know."

"He has a point, ya know." Daniel, who can't feel a thing, whispered to my ear.

I stomped on his foot in return, "Shut up."

I returned to the prisoner, "I want it to come from your filthy mouth. Where-"

"You'll never stop us anyway. So, what's the point of trying to solve our mysteries." He said.

I scoffed, "I know that you know that we're the first kingdom to foil your schemes." He flinched at this. "So I think we have a big chance of beating your kingdom's gigantic, lying ass."

"You really think you've figured it all out, huh?" He smirked.

"What the hell are you saying?" I narrowed my eyes.

"We're always one step ahead of you.", The guys looked at me with confusion in their eyes.

One step ahead?

"Did you think we'll let Sorah get away with our secrets? We're not over yet, your majesty." He taunted.

What is he saying? They're not over yet? What does that mean?

"What's the matter? Did you think we didn't know who's uncovering our secrets? Who's solving the case, planning to expose our kingdom? We know each and everyone of you..."-And what he said next was what feared me the most.-"....including that pretty little scholar girl."

"Isabelle?!" Scarlett gasped. Then her eyes flamed, "What on earth are you saying, you scoundrel?!"

"You made no mistake when you caught me. I was surprised that a kingdom was able to figure out for the first time. I was starting to take the whole world as fools who would fall into our traps one by one. But, you missed something." He snickered.

Scarlett glared at the man like she wanted to tear off his skin, "Why you little-"

"Too bad. It was only supposed to be the four of you, the ones who knew. Then after we destroy you, we leave your kingdom and prepare another plan. But, your mistake? You told your whole nation. And now, we have no choice but to finish them off-"

I grabbed his collar through the bars out of anger, "Why you little rat! Do you think I'll let you hurt my people?!"

He grinned, "Actually, you're letting them get hurt right now."

"W-what?"

"While you're here wasting your time, our plans are being carried out."

My arm shook and my eyes widened, "Impossible. Y-you're locked up. There's nothing you can do."

He smirked, "Let me tell you a secret. I have two occupations: a mole....and a bait."

Bait?

Is he saying that we were fooled?! Is he saying that this was a trap?! No. I was sure that we caught the right guy.

"Aspen..." Scar shook.

He's the bait, then who's the fisher?

No...

"Could there be..." Daniel started.

No. I don't believe it! I refuse to.

Only then, when I saw him close, was I able to notice the thing dangling from his neck.A whistle.

And not just any whistle.

"It's a crane's whistle." Scarlett said, noticing it as well then tearing it off his neck. She should know. They use this kind of whistle to signal an ambush, a partner, a spy....or an accomplice.

How could we have missed it?

The prisoner smirked again, "From the looks of it, I think you've figured it out."

It's true. My suspicions are true.

There are.... two moles.

I gulped as I looked at him, "Does the other know her? DOES HE KNOW ISABELLE?!"

With a glint of sarcasm, the worst kind of it, in his eyes, he spoke, "We know everyone."

I dropped him in shock.

No. It can't be. They know her. They were also after her all along.

Isabelle said it earlier, that someone attacked her, but I didn't pay attention. She's in trouble.

I pulled her into this. Isabelle's life is in danger. The other mole...is targeting her because of me.

"Aspen.." Scar shook in worry, "Isabelle is-"

But I didn't let her finish because I already left the cell. I ran and ran until I reached my horse outside the gates. It was already night-time.I ignored the soldiers and the palace staff who gave me looks as I seemingly ran for my life.But no, I was running for Isabelle's life.

"Isabelle..."

Please, don't let it be too late. Please let it be me to reach her first.

I ran on my horse as fast as I could. I need to get to her.

"Isabelle!"

Please, don't let me be too late.

19

CHAPTER 19

Isabelle

"I'm home," I yelled as I opened the door. I was greeted by my mother who ran to me and hugged me.

"Isa, dear. We were so worried!"

I laughed softly, "Mom, I told you I'll be back."

She eyed me in a mocking way, "Did you really think that that would calm me down? Of course I wouldn't stop worrying about you."

My dad then stepped forward and placed a hand on mom's shoulder, "Gertrude, let the girl be. She kept her promise, alright. She's back in one piece."

"Why are you always taking her side, anyway? Aren't I your wife?" She glared at dad as she put her hands on her hips.

Dad raised up his hands in surrender, "It's not that, dear. I just don't like the way you're coddling her too much. She's a grown up now."

Mother flared, "Are you saying I'm old?!"

"Oy.." Dad face palmed, knowing he can never win an argument with mom. No one can.

"Hey, Lio! Speak to me!"

"Mom, Dad?" I intervened before it gets too far. I smiled at their baby fights. It was always so fun to watch and it would always cheer me up.

"Yes, Isa?" They responded in unison.

I took a deep breath before saying it, "I quit the noble's academy."

And as expected, their jaws dropped, "What?"

After I left the palace grounds, I proceeded to the public library, where my parents thought I would be. I made my letter, one of the most painful things I had to write. But, I needed to. This won't end unless I do this and I know that with all of my heart.

As I grabbed the quill, I almost forced my hand to move, but it wouldn't. I needed it to move and write the things I wanted -no- needed to say, but it wouldn't.

"Come on, Isa. Write!" I tried to scold myself. But what good would it do?

My tears then rolled down my cheeks.

How...

How could I possibly leave the place I love?

That place I dreamed about for a very long time?

How could I give up on it when I've barely started my life out there?

But I had to. As painful as it is, I need to quit the noble's academy. It's where it all started. My stupid, ambitious, and selfish dream to go there started it all.

These lies, these secrets that weren't even supposed to be made, it started because of that dream.

I need to put my family first. I can't do this to them anymore.

"We love you, dear."

"We trust you, Isa."

Those words wouldn't leave my head. It became a dead weight to me instead of encouragements because I knew I didn't deserve it during those times.

I have to give it all up. I have to leave my friends, I need to tell the truth to my parents.

So, with my heart set on this, I started writing.

[Ms. Amelia Yang, my dear teacher,

I'm sorry to say this, but I, Isabelle Almere, am quitting the noble's academy because of unfortunate circumstances. Thank you for accepting me as your student.

Sincerely,

Isabelle]

It was a short letter, but it felt like I've been writing it for hours. Suddenly, I felt a tear roll from my eye.

Why is it so hard to let go? This was just a stupid dream from the beginning. My family matters more than this. So, why am I feeling like I'm losing something that matters the world to me?

"You can do this, Isabelle." I said to myself.

So, with a heavy heart, I made my way to the academy.

The public library was very close to the academy, so it shouldn't take me 10 minutes to get there. But it felt like I was walking forever.

And when I finally got there, I sneaked inside Madam's empty office and I left the letter there. I hurried outside, I hurried to walk out that academy door, because it would be much more painful if I stayed for too long.

And so, I left everything and went home to where I must belong.

Home.

"Why, dear? Isn't that your-"

"No," I cut off dad, "I should be here with you. I know that now. I never should've left. I am your daughter. This is how it should be," I smiled.

Then, my parent's eyes softened as they both came to hug me, "Isabelle. We've been so worried about you. But are you sure about your decision?"

"Yes," I assured them.

Dad spoke, "You don't seem too sure, Isabelle."

"Of course I'm sure, dad," I tried to laugh, but ended up sounding like a horse, "Sorry for causing you guys so much trouble. If you'll excuse me, I'll just be at the farm, doing my chores."

"But it's already getting dark, darling."

I let go of them and walked towards the backdoor and to the farm. But, I won't be really doing my chores. I'll be trying to come up with a plan on how to tell them the whole truth. I may have given it all up, but they still deserve to know.

I grabbed my basket and my watering can to fake my agenda and I set off to the field.

As I walked across the crops, I felt tears rolling down my eyes again.

I miss them.

I miss all of them.

I wondered about what Ms. Amelia was teaching now.

What have my friends discovered new about the case?

Have they figured out the mysterious kingdom yet?

And as these questions invaded my mind, I sobbed.

I was completely lying to myself. I wanted to stay. I wanted to study more at the academy. I wanted to stay with my friends, solving the case. I wanted to stay so bad.

I brought my hands up to cover my face and my tears. I looked up the dark sky as the moon rose up. I didn't even notice that it was already night.

But, for an hour or so, I just kept on working. I need to get these things out of my mind before it makes me crazy.

I have to forget all the things that I want and focus on my family. I can't make them go through the same pain they've experienced in the past; a pain that aches up to this day. By forgetting those stuff that I want, maybe I'll be able to ease that pain so it becomes slightly bearable for them.

Hurting them is the last thing on my mind. That's why I can't find it in my heart to tell the truth because I don't know what's worse yet: lying to them or hurting them by telling the truth?

I can't weigh it, because in reality, the outcome is always un-escapable pain for someone.

After working out in the cold for a few more minutes, I gave up trying to clear my head for I couldn't.

I sighed, dropped my stuff and decided to go back. But what came next, what I heard, and what I saw as I turned around was the most unforgettable, most horrible thing I'll never forget.

Smoke.

Screams.

FIRE.

Our house was in flames. The walls were burning, emitting heat that pierced the cold wind. Fire clouded my vision as the smoke clouded the air. I could already hear the screams of my parents. We were far from the main village. We have no one to help us.

"M-mom, dad..."

My eyes watered, my heart filled with fear as I ran towards my family.

"Isabelle!" My mother screamed.

"Gertrude! Let's go." I heard my father's voice.

"MOM! DAD! NO!" I grabbed a pail of water beside our fence.

I poured a little bit of water on myself and I raced through the burning walls of my house. Fire was everywhere. Our home was literally tearing apart. I desperately called for my parents between coughs, despite the heat hurting my eyes.

I took the pail with me to pour little water to clear my path. In the midst of the smoke and flames, I saw my father trying to help my mom who is passed out.

"D-dad!" I coughed.

"Isabelle! Watch out!" My dad warned as he called out to me.

But it was too late.

A huge piece of burning wood, which previously supported our roof, was already on its way to crush me.

Even though I needed to, I couldn't move. All I could do was watch as the wood fell and hear as my dad calls out my name, telling me to move.

"Isa! No!"

Even though I was to move, it's gonna be too late.

This is it.

It's closing in.

I couldn't do anything more.

So, I closed my eyes as I prepared for my death...

"Belle!"

...which never came.

I opened my eyes as I felt my waist trapped in a familiar hug. This arms, this feeling.

I know this.

I realized that I was already out of my burning house, but I still had difficulty breathing. Still, I tried to speak to him, "A-aspen?"

With evident fear and worry in his voice, he shook my shoulders hard, "Isabelle?! Are you hurt?! Is someone still there?"

"M-my parents..."

Then he turned his face towards the fire, and wasted no time in returning to the danger. I watched helplessly as he bravely jumped into the flames, as if neglecting the damage it will bring upon him.

"Aspen..." I weakly called out as I started to feel the pain of my burns and bruises.

I was so numb from the pain, I couldn't get up, but I strived to hold on to my consciousness. My parents...and my friend safe- that's the last thing I want to see.

To my fear, the flames burst as if there was an explosion.

"MOM! DAD! ASPEN!" I screamed out.

I stumbled as I walked towards the flames, lacking the power that I badly need right now to go and save them.

I felt my limit as my knees touched the ground. But, thanks to my few lucky stars, my eyes managed to hold on, and so did my sense of touch.

I saw three shadows coming out of the fire, one was supporting the other two, and only an idiot wouldn't know who that was. I smiled in relief as I saw them, all safe.

Aspen gently laid my parents down next to me, and I weakly placed my arms around them. They were unconscious but they were safe. That's all I wanted for now.

"Mom, dad..." I whispered as I felt their breathing.

Aspen then walked to me and held my shoulders with his burnt hands, "Stay here for a while. I'm sure my guards are on their way. I'll just go get a cart to get you and your family to the infirmary."

I looked at him and touched his hands, barely having the energy to do so, "Thank you, Aspen."

He nodded, with worry on his face, "Wait here."

I laid down and turned my gaze upon our destroyed home, and my unconscious parents.

What happened?

How did it happen?

My heart, along with my remaining life started to die with the agony.

It's all gone. It took place all too fast.

But what I feared the most, is what would happen next after I wake up. Now that Aspen has showed up, revelations would be inevitable.

I know it's gonna come down to this point, where the truth shall be revealed after. But I didn't expect it to be this horrible and painful. I didn't expect that it's gonna make me lose this much.

"No..." I whispered, because there was nothing more I could do.

Aspen, pulling a big cart from nearby, came back. As he attached it to his horse, soldiers came.

"Your highness!" They saluted as they got down from their steeds.

"Do something about this," He said firmly, "and arrest anyone near the scene."

"Yes, sire!" Then they went on their way. A few soldiers accompanied him an helped him mount my parents safely into the big cart. The soldiers brought blankets and cushions for them.

"Isabelle," Aspen went to me and grabbed me himself. He lifted me up and carried me safely to the cart.

"Are you alrig- Ugh. Sorry, that was stupid. Of course you're not," He uttered with a concerned look.

"I'm fine. I'm just a little bit....scorched," I replied as I grazed his cheek to ease his worry.

Then he put on a very stern, angry, and serious face, "Isabelle, I swear that the one who did this shall pay. I'll never forgive him for what they've done to you. They're gonna pay."

"They?" I asked weakly.

"Shh. I'll explain everything later. Right now, let's get you and your family treated," he said as he placed me in the cart.

"Thank you, Aspen."

He shook his head, "Don't thank me. I shouldn't have let you go."

"It was my decision to leave. Don't blame yourself," I insisted.

He bowed his head low and cursed, "I had the power to protect you at my fullest, yet I wasn't able to. I promised to keep you safe, but I failed."

No. He's wrong. He've already done so much.

I coughed, "Aspen..."

"Rest. We'll get to the infirmary soon," He commanded as he turned his back and faced the road.

I stayed silent instead, and I rested, just as he asked of me.

I was so anxious about what would happen when I open my eyes later, that I don't think I'd want to open them again.

As I closed my eyes, the last sight I beheld was Aspen, the king who saved us, looking at the fire as if he was ready to murder. The rage he had in his eyes that night, couldn't even be compared to the fire. Whatever he had in his eyes, it was more furious than the flames that destroyed our home.

He's angry, for sure, as I am.

I clenched my fists tightly as I let go of my remaining energy, and slept.

Scarlett

"What on earth happened?!"

"A fire. I think it's-"

But I didn't let this king finish because I already know who, "Those bastards!"

An hour hasn't even passed yet when Aspen left the dungeon and rushed to Isabelle. And, this is what we find?!

A few soldiers are with Aspen. The ones I sent him must still be at the scene.

Daniel and I were about to leave when we saw Aspen and his soldiers coming towards the city gates. I was horrified to see what he had on that cart.

"Let's take them to the infirmary," he commanded.

"Oh Isabelle..." I whispered as I gazed upon my friend's state.

I balled up my fists until they turned whiter than snow. Whoever did this to her will pay with his life by my sword!

We hurried to the infirmary, passing by busy villages. It was hard to get through but we managed through Aspen's shouting.

"Get out of the way! Move!"

Talk about thunderstorms. His voice is like one when he's angry.

"Move! These people need help," I commanded the nurses and physicians as we entered the infirmary. We detached the cart and carried it in.

We were about to lay them down on the beds but we heard Isabelle cough. We cringed as we heard her pain. She kept grunting and her closed eyes kept shaking.

"Isabelle..." Aspen cupped her face, "She's burning up!"

I checked her legs and I saw that there were burns all over. Her hand too. I lifted her hand that was resting on her stomach, balling up in pain. But as soon as I did it, I saw blood.

"No," I could only mutter. Isabelle, my friend, was wounded badly. There was a piece of shattered glass stuck in her skin.

"She must've been covering it all along," Daniel said as he observed Isa.

"DAMMIT!"

Daniel and I soon found ourselves on shock as Aspen slammed on the cart and turned the bed over. His was in pain also. I could see that. He must be blaming himself. I understand him. With all the power in the world, he thought he could protect Isabelle from all kinds of hurt since day one.

Yet he's just human no matter how powerful.

I would blame myself too. In fact, I am right now. But, there's no use. It's already happened. All we can do now is make everyone feel better.

And how would we that?

Payback.

I tightened my hold on the hilt on my sword, but it loosened as soon as I took notice of the king's hands. He was burned badly himself too.

"Your majesty, your hand!" One soldier pointed out.

But, he balled them into fists. It turned so white that the burns became unnoticeable.

"I'll make them pay. I'll kill them for sure," ge gritted in a low, dangerous, murderous tone as tears of anger formed in his eyes. I've never seen him like this.

"Let's go to the palace. We'll treat them there," he stormed out as he hopped on his horse, pulling the cart to attach it again.

I held his hand, "But Aspen...Isabelle's parents," I reminded him. He glanced at them in worry, "If they wake up and find out that they're in the royal infirmary, Isabelle could be in trouble. You know that."

"Isabelle..." Aspen whispered as he looked at her longingly in concern. He was about to let go of the cart when Isabelle grunted in pain once more.

He firmed his hold on the cart, "No! She has to be treated by the palace's physician. She'll recover faster there and I could watch over her. I won't leave her again."

"But-"

"Whatever may happen next, I'll take responsibility for it. I'll help her explain. This is on me too. I brought this upon her. It's my duty to take care of her."

Now, he's become a nurse?! Why can't he just trust us with her? That accomplice is still on the loose and there are much worse things to worry about.

He attached the cart to his horse once more and prepared to get on.

I shook my head, "We can watch over her here. Aspen, you can't just focus on Isabelle. You have a lot of things to do," I tried to reason, "You're the king."

But he looked at me with the most serious eyes I've ever beheld, "I'm her friend."

And those were the last words he said to me before he stormed to the palace, taking Isabelle and her family.

That role...it's starting to have the same weight as his kingship.

"I'm her friend."

"Is it really him?" I asked once more.

"Yeah. He was found near the scene, passed out," Daniel raised the whistle that he got from the accomplice.

Finding this bastard was easy enough.

"He also had this," Then Daniel handed me a firecracker.

"Where was he founded again?" I asked.

He raised his brows, then answered straight, "Near the house, passed out."

"Hmm," I thought. Near Isabelle's house?

It's a given that he was the one who lit in on fire. But, why was he found there? I mean, if you weren't stupid enough, if you burned someone's home, shouldn't you have run away once you dropped the oil and matches?

"What if-"

"Scarlett, I-"

"What?!" I glared at him.

"Nothing, milady," he shook, "I wasn't interrupting."

I breathed heavily, "Good."

"But-"

I growled.

"Eep," He bit his lip.

But, calming myself, I sighed, "Fine. Speak."

"Well, I just wanted to tell you that Isabelle's home was not that far from Mount Kenan. It's the-"

My eyes widened, "Second highest mountain in Sorah."

"Yeah."

"So, he must've been trying to signal his kingdom, same with the first spy!" I exclaimed.

"I think so too." -Daniel agreed- "It may also be a possibility that he passed out due to the explosion. That, and also because he tried getting to mount Kenan after. It may have drained him."

It's a good thing we stopped him early. Well, technically, we didn't stop him. He passed out by himself. Boy, if ever he did fire that damn thing, Sorah would be in trouble. But, that's not gonna happen on my watch.

"We need to bring this bastard to Aspen and quick. I bet he's still at the royal infirmary watching over Isabelle," I said as I took the unconscious criminal from the guards and held him by his collar.

He nodded, but then his head remained gazing at the ground. Worry was evident in his eyes.

"It's been three days, and Isabelle hasn't woke up yet." He stated.

I sighed, depressed, "I know. I'm worried too."

Daniel held his head and looked at the accomplice, "You know I just can't help but wonder what's gonna happen to this guy once Aspen, Isabelle, and Isabelle's parents find out."

I looked down at the man and shook him for emphasis, "This guy? Oh, he's dead meat for sure."

"Double-dead meat," He added.

I smiled, "You know, I'm starting to like the way you think."

"W-what?"

Oh shoot.

I quickly covered my mouth and looked away to hide whatever's showing in my face. Did I really just compliment him?

Dang it. I think I did.

I just complimented this guy!

This is getting totally out of character. I need to do something and fast. I refuse to act like a silly teenage girl!

"Scarlett, are you alright?"

"Let's go!" I said, dragging the accomplice towards the dungeon.

"Scar?"

"WHAT?!" I turned around, flaring up. Why am I flaring up again?

He gulped as he pointed his finger towards the opposite direction, "The dungeon's that way."

I mentally face-palmed myself. What is wrong with me? I'm even losing my sense of direction.

I rolled my eyes to cover my mistake, "I know. I was just taking him for a ride....on the floor." Then I dragged him towards the opposite direction.

"Let me help you with that."

He held his hand out to help me, but instead of grabbing the hem of the man's shirt, the idiot accidentally grabbed my hand.

And as always, everything stopped.

Aww, damn. Here we go again. What's wrong with me? The thing pumping blood in my chest is going haywire.

He looked at me with those sorry eyes, "Uh, I apologize for that." He withdraw his hand and balled it into fists as he bit his lip.

My heart is losing control!

"Stay..." I whispered suddenly,

Why is it always like this with him?

"What was that, Scar?"

These things only happen when I'm with him.

Stay..."

"What?"

I brought out my sword, "Stay away from me!"

He quickly took 20 steps back, and held his hands in front in a form of surrender.

"Sorry!"

I withdraw my sword and glared at him, "I don't need your help! Get that through your thick skull!"

Then I continued to walk towards the dungeon, dragging the accomplice behind me.

"Uh, sure. I'll call the king then."

Then he went to the direction opposite the one I took. I looked back at him as he walked away. What does he do that makes me so angry....and weird all the time?

"I think he's giving you the butterflies, miss," a mysterious voice whispered.

I looked down only to see a drowsy, half-awake bastard. He was looking at me in a mocking way that I found annoying.

But...butterflies?

Please! Daniel, that dunce? Giving me butterflies?

"Shut up," then I punched him, knocking him into his previous state.

"That's better."

I continued to drag the prisoner all the way to the dungeon, ignoring the looks the guards gave me and the prisoner.

I hummed some unknown tune since I took the very long way to the dungeon- through the basement.

This is going to take a while.

I thought of Isabelle all the while. She must've suffered a lot. Her house is burned down, she's wounded, she's hurt.

She went through a day what I've been through a thousand train-ings.

She doesn't deserve this at all. I tightened my hold on the man's collar. Oh, if I only I could put this grip on this guy's neck right now.

But, I can't. Not for now. But I will.

I proceeded to the tunnel that leads to the dungeon. Boy, this basement hasn't changed. I touched the burnt brick walls inside. I used my sword to create a spark to light the torch.

"Yup. It's still here."

I cracked a smile as I looked at the black burn marks on the wall. Anyone would think that it looked awful and that something bad might have taken place.

But, sword to my throat, it isn't. Not even one bit.

It was one of the most fun experiences I've ever had.

(10 years ago)

"Daniel, this is stupid. And this late? It's almost midnight!" A little Scarlett de Beville warned the prince once more.

"Stupid is fun!" The prince cheered while he continued to set up what he wanted to show the worried girl.

Scarlett gave a sly grin before leaning in to whisper, "So that's why you're fun?"

Instead of being annoyed, like she was hoping he would be, he answered, "Exactly."

This reply made Scarlett face-palm herself. Anyway, she went to help Daniel, her curiosity about what comes out of this got the better of her.

"So, you just light these things up?" Scarlett asked.

"Yeah, and boom!" Daniel smiled, raising his hands to emphasize a 'boom', all the while grabbing a match.

"Is it a good boom or a bad boom?"

Daniel scrunched his nose, eyeing his contraption, "I'm not sure."

"Really, how stupid can you get? If you're not sure, why do it here in the basement?!" She mentally pulled her hair out.

"Shh. Aspen might hear us." He shushed Scar, putting a finger on his mouth.

The redhead blinked and looked around, "Speaking of, where's Aspen?"

"Uh, he can't be here," he replied with his tongue out, trying to get something from his toolbox.

"Why?" she asked.

"Stop asking questions please," the boy casually said as if he was serious.

But, being friends for a couple of years, Scarlett knew what that meant,

So she sighed and took out her dagger, pointing it at him, "Something you're not telling me, Daniel?"

And of course, who can win against THE 'Scarlett de Beville'?

Knowing the answer would be no one, Daniel frowned in defeat, "I didn't tell him about this scheme."

She quirked a brow in return, "And why is that?"

He widened his eyes and looked sideways as if searching for an answer- or in his case, an excuse- all the while, blushing.

"Um..." he bowed his head.

"Speak," she glared as the little dagger in her hand came closer to the prince's face.

Trying to hide the redness in his cheeks, he gave a stuttering reply, "W-well, I just...I kinda...I wanted this to be, well, sort of, between the two of us...only."

The innocent Scarlett lowered her dagger at the boy's words, "What?"

Daniel stood up to explain more clearly, "I wanted to keep this a secret from Aspen, so I asked for your help here in this basement, where he obviously can't find us."

"So this is-"

"Yup! You were helping me with my surprise for you," He scratched the back of his while plastering a grin on his face.

Scarlett blushed like a 10-year-old girl with a crush, but then she turned her head sideways, realizing something, "Surprise for what?"

Out of nowhere, Daniel grabbed a can and two sticks. He did a classic drumroll and, "It's for your birthday!"

"What?" Scarlett pursed her lips, not quite getting it. Out of all people, it's Daniel.

Not even the officials who were friends with General Aris, his father,

Not even the royal family...

Would forget...that it's not her birthday today, but tomorrow.

"But it's not-"

"I know. I know. Geez, I'm not that stupid, Scar," he frowned at her.

The redhead scoffed, "Yeah, you're way much worse."

Daniel mouthed a 'what the' before speaking with a tinge of childish resentment, "Hey! I did this for you! Don't I get any gratitude around this place?"

Scarlett looked at him, pouting with doubt, but then she smiled, "Fine. Thank you. But, I'm telling you, it's not my birthday."

"I know. I told you that already."

Scarlett blinked. Has her friend been drinking coconuts?

"I don't get it."

"I wanted to do this for you today because..."

"Because...?" She took a step closer to hear him better.

Daniel averted his gaze towards the ground. He closed in eyes in guilt, "I won't be here on your birthday celebration. I'm going on a trip with General Dreyus to Aldon."

Scarlett, hearing this, broke, "Wait. What? But, it's my birthday. You're always on my birthday." She said sadly.

Daniel sighed in despair. He cupped her cheeks in his hands, "I'm really sorry. That's why I wanted to do this as an early present for you, and also in hopes that you would forgive me."

Scarlett started tearing up. It wasn't easy to discover that your bestfriend, one of the most important people in your life, won't be showing up on one of the most important day in your life.

Her lips quivered, "I hate you!" She suddenly pushed him away with much force. She started walking away towards the tunnel's exit, shivering.

"Scar, wait! Don't go!" He stood up and went after her. He touched her shoulder, desperate to stop her. She turned around, but her eyes were as cold as the temperature down there.

"It's getting cold, isn't it?" Daniel asked with much concern as she noticed the shaking of her body.

"Well, it's night. What do you care anyway?" She spatted out with much annoyance.

Daniel just shook his head and chuckled at the way Scar was acting. Nonetheless, he took off his robe and placed it on Scar's shoulders, "You. That's what I care about."

This earned him a hidden blush on the redhead's cheeks.

He kept smiling at her as he fixed the coat on her, "Hey, you're not shivering anymore."

She nodded, "It's not that cold anymore, I guess."

Their conversation was suddenly interrupted by a classic stroke of midnight, courtesy of the classic clock tower in the middle of the town.

"It's time!" Daniel cheered, then he went to his contraption, confusing Scarlett.

The girl followed behind him, "What are you doing? It's midnight already. We're suppose to go home."

"No. Why would we when we're just getting started?" He smirked as he grabbed a match. But first, he took a glance at Scar, then back at the match.

He bit his lip."I think you should go sit on that rock over there," he pointed at the huge chunk of stone sitting almost a 3 meters away from the contraption.

The thing looked dangerous, so for her dear life, she did what was told.

"You ready?" Daniel glanced at her as he held the match.

"Sure."

He smiled, biting his lip in excitement as he lit the thing. He ran to where Scar was and they both waited for the so-called 'boom.'

And when it happened, it was the most beautiful thing she've ever seen.

Lights, colorful sparks, invaded the once dark and quiet basement. The loud booms felt like music to her ears as she watched the scene in awe. No one has ever given her something this beautiful. Her eyes didn't know where to watch. Blue, red, yellow, golden rings appeared everywhere.

She glanced at Daniel to thank him, but she wasn't able to utter a word. She just sat there, looking at the young prince who worked so hard on this for her. If Daniel looked at her right now, he would've melted.

The softest eyes Scarlett de Beville had ever given was right there in that moment.

As if magically, the general's daughter felt it for the first time- a heartbeat. Not the heartbeat that keeps you alive, not the one you feel all the time.

It was different.

It was new.

It was warm.

The young girl was confused, asking herself what on earth was she feeling in the middle of the spectacle. But as she looked at Daniel, it all faded into black as his face colored her mind like a crayon- The face of the boy who almost did everything for her like it's no else's business.

But these warm and childish thoughts were interrupted, "Look out!"

"What?"

The next thing she knew, an explosion took place and they were on the ground. She closed her eyes as he felt Daniel's arms in her back, protecting it.

"You alright?" He asked in concern.

"Yeah." She stood up, dusting the dirt of her skirt.

She helped Daniel up. As soon as he was up, he snickered. The two had black smudges on their faces and their hair looked like a porcupine's body.

Daniel then changed his gaze from Scarlett to his destroyed con- traption, "Aww. It broke." He went to it and picked up some of the debris.

"I'm sorry, Scar. I destroyed your birthday."

Scar shook her head vigorously to emphasize her disagreement, "What? Of course you didn't. If anything you made it special."

His eyes lit up, "R-really?"

"Yeah."

The two stared at each other for a while, laughed, then wiped the smudges off their face.

"Who's there?" A manly voice sounded.

"That's our cue." Daniel uttered, taking Scar's hand as they went to the exit.

They kept running until they reached the outer courts. They stopped in a corner among the big columns of the castle. They tried to catch their breaths as they leaned against the wall.

Scarlett then took notice of the big clock and noticed that it was already past midnight.

"Midnight?" She repeated.

"Happy birthday." She felt a whisper on her ear. She looked behind her and found Daniel smiling at her with his brightest grin whilst holding what seemed to be flowers.

Scarlett, utterly touched, brought a hand to her chest and spoke, "You waited till midnight? You waited till my birthday?"

He took a step closer to her, "I'm always on your birthday, aren't I? I will always be the first one to greet you. I will always be the first one to give you your gift. Remember that. You can always count on it. If there's one person in this world who would remember this special day before anyone could ever think about it, it's me." Then he winked and gave her the flower.

"But you said-"

"I only meant your birthday party. But seriously, why would you think that I'd really miss your birthday? I'm not that kind of friend. I even have your birthday marked on my schedule for the next 20 years," he smirked.

She knows it's a joke...or a metaphor, more or less, that he would never forget her birthday. As if a 10 year old prankster would keep a schedule, right? Still, despite knowing this, she blushed and all, counting on his words.

She has never held on to something so tightly before, until this boy came, promising her -no- swearing to her that there would always be someone to remember her.

"Oh Daniel..."

"Well, you know me. As long as it's you," he shrugged.

Scarlett felt it again- the heartbeat. She felt it again, this time faster. Her cheeks flared, warming her body up despite the cold.

"Let's go home."

The two walked together towards the east wing. But Scarlett stopped for a while, leaving a short distance between her and Daniel.

The prince looked behind him, "What's wrong?"

Scarlett bit her lip, looked at Daniel in the most endearing way, and ran towards him.

"Scar?"

But before he could even take a step, the next thing he knew, a soft kiss was implanted on his cheek as Scarlett leaped in the air to level with his face.

His eyes widened.

His face turned as red as a tomato.

He held his kissed cheek as he looked at his bestfriend.

Scarlett didn't look back, instead she ran towards the defense hall and hid behind the doors.

"Why did I even do that?" she thought to her self as she blushed, and blushed some more.

She looked at the window and saw Daniel still standing on where he was when she kissed her. She smiled gracefully, touching her lips.

Daniel, on the other hand, was still unable to move, and the redness in his cheeks was still present as if it turned permanent.

Scar smiled to herself and muttered, "Thank you, Daniel."

Then she flew to her room, plopped on the bed, and snuggled. She will be having happy dreams indeed, but not as much as the other one though.

(End of Flashback)

Things have changed since those times. I was so young and soft back then.

Yeah, yeah. I may be strong and fearsome, but I'm not all that made of stone. I still have a heart. I can still feel emotions every girl feels. I still like sweet things, I wear dresses if needed and all that fluff. And to my dismay, yes, I could still like a boy. After all, I am a girl.

The memory made me warm inside. I can't believe that it's been that long. Obviously, things have changed now. Most of them at least.

One day, it all just turned this way. Me, always angry and hunting for that guy, and him, always running for his life. But I still could never forget those days, when it wasn't all like this.

I didn't meant for it to be like this between us. It was his fault. It was that stupid prince's fault. Ever since 'that' happened, I never found it in my heart to forgive him. I was utterly hurt because of what he did.

I thought that I could live hating him and chasing him away from my life. But it wasn't as easy as it first seemed. No matter how hard I tried, it always came back to me.

The feelings.

The heartbeat.

My feelings....for that stupid guy.

Fine, given that it's already out, I'll admit it. I had a crush on him back then. And that stupid thing from my childhood is still haunting me up to this day.

Putting up a tough girl act would never be easy, especially around that moron.

But, I'm sure I'll manage. I won't let him get to me again.

"Open up!"

"Yes, Miss Scarlett."

The guards opened the heavy basement door for me and the prisoner. I dragged him an place him inside the cell where the other bastard was.

"Hey. Brought you some company," I said as I threw the guy to his side.

"Y-you..." His eyes widened as he looked at his caught partner, "You were caught."

"Obviously," I rolled my eyes. I locked the door myself. I turned towards the exit, but I my steps were put to a halt when I heard a loud bang on the cell bars.

I turned around once more and I saw the first spy crying out, "Please, just kill us now! Please, I'm begging you! Let us out of here. Please just take us away!" He was crying out so loud, as if he was really scared. He was crying too. His partner was sobbing beside him. His lips were quivering.

"What the heck is going on?" I muttered as I went back to them.

The first spy took hold of the bars. He slipped his hand through it and held my feet, "Please, ma'am! Kill us now. Please don't let them know that we've failed! I'm begging you, just kill us right now."

I knelt down to level with him. I looked at him in a mocking way, "Well, well. You're one to talk big and threaten us using your kingdom's metaphorical power," I sniggered as I repeated his words, "Kill us now? Are you serious?"

He held his hands together as if begging for mercy, "Yes, madam. Just take our life away, right here, right now. Let the country we've sinned against be our grave. I'm begging you."

What the hell is wrong with them? For a minute or so, they looked proud, confident even, about their kingdom's power. Now, after a failed mission, they're cowering like hens?

Does something happen to failed spies in that kingdom?

But, like I should care. They planned to destroy Sorah. Not even Aspen would show mercy for that. Nor will I.

I looked at them straight in the eye, trying to look dead serious, "For what you did to Sorah...suffer."

I got up and left them immediately. As the guards bar the door behind me, I heard them cry out the same words over and over again. I picked up my feet and started walking but they just kept getting louder.

Sure, they're our enemies. But, I'm not that deaf when it comes to people's fears. I may be somewhat strict and vicious, but I have a little bit of mercy and consideration in my system too, of course. I'd be a monster without em.

Their fears sounded real and they looked really terrified. Really terrified. Is their king gonna eat them or somethin'.

Whatever it is that they're afraid of, they've bought it upon themselves by messing with Sorah.

I shouldn't be listening to people like them.

"Please help us!"

I shouldn't care.

Aspen

Daniel came running to me. I was watching over Isabelle while she was sleeping, holding her hand, when he came in.

"You caught him?" I stood up from my chair.

"Yes. Scar already brought him to the dungeon." Daniel affirmed.

"I'll be there immediately," I nodded, clenching my fists.

Finally. I'm gonna make them pay for what they did to Isabelle. They'll pay for it tenfold.

After Daniel went out, I bent down to level with Isabelle's face. Despite the burns and bruises, she still looked her. She looked so peaceful and beautiful. If only she could've stayed like that.

But, no. She couldn't because I needed to drag her into this mess. Some friend I am, making her life miserable. Only God knows how much I'm hating myself for that.

"I'll be right back, Isabelle., I whispered on her ear. She stirred after I said that, making me smile a bit. Did she hear me?

I called in my nurse to watch over her, "Please keep an eye on her for me."

"Yes, your majesty."

I shook my head, took my coat, and went on my way. I passed the room where Isabelle's parents were being treated. I should go and see if they're doing alright.

I hope they wake up soon....but not yet. I'm still not ready to face them after what they went through because of me. I sighed deeply before I opened the door to their room. I then saw Isabelle's mother, sleeping peacefully in her bed. Some nurses were treating her wounds.

I closed the door behind me as I entered the room. The nurses stood up and greeted me. I nodded at them and they continued their work.

I walked over to the bed where Isabelle's father was being treated. "Mr. Almere?"

As I drew the white curtains away ,my eyes widened.

He's gone.

I faced one of the nurses, "Excuse me?"

The nurse quickly stood up, "Yes, sire?"

"Where's Mr. Almere?"

She replied with her head down, "He's at the veranda, king Aspen."

I placed a hand on my chest to calm myself, "H-he's awake?"

"Yes."

He's awake?!

He's figured it out already. I'm sure of it. What would he do? What would he do to Isabelle? What if he's furious?

"You can do this, Aspen. You said that you'd take responsibility for this. You got this," I tried to calm myself.

I promised Isabelle that I'd help her with this, that she won't be alone when this comes. I have to do this for her.

With shaky footsteps, I walked towards the veranda. I clenched my fists as I inhaled every air in my wake.

I took one small step more, then there I was, staring at the back of Isabelle's father.

I gulped an cleared my throat nervously, "Mr. Almere?"

He turned around, but he didn't look at me in the eye. Instead, he immediately turned to a bow.

"Your majesty."

"Please," I quickly took a step, "It's alright. You don't have to do that sir....after all I've done."

He finally faced me, looking at me straight in the eye, "Still, you're the king. I still have to pay my respects."

He bowed once more, then stood up after.

I sighed, preparing my words even though I didn't know what to say, "Mr. Almere, I can explain." I bowed.

What the heck am I supposed to say?!

I heard light footsteps walking away from me. I looked up and saw Mr. Almere's back facing me. He was looking afar with his hands folded behind his back.

"I'm not resenting you or anything, your majesty, if that's what you're wondering. I don't know everything that's going on, but I know just about enough."

I bowed once more, "Mr. Almere. I apologize. I never meant to drag your daughter into this, so please don't resent Isabelle. This is all my fault."

He faced me and spoke, "I don't feel any resentment towards my own daughter. I am a little bit disappointed, though. And she knows that."

"Believe me, sir. She didn't want this. Many times during our quest, she wanted to go back home because she didn't want to lie to you anymore. But, I was the one who kept needing her. I was the one who kept her from leaving."

He sighed, "Typical Isabelle." He chuckled, "I know that you know by now how special my daughter is."

I smiled, "Yes. She is unlike anyone I've ever met. She's smart and brilliant. That was why I kept needing her. She was the only one who could solve our problems."

"I see," He nodded.

I took a step towards him, "Sir, you may not know this. But, you're daughter saved Sorah. We were in the middle of a crisis, but she stopped all of it. It's because of her that we're still alive. I couldn't have done it without her."

"She is indeed a very brilliant girl."

"Yes, sir."

But then, his face turned stern and serious, "That's why her life is danger."

I closed my eyes, swallowing a lump in my throat. It was true. Because I kept needing Isabelle's skills, she got in trouble. Her family barely survived the fire.

"Mr. Almere..."

He folded his hands and shook his head, "This is the reason why I kept Isabelle from meeting people like you, king Aspen, from people with great, dangerous powers. Isabelle possesses almost the same skills and prodigies as you people, maybe even more advanced than what you have. That's why, without a doubt, it would only take a mere contact with you, with the nobles, with the royals, for her to put herself in danger. Take what's happened for example."

"I-I understand," I nodded. I never thought of it that way. Ever since I got to know Isabelle, I've always regarded her as a brilliant woman. I thought that any kingdom would prosper if they had someone like her in their realm. She becomes indispensable to the ones she meet.

I never thought that such brilliance would endanger her life like this. I understand Mr. Almere now. If I am to be in his place, I would do the same thing.

"The thing is, Your majesty, Isabelle isn't really aware of that," he shook his head.

"What do you mean, sir?", I asked.

He sighed and turned his back away once more, "Our fears are her dreams. We fear that she would go too far to pursue her learning and put herself in danger. Her dream is to pursue her learning even though it would mean risking her life. That's the way my daughter is."

"Indeed," I chuckled lightly so that he wouldn't notice.

"She was trying to balance her dreams and our dreams for her. We just want her to be able to live a peaceful and normal life." He faced me again.

"Mr. Almere, if you would allow it, I would like all of you to live in the palace. " I proposed suddenly. When I heard something between the lines of Isabelle's life and safety, I couldn't think of any other way. It's the only choice wherein I can protect her and watch over her family.

"King Aspen...."

I bowed, "Please. I'll do everything to protect Isabelle and your family. You'd be safe here. We still don't know what kinds of danger are waiting out there. In this palace, we could keep her safe from all of that. Please, let me protect her."

He shook his head and sighed," Your majesty, I'm afraid I can't-"

I clenched my fists in desperation," Please. Your daughter is very important to me. She has become one of my dearest friends, one of all the people I can't afford to lose. You don't know how much I'm willing to risk to protect her. So, please, live here."

He sighed heavily and went into the room. He sat down chair before his bed. I followed him and sat on the chair opposite his.

"Mr. Almere..."

"Do what you must do," he said sternly.

"W-what?"

He put his hands on the table between us, "King Aspen, can't you see? As long as Isabelle is here, she can never be safe, especially after what's happened. Now, you're asking that she live in the palace so that you may protect her?"

"Well, I-"

"Not even the palace will be a sanctuary for my daughter. Admit it to yourself, your highness. You can't watch over my daughter all the time. You're the king of Sorah, not her guardian."

I swallowed a huge lump in my throat, "But I'm her friend, a friend who is completely powerful and capable of protecting her. Am I not suppose to do anything?"

"That's not the point, your grace." He looked down, "In fact, you've already been doing too much for a friend. You're starting to value your connection to her more, am I correct?"

"It's not like that, Mr. Almere."

Then he asked me firmly, "Will you be able to give your time protecting the kingdom to protect her? Will you be able to watch her over your own kingdom? Will you be able to assure me that you would always be there for her?"

"I-"

"Always?"

And I wasn't able to speak. He rendered me speechless.

He sighed, "If your answer is yes, then your kingship would be in peril. If your answer is no, then her safety is not assured, even under the king's wings. See, your highness? As long as she's here, as long as we're here, it's not only her who's gonna get in trouble, but also you. If people will be trying to hurt my daughter, they'll also hurt you. And, if people would try to hurt you, what becomes of Isabelle?

I sighed. He had a point, an undeniable point.

The only thing on my mind was how to protect Isabelle. She was very important to me. Sacrificing my time as king never crossed my mind, when in reality, I might have to because I want to keep Isabelle safe with me.

Does he mean that we won't be safe...as long as we're together?

"The king's friend." He chuckled, "How many people would kill for that kind of position?"

"I never thought about it," I admitted. I felt so normal around Isabelle, not a care in the world. I even sometimes forget that I'm king.

"Well, you better start thinking about it, King Aspen, because it's going to matter a lot." He cleared his throat.

What am I supposed to do? Above all, I just want to protect Isabelle. I just want things like this to never happen again for her to live a normal life. Her safety. That's what matters to me right now. I don't want her hurt. I don't want her suffering. I don't want her enduring these anymore. To know she'd be secure. That's what I want. That's what I should think about.

But, above all, also, I want her to be by our side, to be friends with her.

Well, hell. Because that's gonna put her in danger.

So, what do I do?

"Mr. Almere, I just want Isabelle safe," I stated.

"We all do, sire."

I looked up to him, "Then what shall we do?"

He stood up from the chair, looking down, "You said that you still needed her. I'm not gonna deny you my daughter especially now that you say the kingdom's in trouble. Do what you must do..."

I felt uneasy. My heart pounded wildly inside me. It felt like something was about to go down.

"But after that..."

My jaw dropped in shock, and so did my heart. I clenched my fist in mixed negative feelings. I felt angry, and regretful. I tried my best not to lose myself in front of Isabelle's father.

But I was on the verge of failing.

"No," my lips quivered as he stated his condition.

"We'll be leaving Sorah....for good."

20

CHAPTER 20

Isabelle

The first thing I felt was pain down my midsection. Pictures of flames and a glimpse of Aspen's face flashed in my mind.

Oh. That's right. Our house burned down. Aspen saved us and took us to the-

"Aw damn."

Red carpets, a big room, soft blankets, complete medicals?

"I'm not in an infirmary, am I?" I swallowed.

I looked around. This place seemed familiar and unfamiliar. It looked so regal like it was...that it almost looked like...

"The palace."

I'm in the palace. This is no normal infirmary. I'm in the royal infirmary. If I could recall what happened last night (unfortunately I can because unfortunately, I didn't suffer memory loss, which is my wish and unfortunately, it didn't come true) Aspen brought me and my family in a large cart.

That means...my parents must be here too, in the palace. We're all in the palace!

"Great. What a convenient place to die." I said as thought about my parents who will be finding about my trouble-causing circumstances, which I dragged them into even if they told me so, soon enough

I stood up, feeling my headache. How severe were my injuries anyway?

I checked my midsection and there were bandages around it. Wait. That's right. A shattered glass almost pierced my stomach.

I groaned, standing up. I have to get out of here and find my parents, prepared to face them or not.

I slowly made my way towards the door, my hand on my stomach. I reached the doorknob, but someone stopped me.

"Miss Isabelle, you have to rest. You still can't get up yet."

I looked down then back at the nurse in a satirical way, trying point out my standing form, "I can. I just did."

The, I think 40 years older than me, nurse looked at me in concern, "What I mean, miss, is that you've been out for 3 days. Your injuries are no joke and-"

"3 days?"

She took a step back, "You didn't know, miss?"

I deadpanned , "I was asleep."

She laughed lightly, "O-oh. Yes, of course."

Three days. I've been out for three days! What has happened since then? I can't believe I missed so much.

I shook my head to clear my thoughts,"Nurse, if you don't mind, I would like to see my parents." I said, my hand already on the doorknob.

She forcefully placed a hand on the door, "But miss Isabelle, king Aspen asked me to take care of you." Her voice alarmed.

"Aspen?"

3 days? Aspen must also be worried sick. He saved us. For sure, he's injured too.

"I'm Rosita. I was just assigned to you about half an hour ago." She smiled, "I was your first nurse."

"First nurse?" I've been out for three days. She was just assigned to me moments before. Then, those 3 days before, no nurse took care of me?

"I know what you're thinking, miss." She chuckled, "And it's not it. Someone took care of you."

"Another nurse then?" I asked, my hand slipping slowly from the knobs.

"No. It was his majesty who took care of you." She smiled.

My eyes widened, "Aspen...took care of me?"

No way...

Needless to say...I was shocked, as well as speechless. I almost stumbled upon knowing.

I couldn't believe it. The king of Sorah took care of me personally. God, I felt like a burden, a flattered burden.

Yes, I am his friend, but for a king like him to take care of someone like me?

Who am I?

If that's the case...then is he also the one who treated my wounds?

I brought my two hands up to my closely red face, "My wounds are almost everywhere."

Oh dear donkey. What did he see exactly?! What parts did he cover up with bandages?

I tried to scan my own body, feeling my arms, my stomach, and my legs, when the nurse interrupted.

"I've been taking care of the king ever since he was young. I was his personal nurse, you see. I was very close to him. Most of the time, he'd ask me things about medicine so when the time comes, and I wasn't there, he'd know what to do." The nurse suddenly pointed out.

"I see." I nodded.

She shook her head and chuckled lightly, "You don't understand, my dear. I'm the king's personal nurse. That means I am only for the king and I am under his majesty's command. And, he has never treated anyone besides himself. But here I am, assigned to you, miss. And there he was, treating you."

Then, like a stone boulder to me head, realization hit me, "Oh." And that was all I had to say for myself.

She nodded at my words, "You don't realize how special you are, dear. My boy has never done this for anyone. And if anything, you are my first patient in this royal palace, besides Aspen that is."

I found myself stuttering at her words, "I-I'm just a friend, nurse."

"Really?" She smirked.

I nodded, "I'm really just his majesty's friend, nurse Rosita."

"Well," She added, "I've never done this for miss Scarlett or the prince, and they too are his friends."

I forced a laugh, "I'm sure they get injured rarely."

"Yeah, with all those guarding duty and training, I'm sure they've gained no bumps or bruises." She raised her brows.

"Nurse..." I forced a smile in my discomfort, implying that she should stop. I tried my best to hide my redness that's practically spreading all over my face.

She raised her hands, indicating that she's stopping, "Okay. Sorry dear, that was my last." She chuckled, "I'm a nurse, yet I'm making you uncomfortable."

"It's fine. " I lied, feeling my knees weaken a bit, making me stumble.

"Are you alright, dear?", she asked, taking a hold on my waist.

"Y-yes."

What on earth is happening to me? Why does hearing what Aspen has done for me...make me so...

Weak and fluttery all over.

"You know, his majesty-"

"Agh." I stumbled again, but she held me so I wouldn't fall.

I lift up my head, only to come face to face with a knowing smirk on her lips, "I see."

I blushed, "What? What do you 'see'?

"Nothing.", she looked away to look at nothing and muttered, "This is gonna be good."

"What's gonna be good, nurse?" I asked her.

"Oh, it's nothing." She cleared her throat and smiled like nothing happened, "Anyway, if you need anything, just tell me, dear."

I nodded and turned my gaze towards the door, then back at her, "Can I see my parents?"

"Very well." She entwined her arm with my left arm as I used the other to hold my stomach to ease the possible pain as we walk.

"Let's go."

She opened the door and we walked past the main halls slowly. I bit my lip, flinching with every step, but it was bearable. The royal infirmary sure is big. It's almost the same size as the village hospital, but it's rarely used.

Not a moment too soon, we reached a room where I believe my parents were since I asked to be brought to them, and now I'm here.

I put my left hand on one of the door posts, slipping from nurse Rosita's hold. Her hand found it's way to my back, "Are you going to be alright?"

I smiled, "Yes, nurse. I can take it from here."

She nodded in response as she folded her hands, "Okay. If you need me, I'll be waiting for you outside the room."

"Thank you." I whispered as I held the door. I turned the handles, lightly pushing it open. I took a peek, being cautious before I really come in.

Seeing that the coast was clear, that being my mom was still asleep, I went inside. A few medics were still with her and were treating her.

One nurse stoop up and bowed, "You must be miss Isabelle. We're very sorry. Your mother's still recovering."

I put my hands up, "No. Please don't be sorry. If anything, I should be thanking you for making her feel better. Thank you."

She looked up, as well as the other nurses, surprised. They all stopped to look at me. They gave me a light genuine smile before going back to what they were doing.

My lips pursed in confusion. Why do I get the feeling that...it was their first time being thanked? Being appreciated? I mean, yeah, they're nurses and it's their job, so gratitude isn't necessary. But still, they've done so much. Everyone deserves to be appreciated. If anything, especially them.

So for all the people they've helped, they got no thanks.

"We're sorry, miss. Uhh- I mean... You're welcome." She stuttered, bowing her head lower than before.

"What's wrong?"

She bowed lower, "Well-"

I cut her off, "Please don't do that." I said calmly, referring to her bowing, "I'm no royal or noble. I may be your patient by the king's orders but I'm just like all of you. Respect shown once is enough."

She looked up to me.

I chuckled, "Come on. All the way up with your back straight. You're a girl, you must maintain your posture. It's essential for us." I winked.

She smiled, "Yes." Then she did what I told her to do.

"That's better." I took a glimpse at the other nurses who were smiling as well.

I took notice of the other bed beside my mom's. The curtains weren't drawn back. This must be where my father is. I pulled back the curtains, only to see that it was empty.

Was he in another room?

Oh no. Please don't tell me....

"Your father's awake. He's in the balcony."

I hate this life!

I gulped as I faced the balcony, "Thank you."

With my fists clenched and my lips quivering, I walked forward with shaky steps. The sunlight was shining on my eyes, depraving me of a clear view, but I could see his back facing me.

As I was a foot away from him, my fists clenched tighter in anxiety. I gagged with huge lumps going down my throat, and that's not just one lump... huge lumps!

I'm sweating. I'm sweating like a sinner in church! This is gonna be the end of me. He knows now, and I didn't even tell him.

I should've told them earlier, so that it shouldn't have come to this point where our house had to be destroyed first, and we had to be taken to the infirmary.

Why does my dad have to find out like this? Can this life of mine get any miserable?

"D-dad? It's me." I uttered the moment I got close enough. My heart fell as I saw some bandages wrapped around his arms and legs. He looked hurt.

This was all my fault. I'm such a bad daughter.

His back straightened when he heard my voice, but he still didn't face me. Seeing that he doesn't plan to, I turned to face him. I went around him so that I would see the well-deserved and expected look of disappointment on his face.

I bowed down in dismay. I was facing him, but I was unable to look at him in the eye. Who would have to guts to in my place?

"Isabelle." He acknowledged my presence, making me step back a bit.

After that, no words came out of our mouths for a few seconds. Silence completely dominated those few seconds.

But not being able to take the increasing tension anymore, I quickly knelt down, "F-father...I don't know where to start." I trailed off. I could feel my eyes starting to water.

He breathed heavily, once, twice, before making my heart almost explode by the words I've been preparing for ever since this whole thing started, "Why?"

"Well, I-"

I didn't look, but I felt his eyes on me, stern and intense, "We trusted you, Isa."

I sighed in disappointment over what I did, "I know. I should've known better."

"Likewise," he scoffed, "I shouldn't have let you go to that academy, I shouldn't have let you leave the house, if only I knew."

My hands curled into trembling fists at his every heavy word, "I'm sorry, father. I never wanted this to happen."

"No one did." He added. His voice was still as cold as his expression, "I just thought that you were wise enough to think about your actions."

"Father, I didn't-"

But he cut me off when he dropped something in front of me, sliding it so that I could see it clearly with my head down.

I gasped as I saw it. My eyes turned as big as salad plates as I took notice of what was in front of me.

"My lady investigator uniform."

It's the purple one that I first obtained when I signed up to be a temporary investigator.

Dad. He had it all along. Could it mean that...he knew?

I looked up to him, "You knew?"

My heart skipped a beat when he answered me with a firm nod.

I touched the uniform, speaking as I did so, "Why didn't you stop me?"

He gave a shrug before turning his head to look at nowhere, "I know you'd be able to discern what's right for you. That's why I let you go. I hid it from your mother, though."

"So, when I lied about going to the library..."

"I already knew back then." He said, looking back at me.

I tightened my hold on the uniform, consumed by my guilt, "Father, I'm so sorry."

He closed his eyes for a moment, heaving a sigh, "Isabelle, we have forbidden you to be involved with these affairs for a reaso n."-he stated before muttering what I thought sounded like- "even though it was very hard because of how you are. You joining the noble's academy was one of the hardest decisions I had to make, and it burdened me everyday to see you go. I know that you know why. And now, this?!"

I understand why they're forbidding me to have connections with people like Scar, Daniel, and Aspen. I know that all too well, and I don't like being reminded.

I swallowed a lump as big as a camel hump before speaking, "I know, dad. I'm sorry. I just couldn't help myself, but be-"

"I know." He shook his head. His voice as firm as a stone, "That's why I knew that it wouldn't be very long until the rule we gave would be broken."

I shook my head lightly, clenching my fists at the ground close to my knees, "Now, I fully understand....why you told me not to be involved in these. It's very dangerous and, well, bloody, just like you said, but I was too hard-headed."

"I told you." He said, "But, I heard about what you did for Sorah, and I'm proud of you."

I suddenly looked up, "You talked to Aspen?"

"The king? Yes." He nodded.

"Oh." I bowed my head once more.

He chuckled, "Using your prowess at these kind of things, this is what you've always wanted, isn't it?"

"Well, I-"

"Don't speak. I know that all too well."-He touched his beard-"You've always had that wild fire in you. I've always known that my rule would never be able to contain it."

"Dad..." I groaned.

"Well, here you are. You've saved Sorah, but what about yourself, Isa?" He said.

I sighed and closed my eyes, "I-I don't know. All I thought about was how I could help them. I didn't think that anything could've happened to me at that moment."

He shook his head, "What's done is done. There's no changing that now."

This time, I stood up, "But, father, what about the house, and the farm?"

God, that was our life. How are we supposed to live now? This is all my fault. This is what dad warned me about. But, being the rebel that I am, I still went on with it.

This time, he was the one who stood up, standing a head taller than me, "Remember, back at the fire, when you were about to be crushed by that huge piece of flaming lumber?"

"When I was about to die?"-I managed to crack a grin-"Yes. I remember that."

He put his hands on my shoulders, "I thought that I was going to lose you. During those moments, I didn't think about the house, or the fire, or the farm. I thought about you, you and your mother."

"Dad." I whispered in sympathy. Have I always worried him this much? It's unbearable to watch, even for me.

"The house and the farm would be easy enough. A lot of the farm was still left, and we can rebuild the house." He took his hands off my shoulders and turned.

I lit up, "So, we're gonna go back?"

"However"- he cut off- "We can never guarantee your safety, our safety. Not in here. Not in Sorah. Not anymore."

I took a step back, surprised by his words, "W-what do you mean? Are you saying that we-"

"I already told the king, Isabelle." -He folded his hands behind his back as he faced me- But, it seemed that you are still needed so-"

I balled my hands into fists, "Dad, no."

"-after that-"

"Dad, please.."

"- we are leaving Sorah-"

"Dad!"

With the firmest tone I ever heard from him, he said the words, "For good."

I forcefully slammed my hands on my sides, "I don't want to. Sorah is my home. My friends are here."

"Isabelle-"

"No!" I knelt down in front of him and pleaded with my voice breaking, "Dad, please. Let's stay. I promise that I'll do anything you say from now on. I'd even stop studying if that's what you want. I'll stay at home for good."

"Then what?!" He exclaimed, "Even if you do those things, you cannot erase what you've already done. And those consequences will never stop chasing you because of what you did...as long as you're in Sorah."

"Dad!"

"Do you think I'm doing this only for you?"

I looked up at him as he went to the room, sliding the curtains away to reveal my resting mother, with bandages all over her.

"It's not only you who's gonna get hurt, but also the people who worries about you, and the people you worry about. They're all connected to you. This family, or even your friends could get hurt." He said.

"As long as I'm here? Is that it?" I gritted between my teeth, trying to prevent my tears from falling.

"I know you'll understand." He held my arms to help me stand up.

My knees felt weak for a second and I was unable to look at him.

Leave Sorah...for good?

How did measures become this desperate? Do we really have to leave?

I don't want to. I want to stay here for the rest of my life. This is my country, this is my home. Even if it's for my safety, to leave is just...

"Isabelle, you need to do this."

...it's too hard.

"But," -I met his eyes, crying as I wasn't able to control my tears anymore- "It's so unfair!"

I quickly escaped his clutches and ran. The next thing I knew, I was running out the door, out the palace and away from everything.

No.

I don't wanna leave.

Ever.

21

CHAPTER 21

Isabelle

"It's all gone."

After 'escaping' the royal infirmary, I found myself standing in front of our house. Well, what's left of it, or what used to be our house.

Everything was either black or gray. Exactly what I'm feeling right now.

My room, our kitchen, our farm, it's all still vivid in my mind. Now, I can't even recognize it. Not even our staircases and doorposts made it. It's all burned to the ground, pounded into ashes.

I sighed, scooping up a pile of ashes and letting it go like dust in the wind, "How did it happen so fast?"

I dropped to the ground, unable to take the sight. I felt so weak, having nothing left. This house was a piece of me, now it's gone.

Now, I'm leaving Sorah. I don't know what's gonna be left of me after that. I lost my house, will I also be losing my home?

"I-it's so..." I sobbed, my face buried in my palms.

Why me?

I never wanted any of this. All I wanted to do was learn, study, live like any other ordinary human being, be with the ones I love, especially. What did I do to the world the made me deserve this?

I don't know what to do. I want to stay, but after everything, it's starting to be a pain to stay. And I hate that feeling.

I don't wanna leave, but I want to escape.

"Isabelle!"

I turned around at the shout of my name. Passing by the trees was Aspen, galloping on a horse.

I met his eyes, along with the much worried look on his face. I couldn't stand to greet him and run to him. I couldn't move at all.

When his horse stopped moving, he stepped down and ran to me. He stopped just a feet away from me, looking at me with the most pained eyes, whereas I was looking him with tears running down my cheeks.

"Aspen.." I uttered.

"You're awake." He gave a sigh of relief and knelt down to level with me, "How are you feeling?"

I felt his arms suddenly embrace me in a short, tight hug.

I smiled lightly at him, "Well physically, I'm better. But, I'm not really as well."

"I'm sorry." He said, "I couldn't do anything."

"Shhh." I put a finger on his lips, "It's okay. You weren't supposed to. Stop acting like everything's your fault, Aspen. We wouldn't even be here if it wasn't for you."

"But still, I-"

"Agh..." I fake-grunted in pain as I held my midsection. I wasn't really in pain per se.

"Isabelle!? Are you hurt?!" He quickly exclaimed, examining me.

"Nah. I'm just messing with you. Really just wanted you to shut up." I smirked, letting go of my stomach.

He glared at me and shook his head, "You had me worried."

"At least you're not blaming yourself now." Another smirk played on my lips.

"Sorry bout that." He scratched the back of his head, "I just really-"

I stopped him before he could say another stupid speech, "Say another word. This time I'll play dead and never wake up."

Finally, he shut his mouth. But, it later formed into a smile, then into hysterical laughs.

Unconsciously, I started laughing too. Guess, it's contagious. Good thing there's no one around to laugh back at us.

"I really missed you Isabelle." He uttered as he stopped laughing.

As my reply, I just smiled and stared at him in silence.

"Everyday, I hoped you'd awaken. I'd always wait for you to open your eyes."-He gave a smile- "I was so afraid to lose my friend."

I chuckled inwardly. I'd say. You even took care of me, king Aspen.

I caressed his right cheek, " Thank you for everything. I'm here now, okay."

"But you won't be soon." His eyes turned cold and hurt, replacing the worried look on his face before.

That's right. Dad already talked to him about us leaving Sorah.

"Aspen, I-"

"Your father said that it was for your safety."

I looked away, "I won't leave still. Leaving Sorah is not an answer."

Then, out of nowhere, I felt it again- his arms around me, this time tighter than before that I couldn't breathe, but not because of the embrace but because of my heart, which was beating too fast it's starting to get abnormal.

I looked down, unable to utter a word, and rendered speechless.

I started crying, and with every sob, his hug got tighter and warmer.

This time, I hugged him back with the rest of my arms that weren't trapped in his embrace.

All I could think about, all we could think about, was me leaving. It was painful even at the thought.

The time I disobeyed my parents, bad things happened. This time, I had to obey them, but I fear that nothing good is gonna come right after. I fear that things might turn out for the worse instead.

I'll be miserable.

I'll be missing my friends. I'll be missing the farm. I'll be missing the village and those friendly people. I'll be missing everything.

"And I'll be missing...you." I whispered while I was in thought.

"No!" He tightened his embrace, then he let go. He held my shoulders and looked at me sternly.

"If there's one thing I'm not prepared to lose, it's you." He said firmly using a very husky and serious tone.

And somehow, with what he said, I felt brave and relieved. I just don't know if this bravery is enough to defy my parents' orders, and follow my heart.

He faced me, "Now, I don't want you to get in any trouble with your parents again. I just need your help with this last case."

I nodded, "I understand. But what about my father?"

"He told me that I could still use your help."

"But after that I-"

He cut me off, without missing a beat, "There's no way I'm letting you go, Isabelle."

I looked up to him. My heart raced with every assured word. If Aspen is holding on, then I will to. I won't let go. I don't wanna leave. After this case is solved, I'm gonna make sure, just like Aspen's going to, that I stay here...at my home.

He hugged me once again, "I won't let you go. Not ever. I'll fight for you."

"Don't do it physically, okay." I chuckled.

He held my shoulders and looked at me incredulously- "Of course I won't."- only to hug me again.

I put my arms around him, "I don't plan to. I won't go. I'll do my best to stay."

"I'll help you with that, Belle." He chuckled.

"You haven't used that name in a while." I smiled, "I kinda missed it."

"Then I'll use it more often." He replied.

"If you wish." I laughed, "Thank you for making me feel better despite the tragedy I faced."

He tilted his head, breaking the embrace. He helped stand up before he spoke.

"About that, I thought you might want to meet who caused it."

"Someone caused it?"

Well, I believe in proper introductions. And as they say ,'Make a good impression.'

And I ought to give that bastard a hell of a good impression.

"Where's that scumbag?"

Scarlett

"You're awake!" I quickly jumped on Isabelle as I hugged her into oblivion, "I was worried sick about you."

She chuckled as I practically crush her in my arms, "Hey Scarle
tt."-she hugged me back- "Wow, looks like I've been getting a lot of
free hugs lately."

"Wait. What?"-I tilted my head- "but you just woke up."

"Well..." Both Aspen and Isabelle suddenly trailed off. And are
those blush on their faces?

I looked at Isabelle, than I examined Aspen, then I almost lost my
head glancing back and forth at the two as their eyes hurt looking
at each other.

I pointed at them, "Did you two-"

"Scarlett." -An idiot, namely Daniel, suddenly held my shoul-
ders-"Let's just take it easy on them."

dug dug

Damn this.

His voice was so calm and easy as he spoke. He sounded serious
and dominant when he spoke like that. It felt...strange. But what's
more strange, is that me, the stone-hearted daughter of a general,
totally obeyed.

Well, not 'totally' per se.

"F-fine!"- I took his hands off my shoulders, looking away- "You
don't have to tell me." I grumped towards the table to get the keys.

Stupid prince, making me feel all different...and warm...and
- WHAT ON EARTH AM I THINKING?!

"Daniel." Isabelle greeted.

He jumped up and down, about to greet Isa 'happily', "Isabelle!
You're alive!"

But before he could even land on Isa, Aspen palmed his face,
"Of course she's alive, idiot. Now, give her some space." Then he
forcefully pushed him away using the same palm on his face.

"Oww." He touched his face.

Meanwhile, I was enjoying the show. For once I was enjoying their company.

"Hit him more, Aspen." I really wanted to say that if I wasn't too busy looking for the keys.

"Putting that aside,"- Aspen started, snarling at Daniel,- "Scarlett, Isa would want to meet the-"

"Where are they!?" Isa suddenly grabbed a sword out of nowhere and charged towards the basement door.

Luckily, Aspen was able to take a hold of her by holding her waist, "Woah. Easy, Isabelle. That's the basement door. Scar's gonna take us to em."

"Wow, she can be as mad as you, Scar." Daniel uttered in bewilderment.

I finally pulled out the keys, "Isabelle, you make us girls proud."

"Only you." -Daniel muttered under his breath, but I heard him anyway- "Most girls aren't like that."

I glared at him in response, "Try calling a girl fat and think again."

She then straightened up herself, "Sorry. I've been waiting to get my hands on their necks."

She really is my friend, "Good, because I was about to..."-then I noticed something- "..tell Aspen that he can take his hands off your waist now because it strangely distracts me."

Finally, they became aware of this. Isabelle jumped suddenly, blushing for all its worth, and Aspen took a hand to his back and the other to scratch the back of his head in embarrassment.

I crossed my arms, smiling, "Now, we're ready to meet them."

"Captain de Beville, Ma'am." The soldiers stood straight, saluting.

I nodded my head in response, "We'll take it from here, officers. And we'd like a little privacy."

They bowed their heads, "Yes, ma'am."

Using both arms of theirs, they held the levers of the reel as they slowly opened the metal gates, the path to our strictest, secured, and most 'you-can't-get-the-hell-out-of-'prisons yet.

"Scarlett, can I ask you something?" Isabelle tapped my shoulder as the soldiers were still opening the underground gate.

I turned around, "What is it?"

"Would it be possible for a non-officer to punish criminals, in the sight of ranked and revered officials, in the most lethal method converging into something similar to immediate demise, but-"

"Woah, Isabelle. Slow down."

"-these actions are justified by agreeable and righteous reasons. Would that be possible?"

"Uhh...well.."

How could you answer something you pretty much haven't gotten a grip of?

What did she even say again?

I cluelessly glanced at Aspen, my mouth hanging open, my eye-brows knitted.

"What?" I mouthed.

He cleared his throat, "Uh, she's asking if she could kill them."

"Oh, that." I said, the same time Daniel did.

I will never understand the mind of prodigies. I'm glad that we're solving a case about a mysterious kingdom and not studying one of these two's brain. Now, that's almost impossible.

I gave a loud sigh, "Isabelle, as much as I'd like you to, and as much as I'd like to accommodate your needs, namely swords and whips and all, I think..."

"I was thinking we could give them a better punishment." Aspen interrupted.

"Yeah, that."

Isabelle lowered her head in thought. Her eyebrows furrowed, and I know that she's itching to take her frustrations out. So, I went to her and held her shoulder.

"They'll pay for sure. Don't worry."

She nodded, "I'm sorry. I just feel so angry."

"We understand you." Daniel added.

I heard the sound as the metal of the gates collided with its locks on the top of the wall.

"We shall be taking our leave, Captain." The soldiers saluted before waltzing out.

"Shall we?" I offered.

We all marched into the room like a violent four-man mob. Well, most of that violence feel was actually emanating from only one of us, but you get it.

And there they were, sitting with their hands tied. Their feet were also bounded by ropes. As I said, this was the strictest. We put you in a metal cell, and still you have ropes on ya. What can I say, we want prisoners to feel at home.

They looked lifeless, as anyone would expect. They looked like they've lost, which they have.

I stood in front of the criminals' cell, "Isabelle, meet the the-"

"You bastards!" Out of nowhere once more, Isabelle got out a sword and started charging towards the men who still pretended that no one was paying them a visit.

This time, Daniel and Aspen took hold of Isabelle on both of her arms, making her drop her sword.

"Woah, Isabelle. Calm down." Aspen blurted out as he held Isabelle, all the while wearing a surprised and scared look on his face similar to Daniel's.

"Looks like Scarlett's influenced her pretty bad." Daniel muttered, hoping it would get pass my ear I suppose. But, it didn't.

I snarled and got a dagger from my belt. With one expert, swift move, I flew the weapon just a centimeter above Daniel's head.

"Watch your mouth there, you stupid prince." I glared at him, making him shut up.

Finally, after a few mean stares at the captives, and a few heaves of breath here and there, Isabelle decided to calm down.

"Are you okay now, Belle?"

And again, with Aspen's nicknames.

They removed their arms from her to give her some space. She brushed the imaginary dirt of her torso before speaking.

"I'm fine now." Then she glued a glare at the criminal's not taking her eyes of 'em.

"I never saw that side of you before." Aspen commented with a curious and shaky tone.

"Me neither." I agreed.

With her eyes still glued to the men behind the bars, completely ignoring us, she muttered, "I swear I'm gonna kill you."

The boys gulped, backing away a bit. But I was as proud as a mother. I feel like she's totally my soul sister now. I smiled, walking towards the cell and getting the keys.

"What on earth are you doing?!" Daniel exclaimed.

I shrugged, "I can't let her let her steam in. She's frustrated."

"Scarlett!"

As soon as the lock clicked, I removed the keys an swirled it around my fingers, "Relax, guys. I won't let her kill em."

I opened the door. The criminals were still motionless. I smirked, facing Isabelle after I took a long look at the two.

"Well, do whatever you want." I said to her.

She looked at me, then she glared back at the men. She took a step forward, determined to let at least a bit of her pent up anger out. But she stopped all of a sudden, backing away.

"What's wrong?" I asked.

She let out a sigh, "I won't be satisfied." -she went to me, taking the keys and closing the door herself- "I'm gonna hurt them where it hurts the most."

We all looked at each other after she said that. I didn't know that Isabelle could be this patient. If I was her, I could've been slashing their throats out by now. Those bastards are lucky, having added another few moments to their lives.

She bent down, looking at the criminals who paid her no mind, "You don't belong here. It's not Sorah who you failed. You're not our citizens to punish."

This time, the two looked up.

"I'm gonna find out who you work for. And I'm gonna make sure that you make it back to that gruesome place you call home. Let's see if they'll be happy to know that they couldn't add Sorah to their empire because of your shortcomings."

Then, she banged on the bars, making the two flinch. As she stood up, the two men started to scream, repeating the things they've been saying before.

"Please ma'am. Punish us here! Kill us now, I'm begging you! Don't take us back! Please, don't let them know!" One cried.

"They'll punish our families too! Please!"

Isabelle's angered face, as soon as she heard them, was replaced by a curious look.

"What on earth are you talking about?" Isabelle bent down once more.

Aspen went to her and held her shoulders, "Isabelle, let's go. They're just bluffing."

"No!"- One appealed- "Our king is ruthless! He'll kill our families."

I took hold of the bars, "Then, tell us who you work for and we'll-"

Then, I stopped to think about what I'll say. Saying that, 'if you tell us who you work for, we'll save you', wouldn't bring Isabelle the justice she deserves at all. These people hurt her and almost killed her family. We must still punish them either way, if we find out from them or not.

It's better if we solve this on our own.

"Forget it."- I stood straight- "No man, who makes an enemy out of Sorah, shall be spared. That includes you, your damn kingdom, and your devil-sent king."

"Let's go, Isabelle." Aspen urged, shaking his head.

But they screamed once more, "Please! Our families!"

I turned, my hair whipping behind me, "You should've thought about that when you tried to destroy hers!"

They bowed their heads and sighed in dismay that we couldn't kill them here. One of them even cried.

"We had no choice." The first spy whispered.

We ignored them. They're bad guys. They should get what they deserve. We spun and walked towards the door, but Isabelle stayed where she was.

I held back a groan, "Isabelle, let's go."

"Come on, Belle."

But something changed. She didn't look angry anymore. Instead, it looked like she was...pitying them. Her eyes, not anymore stuck in rage, were glued to them as if she wanted to do something for them.

"Isabelle, ignore them." I said. But, she didn't respond.

"What's your name?" She asked, surprisingly, in a calm manner. It even seemed like she wasn't angry anymore.

"W-what?" They stuttered, looking at her with tears in their eyes.

"The two of you. What's your name?" She repeated.

Aspen went closer to her, "Isabelle..."

Before he could reach her, they answered, "We're brothers. We're Siegfried and Stefan Osbern."

She said nothing. After getting their names, she immediately got up and left them, leaving the prisoners puzzled.

She walked past us without saying a word. Giving the men one last look, I closed the gates and called the guards once more.

The three of us trailed behind her, also confused.

When we caught up to her, she was still dead silent, but Daniel asked her anyway.

"Isabelle, what was that for?"

"Yeah." Aspen said.

I was also meaning to find out. But she didn't answer. We continued to walk together until we got out of the prison areas.

Once outside, she spoke with her hands behind her back, and her face in all seriousness.

"We need to find out about that kingdom immediately."

With puzzled looks, we just nodded and agreed with her.

"Then what are we waiting for?"-Aspen started- "Let's start at the library."

I went with them, having no idea what made Isabelle all detective all of a sudden, and I don't know if it had something to do with asking their names.

But, I don't need to know all of that. Even so, I'll help them. I've been aching to find out every bit of this damn mystery anyway.

22

— ◈ —

CHAPTER 22

A^{spen}

I was anxious.

Seeing Isabelle meet the criminals gave me mixed feelings: fear, pride, impressiveness, unease, curiosity, and worry.

That can all be summed up as anxiety, right?

Right now, we're at the royal library, trying to solve our remaining questions, and by remaining questions, I mean the very mystery that started this all.

Who is this kingdom?

"Do we have any leads?" Scar asked Isabelle, who was scanning some books.

Isabelle shrugs, "All we have is the strategist's notebook, and -" she turned to me -"What was that again, Aspen?"

"Quiet Conquerors." I replied.

"Yeah, that." She continued to scan the books.

Daniel jumped, sitting suddenly on a table, making some books fall off, "Well, we could start with big kingdoms. It has conquered 5 already. So, it should've been massive by now."

"There are a lot of other big kingdoms too, Daniel." Scar said.

He frowned as Scar countered his suggestion, "Yeah, I know."

I slumped on a seat, "We wouldn't get anywhere with this. We need to think deeper."

My eyes found their way to Isabelle as she suddenly slammed a book shut, shaking her head.

"I agree with Aspen."

Daniel scratched the back of his head, "Well, where do we start?"

"Quiet Conquerors." Isabelle uttered all of a sudden while holding the strategist's notebook, looking intently on its cover.

I stood up, "They were called that because of the way they conquered lands. You wouldn't even feel their presence or notice them in action. They work their plan of attacks secretly, and before you know it, you're dead in just one bite."

"Sound strange but perfectly reasonable." Daniel nodded.

"Bite?" Isabelle suddenly turned to me. "What did you just say again?"

Scar answered before I could even say something, "He said ,'before you know it, you're dead in just one bite.' Why?"

"Bite. Quiet Conquerors. Bite. Notebook." She kept muttering those words.

We just watched her as she walked back and forth across the room, trying to think.

"What is it?" I asked.

She held the notebook, making us look at its cover. The picture on it was as abstract as it was before, looking like some sort of dangerous boat or a flower. I don't know. It still had unrecognizable pointy shapes and arches. Nothing changed. But she kept looking at it like it did somehow.

"Does this remind you of something?" She said, pointing at the picture.

"Nothing." I answered.

"Not a clue." Scarlett said.

Daniel turned his head sidewards, tilting it a bit. He even took a few steps back.

Daniel's skills in recognizing things and comparing them are very adequate. He is good at judging artworks and the faces of people and stuff, sometimes bluntly, that ends up offending others. Nevertheless, I'd say he's kinda a good critic.

After a few moments of 'examining' the picture, he said, "Nothi ng..."

Scar and I looked at him dumbfounded, "How surprising."

Really thought he was on to something back there.

"Well, except for shark, but that's just my imagination."

"A shark?" Isabelle's eyes immediately widen at Daniel's words, observing the picture once more.

Scarlett and I turned to him, looking at him disbelief, "A shark?"

"I couldn't even see a thing." Scar said.

"You don't see it?" Daniel went to Isabelle and borrowed the notebook. He faced the picture towards us so we could see clearly. But he did one more thing - he flipped the picture.

"See here? It's not really recognizable at first because the picture's like a carefully painted ink blot with only one damn color. But if you look far enough, you can see a shark. It doesn't seem like one at first because it's only the upper half of the shark's body."

I stood up, taking a few steps back. Scarlett did the same, and we saw it.

It really looked like a shark. Its mouth was wide open, like it's ready to eat and kill. So, the pointy lines were its teeth! I see it now. It did look like a shark.

I suddenly remembered the note from the strategist on the last page of the notebook. It said something about a cold-blooded monster. It all makes sense now.

"A shark. It is a shark." -Scarlett exclaimed - "Nice work, Dan-"

At this, my cousin's eyes lit up, finding its way to Scarlett. That is until she changed her words.

"I mean, anyone could've seen that." She coughed and looked away.

I smirked as he frowned, looking as hopeless as he secretly was with Scar.

"Quiet Conquerors. Shark. Emblems." Isabelle started mumbling again.

I walked over to her. I placed my hand on her shoulder, "What is it, Isabelle?"

She turned and faced me with the brightest eyes, "That's it!"

"What?" We all exclaimed.

"Sharks are quiet conquerors! That can be our clue." She said.

"Now that I think of it, it does make sense. Sharks attack quietly, they don't make any sounds, and you won't see them coming. The moment you do, you'll be a goner then." I said, agreeing with her.

Scarlett nodded her head, "I guess that makes perfect sense. But how can that be our clue in finding the kingdom?"

"Emblems." She answered.

"Emblems?" Scar and Daniel repeated.

"Yes."- Isabelle smiled -" Kingdoms, especially big ones, have emblems of animals or flags that represent them. Like in Bethany, they have the raven. In Shen, they have the crane. So in -"

"In that kingdom, they might have a shark in their flag or as their emblem." I finished for her.

The both of us smiled, along with Scar and Daniel.

"Then, let's look for that flag...or emblem." Daniel said as he grabbed a book.

Soon, a large part of the library looked like it was hit by a storm. We ransacked every shelf for every book that had to do with flags and emblems.

Our fingers felt like its bones were brutally pounded from turning thousands and hundreds of pages. Call it exaggeration, but in our defense, we've been doing this for an hour.

And our reward?

Nothing. Yup. That's what we found.

"I don't understand." -Isabelle slumped in a seat - "That was supposed to be a lead."

I sat beside her, "Maybe that emblem was just for the kingdom's spies."

"I guess so." She sighed hopelessly. She stood up and went to a table, taking another look on the strategist's notebook.

"We're sorry we couldn't think of anything, Isa." Daniel said.

Isabelle smiled, "No, don't. In fact, I should be thanking you."

"No." --I cut her off--"we should be thanking you. Despite what you've been through, you're still willing to help us."

"Of course. It's for Sorah. It's for my home." She said.

We smiled at her words. Suddenly, I was reminded that she was to leave Sorah. Scar and Daniel don't know yet.

I'll do whatever it takes to keep her here longer. She belongs here with us. She's a Sorahian. She belongs here with...me.

Isabelle's my friend and she has become so important, too important for me to lose. I'll try, and I'll keep trying.

We are her home. Sorah is our home. And I'm gonna do whatever it takes for her parents to know that.

"And I'll do everything for it too."- I walked up to her and smirked - "Don't forget. I'm the king, and I'm not gonna lose to you."

She raised her eyebrows in a questioning manner, imitating my smirk, "Fair enough, your majesty. Then let's all work together to keep Sorah standing."

She put her hand in front of her, and I placed my hand on top of hers. Scarlett smiled, joining in, liking the optimistic and atmosphere and fighting spirit Daniel, however, pouted.

"That is so lame and cliche."

Scarlett shook her head, "Says a killjoy."

Daniel forced a grin, "But I didn't say that I wouldn't do it." He leaped to us and placed his hand on top of Scarlett's.

"For Sorah." I started.

We all then shouted in unison, throwing our hands in the air, "For Sorah!"

We laughed, straightening ourselves after our gesture. Isa laughed, grabbing the strategist's notebook again.

"Let's go back to this. Maybe we missed something." She suggested, holding it out.

Scar spoke up, "Daniel and I will look for more books while you do that."

Daniel nodded and followed her while I went to Isabelle so that we could go over the notebook again.

"You think we missed something?" She asked me.

I shrugged, "I was kinda hoping we did. Maybe the things we've missed.." - And my eyes brought themselves to hers- "might be the things we need the most."

"To solve this case?"she smiled.

I cleared my throat, "Yes."

She averted her eyes, "I hope so too."

But she stopped reading for a moment to face me. She leaned back against the edge of the table and looked at me with a pair of sad eyes, "Aspen, let's not tell them, okay."

"Who?"

Suddenly, a crashing sound was heard at the back part of the library. It sounded like a shelf got wrecked.

"Daniel! You were supposed to carry the books!"

"How am I to know?! You didn't tell!"

"You're such an- Ughhh!"

Isabelle chuckled lightly, and so did I. I nodded my head at her request earlier.

"Oh, them. Why?"

She gave a loud sigh, "I don't wanna burden them. How are they going to take my absence? Especially Scarlett? She'll go -"

"Yeah. I know that." I looked down. I know that Scar will go full-blown rogue. If there's anything she hates as much as we all do, it's losing her friends and the people she cares about. She doesn't care who she'll apprehend when it comes to those matters. Let it be Isabelle's parents.

"Let's keep it a secret from them for now." She said.

"Sure."

After that, together , we scanned the pages once more. Picture by picture, and word by word. Still, as before, nothing came up. Nothing was sufficient enough to reveal the identity of the kingdom.

To be honest, I wasn't really looking at the notebook. Most of that half of an hour, I spent on looking at her, practically memorizing her face because I don't know if ever I'd see it again.

I know I promised her that I wouldn't let her leave. But the truth? I was as terrified as hell.

Ever since the fire, I've been hating myself, for I couldn't protect her. How on earth am I supposed to make her stay if I couldn't even make my stand because of my shortcomings as a friend who swore to protect her?

And I'm a king at that. Tch.

"We're back."

Scar and Daniel came up with scrolls and tons of books. Actually, only Daniel was the one carrying the stuff. He looked tired and soulless. Scarlett really found a way to cruelly utilize him, huh.

"Found anything?" Scar said as she sat on the table.

"No." Isabelle and I said in unison.

"Oh."- Scar bent her head down - "Well, you think these will help?" She pointed at the mountain of books and scrolls Daniel was carrying.

Isabelle soughed, "Thanks, guys. But I don't think that those would be much help."

At this, Daniel made an audible noise as he dramatically dropped the books to the floor, "Aww, come on! You've got to be kidding me."

We all laughed at his suffering.

Isabelle managed to calm herself from laughing, taking a scroll from the floor, "Okay. I'll at least take a look at them."

Daniel sprawled on the floor, with beads of sweat on his forehead, "If you wish." He said emotionlessly.

Scarlett shook her head, "You're shameful. Those were just a couple of books. And you call yourself a man."

Daniel gave an almost unnoticeable scoff, "Exactly. I'm a man. Not a bookkeeper."

I crossed my arms, "I'm proud that you're starting to help each other out. It's good training, especially know that you two are gonna get married." - At this, Daniel's expression changed from an annoyed one to the face of someone about to be endangered. "I almost forgot that you're enga-"

And I was cut off with a sword to my throat and a deadly stare from a redhead tormentor.

"Say one more damn word, and this goes through your throat."

In the corner of my eyes, I saw Daniel mouthing, "Never remind her."

"Sorry." I choked, "I just thought that -"

Daniel, again, mouthed the words, "No. Don't." And he was waving his hands, telling me to stop if I want to come out alive.

"Nothing. Sorry."

Scarlett, to my relief, withdrew her sword but started glaring daggers at me.

"What the?"

But Isabelle's sudden voice almost blew away the tension. We all looked at her out of curiosity.

"What is it?" We all went to her.

"Nothing. It's nothing. I just thought that it looked familiar." She held her cheek as she observed the scroll intently.

"What's familiar?" I stood beside her to take a look at what she's looking.

"This is a new map, right? The one from 10 years ago?" She said as she pointed to the scroll.

I gave her a nod, "Yeah, that's the latest. Sorah's always updated. But that's just a map of the Southern kingdoms."

She looked back at the map once more, muttering something between the lines of ,"This really looks strange." Or something like that.

She snapped her head up suddenly, making us take a step back.

"Could it be?!"

Wasting no second, she scrambled to get the notebook. She flipped through it and started tearing certain pages one by one, placing them all on the table. That was 5 pages, I think.

I stood close to her, "Isabelle, what's -"

"Just a second." She started arranging the pages she tore from the notebook. She rotated them to the left, then to the right, and sometimes she flipped it as if she was solving some puzzle. She shook her head when she sometimes stopped, as if trying to form something with only a blurred memory as a basis.

Words from the lame, I know. But that's the only way I could describe it.

Daniel and Scar stood closer as they observed her work. She stood still, with a hand on her cheek, trying to figure out what she was doing.

She scrambled the pages once more. She kept shuffling it until the pages she tore from the book formed something scarily familiar.

Once I recognized the picture the pages started to form, I held her hand into a halt as I observed the picture intently.

Startled, she looked at me in a questioning way, but she must've figured that I was recognizing the same thing.

I let go of her hand as I took the map that she got earlier. I placed it next to the pages, and one figure in the map looked similar to the figure the papers formed.

One particular kingdom surfaced:

The kingdom of Massah

"It's Massah." She uttered, "The lands of the 5 fallen kingdoms were adjacent. They were land-locked. And, after they were conquered, it became Massah, 5 kingdoms shattered to one domain."

Of course. It's the closed kingdom, the kingdom with walls. It's the only one that doesn't have any allegiance to any kingdom. They don't even have ports for trading, only battleships and other vessels. It's because they've conquered every kingdom that would supply everything, from weapons to land to food.

No kingdom knows what's it's like on the inside. No one was ever allowed to visit, even the kings. Anyone who was not born a Massite seemed like an enemy to them.

Isabelle let out a scoff, "Why didn't we think of that?"

"The kingdom where no one enters or leaves."Scarlett added.

"Why didn't we even suspect it? It's the most suspicious." Daniel mentioned.

"I don't know." -Isabelle said, grabbing the map - "But, point is, we've figured it out now."

Scarlett nodded, cracking her knuckles, "Now, we can make a move. We can make them pay."

Yes. The case is finished now. We've figured out the mysterious kingdom. It's over now.

"We did it. We actually did it!" Daniel muttered, taking the torn out pages and waving them around as if they were flags.

"Easy, there."- Scar reminded - "We still need to plan things, like how are we gonna 'make them kinda pay' knowing that they are this giant-ass empire with a haul of secrets?"

"Oh. Right."

But, I didn't focus on our victory or what would we do next.

Instead, I looked at Isabelle. And her worried face reminded me of another problem we had to face.

She turned to me, and she wore an expression as troubled as mine, with tears, making her eyes glisten a bit.

Now that it's over...

She'll be leaving soon.

She gave me a slight, disappointed smile knowing this. While Daniel and Scar argued, I only thought of one thing, and one thing only.

Isabelle.

How could I make her stay? I wanted to be her friend longer, longer than the time we had.

"It's not Massah." I blurted out to my own and the other's surprise.

They glanced at me, wearing puzzled expression.

I know that the clues were as obvious as Daniel's feelings for Scar, but I couldn't think straight.

What's going on in my head right now?

Longer. I want her to stay just a little longer. I can't lose her.

What's the point of solving this thing...if I lose my friend?

"Are you crazy?"

It means nothing at all.

Isabelle

Wait. Say what?

What on earth is he doing?

"Are you crazy?" Scarlett complained, "You're kidding, right?"

The clues were obvious. It was definitely Massah. What is he saying? Days ago, he was hellbent on finding out who this kingdom was. I don't understand why he would say that.

"It's not Massah?"....when it obviously is?

He shook his head side to side, grabbing some random books and turning its pages to somewhere, "We need to investigate further. We can't just jump to conclusions."

"Uhh...what?!" -Scarlett placed her hands on her hips - "Conclusions?! These are definite and sure answers, Aspen."

"Yeah." Daniel agreed, "What has gotten into you, man?"

"I won't end it this way!" He suddenly spewed out, slamming his hands on the table, silencing the library. When I saw his expression, dismayed and angry, I finally realized that...

He's not talking about the case, is he?

My hands shook as I bit my lip in worry and distress. He can't take his mind off my leaving Sorah.

It's true. There's no need for me now that the case is over. So, I should go as my father wishes me to. We both know that. And knowing it is like a punch to the gut, repeated.

He then faced me. His eyes were sternly on me, troubled and in distress as I am. I just sighed as I tried to hold my tears.

I can't let Scar and Daniel know. They'll be burdened sick.

"Aspen, are you going coo-coo?" Daniel went to him, knocking on his head as if he was some kind of door. But Aspen was unfazed, still facing me.

"Aspen. We need to make a move. Stop this nonsense. These people need to pay." Scar demanded, but she still got no answer.

Aspen quickly exclaimed, without looking away from me, "And then what?! You'll leave?!"

And I knew that he was talking to me. My eyes widened as he practically shouted for the team to hear.

"What?" The clueless two said.

"Aspen..." -I mouthed.- "No. Please."

"Who's leaving?" Scar asked.

Sending a somewhat telepathic message, I shook my head to beg him not to tell. I don't want them to know. I tried to hold back my tears, biting my lower lip as I tried so. Solving this case doesn't feel fulfilling at all to me, too, given that it's the only thing that's keeping me here, and now it's over.

"No one." Aspen answered Scar to my relief. "Forget what I said."

I glanced at him once more and mouthed a thank you, hugging myself as I went to the table. With the four of us gathered, we tried to think of our next move.

"What now?" Daniel sat on the table, "How do we supposedly make them 'pay'?"

"I don't know yet." Aspen replied, placing a hand on his forehead.

"How bout we just attack them?" Scarlett suggested, twirling a book she found beside her.

"They're an empire, Scar." Daniel countered, "We can't just barge in."

She dropped the book and rolled her eyes, "Duh. I'm a strategist and captain. I know that."

"Sorry."

Scar continued, "What I meant was we can attack them by doing what they do, you know, seize them from the inside."

That was a pretty good suggestion, actually, but that's not gonna be all pretty.

"We can't."- Aspen said- "If we do that, they might attack other kingdoms too. They might have moles in every kingdom, remember?"

"Oh, right." Scar shook her head, "Then what can we do? We have to get rid of the criminals, expose Massah, and protect the other kingdoms."

"We can do it all at once. In one move." I uttered, remembering what Aspen once said before we caught one of the spies.

They turned their heads to me simultaneously.

"What? How?"

I glanced at Aspen, nodding my head. I know that he knows what's going on in my head. He's the one who said it before.

"We only need to warn one kingdom." We said together in unison.

"Massah?" Scarlett and Daniel said as they looked at each other, then back at us.

"Yes." I nodded, "Only that one kingdom."

"How?" Daniel asked.

Aspen stood up and went to a shelf, searching for something. No, it wasn't a shelf of books. It was for other things like stamps, flags, quills, and all.

He got back, holding a bottle, a piece of paper, and a small red flag, "We just need to expose them, but not to the kingdoms. To themselves."

I smirked, as I was thinking the same thing. I glanced at the other two, who were tilting their hands in confusion.

Scarlett crossed her arms, "And exactly how do we do that? Because I'm not getting a single thing."

"Me too."Daniel agreed

I stood next to Aspen as I grabbed the red flag, playing it on my hand, "What he meant was, we just need to -"

"I know what he means. I just don't understand." Scar complained.

"Me too." Daniel pouted.

"Why don't I explain if it's okay with Aspen." I tapped the king's shoulder as he started writing.

"Sure." Aspen smiled, then he went back to writing.

I nodded, and then I started explaining. But before I did, Scarlett and Daniel sat on the floor like children anticipating a bedtime story, with eyes full of curiosity.

I chuckled," Here's the plan. We'll tie the two spies on a boat and have them sent and punished to Massah, the kingdom they work for. We're gonna send them a threat by doing that."

Scarlett clasped her hand and smiled, "Then they'll be too afraid to make another move knowing that the whole world might know them."

"I see now." Daniel nodded.

"We're gonna use their fear of being known, of being seen."- I added -"Even if only one kingdom knows, that's gonna be a huge problem for them. At least, that's what I think."

Scarlett clapped her hands dramatically, standing up, "Isabelle, you're a genius!"

I laughed, "Technically, Aspen came up with it first. I just sorta rephrased."

"You're still a genius. That's it." Scar looked at me sternly, as if she was pissed because I contradicted her.

Typical Scar. She doesn't wanna admit that Aspen was the one behind the plan and that he's a genius too.

"I'm really gonna miss her," I sadly thought to myself as I was reminded of my situation.

"It's done."- Aspen stood up from his chair, handing me the letter.- "What do you think?"

I took it and read it for them to hear,

We know. Don't even ponder about making a move. You may be an empire, but we have a hundred kingdoms behind us. We have your secrets. And we'll keep them as long as necessary unless you change your plans and misbehave.

Remember this, Massah.

We can turn your shark against you anytime.

Then, at the bottom, he drew the symbol of the spies - the shark. But he added angry eyes and a little bit of red. He also rotated the shark, as if indicating that we're the shark now.

I smiled, "This'll do it."

"Yeah, it gave me chills." Scarlett touched her skin, feeling the goosebumps.

Daniel nodded his head, "If I were the king, I'd definitely run."

"Then what are we waiting for?" -Scar headed towards the door - "Let's go kick some Massite ass!"

"Let's go." Daniel ran after her.

"You go get the spies and ready the boat!" Aspen tried to instruct them, but they already took off. The two of us sighed. I know that they'll know what to do.

I walked up to him and handed him the letter. He took it from my hand, rolled it, and placed it inside the bottle he got earlier.

"This it it." I sighed.

"Come on. We still have a lot to do." He passed by me and went to the door.

But, I refused to move. The thought of leaving, even if it's just out the door, was preventing my feet from moving. Yes. I was that scared. My knees shook, and my mind became completely clouded. How I wished to stay. I don't care if it's in this library forever, as long as it's in Sorah.

"Isabelle, what's wrong?"

I embraced myself in worry, still unable to speak. He then tightened his hold on the bottle as he went to me. I used my teeth to bite my quivering lower lip.

"Hey..." - He said calmly - "I'm not gonna -"

"I don't wanna go." -I whisper-cried- "After a few moments, this whole thing's gonna be over, and my parents will take me away from Sorah."

He dropped the bottle and wasted no time. He held my hand and brought it to his chest, "I'm not gonna let that happen, Isabelle."

"Aspen, we're not sure of that."

"But you can be sure that I'll try." He quickly countered, "Don't lose faith now."

He's right. I could not lose faith now. If I wanna stay, I have to try and talk to my parents. If I don't wanna leave, I have to hold on.

"Let's go?"

I dried my tears, picking up the bottle with the letter, "Okay."

I handed him the bottle. He took my hand, and together, we walked out the door.

23

EPILOGUE

Isabelle

A small ship was ready. A few trusted soldiers were with us at the bay, where we'll sail the spies to their demise. And by demise, I mean their home. And by home, I mean their 'worst nightmare.'

We chose to keep this a secret. So, only the four of us and these soldiers know. We didn't wanna scare the people anymore. Not even the royal family nor the ministers were informed. We let them be thinking that everything's okay now, as it will be once this is done.

"Get the spies." Scarlett ordered.

And at once, two soldiers arrived with the spies trailing weakly behind them. Their hands were tied behind them. A few more ropes were prepared for them for the sail to Massah. After they were brought out, soldiers made them climb the ship, where they were tied once more, tighter, in a buoyant, wooden cage on the ship.

The plan was, once we get to Massah, we'll let the cage float to the shores of the kingdom and let the soldiers find them. We'll also leave the bottle tied to the flag on top of that cage.

"I'm ready." Scarlett began to board the ship.

But before she could even take another step, I quickly went aboard first, surprising the others.

"Isabelle, what are you doing?" She questioned.

"I'm coming with you...to Massah." I stated firmly.

She let out a smirk, probably assuming that I was pulling her leg, "Isa, you can't be serious. If this is personal, I'm gonna make sure they're gonna regret what they did to you."

"This isn't personal." - I countered before adding - "Okay. Maybe it is. But I still wanna come."

"Isabelle." This time, it was Aspen, and behind him was Daniel.

I shook my head, "Whatever you're gonna say, it won't change my mind. I wanna come."

"I wasn't going to stop you." - Aspen then took a sword from one of the soldiers - "I'm coming with you."

"What?!" Scar exclaimed.

"Hey, you can't leave me behind." Daniel said, climbing aboard as well.

Scar placed a hand on her forehead and sighed, "Guys, this is a very dangerous delivery, not a leisure hike!"

I chuckled at Scarlett, placing a hand on her shoulder, "Then, count us in."

"But -"

"This was my idea in the first place." - Aspen climbed the ramp - "I should see it through."

Scarlett unsheathed her sword and tried to block Aspen's path, but he blocked the sword with his own as well, looking calm and cool as he did.

"This is my job. I'm the chief. I'm the captain." Scar gritted. Did she really wanna do this on her own that bad? Or did she just want some 'alone time' with the spies? Some terrifying alone time. No one has ever been alone with this girl mad and survived. At least, that's what I heard.

"Well, this was my plan. I'm the king. I am Aspen." He retorted.

Scarlett raised a brow, "What does your name have to do with you getting aboard?"

"Everything." He winked. Seriously, does Aspen have a death wish?

Scarlett blinked once, twice, and then a couple of times more. Finally, she sighed, withdrawing her sword.

"Fine. Climb aboard, but behave."

"Why?" - Aspen scoffed - "This is my ship. If anything, you -"

"Before I kill you, Aspen." She glared, pointing at the ship.

"Just get on!" Daniel and I mouthed at him.

"And indeed I shall." He quickly ran past Scarlett and onto the ship, whilst Scarlett's glare didn't leave him.

She sighed heavily, annoyed. Then, she separated the ramp from the ship and closed the entrance carefully. The soldiers, who were supposed to come, ran to us.

"Ma'am! What about us?"

"Stand guard here and make sure that no one will know." She commanded.

"Yes, captain." The soldiers gave a salute, then took their positions.

After that, we set sail. We ensured that the spies were safe and secured in the cage. And by safe and secured, I meant 'suffering' in the cage.

As we traveled the quiet waters to Massah, we talked about our strategy once more, from how we plan to leave the cage and how we'll sail away without being seen.

"I can cover the back of the ship with a mirror so that it would look like we're invisible." Daniel offered.

"You could do that?" I asked in disbelief.

"Yeah," he smirked . "If you should know, Isabelle, I created and designed this ship... and most of the ships of Sorah. Every ship has a special feature. Some are for hiding, some are for battles, some are for settlements-"

"Settlements?"

"You know, ships that could be a house once it reached land."

"Woah. Wait." I held my hand up. I turned to Aspen and Scarlett, who were acting as if this was normal, "Is he serious?"

Aspen shrugged, "Yes. He's Sorah's specialist in ships, weapons, security, and other contraptions."

As he was saying this, Daniel was nodding in agreement while flexing his muscles and kissing his biceps.

Still, unable to believe, I looked at Scarlett, "Seriously?"

"Though I hate to admit it.." -she said, emphasizing the word 'hate'- "If there's one thing I know about this stupid head, it is that he's annoyingly smart."

"Wow." I said blandly.

"Did she just...compliment me?" Daniel asked in a form of a whisper while he was hiding his face using his hand.

"Well..."

Scarlett suddenly removed his hand from his face and glared at him, "The waters aren't loud enough. I can hear you whisper. And hell no," she said, referring to his question- "I was just stating a fact reluctantly. Are we clear?"

"Y-yes ma'am," Daniel replied.

"Good," she forcefully let down his hand before walking away to check on the spies.

Aspen and I chuckled at their actions. Although, I did pity Daniel as he held his hand, looking at Scarlett in a sad way.

I know that he likes Scarlett so much to endure this. Though I don't know the true feelings of Scar, I can assume that she cares for Daniel. At least, that's me trying to stay positive.

"Is something wrong?" I asked.

He sighed, "We weren't always like this, you know."

"Uh-huh. Years ago, those two stuck to each other like cement, back to when Scarlett was not as tough as stone." Aspen added.

"Wait. So the legendary 'soft' kind of Scarlett de Beville actually exists?"

"Yeah. And I'm sure she's not gone yet." - Daniel answered sadly - "I miss being able to talk to her, and being able to have fun with her, I just miss...us."

"Us?" I repeated.

"W-Well.." -he stuttered, obviously blushing - "I..her..we.."

"They liked each other back then." -Aspen said- "But, it was mostly him who liked her. He would do anything for Scarlett back then. I swear that the only thing standing between those two from being together was their age."

"Really now?" I smirked, amused by their story.

"Can I speak now?"- Daniel gritted - "But he's right, though."

"Of course I am."

Daniel gave him a glare before continuing, "Since it's already obvious, I'll admit it. I'm in love with Scarlett. I've always been."

"Any 3-year-old could've figured it out, Daniel." I laughed.

"And you tried to deny it."

"I was that obvious?" He frowned, annoyed.

"Yes." Aspen and I said.

Daniel laughed too, brushing it off, "Well, as the law says, you can only marry at the age of 18. And that's what I wanted. But, I wasn't gonna wait for that long for Scarlett to know that I loved her."

"So, what did you do?"

He smiled as he seemingly remembered what he did, "I tried to propose to her the day she turned 15."

All that I could think about was... Wow. Who knew that a guy like Daniel would be so thoughtful and sweet? I can't even imagine him giving roses or gifts, let alone a ring. But he didn't look like he was lying, so it must be true. Gosh, it's bringing tears to my heart!

"Aww. That's so sweet."- I cooed - "What did she say?"

Then, his expression turned sad and regretful somehow, "It didn't happen. I never got to propose." -he sighed heavily before adding - "That was also the day she started to hate me."

"Ouch." Aspen shook his head, "two in a row." This earned him a glare from Daniel.

"How come? What happened?"

"Well, I-"

But I never got to know because as soon as he opened his mouth, Scarlett interrupted, "We're almost there."

We scrambled to our feet and went to the edge of the ship, where we could barely make out the forest surrounding Massah because of the fog.

"This is far enough." -Scarlett said - "We'll let them off here."

"Not yet." I quickly said, making the three of them turn to me.

"What's going on?" Scarlett demanded.

If I tell them, they'll stop me for sure... and think that I was out of my mind. But still, this is my resolve.

"I need to talk to them first." I stated, making my way to the cage.

Aspen held my hand and looked at me in a questioning way, "Isabelle..."

"I know what I'm doing. Trust me." I whispered.

He looked reluctant for a bit, but he let me go. I thanked him in the form of a nod, and then I walked towards the spies. I bent down to meet their face.

"What more could you want?" -One of them, whom I recall to be Siegfried, spoke - "You already won. We'll be dead in a few seconds...and so will our family."

I can't believe I'm doing this for the men who almost killed me. Damn this conscience of mine, "Not yet...at least not your family."

"What?!" The others exclaimed.

Both of the spies suddenly held their heads up out of curiosity and surprise, "W-what do you mean?"

I held back a groan as I myself, am annoyed that I've decided to do this, "I'm going to save your family."

Then, tears suddenly formed in their eyes, flowing down to their bruised cheeks. At that time, they resembled sinners about to be saved from the brink of death. They looked hopeful, more hopeful than I'd care to admit.

"Y-you...you'll do that?"

"Isabelle, you've gotta be kidding me?!" -Scarlett intervened - "What the heck are you saving their ass for?"

"Technically, it's their family's ass."

"Haha." -she blurted out sarcastically - "Shall I give you a big clap with that? Because it was so funny."

Daniel, wearing the same troubled and puzzled expression as Scar, came up to me, "Isabelle, do I have to remind you that they almost killed you and your family?!"

"So that's why you asked their names." Aspen stood closer to me, wearing a slightly different expression than that of the two.

I sighed as I tried to explain my actions, "It's not their fault to be born a Massite, Aspen, nor do they have to suffer from that. I find it reasonable if these people" -I pointed at the spies- "died because they tried to commit murder, but their families? That's a different story."

"Isabelle. We can't be sure that we can save them. This country is dangerous and devil-sent." Daniel tried to argue. But I've already made up my mind.

"I have to at least try. If there's anyone who knows what it feels like to lose a family, it's me....or in my case, almost. I know what it's like to have the people you love suffer because of your actions."

"Isabelle..."

I continued, "I need to do this. This is what my heart is telling me to do."

"Then your heart is crazy." Scarlett shook her head in dismay.

"Yeah. It's gone, coo-coo." Daniel agreed.

"I'll come with you," Aspen placed a hand on my shoulder, "I won't let you go alone."

"Okay. If you want," I permitted. I could use a little bit of help. I won't be stubborn about that fact, and it's gonna be pointless to argue with him about it.

"This is unacceptable." -Scarlett complained - "Aspen, you won't stop her?!"

"I'm pro-Isabelle. What can I do?" he smiled innocently, "Besides, I think it's a noble act to save the life of an enemy's family."

"Yeah, and so does bringing them to justice," Scar kept trying to waver us from our resolve.

"Scarlett, I wanna do this. You know that I won't be able to sleep at night if I don't." I said.

"And I'll be having nightmares if you do!"

"Scar..." I kept on insisting.

Aspen walked up to her, "Scarlett, I'm with her on this, and I'm the king. I won't let anything happen to her."

"But -"

"There's no point in arguing with both of us." -he reminded her - "You know we're both stubborn."

Scarlett rolled her eyes, then glared, "Well, tell me something I don't know."

"Will you? Will you really save our family?" We heard a voice say. We turned to the cage and saw Stefan, the other spy, looking as hopeful as his brother as he asked.

Scarlett crossed her arms, "We're debating on it. Hold your hopeful horses."

"I know it's a lot to ask...and to hope for." -he continued - "We can accept our fate in the hands of our king wholly. We've been prepared for it ever since. But our families...please. They don't deserve to die. They're good people. Their only sin was being born in this wretched country."

A moment of silence took over after he stopped speaking. We all looked at each other, then back at the spies. Exactly how awful is this country? Not even sparing the lives of innocent families.

Okay. I'm doing it.

"Isabelle. Don't."

"Please, I'm begging you." -The spy pleaded again - "My son is only 8 months old."

"That does it!" -Damn myself for being a sucker for babies - "I'm going in."

"Me too." Aspen quickly took his sword and followed after me.

"You've gotta be kidding me." Scarlett and Daniel face-palmed.

"W-we live in a cottage near the mountains. It's a little bit far away from the towns, but it will still be dangerous." The spy blurted out.

"Got it."

"There's really no turning back now, huh?" Daniel said.

Scarlett started tapping her foot, glaring at us. Finally, she let out a groan, "Fine! Just come back safe, or we'll kill you."

I gave her a quick hug, "Thank you, Scar."

"Yeah. Yeah. Some supportive friend I am." She reluctantly said, patting my back.

I smiled at her, and then I let her go. Before I jumped into the water with Aspen, I took one last look at them.

"Ready?" He asked.

I smiled, "Yeah." -I looked down a little, then I shivered at the sight - "This isn't as bad as the cliff."

He coughed, "A choice to cower or not, remember?"

"How could I forget? I almost died back then." I glared, but he shrugged it off by laughing lightly.

"I'll be with you." He held my hand. And for an instant, it seemed that my fear of heights wasn't there.

"On 3." He said.

"1." We counted together.

"2."

"Gah!"

And the next thing I knew, I was wet and cold. The taste of seawater almost made me choke, and I added that to my shock and surprise. You now have a recipe for a reasonable irritation.

"That was too early!" I splashed at Aspen as soon as he appeared from the water.

He wiped his face, "That was exactly on three."

"No, it's not."

"Yes, it is. If it's not, then it would be 'after 3' and not 'on 3.'"

Scarlett's voice then bellowed, "Hey! Are you just gonna flirt there or what?!"

"We're not flirting!" We defended. Flirting?! I wouldn't even dare flirt with the king! I would besmirch his good name...and my good name as well.

I shook my head, glaring at Aspen before swimming to the shore.

"Sorry," he said as he swam after me.

9 781944 253936